Surreal in Saudi

Sharon;
Albert Einstein once said: "intellectual growth should commence @ birth & cease only @ death." May this story of my time in Saudi Arabia not only entertain, but inform.
Enjoy!

By M.Doreen

First published by Dog Ear Publishing
4010 W. 86th Street, Ste H
Indianapolis, IN 46268
www.dogearpublishing.net

ISBN: 1-59858-225-9
Library of Congress Control Number: 2006935287

This book is printed on acid-free paper.
This book is a work of Fiction. Places, events, and situations in this book are purely Fictional and any resemblance to actual persons, living or dead, is coincidental.

Printed in the United States of America

Chapter One

"Claire? Is that you?"

"Yes. Who is this please?"

"It's Ian. You know, Rose's friend."

"Oh, Ian. Hello."

"Listen. Listen. Rose and I are in jail."

"What?"

"I don't have much time. I'm okay, but I gotta get out of here and find Rose. She's in the women's prison. This is the only phone number I know by heart, so I need you to call one of my buddies at work. Rose has my business card somewhere. Find it, then call my office and they'll send someone to the men's prison to help me."

"What about Rose?"

"Don't know where she is. I can't help her from inside here. Please, Claire. Call my office.

"Got to go. The matawa are demanding ... ."

"Ian? Ian?"

The sudden jolt from my deep sleep left me dazed as I watched my shaky hand put down the receiver. I stood motionless, staring at the phone.

Was I dreaming? Could this be happening?

I shook my head and walked into the kitchen to check the time. *Two o'clock in the morning. No wonder I'm not awake.* Rose. Poor Rose. In jail. What will they do to her?

I brushed a stray lock of hair behind my ear and felt my stomach tighten. Back and forth, back and forth, I paced the floor, holding onto my waist. Fear gripped me and disorganized my thoughts. Memories of colleagues' voices overwhelmed my consciousness ...

"Saudi Arabia? That's where they mutilate people ... You're crazy. I'd never go because of the way they treat women ... My brother worked as a contractor there ... They chop off hands ... And heads. Stay away from downtown areas on Fridays. The police round up Westerners and push them to the front of the crowds to get a good view of the beheadings … They arrest women for no reason and throw them in jail …They rape and torture them …"

Stop thinking like this. They won't … they can't…

I stood in the living room of the tiny seventies-style apartment wringing my hands. "God help Rose. God help me. What am I going to do?" My words echoed in the room. I had to settle down. Think. Think. Who to contact?

Closing my eyes, I put a fist to my forehead, trying to clear my thoughts. The business card—I had to find Ian's business card.

I walked into Rose's room and looked around. I felt awkward, like a thief scouting out his territory before making a strike. Having arrived in Saudi Arabia just a few days before, I hadn't crossed the threshold of her room. But my fear for her well being overtook any sheepishness. I was frantic to find Ian's card.

I checked on top of her desk, moving books and papers. Nothing. Turning, I saw a tall dresser in a corner. Photos of a little dog were lined up in wooden frames. It was strange, but there were no shots of friends or family, just the dog. I ran my hand along the top surface to ensure a card wasn't laying flat, out of sight. Nothing. I walked to her bureau, scanned the top of it, and peeked into the top drawer. I sorted through Rose's belongings, methodically going into one drawer and then another. Standing up straight, I arched my back and saw a phone on the bedside table. I looked there. No business card.

Frustrated, I brushed my forehead with the back of my arm, fighting back tears. Where to look next? My eyes rested on a door painted the same color as the walls. I didn't see it before. What's behind it? I opened it and saw books and papers piled on high shelves above racks of dresses and skirts hanging in coordinated styles and colors. Needing a better look, I took the chair from Rose's desk and placed it in the narrow space. Balanced on the chair, I pulled papers from between two large nursing textbooks. Hidden between the papers, I found numbers to Rose's embassy and her passport, but no business card.

I jumped from the chair and put the papers on the bed, in case I might need them. I turned and looked through the closet into Rose's bathroom and saw something attached to the corner of the mirror. It was a small card. I approached and saw it was Ian's business card.

My heart raced as I took the card from the mirror and ran down the hall to the living room. I picked up the phone and dialed the seven-digit number. It rang once, then twice.

"Pick up, pick up," I said, tapping my foot and twirling the card in my fingers. Please don't let an Arab answer. He may not speak English well and if he knows Ian's in jail, he won't be helpful. I breathed a big sigh of relief when I heard an Irish-sounding male voice on the other end of the phone.

"Hello? My name is Claire Spencer. I am calling for an employee of yours, Ian, um…" I read from the card, "Ian McGreggor."

"Oh me boss? What's he got 'imself into?"

"He's arrested and in the men's prison."

He laughed and said, "Now don't ye be worried lass. I'll make sure ta boss is all right. Ye just relax and we'll let ye know wat happens by and by."

"But you don't understand. He's in jail and so's my roommate."

"Who, Rose? Now tat doesn't surprise me any."

"I'm worried and don't know what to do."

"Now, now. First tings first. We'll look after ta boss, we will, and see wat can be done for tat lady of 'is. What's your number, lass?"

"It's 426–7765."

The line went dead and I thought of Rose's documents. I had to find the number for the New Zealand embassy. Back in the bedroom, I sorted through the papers. My hands trembled so hard, the papers shook and the words were too blurry to read through my tears. I took a deep breath, rubbed my eyes, and forced myself to concentrate. I found the number, then dialed it, counting the rings until a recorded voice recited greetings and hours of business. I staggered backward, overwhelmed with disappointment. What now?

Tears rolled down my face as I paced back and forth, wringing my hands. I knew I wasn't going to help Rose by getting all worked up. *Be calm. Think.*

I needed a cup of tea, something soothing about a cup of tea.

I took two steps toward the kitchen and it came to me. The supervisor. I could call the supervisor at the hospital.

I rushed into my bedroom and sifted through my hospital orientation documents, looking for the contact numbers. I found them, then studied the paper. They didn't make sense. There were no prefixes. How was I supposed dial these numbers when I didn't know the first three numbers? The operator… I had to call the operator.

I grabbed the phone, dialed zero, and counted seven rings before a male voice with a thick Arab accent answered.

"I need the number to the nursing supervisor, please."

"Da supervisor? But she no have number."

"There must be a number to call her."

"No, sorry miss."

"Look, this is an emergency."

"Emergency? What is emergency?"

"This is a matter for the supervisor. I need to talk to her."

"I tell you miss. She no have number."

"Then how do we reach her?"

"She have pager, miss. What is dis emergency?"

"Could you please give me her pager number?"

"I need to know first what emergency, miss."

I threw up my hands in exasperation. "Would you give me the pager number to the nursing supervisor?"

"What emergency, miss?"

"Oh—never mind." I hung up, feeling discouraged.

The phone rang. I answered, thinking it was Ian with news.

"Please, miss. I need to know emergency."

"How did you get this number?"

"I operator, miss."

"Leave me alone or I'll report you."

"Okay. Okay. I just check you okay. No emergency?"

I rubbed my forehead with my fist and tried to control my voice. "I need to talk to the supervisor. May I have her pager number, please?"

"I cannot give it you. For nurses only."

"I am a nurse. Oh, never mind. Don't call me again." I slammed down the receiver.

It rang again. I hesitated before answering.

"Please, miss, what is emergency?"

Infuriated, I hung up the phone. It rang again. I hesitated.

"'Ellow Claire? David here."

I breathed a sigh of relief.

"Just callin' to let ye know 'e's all right now. We are goin' down to get him out. Should be a couple of 'ours, and then e'll give ye a call. Any news 'bout Rose?"

"Not yet. I tried calling her embassy, but it's closed until the morning. I think I'll walk to the hospital and try to reach the supervisor. It's impossible to call him or her."

"Okay. Be careful now ye hear? Talk to ye in the bye and bye."

I walked into the bathroom and studied my face in the mirror. Crying made my nose red and my eyes swell, enhancing the green in my hazel eyes. Silvery streaks from fallen tears stained my skin. I splashed cold water on my face, ran a brush through my hair, and searched the hall closet for Rose's black Arabic garment. Women had to wear them over their clothes. As ugly as they were, they came in handy at times like these. I slipped it over my nightclothes and wrapped it around my slender body as I headed out the door.

****

    I stopped in the hospital vestibule, confused by the maze of corridors going in several directions. Which way to go? I tried to get my bearings standing in the darkened halls of the enormous hospital. I remembered the warning at orientation, night workers often raped unsuspecting women. I shivered, but pushed on. I had to help Rose.

    I chose a main hallway and spotted the elevators for the upper floors. I exited at the fourth floor and walked into the nurse's station.

    A British nurse looked me over and asked, "What are you doing here?"

    "Who are you?" a man demanded.

    An American woman pulled a chair from beneath the table and sat down. "She's one of the newbies who's gonna work on this unit."

    "What's the matter? Couldn't sleep?" the man teased.

    The nurses giggled.

    "I need to find the nursing supervisor. I tried calling from home, but the operator wouldn't give me the number.

    "Typical," snorted one of the British nurses.

    "Here, you need this. It's a list of the numbers in the hospital," the American offered.

    I took the paper from her hand. "These have prefixes!"

    "Yeah, rare thing that is! In Australia, where I come from, you 'ave numbers to call people. Not pagers. Funny place, this." He laughed.

    "Thank you. Thank you so much for helping."

    "You look pale and a bit shaken. Everything all right?" the American asked.

    "Well, no. My roommate was arrested and I need to help her."

    Everyone in the room froze. I heard several gasps then they all spoke at once.

    "What happened?"

    "Where did it happen?"

    "Was she alone?"

    "Was she with a man?"

    "Do you know where they took her?"

    The American pulled out another chair. "Here, Sit down. You look like you're going to faint."

    I sat down and garnered enough energy to speak. "I got a call from her friend who said they were arrested. I don't know any details."

"Wow. That's scary."

"Tell me. What color is 'er skin then?" the Australian asked.

"What difference does that make?"

"Well, if she's white and blonde like you, they won't go too hard on 'er. They'll take 'er for American, they will. If she's a blackey, it'll be a bit rougher for 'er."

"Oh dear. She has dark skin, but she holds a New Zealand passport."

"The matawa don't care. They won't know where she's from until her embassy gets involved," said the American.

"What's a matawa?"

"The religious police. They can be deadly," a male nurse answered.

The American nurse snapped, "You guys aren't helping. Can't you see she's worried?" She turned to me, "Why don't you page the supervisor? She should be able to help."

"I think I'll call her from home. I'm waiting for a call from Rose's boyfriend to see if he or his company can intervene."

I left the nurses and walked home as fast as I could, afraid of running into security and anxious to call the supervisor.

****

I turned the key, unlocking the apartment door, then picked up the phone and paged the supervisor. I shed the Arabic garment, allowing it to fall to the floor while waiting for the phone to ring. I paced. After a few minutes, I walked into the kitchen to look at the clock. The phone rang, startling me.

"You paged me?" inquired an impatient-sounding female voice.

"Yes. I am not sure who to call, or what to do. My roommate, Rose Casio was arrested."

"Arrested? How do you know? When?"

"I don't know the details. I got a phone call from her boyfriend a couple of hours ago."

"Her boyfriend? What prison is she in?"

"There's more than one prison for women?"

"There are two levels, one for severe crimes like prostitution, infidelity, stealing and that sort of thing, and another for minor offenses. I suggest you find out the prison, then call security and her embassy."

I swallowed hard. "Doesn't someone in the hospital system need to be notified?"

"Like who?"

"Isn't the hospital responsible for us? Aren't they the ones who sponsored us to get into the country in the first place?"

"Yes, they sponsored us."

"You don't sound very concerned."

"What do you expect me to do?" she snapped. "We were told when we came into this country, if you break the rules, you have to pay the price. I have to get back to work."

Irritated and disappointed, I put down the phone. Am I the only person willing to help Rose? I haven't been in the country a week and I need help, but from whom? Those rumors…Would they torture her? Rape her? What do they do to women in prison? I shouldn't think about it…but Rose…poor Rose.

I shuffled through more papers and found the number to the hospital security, then put my fingers in the rotary dial, watching it go around. I shivered, fearing for defenseless, vulnerable women.

"Hello. Dis is secur-it-e-ay."

"Oh…hello. I need to make a report. My roommate was arrested."

"Arrested you say ma'am? Oh ma'am. I am not person to talk. No. Abdul looks after arrest."

"Can I speak to him?"

"No ma'am. He gone 'til morning. I do not know what time."

"Is there anyone else I can talk to?"

"Yes. Khamal. Khamal at prayer. He not be back."

"So if Khamal won't be back, when will Abdul be in?"

"Maybe after prayer. Maybe later. En Shalla. Maybe the next day. En shalla."

I cringed. En Shalla. In God's time. That means it could be never.

"Fine. Thank you."

"Oh ma'am. I need your apartment number."

"Why?"

"So securit-e-ay come and talk."

"What? Now? No. I'll call this Abdul person in the morning. I don't need to talk to security face to face."

"But ma'am…"

"No," I said, hanging up the phone, knowing he wanted more than talk.

As I put down the receiver, the phone rang. I let it ring a second time, then answered, "What now?"

"Aye! Now is that any way to be speakin' to someone?"

"Oh. I'm sorry. I thought…"

"Never ye mind now, lass. I've got good news for ye. Ian's all right, now. Tey are treatin' him well and he'll be free in a short while, dat he will."

"What a relief. Where's he now?"

"We're still at ta men's prison. Tey are goin' troo some procedures and ta like. Don't ye be worryin' yurself over tis now."

"I'm relieved Ian will be free. Any idea where Rose is?"

"Not a word. Tese police types are tight-lipped, lassie. We're all worried 'bout her now. Ye know tat."

"I've been pulling my hair out trying to figure out what to do for her. Her embassy is closed. The nursing supervisor is useless and security is more interested in my location than intervening. No one can do anything until tomorrow."

"Well lass, 'tis nearly four-tirty in ta mornin'. Don't suppose tings'll be done now. I'll get Ian to call ye when tey release him. I tink it won't be too long, I'm sure."

"Thanks so much."

I sauntered to the kitchen and made a cup of tea, then sat down on the big-armed chair in the living room, resting my head against the overstuffed cushion. I felt calm for a moment, then startled when the phone rang. I glanced at the clock and realized I must have fallen asleep. It was past six in the morning.

"Hello, Claire? Ian here."

"Are you all right?"

"Yeah. They didn't do too much. Took my wallet and all the cash I had. They claim there wasn't any money in it, but you know. It's my word against a matawa's. It's okay. They can keep it. Five hundred US isn't too much to pay to get out of there."

"Did they mistreat you?"

"No. Just interrogated me and tried to intimidate me. Called me names, that sort of thing. I think they thought it was kind of a joke cuz it's okay for a man to have a prostitute. After all, if it weren't for the misbehavior of the woman, I wouldn't have been tempted, right?"

"How terrible."

"I know. But hey. This is Saudi Arabia. Any news on Rose? Dave here filled me in. Anybody doing anything yet? I'm worried sick."

"You and me both. I've been doing everything I can, but I'm helpless until business hours. How did you two get arrested in the first place?" I wrapped my arm around my waist and paced.

"Oh boy. I don't know if you knew or not, but we had a pretty serious fight. I left to pick her up because I didn't want the guys at work to hear what was going on. I had some things to do downtown anyway and I thought it would be easier to have Rose with me. We could settle things in the car. You know."

I stopped, clutched the phone, and put my hand to my cheek. "Ian, That's dangerous, a single woman with a man downtown. You weren't thinking."

"We've been downtown together before and had no problem. The thing is, Rose wouldn't do up her abaya. She left it open so everyone could see her legs and you know how offensive that is here. Well, as fate had it, a matawa stopped us. It would've been okay, but Rose mouthed off to him. The matawa was scolding me for not making my 'wife' behave and then Rose started laughing and said, 'As if you can make him tell me what to do'. He told her to cover her head. Rose didn't have a scarf with her, so we went back to the car to get it. When I opened the door, the matawa asked for our marriage license. We should have just walked away. We made a dumb mistake. We still had time to get away, but Rose was calling the matawa names, trying to prove a point. I don't know. You know how she gets sometimes. The next thing we knew, we were surrounded by a couple of armed policemen. I couldn't just leave her there, so we were arrested."

"She mouthed off to him?"

"Yup, that's my Rose. Um …. I have a sort of restraining order to keep away from Rose. If I go anywhere near that prison it will make it worse for the both of us. They'll arrest me again and then who knows what will happen to her. I got off easy this time and I don't want to push my luck, if you know what I mean."

I pulled a chair from the table closer to me and sat down, twirling the phone cord. "Do you know what prison she's in?"

"Yeah. The worst one. I'm pretty sure they'll charge her with prostitution. No sense in you worrying right now. Try and get some sleep and I'll do what I can from this end."

My heart sank. I knew Ian was right and perhaps I should try to get a little rest. I put the chair back and went into the kitchen to make a cup of tea. I sat on the couch, watching the clock, counting the hours and minutes until nine.

****

"Tell us the events as you know them," a concerned-sounding woman said over the phone from the New Zealand embassy. "We'll also need her passport number, if you have it. Don't worry, miss. We have a good diplomat named Mr. Morrison. He's experienced in such cases."

I twisted the phone cord around my finger. "Will she be all right, do you know?"

"Let's hope so. We'll keep you informed."

A tone of uncertainty in the woman's voice increased my anxiety as I hung up the receiver. I tapped my fingers on the table, staring at the phone, then picked up Ian's card, but put it down again. He couldn't help. I sighed, trying to keep calm. Where did I put the phone list the nurses gave me last night? Ah, there, on the kitchen counter. The paper shook in my hands, but I could read the printed numbers. I needed to call security and hoped I could speak to someone who would help.

"Yes? Who is it you want?" an Arabic voice inquired.

"I need to speak to Mr. Abdul."

"He not here."

"Do you know when he'll return?"

"Just minute."

He transferred the call to another male operator.

"What is it you want?"

"I need to speak to Mr. Abdul."

"He at prayer."

"Do you know when he'll be in?"

"No. One minute."

I was on hold again. I lifted my hand to my face and rested it on my cheek. Desperation was choking me. I pressed hard on my cheek, hoping to stop the tears.

"Hello."

"I need to speak to Mr. Abdul."

"I Abdul. How can I help?"

Surprised at how well he spoke English, I breathed a sigh of relief.

"Why did not anyone tell me about this before?"

"I tried all night to get help, but everyone said I had to wait until this morning." My tears dripped onto the carpet.

"In matters like these, I should be summoned. I will speak to whoever was in charge last night. This is bad. Very serious. I will correct it." His voice carried an angry tone.

"What will happen to Rose? Will they hurt her?" I wrapped the black telephone cord around my fist, stretching the coils to control my fears.

"So many questions. Yes, yes. It is serious. Rose will be questioned this morning. She is from New Zealand, so things may not be so rough."

I clutched my chest and swallowed hard, "Her skin is not white, you know. The nurses on the unit last night said that might go against her."

"Not white? And she is New Zealander?"

"That's right. She's very dark."

"Oh, I see. They may beat her or worse. Depends."

I wrapped another loop of the cord around my fist and stared at the blank wall. "Abdul, what can we do?"

"I have good reputation with the prison authorities. I will go down and speak to them myself. A Mr. Morrison, you said, is the man from her embassy? I will contact him and bring him with me. It will go better for Rose if the embassy official is there. I will call you later when I solve this problem."

"You can help Rose? Can you get her out of jail?"

"I have done this many times before. You wait for my phone call. I will call in three...mmm... maybe four hours."

I didn't feel well. My stomach was in my throat and my legs were like rubber. I turned and looked around the sparse apartment and without thinking, walked into the kitchen to make a cup of tea.

I watched the clock, the second hand making its rotations and the minute hand moving in its slow, steady, rhythm as I waited in agony. My imagination paralyzed me. I struggled, pushing images of Rose's incarceration from my mind.

Then I realized, I was supposed to be at the hospital this morning at eleven. I fretted, put down the tea, and rummaged through papers to find the phone number to the unit. I dialed the number.

"Anthony Herd, supervisor D4-1."

"Hello, this is Claire Spencer."

"Ah, Claire. Welcome to Saudi!"

"Mr. Herd, I ..."

"Anthony, please. Aren't you supposed to be here today?"

"That's what I'm calling about. I won't be able to come in. My roommate was arrested and I've been up all night trying to see what I could do for her."

"I see. I don't have a problem with you taking the day off, but because you're not sick, the hospital may insist you make up the shift."

"I don't care, Anthony. I'm in no state of mind to work."

"I didn't hear about any arrest. Did you phone the night supervisor to tell her? And security?"

"I did. I phoned everyone, but no one could do anything."

"The nursing supervisor did nothing?"

"No, nothing. I was frantic and no one helped."

"Hmm. This isn't good. The supervisors have a procedure to follow when someone gets into trouble."

"I didn't think the hospital would turn its back. Oh dear." I paced and brushed my hair away from my face.

"Listen, it's eleven-thirty now. Why don't you come to the coffee shop beside the corner store in about half an hour? I'd like to meet you and we can talk freely there. You never know when the phones are tapped."

"I'd like to meet you too, but I can't stay long because I'm waiting for a call from Abdul, the head of security."

"Abdul is good. He's efficient and cares about what happens to the nurses. By the way, I'm looking at the roster and the nursing supervisor on duty last night was... Karen Smythe. Ah ... she's going home."

"You mean fired?" I stopped pacing and stretched the black cord, almost pulling the phone off the table. I caught it before it fell to the floor.

"No. Last night was her last night to work and she's leaving Saudi to go back to her country today. It's too bad she didn't follow policy. I don't understand why, but there's nothing we can do about it now."

"How could someone be so heartless? Who knows what will happen to Rose in jail?"

"The hospital will intervene. They're pretty good in negotiating with the authorities. Rose is lucky she has a good embassy. If she came from India or the Philippines, it may not be so favorable. I'll meet you later."

****

I stood in the coffee shop entrance looking around. It reminded me of a fifties-style diner, complete with red padded chairs placed at bare tables. A line of hospital workers, holding plates ready to accept mounds of steamy food, approached servers behind glass barriers. Several people sat at tables, eating, conversing and laughing. I was nervous. I didn't know Anthony Herd. How would I recognize him?

A tall, sun-bleached blonde man approached me. He wore a white lab coat and carried a large cup of coffee. His soft blue eyes twinkled as he extended his hand.

"You must be Claire. What an introduction to this country. You've hardly been here a week and already your roommate is arrested."

Anthony directed me to a small round table in the corner of the open cafeteria.

"This is what we call the coffee shop. They make some good meals here, if you like rice dishes. Can I get you a cup of coffee?"

I shook my head and sat on the chair Anthony held for me. I crossed my legs and jiggled my foot under the table. "You must forgive me, I haven't slept much and the jet lag is still affecting me."

"It takes time. So you've finished your orientation and will start on my unit?" he said, taking a sip from his cup.

"Yes, I suppose so." I sighed, tucking a piece of hair behind my ear. "I thought I was going to work in the home health department, but was told there are no positions open."

"Well, you're assigned to D4-1, the VIP unit. You'll be caring for elite of the country, princesses, princes, and any dignitaries who need treatment."

"I haven't worked on the inside a hospital for years and was looking forward to nursing in the community."

"Yes, but you're small and blonde. More importantly, you are a Western woman from North America."

"That makes a difference?" Feeling uncomfortable, I held on to the edges of the chair with both hands and shrugged.

"It's like this. The Saudis like to think of themselves as the most superior humans on the face of the earth."

"They do?" I sighed, relaxing my shoulders.

"Yes, rank and hierarchy are a huge part of this society. You'll see after you've been here for a while. Some Saudis go to countries such as America, Britain, Germany, and Canada to get an education and take advantage of the technology of the West. They're jealous of Americans. By 'American', I mean people from both US and Canada. Most Saudis don't recognize a border between the countries and by 'using' the White Westerner as a servant of sorts, they think they're getting one up on us, if you know what I mean."

"Are you saying because I'm a White Western female, I have to work on the VIP unit?"

"Not 'have' to, but they prefer it and that's why you're not in home health."

"I'm not sure I understand." I wrapped my arms around my waist and leaned against the table.

"Perhaps not now, but you will in time. You're Western, white, and blonde. An image of an American ideal and one the Saudis would love to exploit. Also, your coloring is an oddity."

"The color of a person is important?"

"No, rank and position are."

Anthony cleared his throat and took another sip of coffee. "Now, tell me about your roommate."

I looked down at my hands on my lap. "After only a few days, I don't know her well. We haven't had a chance to talk much. She spends most of her spare time with her boyfriend." I sighed and looked into Anthony's eyes. "I'm worried sick about her."

"I know you are," Anthony said, patting my shoulder. I rested my hands on the table.

"I had one young Arab man who worked as a secretary on the unit. He and a male nurse who used to work here were accused of stealing a prince's watch. It was a difficult and tense situation. Both men were found innocent and it was discovered later the prince's personal assistant was the thief."

"What happened to your nurse and secretary?"

"Before we could prove they didn't take it, the nurse was sent home to England and the secretary was jailed. It took many meetings to convince the authorities not to cut off his hand. He has no family here, so I visited him every day and worked with protocol to get him out."

"That was so good of you. He didn't have his hand cut off, did he?"

"No. I knew he was innocent and he was a good worker. By going down to the men's prison every day, I showed the matawa he was useful. Anyway, after three months…"

"Three months!"

"Yup, months after the truth was discovered, he was set free. Problem was, the hospital administration staff didn't want him to return to work because the prince still felt he needed to prove a point. I spent many hours negotiating with protocol and eventually he was able to come back to work—at a reduced salary, of course."

Anthony finished his coffee and then rested the base of the cup on the table, twisting it towards him. He stared into the bottom of the cup, rolling it between his palms, looking like he was lost in memory.

I was touched by his story and didn't know what to say. I tucked a lock of hair behind my ear and asked, "Who or what is protocol?"

"They are Arab men, handpicked by elite royals who act as liaison officers between the staff and the VIPs. They've spent time in the US, Canada, or other countries going to school and learning English. They're familiar with Western lifestyles so they can explain the cultural peculiarities to the royals and settle any differences. Because they are given many privileges from royal families, they side with the royals, of course. Anytime there's a problem between staff and the VIPs, protocol intervenes. If protocol thinks they'll score points by catering to the VIPs, it's easy to get them to act on your behalf. If not, they won't pay any attention to your requests."

"Do we work with protocol on the unit?"

"Sometimes. They decide who's admitted to the floor and in some cases, who looks after the sick. If you gain their trust, they are pretty good, but some of them can be obnoxious and you have to watch your back. They scrutinize the nurses, interview the families about the care they receive, and if they want to, can make your life miserable."

"Will protocol help Rose?"

"No. Abdul in security will. I'll call him and find out what's going on."

"You don't think Rose will be in jail for months, do you?"

"She could be. Or longer. It all depends on her trial outcome."

"Can I visit her?"

"I'd be careful if I were you. You don't want to be charged with a crime because of your association with her. I'll check with Abdul and we can go from there. Where does Rose work?"

"In the recovery room."

He nodded and a strand of hair fell across his forehead. Brushing it back he said, "Her supervisor doesn't know she's been arrested. I'll tell her."

"Thank you, Anthony."

"That's all right. But listen Claire." Anthony tapped his fingers on the table. "You'll have to come to work on Monday, no matter what happens to Rose. There's no sense in your sitting at home fretting. I have your schedule here." He reached into his pocket. "I've put you down to work three, twelve-hour shifts, Monday, Tuesday, and Wednesday. You can have the weekend off giving you four days of rest and after that return to work. Oh, the workweek is from Saturday to Wednesday and the weekend is Thursday and Friday. Friday is the Islamic holy day. You'll get used to this schedule after a while."

"I understand."

"I'll give you a call later. I believe you're waiting for a phone call and I have to get back to work."

Anthony held my chair and smiled as I stood up. "Thanks, Anthony. For everything."

He put a heavy hand on my shoulder and winked. My stomach somersaulted. Was he being friendly or was it something else? No ... he was a kind man and I was overtired and over reacting. Wasn't I?

****

I trudged home, watching one foot flop in front of the other as I made my way to the elevator. Numb from lack of sleep, raw from emotional upset, my head pounded making me feel nauseous. I turned the key in the lock to the fifth floor apartment and heard the phone ringing. Rushing inside, I picked up the receiver on the old-fashioned phone. "Hello?"

"Hello, Claire. I calling you as promised," Abdul stated. "I found Rose. She in women's prison on Al Jahere road. It not good. This most severe prison, but not to worry. The matawas know her embassy involved."

"Did you see her? Is she okay?'

" No, I did not see her. I will go and try... mmm ... after evening prayer. There will be new staff then. She be charged with serious crimes."

"What's she been charged with?'

"Her official charges are: One—defying a matawa. She refused to cover head. Two—making public noise. It bad in this country to draw attention. She shouting at a man. Very rude. Very offensive. Three—laughing out loud in public and having fun. Four—this most serious. She with single man. They did not charge her with prostitution, but thinking it."

"What will happen to her?"

"It hard to say. Her court date is Wednesday. Her punishment soon after. On Friday, possibly."

"On Wednesday? But this is Sunday."

"Yes, our courts are not like yours. They are swift. You charged with crime in the week, your case be heard on Tuesday or Wednesday. Remember, you guilty until proven innocent. With embassy, it will go better. The officials don't want international incidents. If embassy wasn't involved, it be very bad. Yes, very bad."

An icy chill crept down my back as I hung up the phone. Trembling, I crossed my arms and stared at the floor, feeling small and uncertain. I released my grip then went to the kitchen, trying to digest Abdul's news.

****

The mournful call to afternoon prayer penetrated the apartment as I paced back and forth in the living room, impatient for Mr. Morrison to call. I opened a magazine and flipped through the pages, not concentrating on anything. I turned on the TV, changing one Arabic station after another. I walked to the phone, picked up the receiver, and listened. Good, it still had dial tone. I remembered I hadn't eaten all day and went into the kitchen. I opened the cupboards, but nothing appealed to me. I looked through the fridge and decided to boil a couple of eggs. I needed something to keep up my strength. It wasn't much of a dinner, but it would have to do.

It was eight o'clock when the phone rang.

"Hello. Is this Claire Spencer? This is Mr. Morrison from the New Zealand embassy."

"Oh, yes. Is Rose going to be let out? Did you see her? Is she all right?"

"No, I didn't see her. They wouldn't allow it. The good news is, the Saudis know several people are advocating for Rose. Mr. Abdul is there now and I've an appointment at eleven in the morning. We're negotiating her punishment."

"Punishment?"

"They want to charge her with prostitution. That's serious and could result in a stoning."

"They aren't going to stone Rose?" I could not believe my ears.

"Not with our involvement, they won't. Rose has to make a public apology to the matawa and she may have to pay him a hefty fine. I don't know. We'll see what we can negotiate."

"Poor Rose." I sighed and sat down. "Is there any way I can go and see her?"

"Mmm …You may be able to go on Thursday, after the court hearing. Rest assured, she's safe tonight. Trust me on that one."

"How long will she have to stay in jail?"

"I'm not sure. We're doing our best to get her out, but I doubt she'll be out before Friday. Trust me, we're doing our best."

I thanked him, phoned Ian, and related Mr. Morrison's news.

"It's all my fault. I shouldn't have picked her up that day. I was so angry and I wanted to put her straight."

"Don't blame yourself, Ian."

When I got off the phone, I poured myself a hot bath and tried to relax.

I needed sleep before going to work in the morning. Climbing into bed, I nestled beneath the cozy comforter and prayed, "Please God, keep Rose safe."

Chapter Two

"Welcome to the VIP unit." Anthony seemed relaxed as he addressed the newcomers. "I hope your first week of orientation was helpful."

My mind drifted, thinking about the past week, listening for hours to welcome speeches, preparing for and writing competency exams, followed by a tour of the hospital. Anthony's voice jarred me into the present.

"As you'll see, this is a large unit, approximately one city block on each side of the hall. The suites on the left are for long-term care patients. There are no facilities in the kingdom for the elderly or disabled. Our long-term patients are victims of car accidents and were lucky enough to be injured by a royal. "

"Lucky?" asked one nurse.

"In Saudi, if you injure someone, you're responsible for him for the rest of his life. That's why he's here. Some prince is footing the bill and will pay for the hospital care and whatever the family needs or wants. They're provided with servants, a home, and almost anything he asks. It's a pity someone was severely injured, but his family benefits."

"Aren't there any female long-term care patients?" I asked.

"No. Females aren't worth anything." He cleared his throat. "Claire, I'm going to pair you with a nurse named Barbara. She'll show you around and answer your questions."

A short stocky nurse approached me and extended her hand. "Hi. I'm Barbara. I'll show you around the unit, then you can do a dressing change on the toe of one of our patients."

"Sounds fine."

The rooms had large, comfortable sofas and recliners. Each had its own well-stocked fridge. Sometimes the families and their servants took up two or three rooms.

"Why do they need so much space?"

"For the sitters or servants and to keep the men and women separated. Men and women don't mingle in this country. Ever."

"The servants stay in the hospital with the patient?"

"Yes, Saudis like to be waited on. They're lazy. Another thing, all nurses are called 'sister' and our work is centered around what the patient wants or demands."

"You mean the patient dictates his or her own care?"

"They're VIPs and like to tell people what to do. That includes us, if we let them."

"But how can they know what's good for them when they have no medical background? Don't they know they can harm themselves?"

"Welcome to the VIP unit in Saudi Arabia. Don't look so shocked, Claire. It's not that we don't care, we're not able to. The medical role in the kingdom is reduced to a glorified maid service for both doctor and nurse. Several doctors and nurses have terminated their contracts and gone home."

"But what about ethics and practices?"

Barbara laughed. "Listen. It's hard at first, but let me give you a few words of advice. Don't be too efficient and don't try to change anything. You'll make it difficult for yourself, get frustrated, leave, and no one will give a damn."

I frowned, not understanding what she meant.

"You signed a two-year contract, right? You'll work for a couple of years and then be gone." She swallowed. "You'll soon see what I'm talking about, but they're only bloody Arabs. They don't care about you, so why should you care about them?"

"That's a terrible attitude. They're human beings, deserving care and comfort. No matter who or what they are, I believe in upholding the dignity of every individual."

Barbara laughed. "So idealistic!" She laughed again. "Just watch your back, sweetheart. There're people who'd eat you for lunch." Barbara shook her head. "Go and do this dressing for our patient, Mubaruk. See if you feel the same afterwards."

I withdrew into my own world. I didn't understand. I felt a stubbornness rising from the bottom of my stomach. Or was it outrage?

I opened a blue chart with the name *Mubaruk Al Saud* pasted on the spine and read about his long history of diabetes. He was admitted because he didn't look after his feet and had part of his great toe amputated. I closed the chart, then gathered the supplies for the dressing change, headed down the hall, and knocked on Mubaruk's door. "Hello? Mr. Mubaruk?" I pushed the heavy wooden door open and poked my head inside.

Mubaruk balanced himself on his elbow, hugging his pillow for support, and looked at me sideways. "What you want?" he shouted.

"I'm here to do your dressing."

"No. Not today." He rolled over in the bed, turning his back.

Ignoring him, I set up the room with the dressing tray, normal saline, and other supplies.

"What you want?"

I smiled and said, "Roll over on your back. I need to get at your toe."

Mubaruk glared at me. I put my hands on my hips and watched his dark eyes soften. "I'm not going to leave until you let me change your dressing. It'll only take a few minutes."

He was reluctant to roll on his back. After a few moments he asked, "Where you from?"

"Canada."

"You married?"

I stopped and studied his face, puzzled by his question. I didn't like the look in his eyes.

"You married?" he repeated.

"Why do you want to know?"

"You be my wife, okay?"

"Oh no. No." I shook my head.

"Why, you married? You should be pregnant."

I concealed a silent gasp and didn't respond to his comment, concentrating on my work. Then the door burst open. Five men talking on cell phones entered wearing the traditional long white robes.

"Excuse me gentlemen, but I'm in the middle of something here. Could you please wait outside?"

They laughed and snorted. Two of them sat on a long couch near Mubaruk's bed and observed me. Three others stood at the door, folded their arms across their chests and guarded the exit, occasionally flipping the corners of their red-checked headdresses over their shoulders. They were silent, but had sly grins on their faces. I could feel the tension increasing and sensed they were planning something. But what? I was acutely aware of everyone and every action in the room. My heart raced and my hands were soaking wet inside the latex gloves, yet I forced myself to keep a calm outer appearance, knowing their eyes studied me.

Mubaruk turned to the men on the couch, then looked at me, scoffed, and said something in Arabic. One of the men pointed at me and made a gesture, miming a swollen belly. The men laughed. Ignoring them, I fought the rising panic and wondered how I'd get past the men and out the door.

I secured the gauze dressing with a piece of tape and wrapped the garbage in a plastic bag, leaving the tools on the table. I washed my hands in the sink and took a few steps toward the door, but the men wouldn't budge.

"Do any of you speak English?" I asked.

"Yes, we all do," replied one man.

"Do you know who this man is?" a second man asked, leaning forward on the sofa.

"He is a very important businessman. Very rich."

That was supposed to impress me? I rolled my eyes.

Mubaruk spoke. "Tell me. Why you not married?"

"You would do well to marry this man. He is very rich." He smiled sideways. "You could have many children."

I felt fear rise from the pit of my stomach and wrapped an arm around my waist to steady myself. I didn't trust their intentions.

"You marry him and you will be rich."

"No, I will not marry him. I don't want children."

Annoyed, Mubaruk demanded, "Why you not married?"

"Um … Because my father won't allow it."

The men gasped.

"What you mean, father won't allow? All fathers want daughters to marry. No more troubles."

"I'm the eldest daughter of my family." I hesitated. "Um…we're Catholics and the eldest daughter has to become a nun."

"Oh—so you never married. You are virgin!" The men's expressions changed and they appeared to be in awe of me. I wished I didn't lie, but I was desperate to say or do anything to get out of the room.

"You be my wife," shouted Mubaruk.

"I have to leave." Turning toward the door I said, "Please get out of my way."

A man near the door approached me.

"You should be pregnant."

Another man who towered above me stepped forward and trapped me against the bed. I couldn't move. He giggled and rubbed his hand over my chest, looking down on me as if he possessed me. I felt sick. Gathering my strength and controlling my urge to vomit, I shoved him as hard as I could. He stumbled back, but regained his balance. He looked me up and down, as if I were a prized animal, then grabbed and pulled on my uniform top. I slapped his arm. He wouldn't let go, so I hit him harder. He laughed, then stepped back, and put his hands on his hips, thrusting his pelvis forward and backwards. He took one step closer then another. A second man laughed and copied him.

"We show her how not be virgin!"

They laughed.

My fear was mounting and I felt out of control. From the corner of my eye I saw my dressing tools on the table. I wiggled towards them, then took a pair of scissors and raised them above my head shouting, "Move! Get out of the way!"

The man straightened and crossed his arms as if to test me. "She thinks she going to hurt me with those little things?" He laughed.

The men jeered and egged him on. He reached out to grab the scissors, but I moved, avoiding his attempt, then lashed out and nicked the palm of his hand. He screamed and jumped back. He held his wrist and watched as a single drop of blood fell to the floor. The men gasped and spoke in hushed tones. I was in control. Seizing the opportunity, I raised the scissors above my head, took a step forward, and shouted, "Move out of my way!"

"Okay. Okay, sister. You leave."

They allowed me to pass. I kept the scissors above my head and backed out of the room, staring hard into their astonished faces. The door closed and then I heard them break into raucous laughter. Turning on my heels, I marched down the hallway, ignoring the curious onlookers and headed straight toward Anthony.

When I got to the nurse's station, Anthony greeted me with an inquisitive expression as he talked on the phone. He brushed aside a piece of silver hair that fell across his forehead, and hurried to finish his conversation with the person on the other end of the phone. I waited, clutching the scissors and suppressing tears threatening to spill over.

"Are you all right?" He asked, hanging up the phone. "You look shaken. Come into my office." He offered me a chair. "What happened? Is it Rose?"

I opened my mouth, but couldn't speak.

"Do you want a glass of water?" Anthony leaned out the door to his office and called to the nurse in charge. "Nicole, look after Claire's patients. We're in a meeting."

He closed the door, then lowered himself on the chair and pulled out a bottle of water and paper cups from a drawer. "Why don't you let me have those?" He took the scissors from my hand, replacing them with a paper cup.

I wrapped both my hands around the cup and took a drink.

"What's wrong, Claire?"

"I … I was changing Mubaruk's dressing. Things were going well until some visitors cornered me and threatened me. I was scared they'd rape me right there in his room."

"You were looking after Mubaruk?"

"I was assigned to change his dressing. Anthony, never in my nursing career have I refused to look after a patient. I've looked after all kinds of people, dangerous ones, mentally sick ones, and heaven only knows. I've never been so humiliated or felt so sickened by what happened in his room today. I never, ever want to nurse that man again!" I wiped away a tear.

"Okay. Okay. I don't know why you were assigned to him. I made it clear no female was to work with him. I'll look into this and I promise, you won't have to take care of him again." Anthony leaned toward me with a box of Kleenex.

I took a tissue and wiped my eyes. "I don't understand."

"Just a minute." Anthony walked out the door of the office and spoke to some nurses. They laughed and jested until Anthony scolded them. He returned to his seat and spoke in measured tone. "Your colleagues thought you needed a little initiation to the ward and as a joke, they assigned Mubaruk to you. The good news is they won't do it again, or they'll be written up and suspended."

"Why would they want to do that to me?"

"Jealousy. They are jealous and relish in backstabbing. Another thing, you're paid more than they are. Every nationality has a different pay scale. Canada and the US have the highest. Also, you are pleasant and it seems some can't stand to see anyone happy. It's a strange place, so I'll give you a word of advice. Keep your head down."

"This doesn't sound encouraging. I can't believe the staff would want to hurt one another. Surely, it can't be true."

"Well Claire, people come here for a variety of reasons. Most are running from something. I won't say anything more. If you have problems, come to me and I'll help you."

"There's something else you should know…I… I stabbed one of them with the scissors."

"You did what?"

"I was cornered. They wouldn't let me pass and trapped me. It was a reflex response…I feel so bad…"

"Where did you stab him?"

"In the hand. I don't think he was hurt. I heard him laughing when I left the room."

"Stay here. I have to go and talk with him."

Tears rolled down my cheeks and I trembled. What next? I knotted the tissue, turning it around in circles, staring at my lap through blurry eyes.

In a few minutes, Anthony returned and shut the office door. He sat down and put a hand on my shoulder. "Don't be too upset, Claire. Here."

He gave me another tissue.

"You didn't hurt him. Look at the size of those little scissors. The blades aren't even an inch long. You couldn't do much damage, even if you wanted to. He just got a scratch, that's all, but I'll have to talk to the people in protocol about this incident and have them speak to Mubaruk. What time is it?" He looked at his watch. "Nearly five o'clock. I think you can take the rest of the day off."

"But ..."

"You can't work. You're too upset and you should probably be invisible for the rest of the day." He sighed then asked, "How would you like to join me for dinner in the family dining room? I want to talk to you about your roommate and get to know you a little better."

" Oh ... okay." I stammered. "That would be nice."

"You remember where it is, don't you? Third floor in the hospital?"

"Yes, I think so."

I wasn't sure if he was flirting or if he had a natural glint in his eye.

"Okay. Let's meet at six thirty." Anthony stood up and held the office door. "I don't think you should be alone right now and I don't want you to entertain ideas of going home to Canada."

I exited the office without responding and walked home. How confusing. Was this a business dinner or a date? I was still shaky from the Mubaruk incident and was nervous about Anthony's intentions.

Back at the apartment, I checked the answering machine. No messages. I hoped Rose was all right.

****

Anthony was still in his lab coat when he met me outside the dining room.

"Hello Claire. Where would you like to sit?"

I scanned the room, where hospital staff members occupied most of yellow-clothed, square tables and chose a booth on the perimeter.

"I don't like to be out in the middle," I apologized. "You said you had some news about Rose."

"I spoke to Abdul today. Rose had her trial."

"Already? Oh, I wish I'd known. I'd have gone to give her support."

"You wouldn't have been allowed. Women are not admitted as spectators at court."

"They're not? What was the outcome?" I pushed my hands into the soft brown leather of the bench, shrugging my shoulders.

"It's serious. She was charged with prostitution and being disrespectful to the matawa, along with some other things."

"What will happen to her now? She won't be stoned, will she?"

"I don't think so. Abdul said if she'd kept her mouth shut, things may have gone better for her. She argued with the judge and called him names."

"In court?"

"Yes. She's a feisty one. She's sentenced to pay the matawa and his family the equivalent of fifteen thousand US dollars and to have one hundred lashes."

"One hundred lashes." I covered my heart with both of my hands. "They aren't going to do that to her. They'll kill her."

"They won't give one hundred lashes at one time. They'll give her ten or fifteen the first Friday and continue to give her lashings every other Friday until she's had them all."

"What can we do to stop this?" I was aware my hands were crimping into tight fists.

"Not much. We have to rely on Mr. Morrison and Abdul."

I felt the color drain from my face and looked away.

"If there were anything I could do, I would you know." I felt Anthony's warm hand on mine.

I pulled my hand away.

"Abdul said you can go and see her on Thursday. He and his wife will accompany you. I will too, if you like."

I searched Anthony's eyes. I couldn't tell if he was being generous or if he was trying to win me over. "I don't know."

"I don't mind and besides, you may need a shoulder to lean on." He winked.

"I can manage. I'm a strong person," I said, as I ignored his wink.

"I didn't mean to imply you weren't. I thought you'd like familiar company, that's all."

I squirmed in my seat and studied him. His blond graying hair aged him. I guessed he was ten years my senior.

"I won't press you. You're going through a lot right now. Your roommate got arrested and some Arab men accosted you today. How are you doing?"

"I'm all right." I looked away. "They didn't hurt me, just scared me a little."

"I hope you aren't thinking of going home."

"No, the thought hadn't crossed my mind." I sighed. "Tell me Anthony, how long have you been in Saudi?"

"Five years now."

"Why so long? Do you like it here?"

"It's not that I like it. I need the income to support my family. I have a disabled wife in a nursing home, one son in university, and a daughter who'll be entering college next September."

"I'm sorry about your wife."

"It's lonely at times, but I get along."

He looked into my eyes, until I looked away, uncomfortable from his stare.

"And you? Why did you come to Saudi? Are you married?"

"I came for a change. I was married a long time ago, but he left me for someone else."

My mind raced back to the memory of the pain and isolation. I didn't care about myself, but grieved for my children. Imagine walking out on two small kids, never to contact them again.

"Do you have children?" His question interrupted my thoughts.

"I had two boys. The eldest died of complications of a rare disorder about five years ago. My youngest is out of school and working." I laughed. "I suppose every parent wants their child to turn into something wonderful."

"You look too young to have grown children."

"Well, thank you, but I do."

"May I ask you how old you are?"

"You may ask, but I may not tell the truth."

We laughed.

"You said you came to Saudi Arabia for a change? It's a huge change from anything we're used to."

"Perhaps." I tucked my hair behind my ear. "I'm looking forward to working and immersing myself in an international community and eager to learn different approaches to medical care. I hope to meet a group of intellectuals who, like myself, want to expand their roles in life. I'm anxious to learn more about Saudi Arabia and its people."

"That sounds noble, but you'll be hard-pressed to meet those kinds of people here."

"What do you mean?"

"Most people are looking to make a fast buck or are running away from problems."

I frowned, and reached over to pick up the menu. I tried to read the words, but the red letters on yellow paper blended, forming swirls and shapes. Nothing was comprehensible. I gave up and turned to Anthony. "What's good?"

"You can never go wrong with the chicken. They make a nice side rice and it's filling."

"Okay, I'll order it."

Anthony put down his menu and smiled. "Claire, tell me more about yourself."

"What do you want to know?" I swallowed to prevent a lump from forming in my throat.

"Are your parents still alive? Do you have siblings?"

"Yes, I still have both my parents. As a matter of fact, it was my father who encouraged me to go away for a while."

"Your father?" Anthony moved a glass from in front of him.

"I think he saw how tired I was. After my son Thomas died, things weren't the same. My younger son, Joseph, quit school in grade eleven so he didn't graduate." I tapped my fingers on my crossed arms. "He's one child who should be in university. I'm not saying that because I'm his mother, but because he has such a sharp intellect. I hope one day he'll discover it for himself and hunger to learn."

"I'm having a tough time with my daughter. She wants to quit school and become a beautician. I think she should be a physiotherapist."

"I don't know what Joseph should be. He should just do something. Or be something in the academic world. I think it's been hard for him, with no father—at least not one he could communicate with."

"Didn't your kids see their dad?"

"No. When he walked out the door, he closed it not only on me, but also on the children. I don't understand men who turn their backs like that. Then when Thomas died, nothing was the same. I think Joey misses his brother very much, but he won't talk about it. I sent him to a counselor and he stopped going after a while. I don't know…"

I looked down at my hands, feeling Anthony's eyes on me.

"Your father wanted you to go away because you were tired?"

"Yes, and for other reasons. My dad thought a change would be good for me. He said I spent enough time rearing children and I should go and seek a life for myself. You see, I have a younger brother and sister who were struggling. They came to me for help, since I was the one with the steady income and a permanent address. Not that I minded helping, but Dad said I was enabling and the best thing I could do for them and for myself was to go away." I smiled remembering my father's expression when I broke the news I was going to Saudi Arabia. "When Dad told me to go away and work elsewhere, he meant Texas or some other US state. He didn't think I'd pack up and take off to the Middle East."

Anthony laughed. "This place is different."

"You're here because of your family, too."

"Yes, and I don't see leaving anytime soon. University is expensive and the medical plan only covers so much. The rest I have to pay for and then there's always retirement, and that's only ten years away."

I squinted, realizing Anthony gave away his age. He was fifty-five, fourteen years older than me.

"Claire, I don't want you to get the wrong idea. I'm completely devoted to my wife, Irene. It's rare to find a person I can talk to. Most want to get as much out of you as they can, then leave you to rot. I'm careful with friendships and from the first moment we spoke, I knew you were not like the others."

"What makes you think that?" I squirmed, not quite believing him.

"The fact that you care enough about your roommate, for one thing. Very few would do what you've done."

"I haven't done anything."

"Yes, you have. If it were someone else, they wouldn't care about a missing roommate. They'd leave it in the hospital's hands and the hospital wouldn't notice for three or four days."

"My goodness Anthony, I couldn't turn my back on her. And if it were me, I hope someone would try to get me out of prison."

"Your caring attitude makes you different."

I searched his eyes, looking for clues. Could I trust him? He seemed sincere and I believed he wanted a friendship. I crossed my legs and shook my foot under the table. "If you want to escort me to the woman's prison with Abdul and his wife, I'd like that."

"It's settled. How about nine o'clock Thursday morning?"

"I guess so." I sat back against the soft leather and sighed, relieved someone was willing to help.

****

My thoughts drifted to Rose as I wrote notes in a patient's chart at the nurses' station. No news in two days.

"Hello, Claire."

I turned and saw Anthony, smiling with his hands on his hips.

"Hi, Anthony. Why are you here at this late hour?"

"I had work to catch up on. I've something to ask you."

"You do? Okay." He was up to something.

"Have you been to the souqs?"

"The what?"

"The souqs. That's the Arabic name for store. I thought you might want to do some shopping—to take your mind off things."

"Isn't that dangerous? I mean, being with a man and shopping in those areas? My roommate's in jail for the very same thing. Remember?"

"I didn't mean go shopping with me. There's a lady who works the night shift and I don't know if you met her. Her name is Monera. She's a great Egyptian lady. She said she'd be happy to take you around after visiting Rose at the prison. You need your own abaya, right? It'll be good for you to go, especially after seeing the Saudi prison. I think you'll need the diversion."

I sighed, putting a lock of hair behind my ear. Anthony didn't move, just stared at me. "I'll go because you're asking Anthony. If it were anyone else, I would say 'no'."

"Good. Meet me in the lobby at eight forty-five. Abdul and his wife will take us to the prison. Then Monera will meet you in the lobby later in the afternoon. See you tomorrow."

I watched Anthony walk down the hall. He looked beleaguered and I felt sorry for him.

****

I zipped the long black garment Rose left hanging in the hall closet and was careful to put a scarf in my purse. My hands trembled. Was I nervous about the prison or about being with Anthony?

Before stepping outside, I walked into the bathroom and checked my makeup. I hoped I wasn't wearing too much. I didn't want to be arrested for that.

I opened the exterior door and was met with a wall of heat. A thermometer hanging in the shade showed it was forty degrees Celsius. And it was only April... I dreaded the summer months.

I made my way to the hospital lobby and spotted Anthony wearing tight-fitting jeans and a yellow shirt tucked inside his pants. His rotund belly hung over the top of the belt. Not a flattering picture.

"Ah, Claire. Abdul and his wife are waiting. This way."

A man sitting in the driver's seat smiled as we got into the car. "Hello. I'm Abdul. This is my wife, Heiffa." He pointed to a woman in the back seat.

I turned to greet her, but the woman sat motionless, staring out the window. She was veiled from head to toe and wore black gloves.

"Ah, my wife. She no speak English. She did not want to come, but I insist, or you cannot see your friend."

"If it was too much Abdul..."

"No, no. This my duty and Heiffa knows better. She get over it, you'll see."

Anthony looked at me and shrugged.

The ride took us through the congested downtown section. Cars changed lanes haphazardly and stopped suddenly at red lights. The buildings were squeezed into city blocks and throngs of people walked the paved streets, some disappearing into stores. As we drove from the city, spaces widened and only a trace of civilization lined the paved highway. I looked out the front window, eyeing a single sand-colored building in the distance.

"There! That is prison where is your friend. Now listen to me. You pretend you are this man's wife, yes? You cover hair and do not talk. I do all talking. They may not let you in, but if they are in good mood, perhaps they will. If they do not, I will press them so I can see her. You understand?"

"Yes," I mumbled.

We turned off the paved highway onto a dusty road. A cloud of brown haze followed the van as we pulled up to a large wrought-iron gate leading to the main entrance. Abdul spoke in Arabic over an intercom and the gates opened. We drove to the building and stopped, leaving the van and approached the building. Heiffa lagged behind and Abdul reprimanded her, making her quicken her step.

We walked into an overwhelming stench of stale urine and rotting meat. My nostrils began to burn, making my eyes water.

"Are you sure you want to go through with this?" Anthony asked.

"Yes, I'm sure," I said, straightening my shoulders.

Abdul spoke with one of the guards, flailing his arms in several directions. His facial expressions were almost comical as he seemed to go through a ritualistic display, bargaining for favors. He turned and said, "Okay. Listen. You have ten minutes only. When matawa ask you leave, you go. Understand?"

"Yes."

"You follow that man."

"I'm going by myself?"

"Yes. We are not allowed."

"What about your wife?"

Abdul laughed. "You not get her to do anything. Go, or you miss your chance."

I pulled a corner of the scarf over my nose and followed the armed security guard through a locked steel door and into a long corridor. The unpleasant odors worsened the deeper we trudged into the building. I gagged a couple of times, but reminded myself I was there for Rose and had to be strong.

Naked light bulbs hung on long black cords from the tall ceilings, illuminating the grimy hallway in a dim light. Although I did my best not to brush up against the walls, dust and spider webs left their gray marks on my dark abaya. I was cautious on the hard-packed sand, straining to see and avoided the potholes in the well-worn path. As we ventured further into the darkness, rats scurried past, sometimes running across my feet. I held my breath to stop from screaming. I was here for Rose and I had to know she was all right. My determination drove me forward through the sickening, inhumane conditions.

We passed several empty cells on either side of the corridor. Each of them had a shallow pit in the center for urination and defecation. Decaying rats lay rotting beside skeletal remains and rancid human waste. In the distance, I heard whimpering and what sounded like the cry of a small child.

We came to the end of the hall and faced a large wooden door. The guard pushed his rifle to one side so he could reach a set of keys attached to his belt. He yelled something in Arabic to another man behind the door. He unlocked and opened the door, gesturing me to walk through. I hesitated. If I went through, would they let me out? I had to chance it.

I smiled at the guard as I passed and thanked him. He nodded his head, looking down at the floor. A second guard greeted me with a crooked smile, exposing a missing front tooth. As the guard slammed the door, dust fell from the tin ceiling. I readjusted my scarf to shield myself from the falling dirt.

The stench was worse in these corridors and my nostrils, already burning from the putrid smells, felt like flames reaching deep into my skull. I could taste the repugnant odors in my mouth and gagged. I fought the temptation to turn and run.

I wanted air. There were no windows, just a six-inch space between the roof and the walls for ventilation. I couldn't breathe and choking, concentrated hard to stop from retching. How could Rose survive this?

We passed a cell where Filipino women huddled on the floor. When they saw me, they bounded to their feet and pressed against and reached through the bars. They were dirty, skinny, and pathetic. I jumped backward, escaping their desperate attempts to grab onto me. The guard pulled a long stick from inside his jacket and shouted at them, hitting the stick against the bars. The women screeched and shrank back, then cried out from the darkness. My knees were about to give way when the guard yelled, "Come!"

I said a silent prayer for them, trying to block out their haunting, anguished pleas. Their cries echoed through me, their despair etched on my soul, numbing me. I felt like a traitor as I trudged toward Rose.

The guard stopped and pointed. "There! She there. Ten minutes, you understand?"

I nodded and he sauntered away. I scanned the cell, the sea of women crammed together, looking for Rose. But they all looked the same. "Oh my goodness, a baby! What's a baby doing in there?" I gasped.

A woman stirred, then stood up.

"Claire? Claire is that you?"

"Rose?"

Rose clutched her dusty clothes as she staggered forward. Her long black hair was tangled and matted, her dirty face streaked with tears. The other women in the cell crowded Rose, pushing her into the iron bars.

"Get back," she shrieked.

Rose shoved and they backed up, disappearing into their pitiful places deep inside the cell.

"I only have a few minutes, Rose."

"Get me out of here."

"We're doing our best, really we are."

"Please don't leave me here. Please, Claire, please!"

I swallowed hard and fought to suppress tears.

"Look what these bastards do. Look at the women in here."

I looked around. As my eyes adjusted to the light, I saw several small children. "Why are there children in prison?"

"They belong to the Filipinos. The Arabs don't care about them. Their mothers are charged with prostitution and are going to be killed on Friday."

"Killed?"

"Yeah—stoned to death."

" Stoned! The children too?"

"I don't know. I just know that every one of them was raped. Even the little children."

"Not the children!"

"They are sick people. I *hate* the Arabs. They pretend to be so pious, hiding behind their Qu'ran, using it as an excuse to abuse people. I want them all dead," she spat.

"Rose, you haven't been raped, have you?"

"No way. I won't let these lousy pigs touch me. I fight and scream. Those women don't fight. They've been taught to be submissive. None of the guards have raped me and they won't as long as I have the strength to fight them off."

"Oh, Rose. I wish there were something I could do."

"Just get me out. *Please.*"

"We're working real hard. Trust me, we are."

"Okay. Time go," the guard said.

"I have to go, Rose."

"Claire, get me out of here. Help me!"

Her pleas resonated down the halls, unceasing, lingering, chasing me until I burst through the front doors and into Anthony's strong, comforting arms.

"Claire, are you all right?"

I couldn't speak. The lump in my throat stopped sound from escaping. I took several deep breaths, fighting back tears.

"Hurry, hurry," Abdul said.

He rushed us to the car. Anthony opened my door, then started to climb in the seat beside me.

"You no sit in back with women!"

Anthony hesitated then climbed into the front seat.

"It was that bad?"

"It was much worse than I imagined," I choked on my words. "I'm sorry. I can't keep from crying."

Anthony offered me a tissue. "It's okay. Let it out."

"Women! Always hysterical. That is why I do not like to take them anywhere."

"Abdul, Claire is not hysterical. She hasn't experienced your prisons before and she's in shock."

I straightened. "I'm all right. I just feel sorry for those women. They're being mistreated and abused. Did you know there are children in that prison?"

"Children?" Anthony looked shocked.

"Yes, that is true," Abdul said.

"Why children?"

"They are offspring of prostitutes. They no good."

"No Good? They are innocent children."

"They not innocent as you say. They born with the sin of their mothers."

"Nonsense, they're defenseless children!" I stiffened.

"No! They products of devil's work. They are..."

"That's enough! Let's not get into a debate, right Claire? Abdul?"

I ignored him. "You think those women are prostitutes?"

"Of course! It is different for the nurses at the hospital. They are used to being with men socially. It accepted in your culture. Here, it is not. They Muslim woman and know better. Men and women are forbidden to socialize like Westerners."

Anthony turned around and gestured for me to be quiet. Heiffa stared out the window, ignoring us.

"Rose said the women will be stoned on Friday. If they die, what will happen to the children?"

Anthony gave me another look.

"They won't be stoned, if that what you mean. Sometimes, if children are old enough, they may be useful. The other ones be taken to the desert."

"The desert? To be let free?"

"They taken there and whatever happens, poof! In Allah's hands."

"But they could die!"

"Only if it Allah's Will."

"They do die, Claire. They're taken there to die," Anthony whispered.

A cold chill ran through me. They couldn't be that cruel and heartless, could they? I didn't want to know. I willed myself to stop thinking, to stop asking questions and stared out the window.

Back at the hospital, Anthony and I watched Abdul drive away. I walked through glass sliding doors, escaping from the desert heat into the air-conditioned building.

"Are you all right?"

"Yes, I think so. I'm trying to absorb all of this. Those poor women. And the little children."

"There are some aspects of this culture that are harsh and ugly."

I sat down on an empty bench in the corner of the lobby.

"Claire, Can I get you anything?"

"No thanks, Anthony. I think I'll go home."

"Hey, don't forget about your shopping date with Monera later today."

"I don't feel like shopping. I don't want to go."

"I know, but you must."

"Why?"

"It'll keep your mind off things and you may even see a nice part of life in Arabia. It's for your own good."

I sighed. "Why do you care so much about what I'm going through?"

"Because…" He scratched his head. "I care about my staff."

I chewed my lower lip and sensed he cared more about me than his staff. I remembered his arms around me in the jail and how safe he made me feel. Anthony smiled and rested his hand on my shoulder. Absent mindedly, I put my hand over his. These simple gestures gave me strength, but stirred emotions best left dormant.

****

I poured a hot bath, eager to wash away the prison dirt and settle my nerves. I stripped off my clothes and slipped into the bath, laying back to allow the steamy water to ease my tension. I thought about having to go out again. I didn't want to go shopping, but Anthony was right. I needed a diversion, something to take my mind off the prison.

As I finished drying myself, the phone rang. I threw on my housecoat and ran to answer it.

"Miss Spencer? This is Mr. Morrison."

"How are you? What is happening?"

"We're deep in negotiations, but they're stalling. They want Rose to pay fifteen thousand US dollars and impose restrictions on her. The good news is, they're still talking with us. There's something else you should know."

I pulled a chair from the table and sat down. I felt deflated and prepared for more bad news. "What else should I know?"

"If we can't make a deal with the Saudis, they'll punish her."

"Punish her how?"

"Unfortunately, Chop-Chop Square is looking like a reality. She could be stoned for prostitution."

"Stoned!"

"Hang on—remember the fines. She can't pay them if she's in prison and she has no family here they can threaten. Just the same, I want you to prepare yourself."

"Prepare myself! For what? Her death?"

"It's a possibility. Or she may be in prison indefinitely. I assure you, Miss Spencer, we are doing all we can. It's a delicate situation."

"I understand."

I hung up the phone and stared at it for a long time. Did I understand? No. And I would never understand. I shivered with fear as I went into the kitchen to make a cup of tea.

Chapter Three

I waited in the airy vestibule of the hospital lobby thinking about Rose and dreading the shopping trip Anthony committed me to. I stared into space and then focused on a stocky woman walking towards me, wearing a black silky scarf stylishly draped over her hair. It fell in long graceful folds around her broad shoulders down to the middle of her back and her heavy makeup and tattooed eyebrows highlighted her deep brown eyes. Black eyeliner extending to her temple and henna-dyed lips balanced her weighty features reminding me of pictures I had seen of Cleopatra.

"Are you Claire?"

"Yes, I am." I stood up and held out my hand. "You must be Monera."

"Yes. You are new to the Kingdom, so I decided to introduce you to the culture and the souqs. You have heard the word 'souq' before? It means 'store'. It would do you well to learn Arabic words."

I started to speak, but Monera interrupted me.

"You must pay attention now. It is important you understand. I am going to tell you about Saudi dress and about the culture," she announced.

"That would be great."

"Hush! Listen." Monera leaned forward and looked around. Her eyes rested on a man walking into the lobby. She pulled away from me and walked towards him, waving one hand over her head.

"Faisal, come here."

I saw the confused, sheepish expression on the man's face as he checked over his shoulder then gingerly approached. Monera huffed, stepped towards him and took hold of his arm, pulling him towards me.

"You see how this man dressed?" She said shaking the skinny man until satisfied with his pose.

I looked him up and down. He dressed in Arabic fashion, wearing a white dress shirt that reached his ankles and a red-checked headdress. "Yes…"

"Faisal is wearing a Thobe. Can you say that? Thobe."

I felt like I was in kindergarten.

"Say it!"

"Thobe."

"That is good. See this on his head? The red scarf is called a guthra. It is held in place by a thick black cord called an agal. This is the way the men dress." Monera pushed him. "Thank you Faisal. You go now."

He stumbled, cowered and slithered down the hall. She huffed then turned to me.

"The men can wear western clothes if they choose. Usually the thobe is white but in the winter months he may wear black or brown. During the great Feast of Ramadan, the thobes could be other colors. The thobes are mostly nylon or a cotton blend. More expensive ones are cut from fine wools or silks," she said, batting her eyes.

"Does the headdress or guthra change color, or is it always red checked?"

"The Saudis wear the red, Arab men from other countries or tribes wear black or brown. In the summer months the red-checkered headpiece is often replaced with a pure white one."

"What about the women? Do they always wear these black coverings?"

"It is called an Abaya. The women must always wear the abaya. The abaya has to cover neck, ankles and arms and like the thobes, are made from nylon, silk or light wools. It is most important a woman wear a head covering. See? Just like I wear." Monera twirled around. "You will see some women just cover their hair and other women cover their faces and even their hands. The women cover themselves according to the directive of their husband or father. Some Arabic women expose their face; others have to cover all exposed skin including face, eyes and hands. They do this by wearing a black net over their head and face so they can see where they walk, but their eyes are obscured from anyone's sight." Monera paused, leaned closer to me and whispered, "Within the Islamic religion, it is immodest not to cover and depending on what sect of Islam or how devout one is to their faith, then that determines the degree of cover." She straightened, and raised her arm above her head pointing a finger to the ceiling. "Once a young woman reaches menarche she is marriageable and it is important the woman cover for modesty's sake."

I smiled, suppressing a giggle. Amused, I egged her on. "Do I have to cover my hair?"

"Yes, of course."

"Why do I have to cover my hair when I am not Muslim?"

"Because men should not look at the beauty of a women. They will be tempted to commit adultery with another man's wife, or against his own." Monera looked me in the eye and continued, "The main reason is to keep people from evil thoughts and desires. A woman should always carry a scarf. Modesty is most important and strictly enforced. If you cannot cover your hair, a Matawa may have you arrested."

Monera stepped forward and pinned my arms against my side as if she were going to shake me. "You understand?"

"Oh yes. More than I want to." I replied, nodding my head.

She released her hold and pushed me away from her.

"Anthony said you need to buy an abaya? That is no problem. I will take you to the best souqs where you can get a good deal. I will do this for you because I like to help people, especially newcomers."

"I appreciate this," I said, rubbing my arms, mystified by Monera's eccentric personality.

"Come. I hired taxi to take us."

"Oh, very good."

"Let me tell you about the taxi. Women are escorted by privately hired drivers or are permitted to take a taxi. It is safest for you to take a Hala cab. These are working for the hospital and they will drive you safely. It is not wise to use other taxis."

"So we have to rely on taxis? We can't rent a car or take a bus?"

"Women are not allowed to drive in Saudi Arabia. The hospital does however, provide a free bus service to shops and locations throughout the city and there is a schedule posted on the unit. There are city buses, but they only transport men. Men have the choice of taking the bus, taxi or buying or renting a car. We must go now."

She grabbed my arm and ushered me through the hospital doors. A white cab waited at the curb. Monera opened one of the rear doors for me and then walked around to the other side of the car while I fastened the seat belt. Monera spoke to the cabdriver in Arabic then looked at me. "You always wear that?"

"What? The seat belt? Back home it's against the law to ride in a car without a seat belt."

"You don't have to wear one here, but it is good idea. Some of these drivers are crazy!" Monera reached forward and patted the driver on the shoulder. "We do not speak of you, Mohammad." She sat back in her seat. "How much of the city have you seen?"

"I haven't seen anything yet. The only place I've been to other than the airport is the woman's prison."

"Ah yes. I remember hearing about your friend. Who is on her case from security? Khamal or Abdul?"

"Abdul."

"Ahh…you have a good man in Abdul. He will do his best for her."

I looked at Monera. "Do you know everyone?"

"When you have been around longtime, you know the important ones."

"You don't look old enough to have been around for a long time."

"My dear, trust me. I am an old woman now. I will have my fifty-two birthday. That is old. Yes, I have spent twenty-five years in Riyadh so I know many important peoples."

"Do you have family?"

"My husband and children are in Egypt. They are there. I am here. I support them."

"Even your husband?"

"Yes, you see, when we were very young, my husband had his own business. It was my fault there was a fire and he lost it all, so I have to work to support the family. It is the way it is."

I gasped.

"Don't be so shocked. I have good life in Riyadh. Now pay attention! We are coming to the souqs."

I looked out the widow at the rows and rows of small, congested makeshift stores lined side by side on both sides of the street.

"This area is called Battah. You can get good prices if you know where to go. Come. I'll show you."

"Is this what all the stores are like in Riyadh? I don't always like to shop and if this is what I have to look forward to, I don't think I'll be doing much of it."

"What? You don't like to shop? I never heard of woman who doesn't like to shop. My child, there is nothing else for woman to do in Saudi but shop!"

"I don't mean to sound ungrateful, but I pictured a modern mall."

"Oh yes, we have those. They are downtown. You will get better deals here, you will see."

I felt my shoulders droop and wondered why I didn't feel adventurous. It was after all, that inquisitive spirit that drove me to Saudi. Perhaps Rose's predicament was marring my mood. Rose… Poor Rose. I hoped she was all right.

"So? Are you with me? What do you think, Claire?"

"Oh, yes. Um…it's crowded here."

"This? Oh this is nothing. In the evenings it gets so crowded, you can't walk."

A small group of women approached. They stopped, studied me and then giggled. Monera said something in Arabic and they scattered.

"They know you are new." She explained. "These people are observant. They never forget a face and they know you by what your body signals to them. Come. This way."

Monera led me through a maze of stalls. As I tromped on the hard-packed dirt road, I felt dizzy with the over-stimulation of sights, sounds, crowds and smells. The shopkeepers called out "Welcome! Welcome!" as we passed, adding to the confusion.

"The souqs…they sell the same things in store after store."

"Yes. Yes. It is this way."

"But why? I don't understand how the store owner hopes to make a living with the competition literally next door."

"It is easy for them. You see, most storeowners are related and the brothers or cousins own the same store. At the end of day they divide all the money and the brother who makes the most gets his choice of which souq he wants to sell from next day."

A man jumped out and blocked my path.

"Take a look—only one minute misses. Please. I have beautiful things…"

Monera grabbed my arm and pulled me away.

We walked a little deeper into the maze when Monera stopped and lifting her robust voice over the hustle and bustle on the street, stated, "Let me show you how you buy!"

She walked to one of the stalls and studied the garments laid out on a table. I watched, fascinated as Monera picked one up and negotiated in Arabic with the shopkeeper. He sounded like he was earnestly pleading with her. Monera said something and he bowed his head, opening his palms to the sky, shaking his head 'no'. They agreed on a price and Monera tucked her abaya under her arm. The shopkeeper grinned and turning away, took out a wad of bills and counted his money.

"See? Easy. Now you buy."

I reached into the pile and picked up a black garment. I turned the collar but didn't understand the sizing. I dug through the pile and picked out another, then another. I bought clothes labeled in single digits and these read 55, 60 and 52.

"What is the matter?" Monera asked.

"I don't know what size I am. Is there somewhere we can try these on?"

Monera laughed. "You cannot try on clothes in Saudi. You have to know your size. Come here."

I stepped closer and Monera whirled me around.

"You do like this." She said holding a garment against her back. "See. It fits. Not too long and comfortable in the shoulders. This is your size." She said and looked at the number on the collar. "36! You barter now."

"What? Me barter?"

"Tell him what you want to pay. I showed you, now you do!"

I looked at Monera, then said to the shopkeeper, "Twenty-five Riyals?"

"No. No. That too little," He stated, giving me a look of disapproval. "Not so shy!"

I took a deep breath and said, "Thirty riyals!"

He shook his head.

"Thirty riyals for the scarf *and* the abaya and that's all." I walked away.

"Ok. Ok." He called out after me.

Monera smiled and said, "Ah, you are good. A natural. Next time, you make deal for me with my shopping." We laughed.

It was getting dark and as the hour approached four pm, people poured onto the streets strolling down the narrow walkways, wandering in and out of the souqs. I felt like I was in a dream, out on a Halloween night amongst a sea of women in black and men in white with red-checked head coverings. Veiled woman with nets over their faces and long black gloves, looking like black mummies wearing glasses, babbled in short quick phrases. Some shrieked, talking on top of each other; others yelled. Filipino nannies scrambled after Arab children, struggling with their scarves that often fell from their heads. Men shouted over the women while others had cell phones pasted to their ear. I felt dazed from the unreal people, their guttural, angry sounding language encircling me, lost in the confusion.

Monera wound her way through the maze of endless soups, ignoring the pushing and shoving as people filled the streets. I was feeling small and uncomfortable when a mournful, somber cry echoed and resounded against the cement walls of the surrounding buildings. Only for a moment did the crowds stop and suddenly there was panic.

"What's happening?" I watched in amazement as storeowners shooed shoppers onto the street, gathering goods displayed on the sidewalk and then pulling down rod iron gates. Massive padlocks secured the barriers and when locked up tight, the men turned toward the loud, woeful cries coming over a loud speaker and obeying its solemn call, walked toward the mosque on the corner of the street.

Monera stopped and said, "Quick. We need to sit."

There were cement benches encircling towering tropical trees in a large outdoor planter in the middle of a vestibule in the center of the shopping district. I found a space on one of the seats and Monera sat beside me.

The Arabic women searched for places to sit. Some gazed at us, giving dirty looks. I wondered if I was sitting in their place but dare not move until Monera tell me to.

Monera spoke as loudly as she dared, "This is prayer call. Be glad we are not out during the evening prayer call. That one can be up to an hour. This one only takes fifteen or twenty minutes. It is important for you to understand if you are shopping at prayer time, you have to sit and not wander around too much. The matawa will discipline you if you are being disrespectful. Don't worry. In time you will be used to this."

Enthralled, I expected the Arab people to roll out prayer mats on the streets and the women to go to the mosque. I thought traffic would stop so people could bow to Mecca wherever they happened to be.

"Why do the people driving cars not stop during prayer call? It only seems logical if stores and businesses have to stop then so should traffic."

"No, it is not that way. Those people driving have to make up the prayer they missed."

It seemed like a long wait and when prayer was over, I watched the shopkeepers return to their stores, take the large padlocks off the doors and put displays on the street.

"Come. Come." Monera said. "Hurry, hurry! I am going to take you to a very special area."

We came out of the shack-like souq area, stepped off the hard sand-packed road, crossed the paved street avoiding traffic and onto gray and black marble sidewalks to shops resembling a strip mall. The stores had glass exteriors marking their boundaries and looked cleaner and more attractive. The deeper we walked into the mall, the more elaborate the exhibits. Rubies, emeralds, gold, silver and diamonds gleamed from brightly lit display cases. Light from the overhead chandeliers hanging clumsily from high ceilings lit the treasure houses of gold and precious stones, eliminating the need for illumination in the corridors.

"These are the gold souqs," Monera announced. "You see, all the souqs we visited are owned by men from countries like India, Pakistan and Philippines. No Arab man wants to work in a souq like those. But the gold souq is different. The gold souq is famous for the high quality of gold and the fair and unbeatable prices. These souqs are owned and run by the Arab men from Jordan, Yemen, and Iraq. Come, you will see."

"Not the Saudis?"

Monera laughed. "Saudis do not work!"

"What about the women?"

"Women are not allowed. They are busy having babies. Only the very wealthy ones, or a princess may own a store in one of the malls, but she must hire a man to sell her things. Come now."

We walked to an enormous concrete square with what looked like a drainage ditch on the perimeter.

"This is Clock Square. See the big clock?"

I looked up and saw a clock standing alone to one side of the square.

"The time on that clock is always correct. It is the Saudi 'Big Ben' with one difference. You see the long doors on the base of it?"

"Yes."

"They open and a drawbridge or…um…long stage is stored there. It is for Friday morning events."

"Friday events?"

"Yes. It is so the crowds can see the prisoners. If a person is to be lashed, then he is tied up there and the punishment is given so all can see. This is Clock Tower."

I put my hand over my mouth and felt a cold chill run through me. Clock Tower is the infamous Chop-Chop Square. This is the place they would bring Rose…

"You see the ditch around the square? If someone has his hand chopped off, or worse, then there are sprinklers that come up and wash the blood down the ditch. They drain in that groove there. Look"

I didn't' want to, but did. My hand shook as I tucked a loose lock of hair behind my ear.

"Do they really punish people by lashing them and cutting off their hands and heads?"

"Yes of course. It is the law!"

I looked at Monera. She seemed straightforward and unemotional about these practices. "You have witnessed these, these beheadings and lashes and such?"

"Of course. It is nothing. They do not suffer much and they are deserving of it. Enough now, we must return to the hospital."

****

I took the slow elevator to the apartment concentrating on my aching head and feeling physically drained. I turned the key in the lock and walked to my bedroom, allowing my package to slip from my hand onto the floor then flopped on the bed stretching my arms over my head. I closed my eyes, sighed and drifted into space.

Just as I felt the tension escape me, the phone rang. I sat up and allowed it to ring a second time before going to the living room to answer it.

"Hello?"

"Miss Spencer? This is Mr. Morrison. I wanted to tell you we negotiated a deal."

"You did? Will Rose be set free?"

"Well, yes and no."

"What do you mean?"

"The bad news is she is going to have lashes on Friday."

I clutched my heart. "But that's tomorrow! Can't you stop it?"

"No, that's not possible. If she had a father or brother in Saudi, they'd consider giving her to him so he could beat her into submission. Since she has neither, they feel it's their duty and obligation before Allah. We can't get around their religious beliefs."

I felt sick to my stomach. I stretched the telephone cord as far as it would go, twisting it in my hand.

"Claire? You still there?"

I swallowed hard, and then croaked, "Yes. So what's going to happen to her?"

"The best we could do was to negotiate a plan where Rose receives some lashes tomorrow, for submission's sake, you understand, then once she's out of the Matawa's hands, we can take over from there."

"I am not sure I understand."

"Well, as her embassy representative I'll make sure she's safe until the time is right."

"When the *time* is right?"

"Yes, she won't be allowed to travel for a while, not even to get home. It may take six months to issue her a new passport, one that doesn't have 'prostitute' stamped in it. As long as she has that stamp, she'll have a horrendous time and could land in prison again. You see, if an Arab sees the stamp he can accuse her of soliciting and she'll go to straight to jail, no questions asked. She won't get out next time and there'll be little, if anything that I, or anyone else can do."

"This is awfully harsh." I wrapped my arm around my waist. "Will she be able to come home?"

"That's the good news!"

"Oh?"

"Yes. I've been talking to a Mr. Herd, the man who went to the prison with you?"

"Anthony?"

"Yes, that's right. He's agreed to be the representative from the hospital, and it's important that you pose as his wife again."

"What?"

"Yes. You don't want to make it worse for Rose, and you don't want the Matawa on *your* tail. All you have to do is to go with Abdul, his wife and Mr. Herd tomorrow to Clock Tower. When they've finished with Rose, you'll be allowed to take her home."

My knees gave way and held onto the table. "Go to Chop-Chop Square? You want me to go and witness Rose being lashed?"

"It's the only way. I'll be there too."

"I don't know…"

"If you don't, she'll go back to prison and have lashes again the following Friday."

"I feel sick." My shoulders slumped.

"I know. It isn't pleasant, but it's all we can do. We'll continue to push them, but we have no choice."

"Are you absolutely sure we can't stop this?"

"Unfortunately, no, but we won't stop working on it. I believe Abdul will be calling you this evening. I have to go. See you tomorrow."

I looked at the receiver in my hand and felt the color drain from my face. How could I go to Chop-Chop Square and witness that kind of brutality? Would I be able to live with myself afterward?

"I can't go," I said out loud, returning the phone to its base. "I have to go. No, I cant! I don't even know Rose that well, but I can't leave her. How did I get into this mess? What do I do? What do I do?" I paced back and forth, wringing my hands, too upset to cry.

The phone rang. I stopped in my tracks and looked at it. It rang a second time. On the third ring, I picked it up.

"Claire? This is Anthony."

"Oh Anthony! I just got off the phone with Mr. Morrison. He wants us to go to Chop-Chop Square! We can't! How can we? What are we going to do to help Rose? Is this happening?"

"Claire! Slow down. I know you're terrified…"

"I'm more than terrified! I heard the horror stories and even Monera said she has witnessed heads chopped off and people lashed! I can't go! I'll want to rescue all of them and I know I can't and…"

"Claire! Claire! Calm down, dear. Listen to me, let me help, please." He paused. "Why don't you meet me? I can explain."

"Explain? Explain what? Meet you? Meet you where? When?"

"Right now. There's a park down the road from the cafeteria where we had coffee the other day. I'm calling from the cafeteria now and um… why don't you come here and we'll walk to the park. I think it's better we talk face-to-face."

"I don't know…"

"Come on, Claire. I'll explain what I found out today and I hate to think of such a lovely lady frightened and alone."

I felt the color return to my cheeks and wrapped my arm around my waist.

"I'm all right alone."

"Don't be stubborn, dear. This is something we've not seen before, something we heard of in the news or read about in the papers, but to witness it firsthand and see this cruelty is unimaginable. I'm worried about you and scared for Rose. Won't you come to the park?"

I sighed. He sounded just as terrified as I was.

"The park. Is it safe?"

"Yes. It's hospital property. They made it for the Westerners several years ago. Some Saudis picnic on the grass, but there are places we can wander and be alone to talk. It's nearly eight o'clock, time for the evening prayer so many of the Saudis will have left. Will you come?"

"Ok. I'll see you in a few minutes."

I could almost hear him smile over the phone. Why was my heart beating so fast? He called me 'dear'...Was I fearful about tomorrow, or nervous to meet Anthony?

****

I fiddled with the skirt of my new abaya, trying to keep from tripping over it as I walked to the cafeteria. I saw Anthony wearing a Hawaiian shirt over Khaki colored pants, leaning against a post with his back to me.

"Anthony!"

"Claire? You got here quickly." His cheeks turned red and he cast his eyes to the ground.

"Which way to the park?" I tried to sound cheerful.

He looked up, went to take my arm then pulled his hand away. "Sorry. Habit. I can't touch you in public. Don't want to draw attention, even if we are on the compound."

He led me towards my apartment but turned left, onto a walking path I hadn't noticed before. He stopped, pointed and said, "There's a booth at the end of this path. We can't go through it together. A guard is in the booth and all you have to do is show him your hospital ID and he'll let you pass. If he knows we're together, he won't allow entrance. When you get through, follow the path and you'll come to a park bench. I'll meet you there."

"Ok."

I watched Anthony disappear down the hill. I took a deep breath counting to one hundred before walking towards the entrance. The man in the booth looked at me and studied my ID. He grunted, handed the card back to me and then opened the gate. Once inside, I came to a cement play area where children dodged water spouting in high arches above their heads. Filipino nannies looked tired from chasing the squealing children while a couple of veiled Saudi women sat on a blanket with food spread out in front of them. I walked by, smiling at the children's antics. I felt my heart pound in my chest and my legs were shaking knowing Anthony was nearby waiting for me. I remembered Rose and terror replaced the butterflies. Walking away from the children, I followed the cement trail. I turned a corner and saw Anthony sitting on a park bench, leaning back with his arms spread across the back of the seat, gnawing on a piece of grass.

Anthony smiled then nervously looked around before standing up and approaching me.

"Come with me. There're some caves around the corner."

"Caves?"

"Yeah, not deep caves, more like caverns. There's a little castle built on top of them the Saudis won't go into because they believe it's cursed. There's a great view and we'll be free to talk."

I followed Anthony, climbing crude stairs carved out of the sandstone until we came to the castle. I smiled. "It looks like something you'd see on a mini-golf course."

Anthony laughed. He opened the heavy wood door, looked in and then motioned for me to follow. We went inside and Anthony secured the door with a long piece of wood that was hidden in a corner. "Security. We don't want any unpleasant surprises."

"How did you know about this?"

"You forget. I've been here for over five years and many of the nurses come here for privacy. You learn a lot from overhearing conversations." He winked.

We climbed the stairs to an open balcony and I walked up to the rail and looked out. "Oh...you were right about the view."

"I sometimes like to come here to be by myself. You can see the downtown area over there. See?" He pointed to the right. "And over there is the souq area. It's not lit up as well. Less modern, you know," he smiled.

"I may have to adopt your little get away." I looked over the city that boasted of pink, yellow and green neon lights. I couldn't understand Arabic writing, but noticed the modern architecture in the downtown section. "What are those buildings over there?"

"Which ones?"

I pointed. "The one that looks like an elongated pyramid and the other one that looks like a fast-food chip box."

Anthony laughed. "I haven't heard that description before. The 'chip box' as you call it is the new Bin Laden building. Rumor has it the two towers are wide enough for a plane to fly through. It's still under construction and due to open in a year or so. The other one is the Faisal mall. There are international stores and if you like designer clothes at a good price, that's the place to go."

I took a deep breath, turned my head from the lights and looked at Anthony. I tucked a strand of hair behind my ear and whispered, "I don't want to go to Chop-Chop Square."

"I don't either."

Images of slaughter terrorized me. "Anthony, I can't do this!"

"Claire, they aren't going to chop heads off or stone anyone tomorrow."

"How do you know that?"

"Because they did that last week. This Friday is for lashes. They alternate weeks."

"They do? But that doesn't make it right or any better and I don't want to witness cruelty. I don't want to see anyone being lashed and I especially don't want to witness a stoning!"

"I know. Neither do I, but we have to rescue your roommate. You don't want her to suffer more lashings, do you?"

"Of course not!"

"I spoke to protocol and they told me the lashings are first, then the crowds march to a different area. There's a pit where they put the prisoner, then the crowds throw stones without the spectators getting hurt. We'll have Rose in our custody after they whip her."

"How do you know they'll release her?"

"Mr. Morrison assured me. They made an agreement with Abdul and they won't go back on their word to another Saudi."

I turned my back to Anthony and looked into the distance. I felt him step closer and could feel his breath on my neck. I clung onto the rail and tried to steady myself. He caressed my arms, pinning them on either side with his strong hands then gently pulled me back, whispering in my ear. "We can be strong for each other."

I took a deep breath and felt him squeeze my arms tighter. I turned and his lips brushed mine. I pulled away, facing him, breathing hard. A warm sensation rushed from my heart then spread throughout my body like a fever. He bent down and kissed me. My spirit left, soaring to the skies leaving me exuberant, expectant, longing to be held in his arms. I wanted to kiss him again, but my mind screamed 'no.'

He seemed to sense my desires and helped himself to my lips, my neck, smothering me in an explosion of passion. I bathed in the luxury of his advances, then suddenly pulled back

"Anthony, we... we can't. You're married."

"I know, but I'm so drawn to you."

He took a step closer. I put out my hand and he stopped.

"I can't. I mustn't," my mind screamed.

It was too late. He scooped me up in his arms and before I could stop myself, we locked in a passionate embrace. He kissed me once, then pulled away and looked deeply into my eyes. He pulled me close and hungrily kissed me again and again. I couldn't think. My mind blank, my soul aching for tenderness and comfort returned his luscious kisses and basked in the luxury of his thirstiness and warmth.

He stopped and held my head tight against his chest. I listened to his fast heart beat as my thoughts returned.

"Anthony..."

"Shh..."

"No. Listen."

I pulled away. "We can't do this. It isn't right."

Anthony didn't say a word. He looked down at his feet.

"Anthony..." I stepped forward and put a hand on his cheek. He looked up at me and I saw tears in his eyes. "I understand your struggle, but we can't."

I felt my own tears nearing the surface. I watched him take a deep breath and reaching up, took my hand off his cheek and kissed it. I turned from him.

"I'm sorry. I shouldn't have done that. I have *never* cheated on my wife and..."

"And you are not going to now. At least not with me. I think this whole thing with Rose has upset us and we're nervous and afraid."

"That's part of it."

I turned and looked at him.

"I'm very much attracted to you, Claire. I haven't met anyone like you before."

"You don't even know me."

"Maybe not well, but I'm a good judge of people. You're special."

I turned, clutched the rail in my two hands and looked over the city. "I remember what it was like being left alone. My husband walked out on me for someone else. I was left with two children and I promised myself I'd never do that to anyone." I looked him in the eye. "You have a wife and children."

"They are older, and my wife..."

"Needs you. I'm sorry Anthony. This is wrong. We'd never be happy knowing we hurt others and I will not intentionally hurt anyone. We have to live with ourselves and I want to be able to look at myself in the mirror without guilt."

Anthony turned from me and leaned over the rail. I watched him scan the sparkling lights in the distance.

"You're right. I do love my wife and I don't want to hurt my kids." He paused. "But, but I just couldn't help myself. You must think I'm terrible."

"No, I don't. I think we're scared for tomorrow and feeling desperate."

"I honestly didn't bring you up here to seduce you. I just..."

"Let's just pretend it didn't happen."

A warm breeze freed a silver lock of his hair and he brushed it back with his hand. He stood up straight, turned and looked into my eyes.

"Where do you get your strength?"

I didn't answer. I stepped back and scratched my head. Something didn't feel right. I asked, "What about tomorrow?"

"Abdul will meet us in the lobby and we will travel with him. We'll go and get Rose."

We stood silently looking at each other. I cleared my throat and said, "I think we should go."

We walked down the winding stairs and I watched Anthony take the piece of wood from the door and return it to the corner. His shoulders slumped and he looked like he was in deep thought. He opened the door a crack and looked out. He held the door open and as I started to leave, he grabbed my arm and looked down on me with a sadness I could only interpret as self-pity. I looked into his blue eyes and felt repulsion for him. My stomach churned. Why this sudden and complete reversal of emotion?

He released my arm and I hoped he hadn't noticed the change.

"Um... I'm going to stay here for a while if you don't mind."

"No, that's fine. I'll see you in the morning. When? Nine o'clock?"

"Yeah. That's fine. Good night, Claire."

****

I climbed into bed, lay on my back and stared at the ceiling. My head was whirling. Why did I let him kiss me? How could I desire him one minute then loathe him the next? His eyes. That woeful yearning, the weakness I detected. Why did I turn on those I pitied—not a compassionate pity, but one riddled with contempt? Why did I feel this way? He hadn't wronged me in any way. He was really a very nice, caring man. Maybe it's living in Saudi. Maybe it's Rose, the arrest, the work...I don't know...

I turned on my side.

How could I long for him one minute, then reject him the next? Is it because he's married? Is it because I'm lacking passion? Lacking commitment?

I sat up and stared at my reflection in the mirror. Am I afraid of being left alone? Was it a mistake to come here? Maybe I should break my contract and go home... I sighed and tried to clear my head. I lay on my back and stared at the faded ceiling, thinking.

Go home because I don't want to develop anything with Anthony? Or anyone else? Go home because of Rose? Am I feeling this way because of tomorrow? Afraid of seeing something I don't want to see? No! I'm not a quitter and I'm not going to run away from anyone or anything. I won't leave Rose. Not now. She needs me...but...Why am I here?

I spoke into the vacant room, "You came here for a reason. What was it? Oh yes...If I don't expand my world, let go of old beliefs and face challenges with a positive attitude, it won't lead me to new things in life. Face your challenges positively, Claire. There must be a reason, a purpose for being here... there must be."

Chapter Four

I dressed in my abaya and started for the door, dreading Chop-Chop Square. I didn't sleep last night. I got up several times, made tea and paced the floor. I was sure I was making a well-worn path in the carpet. Imagine lashings. Lashings! How could something like this happen nowadays?

I turned the knob on the door to go out then thought of Ian. Strange he hadn't called.

I went to the phone table, picked up Ian's card and dialed the number.

"Ian here."

"Hello Ian. It's Claire and I hope it's not too early to call. Did you speak with Mr. Morrison yesterday? Do you know what's happening?"

"No. Yesterday my boss reamed me out and I got a two-week's pay suspension. I'm leaving for Scotland this morning."

"They're sending you home?" I paced the floor.

"For a few weeks. My company called my wife and told her about the arrest. I need to go home and smooth things over."

"Your wife? You're married?" I stopped pacing and put my fist on my forehead.

"You didn't know? Yeah, well she doesn't know about Rose, just the arrest and she's worried and wondering why. That sore of thing. What's happening with Rose, anyway? I've been in Jeddah. You know the city on the west side of Saudi? I had to wrap up some business."

I twisted the phone cord around my hand, feeling anger stirring inside me. "She's going to be lashed today."

"What?"

"Yes. She's getting lashes and after she receives her punishment, we can take her home. I'm going to Chop-Chop Square this morning and witness the ugly process."

"Wow. I don't know what to say. Poor Rose. What can I do?"

"What do you want to do?"

"I, Uh…Well, you don't expect *me* to go to Chop-Chop Square, do you? I can't save her and… and her embassy is taking care of everything. There's nothing I can do for her now."

"You could be there to help us get her away. At the very least you could be there to give her your support," I said, controlling my voice.

"See her whipped? No! No I… I can't do that. Besides, I've a plane to catch. Um… You'll be there, right? You're all the support she needs. You've been great throughout this and anyway…"

I could taste the distain I felt for this man.

"What can I do?" He asked.

Giving up, I said, "Pray. Just pray and go and fix things up with your family."

Ian was silent.

"Ian? Are you still there?"

"Yeah. When you see Rose, tell her I'm real sorry and I'm thinking about her."

I bit my tongue, then said. "Have a safe flight."

"Claire? Take care of her for me, will ya?"

"Good-bye, Ian."

I returned the phone to its cradle and zipped my abaya and paced. I'd look after Rose, all right, but not for him.

I pushed thoughts of Ian from my mind. I walked to the door, paused and rested my hand on the knob, then turned the handle. I didn't want to go. I forced myself to put one foot in front of the other, my legs resisting every step. I didn't want to see people in Chop-Chop Square. I didn't want to be with Anthony. I couldn't bare the thought of Rose being lashed…

****

Anthony leaned against a post in the hospital vestibule and smiled as I approached. His blue eyes signaled a yearning, arousing feelings of repulsion from the pit of my stomach. I continued walking towards him, managing to feign a warm smile.

"Morning Claire. Did you sleep?"

"Sleep?" I felt his eyes exploring me, trying to penetrate my thoughts but I ignored his silent communication. "No. I tossed and turned all night. I'm dreading this."

"Ok. Ok. This way." Abdul interrupted. "Claire sit in back with my wife. Anthony, sit in front with me."

I sat beside the veiled woman and fastened my seat belt. She ignored us.

"I will drive us. I know a good spot to park the car and we don't have to walk far. It will be easy for us to get Rose away."

We drove in silence for a few blocks before Abdul spoke again. "I know you think our laws are harsh. Perhaps for some they are, but it is necessary. Rose will survive this and all will be forgotten in time. You will see."

"Some things can't be forgotten." I said.

Abdul parked the car and the walk along the hard, packed sand was short, as he promised. I stepped onto the marbled walkway where a small crowd gathered around the square.

"Come this way."

Abdul led us to a spot facing the tall clock that rose above our heads. The view was very good. Too good. I felt panicky. "Do we have to be so close?"

"It is not too close. We will stand here. The matawa won't make us move and because we are in the front we won't be separated. Just wait for me and I will let you know when it is safe to get Rose and then we can leave."

I looked around. Men and women wearing their Arabic costumes poured around the square. I noticed smiles on some of their faces and wondered how they could look forward to these atrocious acts. I looked at Anthony and sensed his fear. In that moment, I wished to make it better for him, to reach out and comfort him. Why the change? A motherly instinct to protect, comfort and nurture?

My attention transferred from him to the crowds. My soul emanated abhorrence for the people surrounding me. Apprehension tickled my senses and a horrible coldness ran through my veins. My heart was in the pit of my stomach, not comprehending their excitement. I wanted to bolt. Why was I here? I didn't want to be. Why was this happening?

"You're trembling." Anthony said.

"I don't know how to prepare myself for this, I don't know if I can watch."

"You must!" Abdul interrupted. "If you turn your head away, matawa will force you beside the prisoners and mock you and make you watch closely. They may make you hit the prisoners with the whips. Stand still and don't react. Don't move."

"How can I do that? I'm sick just thinking about it."

Anthony leaned against me and whispered, "Where's that strength I know you have? Just tell yourself it isn't real, and it'll soon be over."

I flashed him a disapproving glance. It *was* real.

I startled when a booming Arabic voice interrupted thoughts and conversations. I looked around and couldn't see where it was coming from.

"Look up there." Abdul pointed.

The sound came from speakers mounted on the roof of the mosque. When the loud speaker silenced, two large men dressed in black tunics came up a stairway on the opposite side of the Square and stood in front of the clock. Each had a gun strapped to his side and a whip split into several pieces with balls at the ends of the tethers.

"That is a kinder version of the cat of nine tails. It has leather ends instead of the usual metal spikes." Abdul whispered.

"They're going to hit Rose and others with *that*?"

"Yes. Of course." He snapped.

I envisioned a single whip. This was much worse.

More people gathered. They poured in from all sides, filling in the gaps around the Square. They shoved, pushed and pressed in on us, clamoring, moving as close as they could to the stage.

"There must be a thousand people here! I feel like I'm smothering."

"Stand still." Abdul said.

Anthony looked down at me and reached for my hand. He squeezed it then let go. I looked up at him, but felt nothing.

A van pushed its way through the crowd, honking its horn. People dispersed, cheering as it passed. Young men tried to climb on top of it and others patted the hood and sides as it made its way towards the square. The vehicle reached its destination and two armed guards jumped out of the front seats. They yelled at the crowd, shooting bullets into the air. I shrugged and covered my ears.

"No!" Shouted Abdul over the noise. "Stand still!"

I looked at him and put my hands by my side. I glanced at Anthony. His cheeks burned red and he had a greenish hue around his mouth making him look like he was going to be sick. I had a fleeting surge of compassion and wanted to reach out and hold onto him.

The shouts from the crowd got louder making me feel minuscule and insignificant among the throngs of jeering Saudis. A ripple of terror ran through my blood and I was asphyxiating from the overcrowding and the pushing and the intensity of the crowd.

Don't panic. Don't panic. This is for Rose. I must help her, save her and this is the only way I can. I closed my eyes. *Breathe. Breathe. In and out. In and out...*

"Open! Open eyes!"

When I opened them a matawa stood in front of me, looking me over. He said, "Cover your hair!"

I fumbled in my bag and pulled out my scarf and put it over my head. The matawa looked at Anthony. "This your wife? You make obedient!"

Anthony turned and yelled, "You do as he says!"

The harshness of his voice scared me and I felt tears coming to the surface. The matawa walked away and Anthony leaned over and said, "I hope you know I didn't mean that. It was an act to get him to go away."

I nodded.

"I told you! Keep your eyes open and don't move. You lucky!"

Two more guards with guns emerged and fired their weapon into the air. The loud piercing voice from the speakers rose above the crowd. The shouting, shoving and pushing lessened and all eyes focused on the guards. The men in black tunics opened the big wooden doors at the base of the clock and set up what looked like a bellows. Ropes hung down from the center and four guards climbed on the top of the platform. They raised their guns to the skies and fired three shots in the air. The men in the tunics unlocked the doors at the back of the van and forcibly pulled out women and children. I recognized some of them from the visit to the women's prison. I strained to look but couldn't see Rose.

One of the men separated the older children from the women. Men rushed up the stairs on the other side of the stage and tore babies from their mother's arms. Terrified youngsters screamed, reaching for their mothers, their cries and torment ignored. The women screeched and whaled in anguish, watching their children disappear. Their misery encouraged the onlookers to cheer, shouting louder and faster with every cry of despair.

Horrified, I blurted, "They look like they're celebrating!"

"They are!"

Men and women raised their fists above their heads and chanted.

"What are they saying?"

"Justice for sinners! Punishment for those who offend Allah!" Abdul interpreted.

Abdul's wife joined in the chant, shaking both fists above her head.

More shots fired, this time from a single guard. I strained to see what he was doing. He stepped into the van, shouting, pointing his weapon. A few moments later he pulled on an arm of a screaming woman. I saw dark legs kicking in defiance and the words she was shouting were in English. I froze. The hostile woman was Rose.

Rose was no match for the guard. She equaled the size of one of his massive arms. He yelled at her, but she struggled harder. He threw her down then picked her up in one hand, shaking her like a rag doll. She kicked and squirmed until another guard stepped up and pulled her long dark hair, making her head tilt back as far as it could.

The crowd cheered. I felt woozy.

"Steady, Claire. Steady." Anthony whispered.

Rose swore at the men in Arabic. They kicked her in the ribs. The crowd laughed and cheered again.

I wanted to tell her to stop struggling. They outnumbered her. She's making it worse for herself! Oh my God, Rose…

Rose sat up, her hair hanging in matted strands, her abaya torn and dirty. Her legs were exposed and she glared at the men. I could almost feel the hatred radiating from her.

"Stay still!" Abdul warned us. "Do not react, or we won't get her back."

I felt perspiration trickle down my back.

"Don't move. Matawa coming!"

He just got the words out of his mouth when a matawa stood in front of us. He looked us up and down, then said, "You no like?"

Neither Anthony nor I responded.

The matawa stood tall and addressed the crowd.

"You come up here and see!"

My heart leaped and Abdul stepped forward, speaking in Arabic to the matawa. He looked us over, spit and then walked away.

"Be careful. He knows you don't approve."

I was breathing hard. My chest felt like it was going to explode and my head was spinning. I looked at Rose. She was on her feet, her head hanging so her chin rested on her chest. The men lined the women up then pulled one frightened Filipino woman forward and presented her to the audience. He opened a book and read from it. The crowd laughed and jeered then chanted.

Abdul turned to us. "He is reading her charges one by one."

They dragged the woman to the dangling ropes and tied her hands, securing the ropes around her wrists. One guard hoisted her up so her feet barely touched the ground, stretching her arms above her head. She let out an agonizing cry, which was excruciating for me to listen to.

They forced another woman to the face the crowd and dangled her. They grabbed another, then another and the last one was Rose. Rose struggled, attempting to fight them off. One of the guards turned his gun and hit Rose in the stomach with the barrel of his rifle. She doubled over, gasping for air.

I made a move to run towards her, but Anthony pulled me back.

"It's instinct."

"I know Claire, but do as Abdul says. Stay *still*."

I tried to stand still bracing myself for the inevitable, dreading every moment and powerless to intervene. My heart cried, "Please God, don't let them do this! Make them stop!"

I glanced at Anthony. He had a bead of sweat running down the side of his face. Abdul looked calm.

The men in black tunics stood behind the women, poised, running the tethered whips through their hands. The voice from the speakers boomed out a message in Arabic and the crowd responded in accord. The guards stepped down from the podium and lit incense so smoke surrounded and filled the square. The heavy scent of sandalwood infiltrated my nostrils and combined with the smell of human perspiration from the hoards around me, swirled and confused my senses. I felt like I was going to pass out. When the smoke dissipated, the loud speaker was silent. Four guards sounded their guns in unison, letting their shots escape into the air. The crowd hushed.

I watched the men flex their muscles. They posed, balanced in a formidable stance behind the women. They took one step back and thrust the first blow allowing the tethers to hit the backs of the helpless females dangling like prey after a hunt. They raised their arms and repeated blow after blow. They lashed the women with all of their strength behind every strike, flexing their massive muscles for the audience, boasting their strength and power. Songs of condemnation from the multitudes became louder and louder. The prisoner's cries of anguish, pain and torment reverberated off the cement walls of the surrounding buildings. High-pitched screams rose above the crowd's mantra and disappeared into the sky above.

My soul left. I stood motionless, disassociated from the present, numb to the world around me. I didn't feel. Couldn't hear. Couldn't speak.

The men thrashed them again, and again and again.

Within minutes, agonizing cries dwindled to painful mutterings. The men kept beating them and I watched their silenced, limp bodies sway from the ropes with every lash. Blood dribbled down their backs in steady streams. I could see torn skin between shredded layers of black cloth. The crowd cheered. The men in tunics took a step backwards and surveyed their work. One woman cried out and she was lashed again. The throngs of people egged them on. The men turned and smiled at the crowd. They singled out one or two of the women and hit them again. The crowd cheered. They hit another and the crowd cheered again. They stepped away and walked back and forth parading in front of the people smiling, as if triumphing over an enemy. Their heavy breathing and sweat-soaked tunics impressed the crowd. They marched along the perimeter of the square, looking into their faces, picking out an individual and growling playfully at them. The crowd responded in raucous laughter. The two men paced back and forth and held their whips above their heads. The crowd cheered and chanted, raising their fists to the sky in celebration. One man looked over his shoulder and I followed his gaze to the dangling women. He walked up to Rose, drew his arm back and lashed her three more times. She let out a low, mournful cry. The men laughed and exited down the stairs on the other side of the square, clapping each other on the back.

A guard walked in front of the women and cut them down one by one. They fell, hitting their face on the concrete beneath them.

"Ok. Now!" Abdul commanded.

I couldn't move.

"Claire, come on."

I put my hand on my cheek and felt wetness. I didn't realize I was crying. Anthony reached out and pulled on my arm, startling me. I suddenly got a burst of energy and raced ahead, kneeling at Rose's side. Splattered blood and small pieces of flesh mixed with cloth dried on the concrete. The midday sun beat down and the stench of perspiration evaporating in a steamy mixture of blood and flesh plagued me. I gagged. I pitied the women. They lay defeated, hugging the cement. Some squirmed; others bled from their noses.

Rose was still, her face against the cement. She didn't move and my heart leaped, fearing she was dead. I saw her fingers curl then she made a noise. Abdul had a knife and used it to cut the ropes to free her bound wrists. She turned over, moaning in her effort. "Get me out of this hell!"

Anthony picked her up.

My heart sank. "What about the others?"

"We can't help them, Claire."

Men appeared through the throngs of people with stretchers and picked up the beaten women, loading them into the van. The crowds moved down the stairs, kicking and spitting on the fallen women as they passed. Guards made feeble attempts to stop them.

A Western man came from the crowd and stood beside us. "I'm Mr. Morrison from the New Zealand embassy."

"Where are they taking those women?" I cried out.

"Back to the prison. They have to finish their lashes another week."

I felt sick.

Abdul rubbed his hands together. "Come now. We must go!"

"Put me down!"

I looked at Rose. "Are you sure? Can you walk?"

"It's my back they beat, not my legs!"

Anthony put her down and she stumbled and fell.

I put my hand on my heart. "I think you better let these men help you Rose. You're much weaker than you think."

Abdul looked stunned and didn't make any attempt to help. Mr. Morrison stepped forward and Rose put one arm around his shoulder and the other one around Anthony's.

"Hurry, hurry! Before you are seen," Abdul pleaded.

I looked at him. "What do you mean Abdul?"

"Don't let the matawa see a man touch a woman in public. This is not allowed!"

Anthony growled, "Even when she's hurt?"

"Just hurry!"

"Put down!" A demanding voice shouted behind us.

A large man with a scraggly beard stood with his hand on his hip. He pointed at Rose. "She no go!"

I panicked. "What? What does he mean, Abdul?"

"Matawa wants her in the van with the others."

The matawa pushed Mr. Morrison aside and held onto Rose. I ran forward and tugged on the matawa's arm. "No!"

"Ah!" He shrieked and threw me to the ground. Anthony made a fist and was about to strike him when Mr. Morrison pulled on his arm.

"No! Don't hit him! Wait!" Abdul yelled.

"He can't treat a woman like that!"

Mr. Morrison stepped forward. "Mr. Herd! Please! This man is matawa! You'll make it worse."

The matawa took a deep breath and puffed out his chest. He was still clutching onto Rose. He shook her and yelled in Arabic to the guards. Two men ran forward and took hold of one of Rose's arms. She kicked and screamed, "I'm not going back to prison!"

The guards struggled, pulling her towards the van.

I was frantic. "Abdul! Mr. Morrison! They promised!"

Abdul raised his hand. "Quiet Claire! This is business for man!"

The guards threw Rose in the van. She kicked one of them in the stomach and he struck her hard on the head with a barrel of a rifle.

I started towards the van, but Anthony stopped me. "No!"

The matawa laughed and pointed at me. "I lock her up too!"

Anthony stepped forward. "No! You are not taking my wife!"

"She? She wife?"

Abdul crossed his arms. "If Mr. Anthony say, then it must be true."

The matawa eyed Abdul. "Ok. You go now. Take friends with you. Now! Or I take her!" He pointed at me.

"Quick, quick! Come!"

We followed Abdul to the parked car.

I stopped. "What about Rose? We can't leave her here!"

"See? Woman hysterical."

Anthony raised a clenched fist. "Shut up Abdul!"

"Mr. Herd! Please. I know things didn't go as we planned but Abdul and I will sort things out. Let's not argue."

I turned to Mr. Morrison. "A lot of good your negotiations do when we have to leave without Rose!" I squeezed my purse. "Where are they taking her?"

"Back to prison. Please, Miss Spencer. Let Abdul and I work on this. We'll get her out. We just need to be patient."

I fought back tears. "Patient?"

"We go now. Mr. Morrison is right. We will make deal with the authorities."

"They are lairs!"

"I'll cut your tongue, woman! A Saudi never lies!"

Anthony clenched his fist and took a step forward. "Abdul!"

"Mr. Herd! Abdul, Please."

I flashed Abdul an angry look but said nothing.

"Get in. I will take you back to hospital."

Mr. Morrison held my door open. "I'll call you later." He turned and walked away.

Anthony closed his door, sighed, then asked, "Where's your wife, Abdul?"

"She watch stonings. She'll come home with her cousin."

I gasped. "Anthony, you said they weren't going to stone anyone today."

Anthony said nothing and fastened his seat belt.

****

I stood in front of the hospital watching Abdul drive away until he was out of sight, aware I was alone with Anthony. He reached down and took my hand. I pulled it away.

"You were very brave, today."

"Not any braver than you. I think I should go."

"Claire, please don't. Won't you have lunch with me? Or at least a cup of coffee? I won't keep you long, I promise."

I sighed and said, "I don't feel like eating, but perhaps a drink."

I felt disheartened and couldn't think. I was weak from the shock of seeing the torture of those poor women and the worst part was we returned home without Rose. My legs were like heavy weights walking beside Anthony. He led me into the hospital then to a booth in the family dining room.

"I thought this would be nicer than the cafeteria."

I looked around. The lighting was darker and the tables in the center of the room were bare. I ran my hand along the brown leather seat, then tucked my hair behind my ear. "Not many people here today."

"No, it's Friday. Most people are off."

I fiddled with the utensils and felt Anthony's eyes on me.

"What are you thinking, Claire?"

"Nothing. Everything. I don't know. I'm upset from what we witnessed today. It's hard to believe human beings can be so cruel."

"I know," he said picking up his fork and twirling it.

"I mean, you read about such things in history books, or you hear it on the news, but to see it in person…and to *experience* it…it's too much. They are so cruel, and they *enjoyed* torturing those women. I just don't understand."

"Shocking. There's no other way to describe it." He sighed. "Will you be able to sleep tonight?"

I looked at him. "Of course not. How could I?"

He smiled and reaching over put one hand on top of mine. "This is one time I wish I could hold you through the night."

I pulled my hand away. Repulsed by his suggestion, I stood up to leave but Anthony grasped my wrist.

"Please don't go. I didn't mean…"

I sighed, hung my head then sat down again. I looked down at my hands on my lap, folded them then unfolded them, thinking about bolting for the door. I didn't want to be with Anthony and longed for a cup of tea. My tea. Made the way I liked it.

"You seem upset."

"Of course I'm upset!"

"I'm sorry I lied to you. I thought if I told you about the stonings you wouldn't go."

"I'm able to make my own decisions and how dare you lie to me! I don't need your protection."

He scratched his head. "It was poor judgment on my part. I'm sorry."

I folded my arms and looked away.

"Claire?"

"What?"

"Let's not be at each other's throats. We'll get through this, I promise."

I glared at him but said nothing.

"Scuse me. You want from menu?" A waiter interrupted.

Anthony opened his napkin and placed it across his lap. "Yeah. I'll have your curried chicken. Claire?"

"No thanks. I'll have a diet soda. No ice. Thank you."

"You aren't going to eat?" He rested his chin in his hand.

I blinked. "Anthony, after all we've been through today...I just can't."

"I eat when I'm stressed."

"Lookit, I hate to be rude, but I want to go home."

The waiter came back and filled our empty glasses with ice water. A large drop fell from the jug onto my hand. I picked up the yellow cloth napkin and dried it off then stood up.

"Please don't go, Claire."

I looked down into his pleading eyes and felt nothing. I half smiled then walked out the door. He didn't stop me this time, for which I was glad. Home. Tea. I yearned to be alone.

****

I was exhausted. I stood over the kettle, waiting for it to boil thinking about the day. If only I could stop playing the images of Chop-Chop Square through my mind. How was I going to rid myself of these horrible memories? ...and why did I feel hostile towards Anthony? Why so impatient with him? I had to come to terms with these feelings. I had to work for the man.

I made the tea and sat in the living room, staring out the window. There was a busy street beyond the brownish-orange security wall encircling the boundary of the hospital. Across the road were stables where a brown horse gracefully bent its head to eat hay placed on the ground for him. Another horse emerged from a pink stable and galloped to the bail, pulling out a few straws, disturbing the older horse. I smiled, thinking it was refreshing to know there's still beauty in the world.

I opened the window then staggered back. I forgot about the stifling air.

I looked out and saw birds scattered on the ground and perched in palm trees in the garden. They were gathering seeds and bits of food, singing songs full of gaiety. I listened to the cooing of the doves and the chirping of swallows. Some bird sounds could not be distinguished from others, but there was no mistaking the cry of the rooster. Delighted and mesmerized, I absorbed the scene for as long as I could tolerate the heat. A feeling of peace transcended me as the tension lessoned, leaving me tired yet renewed.

The phone rang, startling me. I closed the window and picked up the receiver on the third ring.

"Hello, Claire?"

"Mom? Hi! How are you?"

"How are you? We haven't heard from you in a few days and were wondering if everything is all right? You're not working today?"

How is it that no matter how old you are, mothers seem to sense when things aren't right?

"I'm fine. No, I work twelve hour shifts so sometimes I have two or three days off in a row."

"You don't sound fine. You sound tired."

"I am. I haven't been sleeping well."

"What's wrong? It's not like you not to sleep."

I couldn't talk about Chop-Chop Square, the prison or the lashings. They'd never understand, then they'd worry and want me home.

"Oh, it's just adjusting to living here. It's different and will take time before I get used to it, that's all."

"Are you sure, dear? Your voice sounds strained."

"No, no. I'm fine," I lied. "How is everyone? Any news?"

I spoke to my mother, then my father and after an hour hung up the phone. Tears ran down my cheeks. I longed to go back home, but I couldn't, at least not yet.

Emotionally drained, I sat on the couch sipping tea with my thoughts and memories my sole companion. I missed my family, yet by speaking with them, felt stronger. There must be a nicer side to life in Saudi. Westerners lived and worked in the country for years, although some of them are strange and perhaps running from something. Even in Saudi there was something to run from…Anthony.

"Am I running away?" I asked out loud.

Running from the memory of my son? Running from my family? Seeking freedom? Ha. That was a joke. What's freedom? Free from stress, worry, pain, responsibility? No such thing.

I took the last sip from my cup, got up and placed it in the sink. I looked at the clock. It was only seven thirty, but I didn't care. I slipped out of my shorts and tee shirt and put on cotton pajamas. I pulled the covers back on the bed and caught a glimpse of myself in the mirror. I stretched then stood in front of the dresser staring at my reflection.

No, I'm not a runner. I didn't run from Rose. I didn't run when my brother got into trouble for his gambling debts. I didn't run when my sister had to go to a detox center for her drinking habits. I didn't run when abandoned by my husband and I didn't run when my beautiful son got so sick.

Why did he have to die? He'd be 22 years old now…and the younger son, Joseph… so much pain in his young life…

Tears fell on the top of the dresser, leaving splat marks on its shiny surface.

People often said I was brave. Am I? There were times I wanted to crawl under a rock. Like now. Like when Anthony gets too close...

I looked deeper into the mirror. "Just because I feel like running from men doesn't make me a runner, does it? Does it?"

I wished I could stop thinking. My head hurt.

I turned and crawled on top of the bed on all fours and snuggled beneath the fresh sheets, pulling the fluffy comforter up to my neck. I stared at the ceiling and chastised myself. I was miserable because I came face to face with the ugly side of humanity. I realized not everyone was good at his core and today was a good example of that.

My parents...they're good people and if it weren't for the values they instilled in us as kids, I know we wouldn't have faired well in life. Yes, some got into trouble, but bounced back. Like rubber balls, always able to bounce back.

I sat straight up in bed. That's it! Things happen. The events in Saudi are external. I'm not responsible for any of this. I have to stop feeling guilty. It happened. It happens, and will continue to happen. Bounce Claire, bounce!

I lay down. Somehow I'd have to find acceptance. Accept this society as it is, but don't give in. I vowed to hold onto my values and stick to my beliefs, that way I would survive.

"What does my mother tell me? 'We make a difference in someone's life by setting a good example.' Please God, let me be a good example."

I rolled on my side and went to sleep.

Chapter Five

I didn't like to sleep in but this morning was different. Images of Chop-Chop Square haunted me. The faces of the terrified women, the agonizing screams and children ripped from their mother's arms… the blood splatters on the pavement… Did it happen? Were those women brutally whipped? Did Rose go back to jail? It was a dream…no, a nightmare. And Anthony. What about him? He lied. Did I sense this dishonest part of his persona and that was the reason I felt repulsion towards him? Could that be it?

The phone rang, rousing me from my semi-conscious state. I swung my legs over the edge of the bed, stretched and then walked to the living room.

"Hello?"

"Morning Miss Spencer. This is Mr. Morrison. I've some news about Rose."

"Will she be coming home?" I choked, wanting to cry.

"Well, no. Abdul, two people from your hospital administration and I have been up all night in negotiations. The Saudi authorities believe she has evil in her and want to get it out before releasing her. I know it sounds crazy, but many Arabs are superstitious."

"Jailed because of superstition? Do you know what it's like in jail? It's awful! I don't know if she'll survive."

"They transferred her out of the downtown prison to one outside the city. The conditions of this new prison are much better and she'll have her own cell. They promised they'd follow the rules and guidelines of the Geneva Convention."

I swallowed hard and wondered if those promises were worth anything. "Will I be able to visit her?"

"I doubt it. It isn't going to be easy to convince them to hand her over, especially since they believe she's possessed. She won't be coming home any time soon. In my experience, women who've been transferred to this prison stay a minimum of six weeks. I know of one case where an Indian National was locked up for seven years."

"Seven years!"

"I'm guessing she'll be there six to eight weeks. At least the conditions are better and she'll be allowed to bathe."

I slumped. "It still sounds awful."

"I'll do my best for her."

"I know you will, Mr. Morrison."

I put the phone down and shivered. Poor Rose. Still in the clutches of those bullies. I felt helpless and wondered if Mr. Morrison had any impact at all with the Arab authorities.

I put my hands on my cheeks then looked down at my pajamas. Feeling dazed, I walked into the bathroom and splashed cold water on my face. The phone rang again. I looked at myself in the mirror, sighed and tucked a strand of hair behind my ear. I let it ring three more times before answering.

"Morning Claire. Anthony here. I assume you heard? They're transferring Rose to another prison and if this is anything like the prison my assistant was in, it won't be so bad."

"Nothing could be as bad as the one she's in now. That was deplorable. If the conditions aren't better, I'm afraid she could die. Not from confinement, but from disease. The stench, the overcrowding…oh…poor Rose." I sighed.

"I know. Lookit Claire, I'm on the hospital grounds. Why not meet me for coffee? You left so abruptly yesterday and there's something I want to discuss with you."

" I…um," I hesitated. "Ok. Where? The coffee shop?"

"Great. I'll wait for you there."

He sounded jubilant. I wished I didn't agree to meet him.

＊＊＊＊

Anthony smiled as I approached. I felt embarrassed and looked around to see if anyone was watching. Being the subject of hospital gossip was not something I relished.

"I meant to ask you, how was your shopping with Monera?" He pulled out a chair.

"I enjoyed it. Thank you. We had a good time." I hoped I didn't sound curt.

Anthony searched my face. "I've been thinking about my situation and I want to run something by you."

"What situation?"

"I've been up all night. I was worried about your roommate and I got to thinking about life in general. My children are nearly out of the house and my wife has been incapacitated for so long…It's no way to live. She's been in a wheelchair for years now. She has all her faculties…well, they're intact, but declining. I was thinking what life would be like if…

"What are you saying?"

"I was thinking about divorcing my wife."

"What? Why? She's dependent on you and you can't abandon her!"

"Is that what you think?"

His defensive outburst surprised me. I sat back in my chair, clutched the edges of the table with both hands, drawing in my breath. His faced turned from a pale white to red.

"I made sure she's had the best care and I'll continue to give her the best, but don't you think I deserve to have a life? I've nothing to look forward to in my marriage. Irene is getting worse and one day I'll be without her. What's wrong with wanting more, a little happiness?"

"I can't answer that Anthony and there's no way I would ever judge you. I don't know all the ins and outs of your situation and I don't want to, but if you're thinking of divorcing her because of me…well… no you just can't do that!"

Feeling panicky, I scanned the room and uncrossed my legs under table.

"Claire, please. Listen. I can't help it. You're the best thing that's happened to me in a long, long time…"

"I am not a thing and nothing has happened. No way Anthony…there's no way we could ever… Stop talking like that. Stop thinking like that. There will never, ever be anything between us."

"But our walk in the park…"

"Forget about it. We were desperate because we thought we were going to witness beatings, hands and heads cut off and heaven knows what else. No. It will never work." My stomach was in knots and I wanted to bolt. I stood up.

"I thought we had something special…" He held onto my arm.

"We have nothing. There is nothing."

"That's not true! Claire, sit down, please."

"I want to go."

"Wait. Sit down."

I looked down at his hand on my wrist. Out of the corner of my eye I saw people looking at us. Embarrassed, I slinked into my seat, tucked my hair behind my ear and glared at him.

"You seem angry. I didn't mean to…"

"I'm not angry. I'm mortified. Please let me go."

He released his grasp. His shoulders sagged forward as he put his hands over his face.

"Anthony, you're not only married, but you're my superior. I don't think we should meet like this again."

"I thought if the circumstances were different, you would want…"

"Well they aren't and I don't want to get into something we'd regret later. I don't want to talk about it any more. I'm leaving." I stood up.

He looked at me and I watched his expression change from one of sadness to one of authority.

"Before you go I need to tell you something."

He cleared his throat and looked as if he were gathering his thoughts. I folded my arms waiting for him to speak.

"We're going to admit a newborn girl to our unit. She's very ill. How would you feel about nursing her?"

"An infant?"

I relaxed my arms, fiddled with my hair then sat down. "I'd love to look after an infant! What's wrong with her?"

"No one knows. They're running tests and she'll come when the neonatal ICU thinks she's stable. I'm going to ask four nurses to look after her so all shifts are covered."

"That sounds good."

His demeanor was a complete reversal of the beaming man that held my chair a short time earlier. His blue eyes had a look of desperation, like he was searching for the words to resume his plea. I felt sorry for him, but refused to console him. I stood up, careful to keep out of his reach and walked out the door.

****

I dreaded gong in to work, but shook off the sleepiness and walked onto the unit to face uneasy night duty nurses.

"What's wrong?"

"Morning Claire! How's your roommate? Can't talk now. We have to figure out what to do with a baby."

"Do you mean the baby from the neonatal ICU?"

"Yeah. She'll be here soon and we have to prepare a room for her."

The nurse walked down the hall. I picked up the clipboard and studied the days' assignment, then heard a voice behind me.

"Morning Miss Claire."

"Hmm? Oh, hello Faisal. How are you?"

"I am fine, thanks be to Allah. Miss Claire, you know this baby that comes to unit?"

"I'll be caring for her when she comes."

"She not here. Protocol wants to speak you."

I walked out and bumped into a tall man wearing a starched, white thobe. He twisted a corner of his red checked headdress and looked me up and down.

"You Claire?"

"Yes? How can I help you?"

"You are the one who care for baby?"

"Yes?"

"Please come. Baby's Uncle wants to speak."

"The baby's Uncle? Not her father or mother?"

"Father at work. Mother not here. Come. Please."

He led me into his office where a man sat in a large leather chair, waiting. He looked up and smiled.

"This is Sully. He uncle to baby."

I extended my hand. He looked at it and appeared uncomfortable then I remembered Arab men are not supposed to touch women and withdrew it. "How do you do? Sorry, it's one of our customs."

He stood up. "What this custom?"

"In my culture, it's polite to shake someone's hand when you meet them."

He laughed, extended his hand and I shook it. He laughed again. The protocol officer cleared his throat and Sully's smile disappeared.

"Sully, this Claire the nurse on duty today."

He took in a deep breath, looking me up and down asked "You married?"

"No, I'm not," I snorted.

"Ah. That is shame!" He shook his head. "My niece, she very sick. I want you tell me if she get better. I need know if she have children."

"Children! She's an infant and I haven't even seen your niece yet. I don't know much about her."

"But you will in time."

The Protocol officer interrupted. "This is very important. It is important to know this baby can have children when she grow up."

"I doubt that can be determined for quite a while and a doctor would be the one to ask, not me."

"No, not doctor. You will be the one with my niece. You will get to know her best. You must tell me if she can have children. You understand?"

"Not really. I don't know if I can do that and I won't be the only nurse caring for her. Why do you want to know if she can have children?"

Sully appeared impatient. The Protocol officer explained, "She new here. She does not know our ways."

"Ah. Then I teach you. Yes, you will understand in time. My son. He will be husband to this baby. If she cannot have children, she will be no good. If she can, then they marry."

"But she's too young…"

"You will know because of improvement. Yes?"

I felt trapped.

"If you don't mind, I need to speak to my supervisor and have him explain things to me. He won't be in until after nine this morning."

"She is very clever."

"My niece will be in good hands. I trust her already. I must go now."

Sully stood up and as he passed me, he chuckled and stuck out his hand. I smiled and shook it. "Good-bye Sully."

He laughed and walked away shaking his head.

"You will not take any patients today. The baby will come. Her room is ready. She be here soon."

"Oh, ok. Thank you."

"What is your name?"

He looked at me and seemed surprised. "It Mohammad. Why? No one ask before."

"I like to know who I'm talking to. Thank you, Mohammad. I'm sure we'll talk again soon." He stood up as I left.

I walked into the nurse's station. The night nurses left and the day nurses were busy pouring meds.

"No patients today, Claire?"

"I'm waiting for a baby from the neonatal unit."

"Oh yeah. I heard about that baby."

****

The morning was long and boring. I flipped through magazines, offered to help the other nurses on the floor but there was little I could do. I looked at the clock. It was after nine. I was there since six and wondered if the baby would ever come.

"Morning Claire." Anthony said as he placed his bagged lunch in the fridge.

"Good morning." I dreaded this encounter. "Anthony, I need to speak to you, please."

"My office?"

"That's fine."

I followed him into his cramped space and sat down.

"Personal or professional?"

Embarrassed, I thought about bolting out the door.

"Claire, before you say anything, I just want to say I'm sorry. I know I've been pushy and haven't been myself."

I felt my cheeks burn and looked at my hands on my lap.

He continued, "I, uh, I've been thinking. You're right. We'd be miserable if we allowed anything serious to develop. I spoke to my family on the telephone last night and I know what my priorities are. I should never…"

"It's ok. We've both been under stress."

He scratched his head.

"I've been thinking." I smiled and took in a deep breath. "Perhaps I should transfer to another unit."

He froze then slumped his shoulders. Turning his head away he said, "You can't. Hospital policy states you can't transfer to another unit until you've worked a year on your original assignment."

"Oh." I frowned. "What if I work nights for a while? Your hours are from nine to five, and mine would be from seven in the evening to seven in the morning. That way we wouldn't see each other. It may make it easier? I could even volunteer to work every weekend and then that would be two less days we saw each other."

Anthony turned and shuffled some papers on his desk. "One of my highlights is knowing you're close. Even though we're too busy to spend time together, just seeing you brightens my day. The other nurses are contemptible. I'm always settling their disputes and helping them with their miserable lives. But you…you're intelligent, no-nonsense type and… refreshing."

I squirmed. "All the more reason for me to work nights."

He didn't respond. I watched him pick up sheets of paper then put them down again. I noticed his hands were trembling. "Anthony, you just said…"

"I know what I said," He snapped. "Lookit," He rested his elbow on his desk and rubbed his hand over his face. "I can't help how I feel."

"Even if we did… I mean… eventually we'd separate and there'd be heartbreak down the road, and not just for us."

"I know, I know. Ok." He sighed. "The next rotation I'll schedule you for nights."

I felt triumphant, but then wondered what lengths I'd go to avoid Anthony. I hated working nights.

Mohammad knocked on the door and stuck his head into the office. "Ah, good. Claire is discussing with you already. I will go."

"No Mohammad, what's happening?"

"She no talk?" He flashed me a dirty look.

"She's just sat down." Anthony said. "Come in. If there's a problem, let's discuss it. Claire?"

"It's not a problem. I met with the uncle of the baby I'm assigned to care for and he wants me to tell him if the child can have children. How can I do that? I don't understand."

Mohammad huffed. "I try to explain, but it is true. She no understand." He leaned towards Anthony and whispered in a low voice, but I heard him say, "She stupid woman."

Anthony tried to hide a smirk. "So, this uncle wants to know about the baby?"

Mohammad nodded. "She is to report to uncle the progress of baby and if she can have children."

I felt my blood pressure rise. "How can I do that?"

Mohammad snorted. "You explain, please. I go. If you have problems, I try."

Flipping a corner of his headdress behind his shoulder, Mohammad walked out, closing the office door behind him.

"I heard what he said, you know."

"It's a cultural thing. Women are stupid because their brain is smaller than a man's. Didn't you know that?"

I crossed my arms. "Oh please! Now what does he mean?"

"They want to know if there's any possibility this little girl will able to conceive when she's of age. If not, her life may not be worth salvaging."

"What do you mean 'salvage'? I don't understand." I folded my hands on my lap.

"They want to know if the baby will show signs of normal development, and if so, then there may be a chance she can have children in the future. Childbearing is the main role of a Saudi woman. If she can't have a child, she's useless."

" Her Uncle Sully said something about this infant marrying his son."

"This little girl has something wrong with her and her prospects of marrying to form a business or tribal alliance are slim. She needs to have a male look after her all of her life. The first man in her life is her father, but her uncle and brothers are also responsible for her until she marries. Because she's not good marriageable material, she'll be given to her first cousin and he'll be her husband."

I put a hand to my cheek. "First cousin! That's incest!"

"There's a lot of incest here. First cousins marrying each other, half brothers and sisters…it's scary. Some of the kids are born with terrible ailments. You know the research part of the hospital?"

"Yes?"

"There are scientists from all over the world who come to study the effects of the genetics of these incestuous offspring. From what I understand the parents of this child are related because of marriages to first cousins for several generations. In reality, they are more closely related than cousins."

"Wow. I don't know what to say." I swallowed and thought of the infant. "Tell me Anthony, what happens if the cousin doesn't want to marry her?"

Anthony leaned back in his chair. "He doesn't have a choice. He can also never divorce her partially because she's family and partially because it's a marriage of honor. Mind you, it's the husband's duty to keep his wife in line, and if she's disobedient, there are no laws against a man murdering his wife or daughters. They don't think of it as murder. You've heard of honor killings? They aren't just for daughters who commit adultery, you know."

I couldn't think. "That's terrible! They don't, do they?".

Anthony hung his head and frowned. I saw images of Chop-Chop Square.

"So…so what happens to this baby if she doesn't develop properly and can't have children?"

"The desert is a big place. Just like the children of the women from the prison…"

"Oh Anthony, no!"

"Claire…"

"Don't say it. Please, just don't say it."

I got up from the chair and walked out of his office heading toward the nurse's desk. I picked up a chart then turned around. Mohammad stood behind me.

"Oh, you scared me." I put a hand over my heart.

"Hurry, hurry. The child is coming."

"Yes, I know, but what is the rush?"

"You must be ready."

"I am ready."

"Chart? Where is chart?"

Anthony came out of his office. "Mohammad, what's wrong?"

Mohammad stepped towards Anthony. "The child. She coming now. Everything must be ready. I want chart."

"Mohammad, we've had this conversation before. You're not in charge of the nurses, and the chart is off-limits to you. Claire is capable of admitting this child."

"It is my duty…"

"To look after the family, not the patient."

Mohammad mumbled and peered at Anthony from under his brow. He slinked away.

Anthony shook his head. "Every once in a while you have to remind them of their duties."

"A little arrogant, isn't it?"

"A little! That's an understatement." Anthony laughed. "You need anything?"

"I don't think so. I won't know until she gets here."

"Oh, here she comes."

I turned and saw bags of fluid swaying from poles and monitors piled up in the crib as two flustered nurses pushed the baby and equipment, fighting for room to navigate the crib down the hall. Two protocol officers on either side of the crib shouted directions, getting in the way and blocking the nurse's path. Behind them walked Sully and behind him, a woman dressed in black from head to toe. Curious visitors and sitters poked their heads out from the rooms, attracted by the noise and excitement.

Mohammad walked down the hallway and led the entourage. He looked at me and said, "Hurry! Come! Come!"

I looked at Anthony.

"Don't go in just yet. Take the baby's new chart into the nurse's lounge and wait at the table. I'll direct the nurse in there."

I sat down and a few moments later, a Filipino nurse entered, tense and out of breath.

"Whew! Crazy bunch. I glad I no work on dis floor. Dose protocol peoples." She put an old chart in front of me.

"I haven't had much to do with them. Anthony keeps them in their place, and things seem to run well."

"It important to have male nurse manager. Dey never respect or listened to woman."

"Tell me about the baby."

"Ok. She dree weeks old now, and de parents are not involve. They cause much problems with de staff, and de doctors work wif de uncle. She born wif no movement on lef side. We not sure she is paralyzed. She can no swallow, but digestive system ok. She can no bend knees, so has stiff legs."

I studied the Filipino woman as she gave her report. Unlike the women in the prison, she was confident and bossy.

"Dey think she deaf and blind, but too early yet. She having seizures and de doctors gave some medication. De parents do no want her have it. Dey refuse. De doctors no allowed to giff anything. Parents no allow tests. No allow feeding tube in stomach. Dey noffing but problems."

I squinted. "The parents refused to give her medications?"

"Yes. You will see dey are trouble. Big trouble. Dey want her die."

"How do you know that?"

She looked at me and sniffed. "You not here long, no? Dey stupid, you will see. Dey big problems for us.

Frowning, I shifted in my chair and crossed my legs.

"Here her chart." The nurse pushed it towards me.

"I'll read through the chart and if I have any questions, I'll call your unit."

"Ok. I go help other nurse. You take over two o'clock, ok?"

"That sounds fine."

I followed the nurse into the baby's room. The American nurse was setting up the monitors and ignoring the protocol officers. One of the officers sniffed when he saw me enter the room. He snapped his fingers and shouted, "You help!"

I put my hands on my hips. "No snapping at me. No, I'll wait until they finish."

"We're here until this afternoon," the American said. "Why don't you go and have lunch?"

"I will. I just want to see the baby and say hello to her uncle."

One of the protocol officers stepped towards me. "You no help?"

The American nurse snapped, "Lookit, protocol people. Leave and let us do our job!"

The men grumbled then left the room.

"You have to be firm with them or they won't leave you alone. You should go and then take over at two."

"I will in a minute."

The two nurses gave me a dirty look. Ignoring them, I turned to Sully.

"Dis my wife. See, Dis my son. He baby Nawaar's husband." He rubbed his wife's swollen stomach. I couldn't see the woman's expression through her black net.

"That child isn't born yet! How do you know it's a boy?"

"Doctor say. We no want girl and have to make sure it boy."

Sully walked to the baby's crib and looked at the sleeping infant. "My wife, she old now. Dis last child. I need new wife."

"That's terrible, Sully. You're old too."

He laughed. "You clever and funny too. You want marry me?"
"No. I'm old."
Sully stared at me.
I smiled. "I better go. We'll talk another day?" I walked out of the room hoping two o'clock would hurry up and come.

****

I picked up the infant and snuggled her. She was so small and soft. She wiggled as I unwrapped the blankets and watched as she stretched her arms. I studied the minute palm of the baby's hand and smiled as the tiny fist weakly wrapped around my little finger. I looked at the baby's legs. They were stiff and hung across my lap. I picked them up. They could move up and down but the knees wouldn't bend. I rubbed a finger on the sole of her foot and the baby squirmed. The baby wasn't paralyzed after all. I returned her to the crib, lay her on her back with the blankets over her.

I startled when the door to the room burst open and two veiled women marched in. The first woman threw her abaya on the couch and came close to me. The second woman carried a basket and placed it on a table, loosening her scarf.

"She no sleep?"
"She did, yes. Are you her mother?"
She nodded.
"Hello. I'm Claire. I'm one of the nurses caring for your baby. It's time for her to be fed, so I'll get it ready."
"Where you from?"
"Canada."
I went to the sink in an anteroom close to the baby's crib and filled a large syringe with formula. Then I attached it to the tube that went into the baby's nose and into her stomach, slowly feeding the infant her formula.

The mother seemed confused and cocked her head sideways, studying me. I smiled at her. "Where Canada?"
"It's a country above the United States."
"Ah. You Amerikey."
"No, Canadian."
She frowned.
"What's your name?"
"Abeer. It means scent of flower."
"That's very pretty. Abeer." I repeated, then asked, "What does Nawaar mean?"
Abeer smiled and looked down at her tiny infant.

"It mean flower."

"Oh, how lovely!"

Abeer's smile faded. "You think my baby live?"

My smile faded. "I don't know Abeer. All we can do is pray."

My heart went out to Abeer as I watched the new mother lean over the crib and kiss her tiny daughter on the forehead. The rims of Abeer's eyes filled with tears. She hid her face behind her veil then left the room followed by her servant.

I looked down at the infant who seemed lost in the large crib and placed the baby on her side, supporting her back with a soft roll. I watched the baby's lungs move up and down in rapid, rhythmical motion, listening to her exhalations that sounded like a song. I reached into the crib and ran my fingers through a thick mass of fine dark hair that covered her round head, feeling the pulse of her fontanel. The baby's skin had a deep yellow tinge to it, typical for Arab babies. I observed her, watching for seizures.

Anthony stuck his head in the room. "How are you managing with baby Nawaar?"

"Oh, just fine. She's so sweet. What are you doing here so late?"

" I had work to catch up on." He looked like a lost puppy.

"I met Abeer today, the child's mother. Haven't met the father yet."

"Seems the father has abandoned his daughter and wants nothing to do with her."

"How sad. I know the mother loves this child very much. Maybe in time things will be different?"

Anthony shook his head. "You're in Saudi, Claire. The father has the last say and if he decides this child is not welcome, then she'll be hidden away for the rest of her life. There are few places that'll look after her and I don't know if this family can afford much."

"But I thought they had money. They're VIPs, aren't they?"

"Yes, but what you don't understand is that families get an allowance from the royals and it may not be enough to cover additional expenses. I don't know what connections these people have, but it'll be interesting to see what happens in this case."

"Interesting? But what about the fate of the child? What about the grieving mother?"

He shuffled his feet. "I don't want you getting attached."

I studied Anthony. He had a concerned look on his face and didn't seem to want to scare me. There was an awkward silence. I tucked my hair behind my ear then looked into the crib and concentrated on the baby. Anthony went to say something when one of the night nurses came into the room. He sighed and stiffened.

"I'll leave and let you two discuss the case. I'll be in my office if you need anything."

****

I slept well, better than I had in a long time and perhaps the rest was what I needed... or maybe it was because I left work last night without Anthony knowing I had gone. Strange I should feel so good about avoiding my supervisor.

I entered Nawaar's room after getting report from the night nurse and saw a tall man leaning over the crib. He held onto a corner of his starched and pressed headdress, hiding his face. I sat as quietly as I could on a chair beside the baby's crib. I pulled a bedside table toward me and laid out the medical chart. I was trying to be discreet, allowing this man privacy yet keeping a watchful eye on the infant.

The man studied the child then clutched the crib's rail, his knuckles turning white. He shook in steady jerks, sobbing. I wasn't sure what I should do. Instinctively, I wanted to comfort him, but remembered it was an insult to touch an Arab man. I looked around for the box of Kleenex. I found them and offered him one. He looked up and took the tissue from the box. He wiped his eyes, breathed deeply and straightened. He looked at me. I felt like I was intruding on this private moment, but couldn't excuse myself from the room. The baby was in need of constant medical supervision and I knew it was dangerous to leave the child unattended by staff, even for a moment.

I looked into his deep brown eyes. He was pretending to be strong, but the pain, sorrow and grief were unmistakable. He turned to sit on the sofa against the wall and I noticed he carried himself like he held the weight of he world on his shoulders. He made no attempt to communicate with me, instead, watched my every move.

I thought it was odd I didn't feel uncomfortable being under his scrutiny. I hoped he saw me as a confidant professional and could sense how much I cared for this little infant.

The baby stirred. It was time to feed her again and I carefully measured the formula. I lifted Nawaar from the crib and looked at the man sitting on the sofa who was staring at me in disbelief. I approached him with the infant cradled in my arms. "Would you like to hold the baby?"

He seemed surprised and looked from me to the baby, then back to me again. "It ok?"

He was overwrought with emotion. I made a gesture for the man to take the child. He awkwardly held the baby, trying to balance support for her head and neck. He couldn't take his eyes off her face. He lifted the baby to his cheek and hugged her. He pushed the baby away and held her in front of him, studying every feature. He kissed her forehead, paused for a moment, looked at her again and handed her back to me.

"You can continue to hold her if you like".

"No," he said. He stood up, avoided eye contact and left the room.

I was stunned. Perhaps it was embarrassing for him to be emotional in front of a stranger.

I changed and settled Nawaar. I didn't return her to her crib, but instead held and cuddled the little girl. The door to the room opened and in walked Abeer followed by her maid. Abeer looked at me with the same astonished look the man had given me earlier. Abeer took off her abaya and unwrapped the black veil that covered her face and head and sat down beside me.

"Would you like to hold your baby?"

Abeer looked up, her eyes filling with tears. "It ok?"

"Of course it's ok. She's your little baby."

Abeer drew in a deep breath and cradled Nawaar in her arms. Tears streamed down her face as she snuggled the infant, showering her with kisses. Abeer rocked back and forth singing to her softly, admiring her, studying her features. I watched Abeer unwrap the baby and examine her tiny hands then her feet as her tears fell in big drops onto the blanket. I reached for the box of Kleenex and offered a tissue. "Abeer, have you not held Nawaar before?"

"N...n...no. The nurse and doctor said no. She too sick."

I was flabbergasted. "What? Who told you that?"

"The nurse and doctor in ICU. They say I hurt my baby. It ok now?"

"Of course it's ok. You hold her for as long as you like."

Abeer didn't answer. She allowed her tears to fall as she rocked the baby.

The maid stood motionless observing the scene. She appeared concerned and I smiled at her.

"What is your maid's name?"

"It Sammere."

When Sammere heard her name she turned and busied herself with unpacking items she brought from home. She boiled water and brewed white beans to make Arabic coffee.

Sammere offered me a cup.

"You like?" Abeer asked.

I looked into a miniscule cup at a greeny-white, perfumy liquid. I smiled at Abeer and Samere then took a sip. It had a strange odor and a taste I couldn't describe. I knew it would be an insult to refuse the coffee and pretended to like the unpleasant liquid. They offered me sweet figs and the combination of coffee and figs wasn't bad. I sipped the two ounce drink from the tiny palm held cup to make it last as long as possible. There was no escaping Sammere's watchful eye and when I had finished the drink, Sammere didn't hesitate to refill my cup, despite polite refusals. I thought I'd be sick if I drank another drop and looked around the room, resting my eyes on the baby's bottles beside the sink. Sammere poured Abeer's second cup. I nonchalantly stood up and wandered to the sink, pretending to work. I put the cup down on the counter, out of their view and picked up a baby bottle, rinsing one out and then glanced at the two women. They were whispering to each other. I waited for a moment and when they weren't looking, dumped the coffee down the drain, replacing the cup on the saucer. I ran the water and rinsed out a second bottle. Picking up the cup in my hands, I pretended to drink the last drop while walking towards my chair. Sammere offered a third cup.

"Oh. No, no thank you."

"My husband here today." Abeer said when she finished her coffee and figs.

"Yes, I thought he was your husband."

She looked up. "You see? You see Raheem?"

"He was here not too long ago. He held baby Nawaar."

"He…?" Abeer looked surprised and her face lit up.

"He hold Nawaar?"

"Yes he did. He held her and kissed her. It was good to see."

"You … you give Nawaar him?"

I nodded.

Abeer cried again. She looked at the baby she cradled in her arms and spoke in Arabic to Sammeer. Sammere stood beside me and rested her hand on my shoulder. She made a fist with her thumb pointing up. I smiled.

"You good," said Abeer. "Sister, you take now."

Abeer handed me the baby and dressed in her abaya and head covering. Sammere dressed and gathered the coffeepot and the rest of the figs then followed Abeer out the door.

****

I entered my apartment after work and saw a flashing light on the answering machine. I played the message, thinking it may be news about Rose.

"Hey Claire! Where've you been? This is Melinda. You remember?

One of the people traveling with you from Toronto? Call me when you get in."

I dragged a chair beside the phone. I hadn't spoken to her since our arrival in Saudi. I dialed the number.

"Claire, is that you?" A friendly voice said on the other end of the phone.

"Melinda! Hi. How are you?"

"I guess we've been busy settling in. Listen. We're getting together tomorrow night for dinner. One of the women I work with arranged it and we'd love it if you could come."

"Oh yes! I am dying to see you again. So much has happened since coming to Saudi there's been little time to do anything normal."

"I know what you mean. Some of us plan to meet around seven and take a taxi to the restaurant."

"You want to spend time with an old fogy like me?"

"You aren't that old, what? Thirty something? I just turned twenty five, so we aren't that far apart in age."

If only I were thirty something...

"I don't finish work until seven. Is there any way I can meet up with you later?"

"No problem. I have to work too, so you and I can go together. How long do you need to get ready?"

I paused. "If I'm not delayed I should be ready by seven forty-five."

"Perfect. How about we meet at the entrance to your apartment building? We can go from there."

"Sounds good."

I felt a sudden burst of energy when I hung up the phone. I pranced into the kitchen and put the kettle on the stove to boil, made a cup of tea and nestled into the couch in the living room. I was excited and looking forward to having some fun for a change. I thought of Rose and felt a twinge of guilt. I hoped she was all right...

****

I picked up my pace as I approached Anthony's office. Why had he sent for me? I knocked and entered. He was wearing his white hospital uniform instead of his usual khaki pants, collared shirt with tie and lab coat.

"Any news about Rose?"

"No not a word, mind you I've been working. No one's left any messages."

"Hmm. I'll give Abdul a call and see if he knows anything. Tell me Claire, how are you?"

"I'm fine." I said then changing the subject, "I'm enjoying looking after Nawaar. I have to tell you about yesterday. I met both of her parents and they held their baby. From what I understand this couple has never held their infant child before. Is that true?"

Anthony looked surprised and studied me before speaking. "I don't know for sure. In some cultures, they don't believe a mother should hold her infant if there is a chance the child won't survive."

"But they need to! If you could just hold your baby once, then at least you had that chance ... but never to hold your child? I can't imagine it."

"We can't argue about cultural and ethical differences, we have to concentrate on the medical management of the infant."

"The medical management? That should include the emotional and the spiritual aspect of this case too. We're dealing with human beings, Anthony and I believe in the holistic approach to care."

"Good luck to you. My advice is not to get emotionally involved. Remember, you're in Saudi Arabia and things are different."

"That's what I keep hearing."

Anthony looked out the door and scanned the nurse's station. In a low voice he asked, "What are you doing tonight? How about having dinner with me?"

I was glad I had plans. "I'm going out with friends tonight."

His face fell. I felt exuberant.

****

I left his office and went into Nawaar's room to take over from the night nurse. "Hi Paula. Anything I should know?"

"Nah," said the Australian nurse. "She's had a good night. Isn't she sweet?"

I leaned over the crib.

"Paula, she's turning blue!"

"What? She was fine all night."

Paula was quick getting the oxygen. I took it from her and put the mask over the baby's nose and mouth and watched as the baby's breathing changed. Her eyes opened, then rolled back into her head. "She's having a seizure and we don't have medication for her. Paula, call the doctor on that phone in the corner!"

I turned the baby on her side and loosened her blankets. Her breathing slowed and her arms stiffened.

"Ok, I've called. The doctor's coming. Oh my. She looks better now. At least her fingers aren't blue. How did you know she was having a seizure, Claire?"

"Just by her behavior. I've nursed special needs children and adults, all of whom had every kind of seizure under the sun." I looked at Paula. The color drained from her face. "Nothing to be worried about, Paula. She's ok right now and will sleep for a while."

The Egyptian pediatrician rushed into the room. "What's wrong?"

"The baby had a seizure, but Claire knew what to do."

"Hmm. That is inevitable, but her parents refuse to give her medications."

"I thought her uncle was in charge of her now. Can't we get him to agree to medication?" I asked.

"No. They are afraid of long-term effects."

I gasped and held a hand to my heart. "What about the effects of the seizures? That's worse than medication side effects."

"I know that! You think I am stupid?" The doctor snapped. "We've been fighting with the parents and uncle. They no care about infant! They spend time arguing about marriage arrangements."

"Oh dear. I have to go to sleep now. Have a good day Claire." Paula walked out, leaving me alone with the doctor.

He pulled his stethoscope from around his neck and examined Nawaar. He listened to her chest and huffed. He tested her reflexes. "The parents think the medication makes it too sleepy, so they prefer the child to fry her brains than to take a simple drug to stop it. They refuse to have a feeding tube put in its stomach. It wouldn't have this thing in its nose and need suctioning and it wouldn't be choking on everything that went down its throat. These parents don't know anything. Stupid people are killing their child. Perhaps that is what they want!"

I put my hand on my hips. How could he call her It? IT? This is a little human being. She has a name... "I don't know, Doctor. I've witnessed the interaction between parent and child and I think her parents do care."

"What would you know! I've been dealing with these people from the beginning. They don't want problems. They want it dead. Stupid people. They think they know more than me, the doctor. This infant is a waste of time!" He left the room.

I looked at Nawaar. I patted her back, my mind blank. The door opened and Sully entered.

"Baby sick?"

"She had a seizure this morning."

"No sister. What mean seizure?"

"Umm...Do you know what 'spasm' means?"

He shook his head. I thought of how I could explain so he would understand. Pregnancy! They understand childbirth.

"Do you understand 'contraction'?"

"Ah. Like born. Pain before born?"

I nodded. "Yes. Sort of. Umm...a seizure is like a contraction in the brain. The brain has a contraction and causes problems in her head and body."

"Ah, I see."

I chastised myself. That was probably the most inaccurate description of a seizure...but perhaps he understands. I wished I spoke Arabic.

"It hurt?"

"It could. There are medications to stop contractions. Contractions in the brain could be very dangerous. With contractions, she may not be able to have children."

"If Nawaar have medication, she ok, and have children?"

"Possibly. The medications will help and Nawaar will have a better chance at a normal life. Do you understand?"

"Yes, yes. She need dis medication. It not make her sleepy?"

"It will, but she'll get used to it and she won't be sleepy after a while. With contractions, she'll sleep even more."

He turned on his heel and rushed out of the room. I heard him shout, "Doctor! Doctor!"

Chapter Six

"Claire!" Melinda said and hugged me.

"So nice to see you! How long has it been?"

"Too long. Claire, we haven't seen you since our week of orientation. Where you've been hiding?"

"I haven't been hiding. I've been running around, visiting prisons, avoiding Chop-Chop Square...

"What are you talking about?"

"My roommate is arrested and I've been frantic trying to get her out."

"Oh...so it was *your* roommate! Yeah, I heard something about that."

"You have?"

"Nothing's a secret, Claire. Any gossip travels the hospital grape vine like wildfire. Gosh. That's one thing I don't want to happen to me ... go to a Saudi prison. Oh look, our cab is here."

We jumped into the backseat.

"This is Hassan. Hassan, Claire. He's my taxi driver and the only one I trust to take me anywhere."

"You need ride, miss? I be your taxi man too. No problem. Here my card."

I took the bright yellow card from his hand and looked it over.

"To the Italian restaurant, please." Melinda said, then turned to me. "We were going to dine on the embassy grounds but the group wanted to try out this restaurant instead."

"Who's 'the group'?"

"Two from our original group from Toronto, my work-buddy from the blood bank, her boyfriend and some guys from the American military base."

"Guys? We'll be with men?"

"Don't panic. We have it all worked out. We women get together with American men from the military once a month. We miss men's company and they miss socializing with women. These are *real* people who just want an evening out. We pick a 'safe' restaurant and have a good time."

"But that's dangerous! What if we get caught?"

"Don't worry. The guys are American *Military*. The religious police will leave us alone."

"How do you know?"

"I told you. We eat at safe places and we always have an escape plan. Come on Claire. Just think. Wouldn't it be good to have male company for a change?"

I didn't crave male company. Lately, I'd been avoiding it.

"Stop thinking so hard. We aren't going to get arrested and we aren't going hide like the Saudi women. This is normal for us and we've a plan to escape, just in case the matawa come. I'll fill you in later"

"It's not like I can get out of this dinner. You've kidnapped me and I have no choice but to trust your judgment … but I warn you, if we get into trouble…"

"Cut it out! We won't."

Hassan pulled up to a restaurant close to the downtown area. I paid my share of the fair with a generous tip and followed Melinda. We opened the door to the restaurant and Indian and Filipino staff greeted us.

"We're with the American Military group," Melinda said.

"Dis way."

We were ushered through the main part of the restaurant to a private dining room in the rear. I stood in the entranceway to the room looking at the long table centered in the middle, with four men and three women munching nacho chips. I noticed a closed door to the left.

Melinda grabbed my arm, "Come on. You remember Anne and Laurie? This is my friend and colleague, Vicky. Let's sit down."

The available seats were in front of the entrance. I didn't want to, but sat with my back to the door.

I looked over my shoulder. "Are you sure we'll be all right?"

"Claire is nervous about being with *the guys*."

A man who had his arm around the woman named Vicky laughed. "You're safe with us. The Matawa won't mess with the US Air Force!"

"Or the US Navy!"

"Especially not the US Army!"

Vicky giggled. "Come on you guys. If you're going to argue, we'll leave. No military talk allowed!"

"Yeah, besides if they have a raid, the waiters will warn us," Laurie added.

I tucked my hair behind my ear. "You put a lot of trust in those waiters."

"They don't like the Saudis any more than we do and they want our repeat business."

"It's just that…"

"Claire! Relax." Melinda chastised, then turning to the others, "Claire's roommate is in jail."

Laurie leaned forward, "That was you?"

"Were you at the prison? What's it like?" asked her male friend.

"She hasn't been raped or anything, has she?" the airman asked.

I swallowed. "I haven't seen her or heard about her for two weeks. I've been assured she's safe and her embassy is working to get her out."

"Getting who out of where?" A musical male voice said behind me.

I froze. His tone struck a cord in my soul.

"Howdy!" He said.

My heart skipped a beat and felt a gush of warmth surge through me. I hadn't even looked at him, yet instinctively knew he was going to be someone special in my life. I shifted in my seat. He sat down beside me. I felt my cheeks burn.

"I'm Jake," he said extending a hand.

I gathered courage and took his hand, looking into his eyes. He smiled, his blue eyes twinkled and my heart jumped.

The Filipino waiter burst into the room

"Quick! Hurry, hurry! Matawa coming!"

Anne turned to the man beside her, "Meet you down the street in fifteen minutes."

"Hurry, Hurry!" He said, clearing dishes off the table.

"Through that door! Don't forget your abayas and purses."

My heart was in my throat. I stood up, looked at Jake then followed the others through the door that was closed moments ago.

"Where are we going?"

"Into the ladies room. Quick," Melinda answered.

We crowded into the single stalled bathroom.

"We can't stay in here. They'll come in!" I thought of the prison, the stench, the overcrowding…

"Everyone, out the window!" Laurie yelled.

Anne took the trashcan and turned it upside down. Melinda climbed on top of it and tried to open the window.

"It's stuck."

"Let me try," I said. "There's no way we are going to that horrible prison."

Anne held my hand while I steadied myself on the square base of the metal can. Reaching above me, I tried to turn the latch. It wouldn't budge. "Anyone got a hairbrush?"

Laurie looked in her purse then handed me a brush with a long handle. I held onto the bristles and banged on the latch. It moved a bit. I hit it again and this time it turned. I pushed the window open and peered out. No one there.

"Give me a boost."

Someone pushed my feet and I pulled myself up, resting my middle on the sill. I put my legs against the wall and managed to crawl up and climb out. I fell, landing on my back. I stood up and Anne fell out, then Melinda.

"Come on—you can do it," Anne called.

Laurie fell. I looked up and saw Vicky poking her head out the window.

"I can't. I can't get up."

My heart sank. I didn't want anyone to end up in jail.

"Don't you guys worry about me. I just remembered! I've a fake marriage certificate!" She disappeared.

"Come on!"

I followed them to the street.

"Watch out. Some of the Arabs will aim their cars at you and try to hit you. They think it's funny," Melinda said.

"You've done this before, haven't you Melinda?"

"Well Claire, it never hurts to have a plan and put it into action."

"I warned you...

"We didn't get caught, did we?" She snapped.

A dark car pulled up beside us. A young Arab man leaned through the window and called out, "Fifty riyal? Ok?"

"You PIG! We are not prostitutes," sneered Anne.

"Sisters, you lie. One hundred!"

Anne and Laurie approached the car shouting, swinging their purses. He laughed, pulled back and they drove away.

"Geesh! It's been an evening, and we haven't even eaten yet," Melinda complained.

An oversized SUV approached and slowed down.

"What? More rude Arabs?"

"No Claire. It's the guys. They'll drive us home."

"But..."

Melinda huffed. "Just get in the car, will you?"

I climbed in and sat beside Jake.

"You gals ok?" the driver asked.

Melinda smoothed her abaya. "Oh we're fine. Some jerks just tried to pick us up."

Laurie added, "They offered fifty riyals—I wonder if they meant one of us or all of us?"

The girls laughed and I looked out the window.

"Hey, what's wrong?" Jake asked me.

"I just don't think it's funny, that's all. It's too easy to end up in jail and that's one place I do *not* want to go."

"I don't blame you. Don't worry, you're safe with us." He smiled.

I wanted to believe him. "I'm not a rule breaker and I don't know how safe we are driving around with you men."

Vicky turned and said, "You're safe because you're in the company of a 'married' couple. The marriage certificate worked. As long as there's a stamp or seal on a piece of paper, the Saudis will believe anything."

They laughed. I was too nervous to jest.

Jake took my hand and caressing it between his and whispered, "Don't worry. See the antennae we have on the vehicle?"

"Yes?"

"Those are for military radiophones. Someone from the base has to know where we are at all times. The Saudis see that and they'll leave us alone. The local authorities don't want to mess with the American Military, not as a small group anyway. You're safer in this vehicle with the five of us than on your compound." He leaned closer to me. "I wouldn't lie to you."

I smiled. "Somehow, I believe you."

He didn't release my hand and I hoped he wouldn't.

We drove onto the hospital property and stopped in front of my apartment building. Jake squeezed my hand then let go. As I prepared to get out, he asked, "May I call you sometime?"

"I'd like that. Um…here's my phone number."

"Eww," said the others in unison.

"A romance on the horizon?" Melinda teased.

"Good night Jake. Good night everyone."

****

"Claire, I need to see you. I've asked Barbara to look after Nawaar while we meet and discuss your six week review."

I followed Anthony into his office.

"Come in. Sit down."

I sat down, waiting for him to speak. I noticed he had tidied his workspace and the piles of papers were gone. A single folder lay on the desktop.

He cleared his throat. He looked at the folder, went to pick it up then hesitated.

"You said it was my review?"

"Yeah. Policy. Everyone gets a review after six weeks to determine if they pass the probation period."

I crossed my arms. "Are you hesitating because you want to send me home?"

"Gosh no! I'm sorry." His face reddened. "I haven't seen much of you lately and I'm missing you."

"Anthony, please…"

"I can't help it. I, uh…spoke to my wife about separating."

"You did what?"

"Yeah. I can't go on like this. I'm so lonely and if we divorce the government will cover her medical needs."

"Anth…"

"I know. Sounds cruel but Irene was agreeable. She told me she was surprised I'd stayed with her this long. It's not like we wouldn't be friends…it would give us financial reprieve and I could have a life."

I felt my hair tickle the nape of my neck. "And your children? What do they think?"

"They haven't been told yet. I'm planning on going home for a five-week holiday next month. It'll give us time to sort things out and plan for our futures."

"I'm sorry things are turning out this way for you and I hope you'll be refreshed after your holiday."

He sighed. "Will you at least think about having dinner with me sometime?"

I studied his face. "I'll think about it."

He sighed. "Ok. Your review."

Anthony pulled the folder towards him. My heart beat fast. I crossed my legs and shook my foot.

"You've done a great job with the baby. You managed to get the Uncle and parents to agree to medications when no one else could, discovered the baby can see and hear and are bonding with the family."

I smiled. "Sharing photos of my family opened the door. Abeer is curious about life outside Saudi."

He tapped his fingers on the desk. "It's good the parents are taking the child home on the weekends."

"I think her trips home are helping in her development. Did you know the physiotherapist was able to bend her knees this week?"

He stiffened. "My concern is you're getting too close."

My face fell. "I know. I can't help it. She's so precious and I like her mother and her servant Sammere. Did you know Sammere is starting to speak English? She's a smart woman. Her father is distant, but he comes regularly and her uncle never misses a day."

Anthony turned from me and looked at his calendar. "There's a very important Princess coming to the unit."

"Oh?"

"She was vacationing with her family in the US and had a stroke. She was rushed to hospital and when she was stable enough, they flew her to France."

"Why France?"

"She loves the French and has personal physicians in Paris. She'll be coming to the Faisal Hospital soon and I'd like you to be on her case."

I hung my head. "I don't know…what about Nawaar?"

"You can still look after her but I think it would be good for you to look after some of our other patients."

"Why? I'm happy looking after the baby."

"Precisely. I think you're too attached."

I leaned forward. "Too attached? No Anthony, please don't…"

He looked away. "My mind is made up. This Princess comes from one of the most important families in Saudi Arabia and her family is demanding the best nurses care for her."

I crossed my arms. "I'm not interested."

Anthony looked at me. "I'm directing you to care for her."

The sternness in his voice shocked me.

"You and Paula are the chosen nurses and I think you two will work well together."

"Chosen nurses?"

"Yes. Protocol approves of you."

My heart sank.. "When will this Princess come to the unit?"

"It could be next week or the week after that. We won't get much warning but I want you to be prepared."

I swallowed. "Very well. I should get back to Nawaar." I stood up.

He pushed the folder towards me. "I need you to sign this paper before you go. It states you agree with my assessment of your work."

"We didn't discuss my work."

"No, but as you can see you got an excellent review."

I looked at the papers, signed them and left his office.

****

I pushed open the heavy wooden door to Nawaar's room.

"Good, you're back. The baby's Uncle was here and he said something about matawa coming and praying for the baby. He'll be here in a few minutes."

"Thanks Barbara. I'll feed the baby before they get here."

I turned to wash the baby's bottles when I heard the door to the room open and Arab voices. I poked my head around the corner.

"Ah! Sister. This matawa. He pray for Nawaar," Sully said, sitting on the couch.

The matawa was an older man with a gray scraggly beard. I approached and went to shake his hand, then thought better of it. "How do you do? Do you speak English?"

The short man looked at me and smiled. His wife approached me speaking in Arabic. She had a big smile on her face. I smiled back and put my arm around her shoulder, giving her a little hug. She giggled.

The door opened and Abeer, Raheem, Sameer and a younger matawa with three wives came through the door.

"Hello sister," Abeer said smiling.

"Good morning everyone."

Raheem nodded his head and the younger matawa looked me over and grunted. He turned and spoke to Raheem and Sully. The older matawa said something and the younger one looked at me then sneered.

"Sister. Come. Sit here," Abeer directed.

I sat beside Abeer on the couch. Sully's wife struggled to sit on the other side of me. She looked uncomfortable wiggling into the couch, caressing her swollen belly.

"Fatima having baby. It boy."

"Yes, Abeer, I know. Isn't it exciting?"

Abeer rubbed her hand on my leg and Sully's wife gave me a hug. I felt warm and welcomed by the family.

The elder matawa spoke in Arabic. Smiles disappeared, focusing on him. The younger matawa put two chairs beside the crib.

Raheem turned to me and asked, "It ok hold Nawaar?"

"Yes, of course."

Raheem took the baby from the crib and placed her in the older matawa's arms. He smiled at her then removed her clothes.

The younger matawa lifted his face to the ceiling and chanted. He looked down, opened his Qu'ran, continuing his solemn song. The older matawa joined him in the chant and blew on the infant's bare chest.

Confused, I turned and looked at Abeer, but her attention was on the matawa and her infant. The older matawa spit on Nawaar. Alarmed, I drew in my breath but dare not move. The younger matawa took the infant and spit on her, then chanted, then spit on her again.

I couldn't believe my eyes. Sickened by the ritual, I turned to Abeer. Abeer reached over and patted me on the knee. I held my waist and crossed my legs, jiggling my foot.

The matawas finished their prayers and laid the saliva-covered child in the crib on her back, leaving her wet and exposed. They walked out of the room as abruptly as they came in, with their wives following behind. Abeer, Sameer and Sully's wife stayed on the couch.

Someone knocked on the door. I ran to the crib, placed a blanket over the baby then opened the door a crack. A protocol officer and Anthony stood outside.

"Please sister, ask woman to cover."

"Oh, ok."

I turned to Abeer and Sameer. The women panicked, put on their abayas and when their veils were in place Abeer nodded. I let the protocol officer in. They greeted each other in Arabic then the officer addressed me. "They say you good nurse."

I smiled. "Please tell them it's a pleasure to care for Nawaar."

I prepared a bath for the baby as they conversed.

"Anthony, they spit on her." I whispered.

"I see that. It's a religious ritual where the Muslims believe they are imparting their strong spirit into her, hoping she'll be healed."

"I think it's disgusting. What if they have something contagious? They'll make her sicker."

"I know, but it's their way."

"Scuse. Parents going to take Nawaar today to medicine woman."

"Medicine woman?"

"Yes. Family want infant cured. Medicine woman pray and give traditional medicine."

The protocol officer left the room. Abeer said 'hello' under her breath to Anthony, as she and the others left.

"Anthony, do you know anything about Saudi's traditional medicine?"

"Not much. There's nothing we can do to stop them. They're the parents and let's hope that whatever they give her won't be in conflict with the medicines she's already taking."

Anthony left leaving me alone with Nawaar. I bathed, fed and settled the baby then wrote notes in the chart.

****

"Howdy!" Said the cheery American male voice on the other end of the phone.

"Jake! So glad you called."

"Nice to hear your pleasant voice. I wish I could see you, but we're locked down."

"What does that mean?"

"No one can leave or come onto the base. There was a bombing downtown and an Englishman and Australian were killed. Didn't you hear?"

"No. I've been at work, oblivious to the outside world."

"They weren't the targets. Two American Ambassadors were visiting a member of the royal family and the terrorists missed their target. We're locked down until the smoke clears, so to speak."

"Wow. That's scary knowing violence is so close."

"We're in the Middle East and things are unpredictable. I'd stay away from downtown for a while, if I were you."

"Thanks for the update."

"I've a little more bad news."

"Oh no. What?" My heart sank.

"I have to go back to the US for a month then travel around the Kingdom for a few more weeks. We're launching a vaccine program and I'm one of the officers in charge of overseeing the operation."

"What are you doing with the vaccines?"

"We're delivering them to the hospitals and outlying clinics throughout the country."

"Wow. You military people do very good and essential work."

"We do indeed. It's too bad the media only reports the bad stuff. You watch. When the media gets their hands on the story of the car bomb, they won't look past this radical's actions or intentions."

I hesitated. "I'll miss you when you're gone, even though we've been out to dinner once ... and that was interrupted by the matawa."

He laughed. "I know. I'll miss you too. I have to go now, but when I'm gone I'll think of you."

His words uplifted my spirits. I smiled, walking to the kitchen feeling light and exuberant. My smiled faded, reminding myself how I run when romance heats up. I didn't want to be in the same situation with Jake as I was with Anthony. Did I want a relationship with Jake? Why was I thinking like this? I hardly knew the man.

I poured boiling water into a teapot and thought of Anthony. I couldn't understand why he made me feel like shrinking from him when he got close. How could I want his attentions one minute then feel repulsed the next? It didn't make sense. Why do these feelings surface when I meet men?

I poured the tea into a cup and added milk. Why was I fretting? I didn't want a relationship with anyone and especially not in Saudi. Hmm…Jake. He could have a girlfriend or several of them. Even worse, he could be married!

****

I walked into Nawaar's room. Jill, the nurse working the night shift looked up.

"I'm glad you're here. I can't wait to go home," Jill said.

"Tough night?"

"No, the night wasn't too bad." Jill snorted. "Look what the parents did to the baby's neck."

I walked over and pulled back the cover. "Oh my goodness!" Overwhelming feelings of outrage and sadness flooded me. "That baby's neck is burned!"

"Cauterized. Her parents took her to a witch doctor. Her neck was burned because they believe it'll release evil spirits and she'll be 'normal'. I've felt sick all night."

"Oh, the poor little thing. It must be painful," I said, reaching into the crib and picking up the baby.

The door to the room opened. "Morning!"

I looked at Paula. She was breathless, cheeks reddened and her long dark hair was pulled back in a ponytail, highlighting her sharp features.

"Paula, you're here too?" Jill asked.

"Yeah. Anthony told me to be here in the morning."

"Ok. There are too many nurses. I'm going home to sleep."

"'Night Jill," Paula called after her.

I asked, "We're *both* going to look after Nawaar today?"

"I don't know. I guess so."

The door to the baby's room opened. It was Raheem. He stopped and looked from me to Paula, then back again.

"Baby, she good? Better?" He asked.

Paula tilted her head. "Better?"

"She ok now?"

"Nawaar is ok except for the burn on her neck," I answered.

"Burn? What burn?"

I watched the color drain from Paula's face and her green eyes open wide when she looked at Nawaar's neck. "She was *cauterized* by a medicine woman yesterday. It's supposed to rid her of evil spirits." I cuddled the baby in my arms. "Isn't that right, Raheem?"

He appeared angry.

"Put child down!" He ordered.

His outburst startled me. "You don't want me to hold her?"

"Put down!"

I put her back in the crib, trying to keep tears from surfacing.

Raheem walked to the crib and pulled the blanket back. He picked up one leg and tried to bend her knee, then the other. The baby cried. "Hmm. Same, same."

He wrapped the baby in a blanket and in one swift move yanked the feeding tube from her nose.

"What are you doing?" I gasped.

The baby howled.

"Where're you taking her?"

Raheem pushed his way out of the room with Nawaar screaming in his arms.

Paula and I exchanged glances.

"Nawaar can't live with out that tube! She'll starve," cried Paula.

I rushed after Raheem and grabbed the handle of the door, but it pushed against me with such gusto I stumbled backwards. I caught myself and saw Abeer standing there with her face exposed.

"Baby Nawaar! Where she?" She sounded desperate.

"Raheem took her."

"No! No," she wailed.

Abeer bolted out the door, screaming and running towards the elevators. Patients and sitters emerged from their rooms, staring at the hysterical woman. I chased Abeer but couldn't catch up. Abeer stepped into the elevator and frantically pressed buttons. The doors closed. I stopped in my tracks, breathless, feeling helpless and confused.

Mohammad ran up to me. "What wrong?"

"I don't know." I choked. "Raheem came into the room, pulled the feeding tube out and took the baby. Then Abeer came and ran after Raheem. What's happening, Mohammad?"

He looked down at me and stiffened. "He do what father do. He brave man. Very brave man." He said, then turned and walked away.

Paula walked up to me. "What's going on?"

"I'm not sure and I'm not sure I want to know. Let's go back to the room."

I was shaking. I couldn't comprehend Raheem's actions. That was his little girl…his first-born baby. I took a tissue from the box, sat down on the couch and sobbed.

"Claire, tell me what Mohammad said. What's happening? Why are you crying?"

"He said Raheem is a very brave man."

"I don't understand."

Anthony rushed into the room. "I got an emergency call from Mohammad. He told me what happened. Are you two ok?"

"I don't know what's going on." Paula said.

He sighed. "Sit down. Let me explain."

Paula sat down. I turned my head away.

"The family was looking for a miracle cure for their little girl. They had the matawa pray over her and to impart their 'spirit of strength' and then they took her to a witch doctor to rid her of evil spirits. Raheem made the decision that Allah was not going to intervene, so according to what Protocol told me, he did what any good father would do. He took her to the desert and left her in Allah's hands."

Paula jumped to her feet. "You mean he left her there to die? Oh no! No! Can't we stop him? He can't! He can't!"

"Paula, we…"

Paula grabbed his arm. "Anthony!" She flopped on the couch and wept.

Anthony gave her a Kleenex.

I put my hand on her shoulder but the lump in my throat wouldn't let me speak. My eyes burned from the salt in my tears and my aching heart occluded any thoughts.

"Um…I am going to let you two be alone for a while. Why don't you both take the rest of the day off? We can manage here."

I stared into space. I was numb. No thoughts, no feelings, like an empty shell, void of emotion. Paula was silent, wiping an occasional tear from her face. The door opened. It was one of the nurses.

"I heard what happened. Are you two all right?"

I couldn't speak. Paula looked up and said, "No. A child is being killed! Dying cruelly in the desert. I'll never be all right again!"

The nurse looked sympathetic. "Why don't you two go and have lunch. You've been in here for a long time, and you need a change of scene."

I cleared my throat. "What time is it?"

"It's eleven thirty."

"We've been sitting here all this time? Wow, but I suppose you're right." I sighed and my mind cleared. "There's nothing we can do for little Naawar. Come on, Paula. We should go."

Paula sighed and stood up. "Ok."

We followed the nurse out of the room. Paula stopped and looked at me.

"I don't feel like eating, if you don't mind. I want to go home."
"Yeah, me too.

Chapter Seven

I walked into the restaurant looking for Paula. I felt better today and assumed Paula did too. We wanted to get to know each other better, especially if we were going to look after an important princess.

The lights in the restaurant were dim and I scanned the crowded room, hoping Anthony wouldn't be there

"Table Miss?"

"Yes. Thank you. I'm waiting for…oh Paula, there you are!"

"Dis way please misses."

He led us to a booth and I slid along the brown leather, making myself comfortable. I picked up a menu the waiter left on the table and studied it. I smiled, thinking this time I could see what was written on it. Did Anthony affect me that much?

"I'm dreading going back to work. You know they're going to be asking questions," Paula said, interrupting my thoughts.

"You don't have to answer them. If I don't want to give people information, I skirt issues and don't disclose anything."

"I've been watching you."

"You have? Why?"

"I couldn't figure you out. You're always pleasant but aloof with the staff, yet a great nurse."

"Well thank you, I think."

"That's not an insult. You're a deep thinker, rather conservative and not aloof at all. You don't let those mean, nosey nurses get too close and you handle them well. You know how hard it is to be discrete in the hospital community. Everyone wants to know everyone's business, then when they get information they try to turn it against you."

"I've been preoccupied with other things to get involved and besides, I like my privacy." I cleared my throat. "Tell me Paula, where are you from?"

"Melbourne Australia. It's beautiful and I miss my family very much."

"I think we all do. I'm from the West Coast of British Columbia, Canada. I live on the Island in a city called Victoria, the capital."

"It must be cold."

"Heavens no. My home has stormy beaches, majestic mountains and year-round gardens full of color and vitality. Lush green fir forests are within a minute's drive from the city center and outdoor adventure is a big part of the British Columbian's daily experience. I think the Island must be Canada's best-kept secret. Warm in the summer. Pleasantly cool in the winter. Rarely any snow. We may get a sprinkling of snow, but it disappears in a day or two and we don't get the rain like Seattle or Vancouver. It's known as the 'garden city'."

Paula laughed. "You sound like a commercial, but it sounds lovely."

I giggled and played with the utensils on the table. "It is. Living on an island, we're surrounded by clear blue water and we even have sand castle competitions. Any kind of outdoor activity you can think of is in abundance on the Island."

"Why did you leave?"

"I haven't left forever. Just needed a change that's all. How about you? Why did you come to Saudi?"

"I needed a change too. Family problems, you know. I don't need money. My family is well off. I just needed some time away to think."

"I don't know if Saudi is the place to come to think. It's been stressful for me so far."

"Oh yeah. Your roommate…"

"You must have had difficulties with adjustments to the customs and lifestyle of the Saudis."

"Not really. My father's side of my family is from Malta, so I'm at home with some of the traditions. I can't speak the language fluently but I can understand what they say and communicate in 'baby language'."

"That's a huge advantage. What about your mother's side of the family?"

"She's from France. I'm first generation Australian."

I crossed my legs under the table. Now I understood why people thought Paula was a snob. It was her French mannerisms. "How long have you been in Saudi?"

Paula frowned. "Five months. It's ok and sometimes I enjoy it."

"I don't think I'll enjoy anything until I know Rose is safe."

"Scuse, misses. You order?"

"Hmm…I'll have your chicken please with a glass of water."

"I'll have the same."

"Same, same? Ok, misses."

We handed the menus to the waiter. He took them, bowed then left.

"Paula, tell me about the sitters on the unit. What do they do?"

"They're supposed to protect the family member from danger or warn the women to cover at the appropriate times. Having a sitter means there's always a witness in case they're accused of something and women can never be left without a chaperone. The men in the hospital environment are among other men's wives."

"Is that because the men don't trust the women?"

"No one trusts anyone. Seems life revolves around sexual activity. It's what the men talk about, what the women discuss … sometimes I wish I didn't understand what they said. It's like being in a room full of teens! It's an act, and they laugh, joke and berate sexuality. It's disgusting, but a woman cross the line? Whew! And it's *always* the woman's fault."

I uncrossed my legs. "Why do the men have sitters?"

"I think it's a prestige or status thing. Some Saudi men think they're superior and want attention when they're sick, and someone to be a slave to them. They um…if they can't afford to hire a sitter from Egypt, Jordan, Sri Lanka, Philippines or other nation, they may be assigned a relative. You can tell which sitters are hired and which ones are related. The relatives are treated better of course, and have a bed to sleep on and eat their meals with the patient. The hired sitters are treated badly. I'm sure you've noticed that most of the sitters are Filipino. Cheap labor. "

"It's very sad. It's good to see the nurses on the unit give them pillows and blankets so they don't sleep on the hard floor."

Paula took a sip from her water glass. "Although some prefer to sleep on the floor. They're used to sleeping on the hard desert sand. But still, they're happy their employer is a patient at the hospital."

"They are?"

"Yeah. These sitters have no rights you know, Claire. They're at the mercy of their employers. Some could be beaten, tortured and have basic necessities denied them. Sometimes they go for long periods without eating, drinking or sleeping. Remember, Filipinos or other Asians are liked the least amongst other groups of people and some of those women are abused in the most horrible ways. They're happy their employer is in hospital because it's the only time they get a regular meal and it's a holiday from some of their duties at home.

"We don't know how fortunate we are, do we?"

"That's true, but don't forget our fathers and forefathers shed their blood for the freedom we enjoy today."

"You're right. I think all groups of people have suffered at the hands of one group or other throughout history. Human beings are cruel creatures." I sighed and folded my napkin, placing it on the table.

"How was your meal, Paula?"

"Very good. Now all we need is a nice glass of wine." She sighed. "Too bad alcohol is forbidden in the Kingdom. Did you know if a person is caught with alcohol he is doomed to have his head cut off? It's a serious drug offense."

"Seems like all offenses are serious in this land." I thought about Rose.

Paula flipped her hair over her shoulder. "Are you looking forward to caring for this princess? She's a very important person in the Kingdom and her husband has a high position in the royal hierarchy. The tribal history is fascinating. They're from one of the branches responsible for unifying the Kingdom. This Princess's husband is either the cousin or cousin-in-law of the Crowned Prince. I'm not sure which—the lineage is confusing, but they are very, very important."

"Status doesn't impress me much, but it'll be interesting to observe the 'upper class.' How did you find out so much about the princess? I don't know anything about her."

"I worked nights and have a friend in the night supervisor. He filled me in."

"Anthony hasn't said much to me. Mind you, I've been preoccupied."

"I'm glad we'll be working together. I like you, Claire. I'm also glad neither one of is in our twenties."

"How's that?

"I think you have to have a bit of life behind you to appreciate this culture. Some of the younger ones want to go to parties and find a guy. Even some of the older ones want to do nothing but socialize. Very few are interested in the culture of the Arab people. I'm forty-two and I'm guessing you're around my age."

"You're a year older than me, not that it makes any difference. It's good to have a friend and I think we're going to have a good time together. Let's go, shall we?"

We walked down the corridor to the elevators. Paula stopped, held onto my arm, pointed and said, "Claire, there's Anthony."

Anthony heard his name and turned around. His tie was loose around his neck and his black pants, wrinkled. He carried his lab coat over his arm. I noticed the deep stress lines and dark circles under his eyes making him look older than usual.

"Hello you two. What are you doing here so late?"

"Late? We just finished lunch," I said.

"Lunch?" Anthony looked at his watch. "It's after six and I'm on my way home."

"Six o'clock! Claire, we've been talking for hours!"

We laughed.

"Well, it's good to see *some* of my staff can get along. Listen Claire. I got a call from Abdul today about Rose. How about a cup of coffee and I'll fill you in?"

"I'll let you two discuss your business. I have to get home. I'm expecting a call myself. Claire, it was a pleasure and I hope it's good news about your roommate."

She walked down the hall and disappeared around the corner.

Anthony smiled. I tucked my hair behind my ear. "Good news, I hope?"

"Let's go to the cafeteria."

I didn't like the way he avoided my question. I worried about Rose as I followed Anthony across the compound to the mini-mall.

"How about our usual table in the corner? Do you want anything to eat or drink?"

I sat down before Anthony could pull out a chair for me. "No thank you."

"I'm going to get a plate of food. Be back in a minute."

Anthony stood in line and took generous portions of rice and meat from the buffet. He walked back to the table, stuffing a piece of chicken in his mouth before sitting down.

I shook my foot under the table. "What's happening?"

He took a deep breath and looked down at his hands. "Looks like Rose can get out the day after tomorrow."

"She will? Can we go and get her?"

"No Claire. It will be the same arrangements as before."

"What are you talking about?"

"She has to go to Chop-Chop Square again."

"No! I thought we were past that."

"She's been feisty in prison and 'badly behaved'. The Saudi Authorities feel she needs discipline and accused her father of not rearing an obedient daughter. They won't let her go until she's lashed. They want to beat the devil out of her."

"This is insane. Haven't they punished her enough?"

"Don't think so, Claire. Abdul wants to meet us in the lobby at eight o'clock on Friday morning and we'll go from there."

I looked at Anthony. Last time we were in this position, Anthony took me to the park and we kissed.

"Are you all right?"

"Um…yeah, I think so. I just haven't had time to process this yet."

"Do you want to go for a walk?"

"No! I mean, no, thanks. I think I want to go home. I think I'll be able to face this better now that I have a greater understanding of Saudi ways. Maybe I'm lying to myself, I don't know. At least Rose will walk away from this alive... Nawaar couldn't walk away. She was helpless. Completely dependent..."

"Claire, you're rambling. And crying. Are you sure you want to go home now?"

"Yes. Very sure."

"At least let me walk you to your apartment."

I stood up. "No. Please. I have to go." I ran out the door.

****

The telephone woke me from a sound sleep. I rolled over and looked at the clock. "Seven thirty in the morning. Ok. Ok. I'm coming."

I answered the phone.

"Miss Spencer? Mr. Morrison here. Rose is free."

"What?"

"Yup. Got her out earlier this morning and she's in the hospital as we speak."

"She is? Is she ok? How did you..."

"Abdul worked his magic. He got them to agree to accept a hefty bounty for her and they let her go."

"You mean ransom? They took money?"

"Yes, a lot of it. Fifty thousand American dollars bought her freedom."

"Wow. I can't believe it."

"The hospital agreed to pay the fine, but Rose is going to have to work to pay it back and that's money on top of the first fine." He paused. "I think her prison antics contributed to freeing her. She kicked a Matawa and knocked out a tooth."

"Really?"

"They're happy to be rid of her. She's out and that's the main thing."

"Where is she?"

"In the hospital. I have to go. I'm happy this worked out well. Goodbye, Miss Spencer."

It seemed too easy. Money. If that's all they wanted, couldn't this have been negotiated earlier, sparing Rose the indignity of Chop-Chop Square?

The phone rang again. I let the answering machine pick up.

"Claire this is Anthony. Just calling to make sure you're ok. If you get this message, perhaps you'd like to have coffee with me at nine-thirty? I'll look out for out."

"Nope, Anthony! I'm going to see Rose today. Don't want to see you. Sorry." I said to the machine.

I had a quick bath, put on a short sleeveless cotton dress, slipped the black abaya over my clothes, put on my brown leather sandals wiggling my manicured toes and walked to the hospital. I went to the information booth and waited for the man behind the desk to get off the phone.

"Yes, can I help you miss?"

"Could you please tell me what room Rose Casio is in please?"

"Yes. Yes. One minute."

I looked behind me and saw Anthony coming down the hall. I stepped to one side hoping a pole would obscure his view of me.

"She on second floor, room 245."

"Thank you."

I walked towards the elevator.

"Hey! Claire!"

Shrugging my shoulders I stopped and turned around.

"How are you? Rose is free, you know."

"Yes, I know."

He bent towards me and said, " I thought you would've called me."

"You did? Why?"

"You were upset when you left yesterday. I thought you'd want to talk, you know, about Chop-Chop Square and Rose's ordeal? The baby?"

"No. I don't want to talk about it. I want to forget about it."

"It'd be healthy if we debriefed."

"Anthony, I don't want to talk. Perhaps a counselor would be helpful, if they have such things in Saudi."

He had a hurt look on his face and I shuddered recognizing the yearning in his eyes.

"Are you all right? You seem distant."

The elevator doors opened.

"Please Anthony, I have to go."

"Where are you going? To See Rose? Let me come too."

"No! I mean, I think one visitor at a time is enough right now, don't you?"

"You don't want to be near me, do you?"

My frustration was mounting. I had to let the elevator go.

"Why don't you come and discuss what you're going through over a cup of coffee. I think the circumstances surrounding your roommates' arrest and her confinement are affecting you. Come on. Let's talk."

"I don't feel like talking right now."

"Come on, it will do you good."

I sighed. He was still my boss and I had to be careful. "Fine. Let's go."

I felt miserable trudging beside him to the cafeteria. He spoke to me, but I didn't respond.

"Let's sit over here."

The cafeteria was busy and he chose a table away from the other patrons.

"You haven't heard a word I've said, have you?"

"No, I guess I haven't."

The look in his eyes changed and I sensed his annoyance.

"What is it with you?" He said in a hushed voice. "You come onto me and then reject me. What are you? A black widow?"

I stood up. "I beg your pardon! I did not 'come onto you'. If I remember correctly, it was the other way around. It was a mistake. A terrible, terrible mistake."

I turned to go and he grabbed my wrist. I looked around the cafeteria. No one was paying attention. "You're hurting me."

"Sit down!" He said between his teeth.

Alarmed, I sat down. He let me go and relaxed his shoulders. I felt my cheeks burn hot and wanted to run away until I saw tears in his eyes. I felt pity for him. That same pity I can't justify; it lacks compassion and breeds contempt.

His shoulders sagged. "I'm sorry. I don't know what got into me. I get the distinct feeling you're running away from me, or blaming me for something. I can't bear the thought of you rejecting me... and I could use a friend."

I let out a deep sigh. Why couldn't I be nicer to him? I looked down, held my hands in my lap and played with my thumbs. "I'm sorry too, Anthony. Things are confusing for me right now. I just need to be by myself to think things through."

"That's the worst thing you can do—be by yourself, I mean. Don't you want to find a way to make sense of everything?"

"I don't know if we can make sense of it and it's just the way it is. The people of Saudi Arabia relish in cruelty and brutality and we can't change it."

"That's true, but Claire I can see you're still in shock. I'm in shock."

I drew in a breath and sat up straight. "Anthony, I can't do this. Please. I need to see Rose."

"Why are you so cold?"

"Cold?"

"Yeah. You need to talk."

"Who says I need to talk to anyone?"

"It's not all about you, you know. Why do you think I agreed to go and watch Rose be whipped and be by your side throughout this whole ugly mess?"

"I don't know. Because you're representing the hospital."

"And why do you think I put myself in that position? I could've let someone else do it, or I could've let you go to the Square by yourself."

"I didn't think…"

"No, you didn't. What about me? My feelings? My needs? I can't brush things off so easily."

"I'm not brushing anything off. I just…"

"You just want to go and pout and be by yourself. Poor little Claire."

"Don't be condescending."

Anthony hung his head then looked into my eyes. I gripped the edge of the table, pulling back from him.

"Don't you think if we leaned on each other it would make it easier? You should know better."

"What do you want from me? I should know better about what? I don't need lectures from you and I don't know how to make this any clearer. I don't want to develop anything with you. I don't want emotional support from you and I cannot give it to you. Why can't you find someone else to talk to?"

"You can't be serious. You know as well as I that no one outside Saudi would understand. Even people inside the Kingdom wouldn't understand." He sighed. "Am I that much of a monster?"

I looked away then back again. "I…I don't mean to hurt you Anthony, but please. Please stop pushing me."

"Pushing you?"

"I don't want to develop a romantic relationship."

"But I told you. My wife and I are separating."

"Lookit. You do what you have to do, but don't put me in the picture. You're going to need time to sort things out."

"Can't I do that with you by my side?"

"No. It won't work. You need at least a minimum of five years before you even think about getting involved with someone else."

"Five years!" He grabbed the table with both hands.

"That's right. I wouldn't consider a romance with someone fresh out of a relationship. Anthony. Please. Stop. I cannot. And the arrest? The lashings? The disappearance of baby Nawaar? You're right. No one would ever understand."

He looked defeated.

"Tell me Claire. How are you going to get past all of this?"

I looked straight at him. "One foot in front of the other. Right now, I want to go and see Rose." I stood up.

"Claire?"

"What?"

He looked at me, paused, then sighed. "Nothing."

I started to walk away. Feeling sorry for him, I turned back.

"Anthony, I'm sorry. You're a good man, but…"

"It's ok Claire. I understand. You're right. I think I am…I don't know…I'm not myself these days."

"Maybe your trip home will put things in perspective."

"I hope so." He sniffed and half smiled. "I haven't been out of the Kingdom for over six months. You need to get out and see the 'real world', otherwise you'll go mad." He stood up. "Claire, I still think you're special and I'm sorry. I would never…"

"It's ok Anthony. I have to go."

****

Rose sat up in bed, spreading bright red lipstick on her mouth when I entered her room. I felt sheepish for neglecting to bring flowers or a card and decided to make sure there'd be something special at the apartment for her when she returned home.

"Hi. What are you doing here?"

"What do mean by that? I came to see you."

"I'm fine. I want to go home."

"I'm sure you do. How are you?"

"I said I'm fine! Where's Ian? Why isn't he here?"

"Ian? I don't know. The last time I spoke to him he said he had to go to Scotland."

"Scotland! He didn't' even say good-bye!"

"He did say to tell you he'll be thinking about you."

"Think about me! That doesn't do any good."

She whipped back the blankets and jumped out of bed. "He should be here with me." She started to dress.

"What are you doing?"

"I'm going to the airport. He owes me an explanation."

"Rose! He left weeks ago."

"Oh." She took off her clothes, put the hospital gown on and climbed into bed.

"I guess I'll have to stay here." She pouted.

I studied her. I expected her to be subdued or in deep thought. Instead, she seemed animated…wired. Was this how she reacted to severe stress?

I cleared my throat. "Have you been able to talk to anyone about your prison experience?"

"Oh that. Yeah. Some doctor came in this morning and we talked."

Her attitude changed. She hung her head.

"How are you, really?"

She cried. I sat on the bed, holding her hand.

"I want to go home."

"Home? Home to New Zealand or home, the apartment?"

"The apartment. They said I can go tomorrow morning."

"Tomorrow?"

"Yeah, why? Don't you want me home?"

"Oh Rose, of course I want you home. I thought they'd keep you in longer, that's all."

"There's nothing wrong with me and I want to get out of here."

"What about your back? What about…"

"I said I'm fine, and I'm going home."

"All right then. I'll come here we can go home together tomorrow. Ok?"

"Ok."

****

I was in the middle of cleaning up after dinner when the phone rang. I looked at the clock. It was after ten.

"Hello?"

"Claire? This is Abdul. I have Rose."

"What do you mean you have Rose? Isn't she in hospital?"

"No. I had to take legal papers for her to sign. She insist going home. I'm in lobby of apartment. Can you come and get her? Please?"

"You are? All right. I'll be down in a couple of minutes."

I raced around the kitchen put some food away and turned off the burner on the stove. I ran into my room, slipped on my shoes and darted out the door. I got on the elevator to the bottom floor and when the elevator doors parted, I walked past the pool area and opened the tall glass doors leading into the lobby.

"Claire! Here she. She tired, but she ok."

"Thanks Abdul. I'll take care of her."

Rose wore a new abaya and kept her eyes downcast. We walked in silence to our apartment. I opened the door and as soon as Rose entered, she broke into tears. "I'm sorry. I'm so tired. So mad. So confused. I'm glad I'm home."

My heart melted. "Let me help you, Rose".

Rose looked at me. I helped her take off her abaya and hung it in the closet. Rose walked to the couch and sat down.

"Can I get you something to eat? Something to drink?"

She shook her head. "I want a hot bath."

I ran a bath for her and while Rose washed, I made a couple of sandwiches and a cup of tea. When Rose resurfaced she was in her nightclothes carrying a fluffy blue blanket. She curled up on the couch, wrapped the blanket around her and stared into space.

"Rose, do you want to talk about it?"

Rose buried her head into her knees and cried.

The phone rang. Exasperated, I wondered who'd be calling at this hour? It was ten thirty.

"Hello?"

"Hello, Claire? Ian here."

I stiffened. "Where are you?"

"In Riyadh. I didn't go to Scotland after all. I begged to stay and they let me. Can I talk to Rose?"

I bit my tongue. I wanted to ask him where he's been all this time. Why wasn't he supporting Rose? How did he know she was free? Funny…when Rose isn't available she's forgotten. Now that she's home he wants her? He's a cad!

"Rose do you want to speak to Ian?" I asked, trying to mask my anger.

Rose shook her head 'no'.

"She doesn't want to talk right now."

"She called me earlier and I'm returning her call. Is she ok?"

"Physically. She's just returned home and I'd like to settle her in."

"I'll call her later then."

I put the phone down, pushing unkind thoughts of Ian from my mind.

Rose had her face buried in her knees. She suddenly lifted her head and stated in a faraway voice, "It's all his fault…"

"Come on Rose. Have something to eat. Have a sip of that tea. I made it just the way you like it, with lots of honey."

She took a sip from the cup.

"How's your back?"

"It's sore, but the doctor said it will heal ok. I'll have scars."

"I'm so sorry. Did the doctor give you any medications?"

Rose nodded her head and pointed to her purse. I saw the leather bag in the corner of the room and opened it, finding two vials filled with pills. I read the labels. One was an antibiotic and the other a sedative. "I think you should have your medication and go to bed."

Rose didn't object. I administered the drugs, helped her to bed and then came out to the living room, unplugged the phone so no one would disturb us. I picked up Rose's bottles of pills and was walking to the kitchen to put them away, when I stopped and read the labels again. The sedative was a mild sleeping pill. I stared at it for a moment then decided to take one. I was under so much stress and perhaps if I had one good night's sleep the memories of the lashings would end for just one night.

I put the medication away then dressed for bed. I was going to read, but when I crawled beneath the comforter, I was feeling the effects of the pill.

****

I woke up to loud banging and cupboard doors slamming. Half asleep, I dashed into the kitchen.

"It's all his fault!" Rose shouted. "He got me arrested!"

"Do you mean Ian?"

"Who else? If he just knew what was good for him. If he would just stop playing games!" Rose took a glass bowl from the cupboard and threw it against the wall, shattering it into pieces.

"Oh... you better let me help you. Why don't you sit down and I'll make you a cup of coffee before you hurt yourself."

"OOOOH! I'll kill him! He wouldn't listen. He thinks his marriage is so precious. He thinks I wouldn't know how to be a mother to his kids. How does he know? They haven't even met me." She picked up a cup and threw it.

"Rose! Come and sit down. Please." I directed her to the living room, but she wouldn't sit down. "Tell me, are you mad at Ian because he's married?"

"Well—if he listened, I wouldn't have called him and he wouldn't have taken me downtown."

"I'm not following you, Rose. Is that what your argument was about? His marriage?"

Rose flashed an angry look. She pursed her lips and squinted making the black centers of her eyes disappear behind her long lashes. She whirled around and I feared she was going to break something else.

"Why don't you go and sit down?"

"Ahh!" She stomped her feet. "He never told me he was married! He's a liar!"

I saw fire dancing behind her dark eyes before she turned them to the floor. She relaxed her expression then thumped out of the kitchen and flopped on the couch.

"Ahh!" She screamed, then buried her face in her hands.

I stood motionless for a minute, not sure how to approach her. I sat on the couch beside her.

"Rose, why don't you tell me what happened."

Rose turned her head away.

"Humph!" She sobbed using the back of the couch as her pillow. "Leave me alone!"

I went into the kitchen, put grounds and water in the coffee pot, got the broom from the closet and swept up the broken pieces of glass. I returned and stood in front of Rose with fresh brewed coffee. "Here. Drink this. Now come on, talk to me."

Rose lifted her head and reached for the cup. She placed it between her palms and warmed her hands. She looked as if she were about to drift back into her despondent state, then cocked her head to one side and brushed her straight black hair over her shoulder. "It was awful. They took all my things. My wallet. They stole money out of my wallet, and I want it back. Who do they think they are, anyway? Then they led me to a real small square room. It wasn't much bigger than our closet. It didn't have any windows and the walls were filled with fabric or something like that and covered with tinfoil. I think it was soundproofed. There was nothing in it but a chair in the middle and they made me sit on that then shone a bright light in my face. Because of the foil on the wall it made it bright and it was stuffy. I couldn't see a thing. Then a matawa came in and talked at me."

"You must have been scared."

"I wasn't scared. I got mad at him and yelled. I wanted some air and I told them that! He started yelling at me—so I yelled back. I suppose I shouldn't have, but I couldn't help it. He was talking to me, but not making sense. Another Arab shouted at me and said 'don't you understand English?' I told him that wasn't English, I didn't understand a word the man said!"

I held my breath and listened. "This was the first prison? Did they hurt you?"

"They got mad at me. I kept telling them I didn't know what they were saying. I insisted they get someone who could speak good English. I guess they didn't like that too much and they hit me across the head."

"Oh no! Did they hurt you?"

"It made me fuzzy. But I was all right." She stopped and sipped her coffee. Her expression softened. "Then they put me in a big room. I mean …it was just a huge empty room. It was like a large warehouse with a dirt floor and tin roof. There were other women and children."

"I was there. I came to visit you, remember?"

"You came? I thought that was a dream."

"It was no dream. Anthony Herd, the supervisor from D4-1, Abdul and his wife and I came to see you. They wouldn't allow the others in, but I spoke to you. Don't you remember?"

Rose turned away from me and pulled her knees to her chest. "I sort of remember. Did you know there was a smaller room attached to the large one? There were bunk beds in it, one piled up on the other but they were so dirty and stinky, I couldn't lie down to sleep, so things are kind of a blur."

"The conditions were horrible, I know."

"In the day the guards came and took out the women one by one." She continued in a small voice. "They said they were questioning them. The poor things were so upset and all they did was cry. Some of them were zombies. I think they were raping them. I know they were raping two of them for sure." She sighed then rocked back and forth, hugging her legs. The blanket fell to the floor. She spoke between her knees. "The ones with young boys, you know, about six or older? They were abusing them too. Some of those poor kids just lay there…they didn't move. Even when the guards came by to take them out again, they didn't move. Then they were hit and kicked…it was awful. Some of them were wishing they could die."

"Oh Rose. That's sickening."

"What can we do? There must be something we can do?"

I thought for a moment. "I know *Amnesty International* is trying to gain access into Saudi. Stories like these do leak out. I read an article describing the impermeability of getting across the border, but acts like these won't go unpunished. You know that, don't you, Rose? When you are feeling better, you should write to them and tell them about your experience." I paused, then asked, "And you. What did they do to you?"

Rose sighed. She dropped her head to her chest and continued. "They took me out like the other women, but they didn't rape me. I think they knew I was from this hospital. Besides, when I yelled at them it scared them. I wasn't going to let some filthy Arab put his hands on me! The women from the poorer countries don't know how to stand up for themselves like we do, so it made the men afraid. I just kept shouting 'Harram!' Which means forbidden. It worked."

"I think your attitude stopped them from hurting you any more than they did."

"That was in the first prison. It was better in the second one. I had a cell to myself, but it still didn't have a sink or toilet. It had a hole in the floor and they gave me straw to put over it."

"Were the conditions better there?"

"Oh yeah. I got to bathe once a week. They put a bucket of cold water in my cell and gave me a towel. No soap, so I didn't get very clean. The guard on duty used to stand around to watch me bathe. At first I tried not to let him see, but then I decided I would show him everything."

"Rose!"

"Who cares? I'll never see him again. I got him all worked up and the stupid guys would start to undress and come into my cell. I kicked them where it counts! I laughed as they squealed. It was pretty funny and like stupid pigs, they did it every week. I wanted to get the keys and escape, but I never could."

"Rose, you were crazy. What if there was more than one? You couldn't fight two of them."

"I'm not stupid. I wouldn't do it when there were two or more. I'd be discreet then."

"Was there anyone else in the prison with you?"

"Not in my cell. We had our own, but I could see three others across from me. They were from Africa, I think. They didn't speak English, but when they saw how I kicked and screamed and scratched the guards, they copied me. I think it saved them from being raped. It was funny when we decided to scream at the top of our lungs. The guards couldn't stand it! There was an echo. Have you ever heard women's high-pitched screams echoing? It could break eardrums!"

I smiled. I could imagine the scene.

"Sometimes they'd take me out into a little room and tried to make me sign a paper. I think it was a confession to being a prostitute. I didn't do anything wrong, and I didn't care what they did to me. I wouldn't sign it and they got angry and tried to force my signature. I sat there, crossed my arms and refused. I told them they were stupid, and they were pigs. That's when they got really angry, and kicked me hard. It hurt and I bled, but I was not going to do as they said."

"Wow. You were brave, Rose."

"No, not really. They kicked me and hit me a lot but not like some of the other women. I don't think they liked me very much, so they didn't touch me. Sexually, that is."

"I'm so sorry you had to go through this."

"The beating wasn't so bad, you know. I mean, it hurt like hell when they first started to whip me, but after a while I didn't feel a thing."

"How's your back now?"

"A little tender, but not so bad. The doctor said I got an infection in some of the wounds and they bandaged them up. I'll have scars on my back. I don't care."

I didn't know what to say.

"Are you making a cup of tea? I'll have one too."

I returned from the kitchen with two hot drinks.

"You make a good cup of tea, Claire." Rose took a deep breath and let out a long sigh. "I have restrictions you know."

"That's what Mr. Morrison said."

"I owe the hospital a fortune, but I can pay it back in two years. The embassy is going to help out some. I'm not allowed to leave the hospital grounds for six weeks."

"What about shopping? Going to the grocery store?"

"I'm allowed to go to the grocery store. I'm also allowed to go shopping in the day, but the security will be recording my every move until my contract ends. I'm also not allowed to travel and my passport will have "prostitute" stamped in it. Mr. Morrison said he'll get me a new passport, then I can travel. He also said that if I wanted to he could get me out of the country real fast."

"Are you going to leave?"

Rose looked away.

"What is it, Rose?"

"This is my home. There's nothing for me in New Zealand."

"What do you mean nothing?"

"My family is Hindu and I refused to marry a man my parents picked out for me. My father disowned me years ago and kicked me out on the street."

"What? How old were you?"

"Fifteen. I decided I would show them! I finished high school then got a scholarship and went to nursing school. I worked for a few years and came here about a year ago. I need to save money to buy a house."

"How did you support yourself after your father threw you out?"

"I'm not stupid. I knew from about the age of eight that I was supposed to marry that man. I didn't want to and I knew when I refused my father would reject me. I saved every bit of money I could get my hands on for years. When he threw me out, I had over twenty thousand US dollars."

"Twenty thousand!"

"Yup. I took money from his safe from time to time. Why are you looking at me like that? He was the one who threw me out! It was part of my dowry. Why should I let my father give it to someone else? It was mine.

Besides, I had to survive and I was not going to starve."

I swallowed hard. "No, it's just that you had incredible foresight for such a young girl. Good for you."

"So, this little prison thing doesn't bother me," she said, flipping her hair.

"*Little* prison thing? Rose how can you discount it so easily?"

She shrugged. "What's the big deal? It can be worse on the streets. Yeah, the lashes were painful, but at least I'm free now and I refuse to suffer like those other women. Nope, not me. I know how to take care of myself and I've just proved it again."

I looked at her sideways. I didn't believe her. No one was that tough, were they? "I was worried sick about you. There were several people who worked hard to get you released."

"I know. I should thank them, I guess." She pouted. "But it's not like I asked for help. I don't want to owe anyone anything."

"How would you feel if we did nothing? If you were left there to rot?"

"I knew someone would come and get me out. And if they didn't I'd figure a way out. I know how to take care of myself." She folded her arms.

"Rose, you must have been scared when you were locked away. I remember how you begged me to help get you out."

She sat up straight. "Scared! No one can scare me. You saw me. You saw how I can fight. I 'd fight them to the bitter end, if I had to."

I bit my lip.

"Even if they killed me, they wouldn't break me. My father couldn't, they couldn't—no one can."

"You're strong, Rose. I know I couldn't bounce back from that kind of experience as quickly as you seem to have."

"What am I supposed to do? Sit around and be depressed? No way. Besides, I had my little chat with the psychiatrist. He's useless. Wanted to know about my family history. I told him it was none of his business." She stood up. "He wouldn't stop asking me questions and I got sick of it. I told him to leave me alone. How can an Egyptian understand anything about my world and my feelings?" She paced. "Stupid. I'm surrounded by stupid people in a stupid society." She turned, "I didn't mean you. And another thing, I am not going to obey their stupid rules. Screw the courts of Saudi!"

"Rose!"

"No worries. I figured out a way to get off the hospital grounds without them detecting me."

"Are you crazy?"

"Who's going to know?" She flopped on the couch. "Anyway, if I do get arrested again—which I won't—I'll be sent home. Mr. Morrison told me that. He also said I was to come next week and he'll arrange that new passport. They'll never know, so when I do need to leave the country or go on vacation, it won't be a problem." She tapped her cheek with her fingers. "And you know the tunnel that leads to the housing on the other side of the hospital? There's a way to get off the hospital grounds without the guards seeing you."

I put my hand over my heart. "You'll be taking terrible chances."

"I'm not going to let them dictate my life to me. Besides, I need to see Ian."

"Ian? I thought you were angry with him."

"Yeah, well." She looked into space and smiled. "This experience will bring us closer together. I just know it. And we need to plan our wedding."

"Wedding?"

She looked at me. "Of course! You don't think I'd waste my time on him if he wasn't going to marry me, do you?"

"But he's already married."

"Not for long."

My mouth fell open.

Rose jumped off the couch and skipped to her room.

I was stunned. Rose just spent weeks in a prison, was whipped and is now planning a wedding to a married man? Didn't she care about consequences? Maybe her experiences left her mentally unstable...or was she always like this?

Chapter Eight

I dragged my hastily packed suitcase down the long hallway of King Faisal Hospital keeping pace with Paula. I was surprised when I got a phone call last night from Anthony telling me I was going to Jeddah. When he told me about caring for the Princess, I didn't realize he meant at her palace.

Our bags made a loud clatter as we passed over the seams in the marble floor. I ignored the stares of hospital workers and visitors as I giggled in nervous excitement on the way to the private elevators. I could hardly see stepping into the dimly lit elevator reserved for the royal families. When the doors opened on the fourth floor an unfamiliar Arab man greeted us.

"Hurry. Hurry!' He said in broken English. "They waiting."

Paula protested, "We didn't have time to pack properly and we don't know what's expected."

"You will know. Yes, yes. You are nurses. You must nurse! Trust me. Now, hurry. Hurry."

He led us into one of the meeting rooms on the VIP unit and I viewed the traditional layout of the furniture lining the walls. The Queen Anne-style chairs and over-stuffed sofas boasted of blue and gold paisley patterns with wooden legs painted to assume an antique finish. An Arabian multi-colored woolen rug centered on the floor depicted a battle fought centuries before and the shapes and vivid colors reflected the flamboyant, mismatched Middle-Eastern tastes. A mahogany desk placed in front of a window on one end of the room had a pile of folders sitting off to one side.

Anthony sat on one of the couches studying some documents. He looked at us and said, "Oh good. You're both here." He stood up. "I want to introduce you to Saloman, the head of protocol.

Salomon peered at us from under his red-checked headdress and nodded as he lifted the skirt of his stark white thobe and sat down behind the desk. The edges of the red-checked headpiece fell forward and he tossed them over his shoulders. He adjusted his headpiece and pointing, signaled we sit down.

"Prince Mohammad wants you two go wid de family dis day. Dey leaving by private jet to palace in Jeddah." Salomon began.

I asked Anthony, "What arrangements have been made? Everything is happening fast and we've haven't had time to think."

Salmon cleared his throat. "What does it matter? You are looking after important lady."

"Salomon, " Anthony answered, "I need to go over some things." He turned to us and continued. "You'll be caring for Princess Linyaa in her palace in Jeddah. She has multiple medical issues."

Paula interrupted, "Does that mean this family is responsible for us? I don't know about leaving the hospital."

"Just let me finish, Paula. We don't have much time."

"Mr. Anthony, dis is waste of time. The womans, dey will know what is expected."

"Salomon, I want to review the contents of the contractual agreement. As soon as that's done, they can decide if they want to do the job."

"Mr. Anthony! Dey must go. De Prince, he want!" Salmon flipped his headdress over his shoulder.

"I understand your concern, but please, let me continue." He cleared his throat and turning, said, "The hospital is still responsible for you. You'll continue to receive your pay from here, unless you resign and work for the family. I advise against that, unless you make a commitment to them for at least five years."

"It is good to work for family." Salomon interjected.

Anthony looked at him sideways. "As I was saying, Prince Mohammad is the eldest son and you'll report to him. He'll take care of your living arrangements and has guaranteed your safety. If there are any problems, there's a new Faisal hospital in Jeddah where you can get in touch with Salomon or another protocol officer."

"Are you sure we'll be safe?" I felt uneasy about what I was agreeing to.

"You don't think I'd feed my staff to the wolves, do you? No, you'll be fine."

"Dis hospital make contract with royal families all de time. De family must agree to certain conditions, you understand, or dey not get Western nurses." Salomon leaned forward. "Dey want de best nurses."

Anthony cleared his throat. "This family hasn't had Westerners in their home before, so you'll have to win the staff over. There are two American nurses who'll be with you for a week or two before you're left by yourselves."

Paula sat up straight. "Americans?"

"Yes. They've been with the Princess since she had her stroke in the US and they'll pass the baton, so to speak, when it's time for them to leave."

"What about time off?" Paula asked.

"Yes, yes. You ask Prince Mohammad. He give. You work for dree months, then der is review. If Prince Mohammad like, you stay. If not, you go."

Anthony stood up. "These documents I hold in my hands are the signed contracts. I've reviewed them and everything seems to be in order. Any questions? Are you agreeable?"

Saloman appeared impatient. "Dey must go. De Prince, he pick you both. We discuss all matters wid family. Dis is delicate matter and must be careful not to insult. You understand? Dis is new for dem, and you representing dis hospital, and your countries."

"Ah…Salomon, I want them to have a choice here. They are not servants."

He looked at Anthony. "Yes, yes. Dey nurses, not servant. I understand. De Prince want de best, and dese de best." He turned and looking from me then to Paula asked, "You go, yes?"

"Of course we'll look after this important Princess," Paula said.

I looked at Paula, then nodded.

Salomon stood up from behind his desk, walked to the door and opened it. I dragged my suitcase past him, into the hall and sighed. " Paula, I don't know about this."

"Don't be silly. This hospital has these royal assignments all the time. I'm so happy I get to go on one. There are nurses I know who've had the greatest experiences. Aren't you excited? We're going to work for a very powerful family. Imagine us on a royal jet! People back home would never believe it."

"That's true…."

"Claire, think. We are *the* nurses for Princess Liynaa, one of the main lines of royals in the Kingdom. I wonder if the 'regular' Arabs will look at us differently now we can name drop?"

"Are you serious?"

"Come on Claire. It's just as Anthony says. He's working out the final deal with Salomon. We'll be fine and it'll be good to get away from the compound for a couple of months." She elbowed me in the ribs. "We're the nurses to a Princess! We'll be respected throughout the Kingdom."

I couldn't respond. I had a knot in my stomach. Perhaps she was right. I remembered Paula telling me her father came from Malta and she may know more than most. This could turn out to be the opportunity of a lifetime.

A protocol officer ran up to us. "Come, come. The Princess. She ready now." He led us towards the elevator. "You must hurry. Downstairs. Hurry! They waiting," he said and danced around as if there were a fire, pushing the down button.

I exchanged glances with Paula. We followed the man into the elevator, down to the main floor.

"Why do they always repeat words twice, Paula? Rather funny, don't you think?"

We giggled.

Saloman used his private elevator, arriving downstairs before us. He took his place in a line with other traditionally dressed Arab men. They stood on either side of the exits, directing us to a parade of shiny, new vehicles parked in the circular driveway outside the main door to the hospital. The cars were all white except for a large silver van designed to transport the Princess. I stood in silence inside the vestibule of the hospital watching men load the Princess's van with a wheelchair, gurney, luggage and when the men stepped out, her attendants, the American nurses and a doctor climbed in. Two men approached us, took our small bags and signaled for us follow. He led us outside, rushing us into a large white Mercedes. Paula and I nestled into gray plush seats and secured our seat belts, grateful to be out of the heat.

I couldn't suppress the mounting excitement as the car left the hospital grounds. Peering through the darkened glass, I watched people on the busy streets and marveled at the modern architecture. Nervousness encroached dimming the adventure as I thought about living in a palace in a new city, faraway from the safety of the hospital.

We arrived at the Royal terminal and waited while the Princess got onto the aircraft. A man directed us up a flight of steel stairs and past Arab men sitting in first-class seats in the back. We went through a door separating the middle section of the plane from the rear and Philippine and African women sat in a group on the right side. Along the windows to the left, was a beige velour sofa, where we settled. Paula and I faced the women and could watch them without infringing on their privacy. I recognized some of them from the hospital; others I hadn't seen before.

When I had secured the seat belt, I turned my head towards the front of the plane straining to see what was behind the partially open curtain separating us from the Princess. To my amazement, I saw a narrowly-designed intensive care suite, equipped with an electric hospital bed, monitors and emergency medication cart. I was hoping I could get a better look at it but didn't dare move. I could see a glimpse of the Princess beyond that area along with her doctor, a couple of her loyal attendants and the two American nurses.

We were on the plane for an hour when it landed in the private zone reserved for the royal jet in Jeddah airport. The women sitting opposite us put on their abayas and filed past, into the rear section. A couple of the younger ones giggled, exchanging glances with the men but stopped when an older women gave them warning looks.

"What do we do?"

"I don't know, Paula. I'm not going to move until someone tells me to"

"Oh Claire, look!"

I turned my attention to the men's section. A handsome gentleman climbed aboard. He stood out, not only in looks but in dress. His starched white thobe fell in sharp pleats over his polished black leather shoes, making the other men's thobes look yellow in comparison. When he moved his arm, a hint of gold flashed from the French tailored cuff. His head was bare and his short, dark brown hair parted on the left. His fine features differed from the heavyset appearance of the Arab male. He was tall and lean with a straight spine, which made him look impressive.

"Ew! Isn't he handsome."

"Paula, I think he's someone important. Look at the men kiss his shoulder as they pass."

"He doesn't seem interested in their homage. Claire! He's looking this way." Paula flipped a loose strand of dark hair and straightened her shoulders. I watched his eyes scan first Paula, then look at me. My stomach tightened and I felt a prickling sensation on the nape of my neck. A smile crossed his lips, which made my heart skip a beat. I shivered. I could almost feel what he was thinking and shied away from the look in his eye. I knew that look of lust and wanted to run, but there was nowhere to go. Perhaps I was misreading him and hoped my instincts were wrong.

"Claire, he likes you."

"I hope not, Paula."

"You're blushing."

I put my hand on my cheek.

He made a gesture, dismissing the men. They backed away, bowing and left the plane in a single file.

He approached us. My heart beat hard in my chest.

"You must be my mother's nurses. Come with me."

Paula whispered, "He's one of Princess Liynaa's sons."

We followed him down the stairs and onto the tarmac. I was feeling more nervous than I did before.

"Come, follow."

The servants stared at us. Some gasped, then whispered. I ignored them and continued to follow the tall stranger. The Prince yelled at the women. For a moment, they seemed confused then stopped their chatter and scurried into their appointed van. The Prince looked around then yelled at the men, making them run in several directions.

I startled when he yelled.

He looked down at me. "Don't worry. Those people need to be told what to do. You two come with me."

He led us to a shiny black Mercedes convertible. Paula drooled over the car and asked, "Is this yours?"

"Of course." He replied. He opened the door and pulled back the seat for us. Paula went in first. As I tried to follow, he pulled on my arm.

"You in front."

"I didn't think women could ride in the front."

"You do as I say. I am Prince Sultan. No one," he said, pointing to the sky, "No one tell me what to do!"

I got into the car and put on my seat belt. As Prince Sultan walked around to the driver's side of the car, Paula whispered, "Ew! These are all leather seats. Very soft."

Sultan closed his door and turned the key.

"You do have a beautiful car, Sultan," Paula said trying to gain his attention.

"Of course. I am deserving of this"

"Oh, yes you are! You must have worked real hard for it. So, what do you do with your time?" Paula pressed.

"I do my work. I go hunting."

I was embarrassed and nervous, and wished Paula would stop flirting.

"What do you hunt?"

"Antelope. I take my falcons and hunt small game."

The Prince looked at me and continued, "I have prize falcons. Perhaps you will see them sometime."

I turned to him and smiled, not uttering a word.

"I would love to see them too."

"Only special people can see my birds. Now Look. Have you seen Jeddah before? My cousin is responsible for the art. He went to school in France and came back and had these sculptures made. Look."

I looked out the window. Gigantic colorful sculptures rose up in the middle of traffic circles and large intersections.

Sultan pointed. "Those are called gawa pots. Arabic coffee pots."

The large decorative urns complete with sugar bowls and trays stood over forty feet high. We passed sculptures of airplanes, cars, tall giraffes and unidentifiable structures. I thought they were odd and looked like paper Mache projects from grade school, only these were constructed from cement and painted bright colors.

I noticed men driving by Sultan straining to see who was in the car. It's uncommon for a woman to be in the front seat of a car and especially one who is not veiled. It made me feel uncomfortable.

One driver tried to cut the Prince off as he approached a busy intersection. Sultan honked his horn and waved his finger in a disapproving gesture. "I could make trouble for him. He knows who I am, but because tonight is special I will let him get away."

He laughed an evil laugh. I shivered.

He looked at me. "You afraid of matawa, the religious police?"

"I don't want to get arrested for being in the front seat."

"I told you. You with me. The Matawa will not bother you. I will protect you both. Let me tell you this. There is school for Matawa in Riyadh. Sometime the law permits men who have committed serious crimes and who were to be punished with cut off of hands or head can, how you say, be given second chance if turn from evil and become a religious police."

"What?" Paula interjected. "You mean religious policemen are reformed criminals?"

"Not all, but some. They have religious reversion and now men of Allah. They now good."

"No wonder some of the Matawa are mean and unpredictable. The country is kept in order by a bunch of "reformed," hardened criminals!"

Prince Sultan looked in the rearview mirror and gave Paula a dirty look. He reached over and put his hand on my arm.

"You like Jeddah?"

"I don't know how to answer that, Prince Sultan." I pulled my arm away. "I haven't seen much of the city."

"I like it here. Better than Riyadh. People are freer here."

"I notice some of the Muslim women are wearing colored abayas."

"This is true. That is because they are from other countries. Saudi females wear black. It is better."

"Claire, wouldn't you like to wear a different colored abaya?"

"I don't care."

The ride to the palace seemed long. I stared out the window and watched as we left the downtown district and entered upper class residential areas. Cement walls in the same decor as the mansions encircled the properties, making them impermeable. Some estates extended for acres, while others were no more than half a city block.

We made a couple more turns, drove into a short brick driveway and waited for a ten-foot black iron-rod gate to open. Sultan drove past the electronic gate, past a guard who sat in a hut to one side and headed towards a mansion. The driveway came alive. Men in thobes appeared from nowhere, clearing the way for the Prince. One walked to the car and opened the Prince's door, but Prince Sultan said something in Arabic and he retreated. The Prince pulled his seat forward to let Paula out. I opened my door.

"No. Wait."

Prince Sultan rushed around to the other side of the car, leaving Paula and held the door for me.

"Go in," Prince Sultan said.

We went up three steps through white double doors with gold trimmed moldings and walked into a massive foyer. I gasped. "The entrance hall is enormous! At least the size of a double car garage."

Two Chinese vases placed on either side of the hall stood taller than the doors.

"Ming," Paula whispered.

"They must be eight feet tall. And the ceiling has to be forty feet or more above our heads. Look at that gigantic chandelier. Wow!"

"Claire, have you ever seen anything like this?"

There were large double doors to the right that opened like an accordion. To the left were matching doors and facing us was a hallway that went deeper into the living quarters of the palace.

Prince Sultan came from behind.

"You stay in here." He pointed to the room on the left.

My mouth fell open when I entered. The room was larger than the entranceway, with long sofas lining the walls. To the right was a space between two French brocade chairs with carved mahogany frames and Queen Anne-style legs.

"Claire, I've been to the Louver in Paris several times. This room is a meager attempt at copying French styling, but they failed to meet the criteria of the French décor because of the heavyset Middle Eastern furniture against the walls."

"I don't think I've ever been in such a large room before. It's the space that's taking my breath away, but I see what you mean about the décor. It doesn't flow."

The walls were a pale yellow adorned with white decorative moldings bordering the ceiling with inlaid gold leaf.

"There's a lot of money in this room, Claire. Those tapestries? The silks over there on that wall?"

"Where?"

She pointed. "The ones about five feet by seven feet? They'd cost a fortune."

I realized as I sat down beside Paula the sofas were much longer than any I was used to. Against the walls in the corners were mahogany tables matching the woodwork on the furniture. Silk rugs and murals hung on the walls displaying woven stories of Arabic battles from history. Others depicted tribal lineage. On one wall were large framed pictures of the present King of Saudi Arabia, his sons, and painted pictures of Liynaa's five sons. There were no paintings of wives or daughters; not even a portrait of Princess Liynaa herself.

I heard a commotion from beyond the entrance to the room. A young lady poked her head in, then entered.

"Welcome. My name is Haifa. I am the daughter of Prince Sultan."

I guessed she must have been around eighteen or nineteen.

"You speak very good English," stated Paula.

"Yes. I grew up in America."

"You did?" I asked.

"Yes. Many of my cousins were born there too. In England or France as well, but America is the best."

"Why America?"

"Because we can go to school and get an education then come back and live better in Saudi Arabia. Saudi Arabia doesn't have what America has. My father and mother can also travel and go to America because their children are American born. It's the easiest country for children to get passports."

"Did you go to school there too?" Asked Paula.

"Yes. I was born in New York. My brother in California. We are Americans. My father has decided that I've had enough school. My brother Faisal will be returning to America to go and study to be a doctor."

"How nice," said Paula. "How long have you been in Saudi?"

"I've been here two years, and no, I do not miss America. My father wanted us to have American passports so we can travel, but my home is in Saudi. Because I'm American I will have a better and richer husband." Haifa stated.

I wondered if she meant what she said, or if she resigned herself to her role as a royal.

We heard male voices in the hallway.

"I must go." She disappeared.

"What did you think of that Claire?"

"I don't know. It disturbs me someone would settle into another country, have children, take advantage of the education systems, resources and everything else it has to offer, not contribute anything then return to their native homeland."

"It's selfish." Paula thought for a moment then asked, " What are you thinking?"

"I wonder if we were supposed to stand or bow or something since Haifa is a Princess. I see the servants bow to the royals."

"We're not servants, Claire. Besides, if we act subservient, they'll treat us that way."

There was turmoil in the hallway and I could hear the swooshing sounds of the skirts of thobes walking towards us.

"I Prince Mohammad, the eldest son," he said, entering the room.

He glared then squinted. "Come!" he said.

We followed him into the hall beyond the entrance, turned right and walked a long way before coming to the Princess's suite. It had dull lighting and furniture pressed up against the curtains. Princess Liynaa was in her bed, looking relaxed. The two American nurses stood to one side and an elderly lady sat on the Princess's left, reading the Qu'ran. Prince Mohammad signaled to the Americans to come. All of us followed him through a curtain into a sitting room. The room was round with a parquet floor in dark rosewood and the furniture, walls and décor were the same theme as the living room, but on a smaller scale. Instead of the long sofas, there were several tall backed chairs placed against the walls. The Prince indicated everyone sit down.

"You tell what you need," The Prince stated.

"Well," said, one of the Americans, "I've been looking after the Princess in the day, and Leslie at night. We want to break in these two nurses before we leave in two weeks."

"You work it out. My mother to have best of care!" Shouted the Prince.

His gruffness startled me. I tucked my hair behind my ear.

"Where are our quarters?" asked Leslie.

"Yes, yes, I show you. These are arrangements. You have one day off a week. I have driver for you. I will give anything you need."

I noticed Prince Mohammad didn't look at Paula or me. He directed his comments to the Americans.

"We will have to prove our 'worthiness' before the Prince will acknowledge us. That shouldn't be too hard." Paula whispered.

The Prince yelled something in Arabic and two Filipino women appeared. Prince Mohammed gave them instructions in Arabic and they groveled, answering "yes, yes" to his every command.

"You follow those." He said, pointing to the women.

We went out of the large room into a narrow hall, walked down a corridor passing several closed doors. One of the doors was open and being curious, I peeked inside. It was another enormous suite.

"No! No!" Said one of the ladies. "Princess sister room."

We continued a short way and came to a French glass door that opened to a concrete courtyard with garden area to one side and an oval shaped swimming pool in the center. Once outside, we could see the glass patio doors that went into the Princess's private quarters. I didn't notice the exit when I was inside the Princess's suite because heavy curtains and large pieces of furniture obscured the exterior view. The beige curtains pressing from behind the glass spoiled the look of the well-designed courtyard.

From the outside, the pool and blossoming gardens were neatly arranged and areas for poolside leisure immaculate. The elegant patio was empty except for a few lounge chairs at the poolside.

There were two villas on either side of the terrace. The Filipino ladies led us into one of them. She opened the door to a large living room where two paisley couches sat against opposing walls and between them, a large screened TV. One of the Filipino ladies went past the TV to a hallway and opened a locked door to a bedroom. She then opened a second door to a second bedroom. The other Filipino woman opened a third locked door on the other side of the room, exposing a small kitchen. She said, "This is for you. You make coffee or tea. Cook bring breakfast and lunch."

The first woman pointed to the American nurses and said "This your room. You share." She then pointed to Paula and I, and said, "You share this one."

Paula went inside the room and came out looking shocked. "There's only one bed."

"Yes. You share."

"No way." Paula retorted. "I may like you, Claire, but I'm not sleeping with you."

One of the Americans looked at the servant, "You expect us to share a bed?"

"Yes, yes. You share."

"*No way!* We want to speak to Prince Mohammad. Now," said the other American.

The servant looked frustrated and said "No Prince Mohammad. You share."

The American nurses said in unison, "We want to talk to the Prince *now*."

The Filipino ladies cowered and seemed confused. They fled the villa.

"I'm Tanya. You have to be firm if you want anything done."

I noticed two other locked doors. "I wonder what's behind those doors?"

"Probably other bedrooms."

Prince Sultan barged in.

"What is matter?"

Paula said, "Your staff expects us to sleep in the same bed. I can't stay here if you expect me to share my bed."

"They told to open whole villa. Every room!" Prince Sultan turned and shouted to a skinny man wearing a yellowed thobe who paused at the entrance. The man hurried away and came back a few moments later with a set of keys. He unlocked the other two bedroom doors. Prince Sultan went from room to room inspecting them, then pointed to Leslie and ordered "You here."

He pointed to Tanya. You here."

He then looked at me and stated in a more gentle tone, "You choose what you want."

Sultan spoke to the male servant in Arabic then turned to us and said, "The cook will bring breakfast to you here. Lunch to you here too. Mohammad expects everyone for dinner at ten pm. Ten o'clock sharp! Anything else?" He looked at me. "You will be happy here."

Prince Sultan walked out of the villa as another male servant entered carrying our luggage on a trolley. He dumped the suitcases in the living room and left, closing the villa doors behind him. We sorted through the luggage, picking out our bags and went into our rooms.

I chose the bedroom furthest away from the rest of the villa. It was painted a soft peach and the white trimmed window looked out into a garden with several palm trees. The room had a king-sized bed, furnished with a dark stained desk and chest of drawers. The walk-in closet had built-in drawers and oodles of space, and on the other side of the closet was a marble bathroom, complete with separate shower, two sinks and a jetted tan colored tub. The bathroom was large enough to be a small bedroom of its own.

"Claire? Can I come in?"

"Yes, of course."

"Oh! I like your room. It's just like mine, but the opposite plan. I think we did better than the American nurses. It helps when you have a prince after you."

"I don't have a prince after me."

Paula smiled. "Better unpack. Meet you shortly to raid the kitchen?"

"Ok. I want to change and freshen up first. It's been quite a day."

****

A servant burst into the villa. "Hurry, hurry. It time for dinner! Go! Go! The Prince, he waiting."

"Where're we going?"

"Dinner! Hurry!"

"I'm not hungry."

"Claire, we can't refuse."

We walked through the halls to the main entranceway, through the accordion doors into the dining hall and saw tables pushed together, forming one long eating surface. The tables, laden with heavy silverware, starched white linen and napkins and full glasses of buttermilk looked bare without centerpieces. Seated were Prince Mohammad, his wife, Prince Sultan, Heifa and Prince Turki. Princess Liynaa was in her wheelchair at one end of the table with a servant standing either side of her; one feeding her, the other wiping her mouth as needed. The American nurses sat opposite the Princes.

Prince Mohammad stood when Paula and I entered and smiled. His cordial welcome surprised me, but I graciously accepted the chair he indicated I sit in, directly across from Prince Sultan. I heard rumblings from behind me and turned around to look. The servants were huddled together, whispering and by their body language, it appeared as if they were disapproving. Prince Turki shouted at them. They popped their heads around the corner and were quiet.

" Hoooowwwwwdy!! Ho ho!" Said Prince Turki. "You must ignore them. They don't know anything."

I gazed at this enormous Prince and tried not to gawk. He must have been at least six hundred pounds.

"Food will come in a minute. Anyone from Texas?" Turki asked. "That's where I lived when I was in the US."

Tanya said, "I'm from New York."

"I'm from Philadelphia."

"And you two. Where you from?"

Before we could answer, doors swung open behind the royal family. A procession of men dressed in black tuxedos with pressed white pleated shirts and black bow ties, carried large silver trays piled with mountains of meat, rice and vegetables balanced above their heads. They formed a single line behind Prince Mohammad then stood still, staring straight ahead. When the Prince was ready he signaled and was presented with one tray of food then another, helping himself to generous portions. Once the Prince made his selections, the food was offered to everyone else and the room became busy with servants running from one guest to another, placing food on people's plates with large silver tongs. The family didn't wait for everyone to be served before devouring their food. They didn't speak; just concentrated on eating.

Prince Turki refused food. He said something in Arabic and another man dressed in a black tuxedo came from the kitchen and placed a large bowl in front of him. He looked at me and stated, "My doctor said I have to lose weight and I have been put on a diet."

I smiled, covered my mouth suppressing a laugh and whispered to Paula, "He may have been told to go on a diet, but the portions of food are so large the Prince will gain instead of lose."

When the Royals finished eating, the waiters returned their trays to the kitchen and then pushed out a large trolley with an assortment of desserts. There was an Arabic dessert that was like shortbread with a thick honey sauce and was a favorite with the family, but I found it too sweet. They had figs and cakes and if desired, ice cream was served on top of French pastries.

Prince Mohammad and his wife finished their meal ahead of everyone else, and left the room.

"Are we slow eaters, Paula? Everyone, even the Americans have left."

"I don't want to rush my meal."

The waiters returned and removed silverware, glasses and replaced the fine china with cracked and chipped plates. They put trays of food in the center of the table. The women servants waiting outside the dining room filed in and sat around the table. I noticed some of them were elderly and used two canes to walk.

"Paula, those poor souls have terrible heart conditions. Look at how swollen that woman's ankles are! You can't even see her feet."

"It's amazing she can walk."

Plates passed from person to person until everyone had one. The dining room was a feeding frenzy. Arms reached across the table, hands grabbed the food and the chatter was endless. They reached into the center of the platters with one hand, picked up large portions of rice, rolling it in their palms, squishing it then eating the mush. Some of the women stuffed their faces first and then piled food on their plate. They returned the mush back to the main plate and mixed it with fresh food. Sometimes half-digested morsels landed on their plates from their mouth, and they would pick them up, return them to the center plates, roll it, squish it and eat it again. It was revolting. The women sitting beside me saw I wasn't eating. She took food directly from her mouth and offered the half-chewed glob to me.

"Oh no, no, no, no. I couldn't," I said, shaking my head and feeling sick.

I got up from the table. Paula followed.

Haifa was standing outside the dining room, grinning at us. "You must eat quickly to avoid them."

"So we see."

Haifa smiled then said, "The two American nurses went back to the villa. One is changing because she is looking after the Princess overnight and the other went to bed. You two please, my father wants you to have a rest tonight."

She gazed into the living room. I followed her look and saw the family seated in the room.

"Come with me."

We sat on the pink velvet couches, facing the sons of Liynaa. Sultan, Turki, Mohammad sat under the portrait of the King and portraits of themselves. Their wives were sitting next to them. I realized those chairs were designated places of honor for the princes and noted two of Liynaa sons were missing; she had five sons in all.

Princess Liynaa slumped in her wheelchair with an attendant on either side. The Princess was blind and appearing tired, was listening to everything that was going on around her.

"Ah, it is time for chi. Where are the chi girls?" Haifa said.

The Princess tried to sit up straight, but couldn't. One servant pulled on her arm.

"What's chi?" I asked, wondering if I should get up and help the Princess.

"It's tea."

Mohammad called out and two girls appeared, carrying a tray of small glass mugs containing no more than four or five ounces of hot tea. The minuscule cups had matching glass saucers with little 18-karat gold spoons and a twig of mint in each glass. The chi girls went first to Princess Liynaa, who refused, then offered the tea to the princes. They each took a delicate mug and put a sugar cube between their teeth and then sipped the tea through the cube.

"You want?"

I took a glass of tea, and so did Paula.

Tanya returned. She looked at the two attendants either side of Liynaa, smiled and greeted them.

"The Princess looks tired." I pointed out.

Tanya glanced at me then walked to the Princess and said something to the attendants. They got to their feet, fiddled with the blanket covering

Princess's knees and pushed the wheelchair out of the room.

Prince Mohammad stood up. His wife stood beside him and they followed Princess Liynaa and her entourage. Prince Turki struggled to get to his feet. He took a cane in each hand, placed them firmly on the floor and dug the rubber stoppers at the bottom of the cane into the floor. With his arms extended above his shoulders, he rocked back and forth until he had enough momentum to stand on his feet. He balanced himself, then shuffled. Before each step, he planted one of his canes into the floor, making a heavy thump, then struggled to move a few inches forward. His left foot sometimes dragged and he'd have to balance himself before taking another step.

Sultan was still drinking his tea. He gazed over the top of the mug and looked at me. My heart pounded and I pretended not to notice.

"So Prince Sultan," Paula said, "When are we going to go for a ride in that car again?"

Prince Sultan looked at Paula and said, "Maybe tomorrow. Maybe never. It is now my son's."

"Your son's car?"

"My father uses a car for three months, then gives it to my brother. My father wants to always have a new car."

Sultan put down his mug, stood up and looking sideways at me, paused, said something to his daughter and then left.

"You must know where to wash your clothes. I will get Joyce to show you." Haifa called to one of the servants. "I must go home."

"You don't live here?"

"Oh no. This is my grandmother's palace. I live with my mother at her palace. She isn't here tonight. My father will drive me home."

A young Filipino woman entered the room. Haifa barked something in Arabic and then left to go with her father.

"Hi. My name is Joyce. I've been told to show you where to wash your clothes."

I guessed Joyce was about twenty-five years old. Her shiny black hair was shoulder length and her skin golden, free of blemishes. She was a pretty young thing, but there was something sad emanating from her dark brown eyes.

Joyce led us out of the room, down the hall, and turned into another hall, leading to a set of stairs. As we descended, I noticed the pale yellow paint ended and the walls were open, exposing wooden joists. We stepped into the dark, damp basement. Single light bulbs swayed from long cords attached to the ceiling with cup hooks and in one area, different sized mattresses were lined up on the floor. They had no sheets or blankets and large stains were embedded into the fabric. The other side of the basement had ropes attached to wooden studs where the servants made crude drying racks for their clothes.

I scratched my head. "What are all these old mattresses doing on the floor?"

"This is where we sleep," said Joyce.

"What?"

"This is where all the ladies of the household sleep. We are servants and slaves of Princess Liynaa and we are lucky to have mattresses."

"Slaves?" I was shocked. "I didn't think Saudi had slaves."

"They are here, but the family denies they are slaves. They come from poor places. Their families sell women for money. The Royals buy them and make their family very wealthy. The slaves do not get money for their work or holidays. I am lucky. I am not a slave. I have contract with my agency in Philippines. I get paid and I get to sleep on one of those mattresses with the others."

"Where are your blankets?" Paula asked.

"We have to hide them so they aren't stolen. The newest ones don't sleep on mattresses. They have their blankets in that corner there and sleep on floor. There." Joyce pointed to a moldy area covered with worn blankets. There were no pillows, cushions or anything for comfort.

"They fight over the blankets at night. It is hard to get sleep at night."

How many sleep there?" Paula asked.

"About twenty or thirty. I don't know for sure. Those women come and go. Sometimes the men from the men's palace want or need slave. Sometimes they don't come back. Sometimes they come back and they have bruises and cuts all over."

I gasped and was distraught. I thought about the king-sized bed and the fuss we made about having separate rooms.

As we walked along, I noticed a room with toilets and sinks in it.

"Is that your bathroom?"

"Yes."

"Where're your showers?"

Joyce stopped and looked at me then Paula. "We don't have baths. We wash at sinks."

I exchanged glances with Paula. We followed her to the laundry area where Joyce demonstrated how to use the oversized washers.

"You are lucky. We not allowed to use the dryer and sometimes we not allowed to use washers. It just depends."

I wanted to ask what it depended on, but thought better of it. What extremes behind these palace walls!

Chapter Nine

Paula and I walked into the anteroom of Princess Linyaa's suite, where closed curtains and a sliding door separated the inner chamber from the sitting room. Tanya curled up on a brocade chaise lounge, sipping a cup of the mint-flavored chi. On the oval table in front of her were chocolates from France and Germany, wrapped in foil with a picture of the King on them. Some of them had pictures of Princess Lyinaa's sons.

"Have one," Tanya said, pushing the tray towards me.

"Oh, no thanks," I said, waiting for Tanya to show us her routine.

Paula sat down on a chair, crossed her legs and scowled.

Tanya unwrapped one of the chocolates and popped it in her mouth. When she finished, she licked her fingers and looked at us sideways. "You don't need those starched uniforms. We wear our sweats." She reached for another chocolate. "The work is simple. You just give out the meds. Right now I'm waiting for the servants to finish washing and dressing the Princess and then I'll show you where everything is."

"You mean you aren't overseeing them?" I was shocked. "The Princess is frail."

"No. I don't want to interfere."

Paula huffed. "We're here because the Princess needs our intervention in caring for her, not just to give out pills."

Tanya stuck her nose in the air. "When we leave you two can do whatever you want. Leslie and I've been working with the Princess for the last three months. This is the first time we've had her out of an institution and it'll be your jobs to figure out how to work with the servants."

Paula squinted. "Why were you hired?"

"To coordinate her care. The problem's her servants. They hover and are always looking over your shoulder. They're impossible. Leslie and I found if we keep our distance it's easier for everyone."

"Easier for who? Sounds like you let them dictate to you." snapped Paula.

"I don't know what to tell you. It's different, that's all and we're glad to be leaving."

Paula whispered in my ear, "Yeah, lazy Yanks. They'll have to do work and that's why they want to go."

I frowned and wondered why she disliked them.

A tall, dark-skinned Chi woman entered the room smiling, carrying a silver tray with glass mugs filled with tea and mint sprigs. Her dark hair was tied back with a yellow scarf matching the colors in her ankle-length skirt. She offered a cup of chi to Paula who accepted, then to me.

"No thank you."

"You no like?" Her smile vanished.

"Yes, but not right now thank you."

"Where you from?"

"Canada. And you? Where're you from?"

"Ethiopia."

" Do you like it here?'

"It ok. You married?'

I smiled. Such a common and seemingly important question.

"No, I'm not. Are you?"

"Oh yes. My family Ethiopia. I work here so they have house and go school."

"Your husband and children aren't here with you?"

"No."

"Do you ever see them?"

"Umm." She struggled to find the words. "Once year. Three weeks."

"You must miss them."

"It ok. I have work. I not slave. I get money one time in year and take home to family. You understand? I free."

"Yes, thank you. By the way, what's your name?"

She smiled, exposing a broken tooth. "Leila".

She turned and walked away, her long cotton yellow and brown paisley skirt swaying from side to side in rhythmic motion.

"That's a typical story." Tanya stated. "The slaves work in the kitchen, or wash the floors or do the 'dirty' work. They're the ones that don't look at you when you pass and are the property of the Royal family. The Royals deny they're slaves because they believe they've done a good deed in paying a handsome price for them, rescuing them from abject poverty. They're not free, can never travel or make decisions and from what I've seen, this family treats them well." Tanya popped another chocolate in her mouth, then said, "The Princess's handmaids are not slaves. They work to support their families and extended family and even whole villages. It's a great privilege and honor to work for a Saudi Royal."

My heart sank. I remembered Joyce talking about the slaves.

"I thought slavery was abolished in Saudi Arabia," said Paula.

"Officially there's no slavery, but it exists. Oh, by the way Claire, I noticed how Prince Sultan looked at you last night at the table."

"Looked at me? How?"

"It's obvious he likes you."

"I hadn't noticed." I lied, feeling my cheeks burn hot.

"Be careful. Some Saudi Princes take women away."

"What do you mean? Kidnap them?"

"Yup. Sometimes women are hidden. Others are forced to marry them. They'll entice a woman by showering her with jewels, travel and anything to buy loyalty. The woman are not free and have to do everything the Prince wants or he'll have her killed, kill her family, or both."

"Prince Sultan wouldn't do that to Claire," Paula huffed.

"I don't know. She's pretty and blonde and if she can have children, well…you just never know. This family however, seems to be decent. He may pursue you on the up and up."

"Ew, Claire! Imagine you married to a Prince." Paula beamed.

"I don't want to even think about it. It scares me." I tucked my hair behind my ear. "How do you know all of this?"

"You learn a lot by living with people. I've also worked on other Royal assignments. You do know this family has never had a Westerner in their home before? You guys are breaking new ground. All I can say is 'good luck'."

Paula looked at her. "Why do you say that?"

"Can't say, but the household is different to anything I've experienced. The Princess is sweet, but her servants…"

One of the maids opened the curtains and indicated we go into the inner chamber. The Princess was in her wheelchair, scented with a light perfume. Her long, thinning hair, red from henna dye, hung in loose strands past her shoulders. From a doorway to the right of the Princess's bed a Thai girl entered, carrying a comb and brush on a marble tray. She said something in Arabic and bowed towards the Princess. Two older women standing either side of the wheelchair stepped aside, allowing the girl to place the brush and comb against the Princess's hand. Princess Liynaa nodded 'yes'. The girl untangled and smoothed her hair, parting it at the back. She braided one side and then the other. When she finished the two older women stepped closer. One of them examined one braid and the other examined the second one. They took a moment, said something in Arabic to the Thai girl then she smiled, bowed and walked backwards, exiting the room.

"I'll show you where we keep the medications. You need this key to get into the cabinet, although it's rarely locked."

She pulled out several bottles of pills.

"We read the labels and give them out at the right times."

"Don't you have a chart or a record of what and when you gave the meds?" asked Paula.

"We aren't that formal."

"But you should be more professional. Isn't that right Claire?" Paula seemed hostile.

"Umm...Yes." I cleared my throat. "Why don't we write down all her meds and put a chart together? We'll review her medical condition and develop a plan for her daily care."

"It's obvious these two didn't," snapped Paula.

"Lookit. We just do what we have to." Tanya glared at Paula.

"Let's not argue, ok? You do what you want and we'll take over from you when you go back to America," I said pulling on Paula's arm. "Let's go to the villa."

We walked out of the suite. Paula was fuming. "Can you believe that?"

"Shh. Wait until we're round that corner."

"This Princess is delicate. She's diabetic and needs her blood sugar checked. She has kidney disease and heart disease, is blind and paralyzed on the left side. They call themselves nurses? They don't even do a daily examination!" Paula quickened her step.

"I know Paula, but there's no use in getting upset over it."

"Did you see what they wear? Jeans and a sweatshirt! No wonder they've problems with the servants."

"It must be confusing for the staff. Rest assured, we'll always wear our uniforms and be professional."

"I bet they're on this assignment for the money and nothing else."

"I don't know. Let's forget about them and have a cup of tea, shall we?"

"I swear, Claire, you live on that stuff."

****

I felt relieved stepping outside the villa after dinner. The intense humidity from the day lessened, but it was still hot, even at eleven at night.

"I'm restless. Do you want to go for a walk, Paula?"

"Where? I don't think we can leave the palace."

"I'm sure the Royal family wouldn't mind if we walked the grounds."

We strolled through the palace, past the curious household servants who stared and whispered. We ignored them and opened the heavy exterior doors, stepping outside into a wall of heavy air.

"At least its cooler than earlier today."

"Not cool enough," I sighed. Come on Paula. Let's go this way."

We walked in the middle of the bricked driveway, past the locked gate where we entered the night before. On the corner by the exit was a grassy area where a man knelt, saying his prayers.

I stopped and held onto Paula's arm. "We better be quiet. Don't want to disturb him."

"Claire, let him finish before we go any further. If you walk in front of someone while praying they believe you've blocked the ears of Allah."

He sat up and rested on his knees. He looked at us for a moment and then stood up. He was tall and thin with a white, manicured beard that matched the streaks of silver in his hair. He wore a pale yellow thobe with a turban-like headdress. His garments accented his natural coloring, giving the illusion that glowing light surrounded him.

I shivered. He smiled then extended his hand He had a mystical presence that infiltrated my soul, raising goose bumps on my skin. I sensed he was someone I could trust. I smiled, gave him my hand and he covered it with both of his. Closing his eyes he raised his head towards the sky, tilting it back as far as he could. He uttered a few words in Arabic. He took in a deep breath, tilted his head forward keeping his eyes closed then after a few moments, opened them. He smiled down at me like a father would smile on a favored child. He put his hand over his heart and said in almost a whisper, "Kwyess galb."

He then took Paula's hand, covered it with his other one, closed his eyes and tilted his head back. When he opened his eyes he smiled at Paula and asked "Enta moammarida?"

Paula conversed with him in Arabic.

"He said you have a good heart, and he's asking if we are nurses."

We shook our heads "yes."

"He says he's from Pakistan and is the Royal Matawa."

"I didn't know there were religious men specifically for the royals."

The man took a couple of steps backwards, then walked across the grass to a small white building.

We smiled at each other then continued our walk. The driveway was broad, just as wide as a street and we followed the curvy roadway until we came to another palace.

"I wonder who lives there?"

"Look, the road forks. Which way do you want to go, Paula?"

"Doesn't matter." Paula grabbed my arm. "Look out. A truck's coming."

"Hooowwwdddyy!"

"It's Prince Turki."

He stuck his elbow out the window and asked, "Where you'all going?"

"No where. Just walking," replied Paula.

"It's all right to walk around your property, isn't Prince Turki?" I asked.

"Oh yes, yes. You walk. Stay away from the front gate. Don't want people to see what happens inside. You have to be careful," he said. "People will shoot you."

Paula and I exchanged glances.

"Yes, it is ok to walk. Walk is important exercise." Prince Turki looked down the road. "Look there. He pointed at another palace in the distance. "That is my palace. Prince Sultan's behind you. The King's Palace in the middle. The men's palace down that road."

"Do all the princes live on this property?" I asked.

Prince Turki laughed so hard he started to cough. When he stopped, he said "All the sons have palace here. We no live here. My father, my mother, and my father's second wife sometimes. Her palace over there."

"You have another palace?"

"Yes. Several. Prince Mohammad lives here with his first wife. It is complicated. The wives of my father have palace each on same property, but only my mother live here. It is not good to mix wives." He winked. "We come to visit and the male servants live in men's palace. Dat is where male servants live that serve our food and take care of my father and do things for my mother if Mohammad wishes. All matters concerning my mother, Princess Liynaa, taken care of by Mohammad." In a falsetto, Turki continued. "That is why Mohammad lives here. He is big boss." He let out a raucous laugh and started to drive away then stopped, stuck his head out the window and shouted, "Hide yourselves from gates!"

He pulled his white truck in front of his palace and opened the door. Out came one cane and then he labored to turn his fat belly from under the steering wheel. I could hear his heavy panting from where I stood.

"Paula, we should continue and not watch Prince Turki struggle."

"Yeah. Don't want to embarrass him. Do you think he can get out?"

We giggled, choosing a road away from the front of the palaces.

When we were out of his sight we broke into laughter and mimicked Prince Turki's grandiose gestures.

"Hoowwdy!"

"Stay away from the gate."

We skipped down the long, dark drive, until another palace came into view. It had a large veranda on the front, with stairs going up on either end. Men gathered in small groups talking and smoking.

"Shh. Don't attract attention."

I linked my arm in Paula's and pulled her along. "Let's get out of here. I think the Princess's palace is down this road."

One of the men noticed us. Their conversations stopped and they moved toward the edge of the veranda.

"What's the matter?" Paula said under her breath. "Haven't they seen women before?"

"They aren't used to seeing women taking a walk. I don't think anyone exercises and besides, we're not wearing abayas and our arms are bare. We're naked to them and you know how exposed elbows and nude necks are such a 'turn on' for those guys."

The men laughed and shouted in Arabic.

Embarrassed, we kept our heads down walking past as fast as we could. When out of their view, we ran back to Princess Liynaa's palace and entered through the main doorway, ran through the halls, ignoring the stares and whispers of the servants, until we reached the villa. We entered and found Tanya curled up on a sofa, sipping a hot drink.

"You two caused quite a disturbance."

"What do you mean?"

"No one goes for a walk. Everyone thinks you're strange."

"Well let them," snapped Paula. "I'm getting ready for bed."

"I should get ready for bed myself."

I went into my bedroom. The air-conditioning was running hard, but there was still condensation on the windows and on the walls.

Damp! Damp! Everything damp! The bed, the sheets and the blankets. I hated humidity. I couldn't sleep in this. I pulled my blue cotton nightgown off the hanger and even that was damp. I changed anyway then waited and hoped Tanya went to bed so I could make a cup of tea. I peeked out my door and saw Paula tiptoeing past.

"Oh Claire, it's you. I was hoping you'd still be awake," she whispered.

"Everything all right?"

"Yeah. I was just wanting a drink." She straightened her shoulders. "I've been thinking about the men we walked by. They've been separated from their wives for long periods of time and we're a novelty."

"I think we should be careful. Perhaps if we go for a walk again, we should wear an abaya."

"No way. We just won't walk by the men's palace again." Paula said. "Are you tired? I'd love you to make me a cup of tea. You make it taste so good and it would sooth my nerves."

I went into the kitchen, made tea and returned to the living room with two large mugs. I settled on the couch across from Paula. Paula let out a sigh and then wrapped her feet under her.

"I don't know why we aren't in bed but this is so nice."

I smiled. Paula continued, "I'm glad Tanya went to bed. I'm enjoying our privacy."

"Yeah. What little we have."

I drifted into one of my dream worlds, allowing the events of the evening to wash over me. I smiled remembering Prince Turki's instructions to stay away from the gate and the controversial walk that stirred up the household.

"I've been thinking," Paula said, interrupting my thoughts, "I don't know why, but I feel close to you. I know we haven't known each other for that long, but I've come to admire you."

"Well, I like you too."

"Everyone watches. They talk about every little detail. It gets tiring, but um… I mean, you never went to parties and you didn't mingle much with the people we work with. I like your private ways. You seem to know where you're going in life."

"I do? I've had to make some hard choices and try to look for the positive in everything. It's difficult to come to terms with atrocities like baby Nawaar and Chop-Chop Square. I've learned that sometimes there isn't a positive side. We just have to accept life as it comes at us. I don't know." I took a sip from my tea. "When it comes to socializing, I guess I'm just cautious and like to spend my time reading or doing something creative. I don't like parties and I don't like to feel I'm wasting time. Life is too short."

" You just seem so…so grounded and wise. I couldn't go to The Square like you did… I feel…I don't know… a little lost right now." A tear rolled down her cheek.

I leaned forward and put a hand on her knee. "Paula. What's wrong?"

"I wonder if I should've come to Saudi. I miss my family so much."

"I know it's hard to be faraway. But tell me, why you are having second thoughts about coming here? Is it this assignment?"

"I've a husband in Australia." She muttered under her breath.

"You what?" I realized my response might be a little explosive. "You're married, Paula? How did you wind up in Saudi?"

Paula sighed. She stared into space then took a sip of tea. "We were married for eighteen years. Most of those years were wonderful. Monte was always generous towards me, but he didn't understand my desire to have children."

I settled back into the couch. "Didn't he want children?"

Paula wiped her eyes. "When we first married, we both decided we didn't want to have children. Life with him was wonderful. Monte knew all my likes and dislikes and made me laugh every morning. He's a business-man and coordinates the concierges for the big hotels and he took me everywhere. He travels often and children wouldn't fit into our lifestyle." She sipped her tea then smiled. "We've been to so many places. We'd stay in five-star hotels for free and while he was at his meetings I'd go and have spa treatments or lie on the beach. We'd meet people from around the world. It was a wonderful life and he spoiled me rotten. I did love him."

"Sounds like you had the perfect life. What changed?"

"My younger sisters married and had children. They're beautiful and I'm so proud to be an aunt. Monte enjoyed being an uncle to them too. Then my sister Patricia had a baby girl born with Down's Syndrome. The baby got pneumonia and died. That's when I decided to become a nurse. I wanted to look after sick children."

"That must have been hard for you to lose a little niece."

"Yeah. And Monte was great in consoling my sister and brother-in-law. He used to say 'I'm glad that didn't happen to us'." Paula stopped and stared into space. She half laughed and flung her head back. "I finished my nursing and went to work on a dialysis unit for pediatrics. I enjoyed it. The work interfered with Monte's and my lifestyle, but we worked around it. Then Patricia had another baby born with cerebral palsy. Deprivation of oxygenation to the brain during the birth left this little one disabled. My sister and brother-in-law were overwhelmed and couldn't deal with having a second baby that was sick. I wanted to adopt this little girl and Monte didn't. It was the first time we fought, and we argued bitterly. I adopted lit-tle Rosemary anyway. Monte wasn't happy, but he'd do anything to please me. He of course, continued to travel but I stayed at home. He left me for longer and longer periods of time. I didn't mind. I loved that little girl." Paula stopped. "I'd like another cup of tea please."

I got up and put the kettle on. It was late. I could feel the heaviness of the hour signal me to bed, but I dare not think of that now. Not when Paula needed someone to listen to her.

I returned to the living room. Paula was staring out the window. "Oh thank you. I needed this." I noticed Paula was shaking and had small beads of perspiration on her forehead.

"Are you all right?"

"I could use a drink."

"You mean alcohol?"

"Yeah." She said in her Australian accent. "There's something else you don't know about me. One reason I came to Saudi was to get away from alcohol. I'm not an alcoholic—don't get me wrong. When the baby died and Monte turned against me, I turned to alcohol. I saw a psychiatrist for about two months and he prescribed valium. With those pills I could relax and I didn't need to drink. I could enjoy a glass of French wine again without getting drunk. Now I'm scared. I've had more alcohol in Saudi than I ever consumed in Australia. So many parties! There's alcohol everywhere I go."

"Then why do you go to the parties?"

"I have to go otherwise I wouldn't see my boyfriend."

I sat up and leaned forward. "You have a boyfriend? Here? In Saudi?"

"Yeah. But I needed to get away from him for a while. I thought this Royal assignment would help me stay away from the drink, but I think I'm craving it more." She sniffed and tears rolled down her cheeks. "I don't have any valium to calm my nerves and I don't have any alcohol. I need something to relax me. I'm not sleeping at night and I don't know what to do. My mind won't stop. I miss my mother and my sisters and my little nieces and nephews. I need to sleep."

I was silent. What could I say to her?

"Oh Claire. Please. Please don't tell anyone. No one knows but you."

"Why would I tell anyone? I wouldn't say anything unless it was a matter of life-or-death."

I put an arm around her shoulders and assessed her like a nurse would her patient. She had mild withdrawal symptoms, but what if they got worse? What if she went into full withdrawal? What could I do?

I sighed and pulled away. "Finish telling me your story about Monte and Rosemary. What happened to Rosemary?"

"I have to tell you something first. You remember when we were checking the Princess's medications and reorganizing them?" Paula swallowed. "I noticed she had ativan. I took two pills."

I felt the color drain from my face. "You took the Princess's anti-anxiety medications? Are you crazy? If we got caught...oh Paula! I don't want to think about it. Ativan is a forbidden substance in this country. We could lose our heads—literally!" Chop-Chop Square flashed before me. Those dangling ropes...the screams...the blood...

"Don't worry. No one counts them. I only took two. I knew I'd go through some withdrawal." Paula leaned forward so she was almost kneeling on the floor. "Claire, don't you understand? I need them. And in this country, well, I can't get them here."

I covered my face with my hands and felt panicky.

"Claire. I' sorry."

Fear, disguised as a warm, sprawling sensation tickled every nerve in my body. I stood up. "Sorry isn't good enough! I don't want to get into trouble for your actions."

"You don't get it. I knew if I could relax and get some sleep, everything would be ok." Paula got to her feet. "My nerves are on edge all the time without the help of that medication."

"Medicating yourself is not going to help you deal with the loss of your niece. I lost a child too and believe me, it's better to face your grief than to run from it!"

"I'm not running! Claire! Look at me! I'm shaking and sweating," she shouted. In a calmer voice, she said, "I know I'll need two doses and I want you to give them to me. Please Claire. It's just to help me over this little hurdle." She sat down. "If I could just have one or two good night's sleep…"

"What! You want to give the pills to me?"

"Yeah. So you can give them to me when I need them. You know a drug addict wouldn't admit what I just did and wouldn't be willing to give the drugs to someone else. I am not addicted." She insisted.

"You want me to give the ativan to you when you feel you're having trouble? Then what? What guarantee do I have you won't take more medication from the Princess?" I paced.

"I need a little help for the next night or two. Besides, I've thought about that. I don't blame you for not trusting me. I'm desperate, Claire." Paula took a deep breath, "This is the plan: I thought if we get a new lock for the medications and if the Princess needs her ativan, then you give it to her. I won't be able to touch it. We can count it together every day." She sucked in her breath. "I'm not a drug addict, you know. The hospital trusted me to give out drugs like these. Please, Claire. Please."

I felt throbbing in my neck. My arms and legs ached from the fear and memories of Chop-Chop Square. I felt trapped. I paced for a moment, looked at Paula then sat opposite her. "All right! All right." I sighed, feeling deflated. "I suppose we're both going to be blamed if you get caught. But believe me Paula, I won't help you if you get in over your head." I felt sick to my stomach. "Ok. Get me those pills."

Is she an addict? An alcoholic? I'd have to watch her. At least the ativan will stop withdrawal symptoms, so those fears are quenched. What am I thinking? I needed to rely on her, trust her…but how? The American nurses will be leaving soon. Then what? The household isn't used to Westerners… If we didn't gain their trust, our job would be a nightmare…

"Here." Paula handed me two tiny white pills.

"I don't like this."

I slipped into my bedroom to hide them. Where am I going to put them? Careful. The maids come in, make the beds and clean the bathroom every day. Would they go through my clothes and other personal belongings? I can't take chances. I wrapped the pills in tissue paper and hid them in the pockets of one of my uniform pants. I doubted they'd look in there and I'd be sure to wear that uniform tomorrow.

I wandered back feeling like a criminal. Paula sat in the same place playing with her fingers.

"I am not giving you one tonight. It's too late."

"I apologize, Claire. My life hasn't been the same since Rosemary died."

"I know. It's never the same after a loved one dies." I stopped feeling bitter and sighing, sat down. "How did it happen?"

"Rosemary was a vibrant little thing. We had her for three years. She always smiled and she was so sweet. She learned to roll over and when she was two, was able to sit for short periods. You should have seen that radiant smile! And to hear her call me 'mommy'… I miss her so much." Tears rolled down Paula's cheeks. "She got sick one day. She spiked a fever and I rushed her to the hospital. They didn't know what was wrong with her at first and the hospital ran lots of tests. She was diagnosed with meningitis. She got sicker and weaker. I quit my job and spent every moment I could with her. I would hold her and rock her. I remember how her frail little body relaxed in my arms and even when she was so sick, she'd open her brown eyes and smile up at me. We had our special little songs and she loved the story of the three bears." Paula smiled through her tears. "She'd always growl when papa bear came home from the forest to find his porridge gone. You know the story? She loved that part. As the days went by, her growl got weaker, until it was a purr and when she couldn't make any sound, she'd just open her eyes. One day she didn't open them at all… She died in my arms, listening to her favorite story." Paula sobbed.

I reached over and patted her on the lap. I left the room and returned with a couple of Kleenexes. While Paula sobbed, I studied her.

Paula is a good-looking woman and very intelligent. She seems fragile, almost translucent. The pain she buried deepened the lines on her face, aging her. I had an image of a delicate silk scarf blowing in the wind, caught on a branch of a leafless tree. Once treasured and now forgotten, holding on by a thread. I know her agony. It torments you, swirls around you, strikes when least expected. I wished I could give Paula strength and wipe away the pain. I was all too familiar with taking in an enormous gulp of air and not having the energy or will to exhale. That horrible, numbing, frozen place between time and space, surrounding you with overwhelming grief and sorrow, paralyzing your soul. Then you feel a heartbeat, giving the signal that life goes on and you find a way to move forward, to live with the pain. It's so hard. So very, very hard.

"I'm sorry, Paula."

"Yeah. I guess it was meant to be." She sighed.

"How long ago did she die?"

"On Christmas Eve."

"This past Christmas eve?"

Paula nodded.

I was stunned. This is the beginning of September. It hasn't been a year since the death of her adopted daughter. No wonder Paula is having difficulties. She's still in the throws of profound grief. Her psychiatric visits were probably to help with her grieving and alcohol was an excuse to drown her pain. The valium would help her sleep so she wouldn't have to lay awake at night and think. Did Paula run to the Middle East trying to escape her pain and problems? They'll catch up with her sooner or later, especially in a place like Saudi where there are few distractions.

"When Rosemary died, my marriage broke up."

"What? Was Monte not supportive?"

"Oh yeah. But he'd want me to come home when I needed to be with Rosemary. He'd visit us at the hospital, but it was always the same. He argued with me, wanting me home on the weekends and then complain I didn't spend enough time with him. I think he was jealous. Can you believe he stopped going out of town on business trips to be closer to me? And when my baby died, he didn't say anything. He just stood there. Even at the funeral he was silent. Then he went back to work three days after the funeral. Three days! I don't think he felt anything. I think he was glad she was gone."

"Paula! You don't mean that. He was your husband and you said he loved you very much."

"He loved me before Rosemary came into our lives. When she got sick, all he did was work. He even set up an office and worked from home. He was there, but he didn't help."

"You said he stopped going out of town. Don't you think that by being closer he may have thought he was helping by just being there?'

"That's what he said. We started arguing bitterly after she died. I don't think he grieved. I don't think he cared."

"Do you believe that, Paula?"

Paula flashed angry eyes towards me.

"What did you expect him to do?"

"I expected him to hold the baby and rock the baby and be with the baby like I was."

"Didn't he hold her?" I scratched my head.

"He did sometimes. But he continued to work."

"Do you think he should have stopped work altogether? Are you angry with him for continuing to provide a living for you?"

Her shoulders slumped. "I don't know. But he didn't even shed a tear for her."

"How much time did you devote to him when the baby was sick?"

She folded her arms. "I didn't have to give him my time. He's an adult and he can care for himself." Paula wrapped her arms around her waist. "But Rosemary was so little, so delicate and she needed me."

"Maybe Monte needed you too." I sighed. "Remember Paula, we grieve in different ways. Just because he didn't sob an ocean full of tears doesn't mean he didn't grieve. How do you know he doesn't feel that same void you do after losing the baby?" I reached out and put a hand on her arm. "Oh Paula. He may be hurting just as much as you. He may not know how to show it, or he may be afraid to express it especially if you haven't included him in your pain and loss. If he loved you as much as you said he did, then he is hurting."

Paula stuck out her bottom lip. She stood up and announced, "I'm going to bed!" She slammed her door.

I stared into space and hoped I didn't' say too much...Poor Monte. What about Paula? Would she be angry with me in the morning? And those pills...what was I going to do with those pills? I put my head in my hands. If I could only stop thinking... I stretched my arms over my head and walked to the bedroom.

Chapter Ten

I opened my eyes and wondered why I was awake at seven-thirty in the morning. I only got three and a half hours sleep. I stretched then thought of Paula. I hoped she'd be in a better mood this morning.

I washed and dressed then walked out to the living room. Paula was sitting on the couch sipping a hot drink. I grinned at her. "I'm surprised to see you up, Paula."

"Yeah. I couldn't sleep." Paula sighed and took a sip of her drink. "There's tea in the pot. Would you like me to get you some?"

"Oh thank you. No, no. I'll get it myself."

I went to the kitchen and stretched. The late night zapped me of my usual energy and I didn't want any confrontations today. They were so unsettling. I poured the tea into the biggest mug I could find adding a little less than half a cup of milk and thought about comments people made about my 'milky tea'. I didn't care. I don't like my drinks too hot or too cold.

I settled on a couch opposite to Paula. We sat in silence, sipping from our cups and staring into space. Paula broke the silence. "I'm not mad with you, you know. I was shocked by what you said and didn't think of it like that before."

I listened, but didn't respond.

"I don't know." Paula continued. "I had to get away. I had to get away and think. Monte didn't want me to go, but I couldn't stay. Last time we spoke we talked about getting a divorce. Now I have Nils."

"Get a divorce? You mean you're not divorced?"

"No. I don't know if I want to divorce Monte. I'm thinking about it and having discussions with him. He doesn't want to but I don't know if I can go back to what we had. It's another reason I came here. I need to be alone, away from his influence. Before Rosemary, we had a good marriage and no one understands me like Monte. Ahh…now Nils." She played with the handle on her cup. "He understands me like Monte used to and he makes me feel things I haven't felt in years."

I tried not to show emotion thinking of the man left behind in Australia. That poor man. He lost little Rosemary, now is losing his wife. Paula fled from him knowing he couldn't follow her. Saudi Arabia closes its borders to the outside world; it has no tourism. I doubted Paula would go through the six to eight month process to get him a special visa allowing his entry into the country. I shook my head and asked, "Who's Nils?"

"He's a man I met here. He's from Norway and he's been my savior."

I was afraid to ask, "Your savior?"

"Yeah. I met him at a party. We were instantly attracted to each other and he's the only man I can talk to. He took care of me the first night we met. I had a little too much to drink and he took me to his flat. What a gentleman! He let me sleep in his spare bedroom, cooked me breakfast in the morning and we spent the day together. We've been seeing each other for over three months." She smiled and stared into space. "When I'm with him I don't think about Rosemary or the miserable existence of living in Saudi. He makes me laugh and he makes me feel safe."

I shuddered.

"What's wrong, Claire?"

"When women tell me their men 'make them feel safe', I take it as a red flag."

"Why? He does! I know I can trust him."

" Hmm…I hope he doesn't hurt you, that's all." I hesitated. Paula was fragile. "Tell me Paula. Is Nils married?"

"No, he's not. He never has been."

"And you believe him?"

"He has no reason to lie to me. His friends approve of us and I'm sure if he were married, I would know by now. We spend all our spare time together."

"Does Nils know about Monte?"

"Yes."

"Does Monte know about Nils?"

"Yes. But he said he understands and hopes I'll give Nils up and go back to him. That's another reason this assignment is good right now. I'm away from Nils and I can think about what to do. What do you think I should do?"

I jumped back. "I can't tell you what you should do, Paula. Umm…I do think however, you should finish your business with Monte first. It's only fair to everyone and it will spare unnecessary heartbreak."

Paula thought for a moment and then asked, "Where did you get your wisdom?"

I laughed. "I don't know if I'm wise or not, but I credit my mother. She's the wisest person I know."

We finished our tea and changed into our uniforms. I checked my pockets and breathed a sigh of relief. The pills were still in the pocket.

****

Prince Mohammad sat on one of the Princess's brocade chairs, speaking to a man who dressed in a starched white thobe and the gouthra he wore wasn't red checked like the Saudi Arabs, but pure white with a black leather igal to hold the headdress in place. I recognized him from the royal jet and when Paula and I approached, he stood up. He wasn't any taller than me, pale in comparison to Mohammad and had a square body and face with pudgy cheeks.

"Hello. Hello. I am Doctor Keerani. You are de nurses from Faisal Hospital," he said, extending his hand first to Paula, then to me.

"I am doctor to Princess." He announced with great pride. He turned to Prince Mohammad and spoke in Arabic.

"I am telling Prince what I say. Now. Now. The Prince wants to know if there is anything you need."

I thought for a moment and then asked. "We need to communicate with our hospital. Are there phones we can use or Internet?"

Dr. Keerani wrinkled his nose and then translated.

Prince Mohammad made large gestures and spoke at length. When he finished, Dr. Keerani continued, "There will be phones put in your villa. There is no Internet service this part of Jeddah. The Prince has generously said you can call to hospital anytime you like. It goes through Prince Mohammad's assistant, Mowark. Mowark will make telephone connections to hospital for you."

"What about calls to home? And what about calls to our friends in Riyadh?" asked Paula.

Dr. Keerani appeared anxious. He half-bowed towards the Prince then relayed the request in Arabic.

Prince Mohammad replied in English "Yes. Yes. You call anytime. It important to call father. I command Mowark and he arrange. You call anytime, for as long as you like. Anything else?"

"What about time off for Claire and I?"

"Work that out yourselves! Remember, my mother not be without nurse!"

"Thank you Prince Mohammad." I squirmed. "We'd like to report to you weekly on the progress of your mother. It that possible?" I asked.

Everyone in the room looked stunned.

Prince Mohammad rubbed his dimpled chin, then in Arabic spoke to the doctor who still looked shocked.

"The Prince said yes. He expects report every Saturday morning when he visit his mother."

I noticed a smirk cross the Prince's face before he left the room.

"Claire, what do you mean we'll give him a weekly report?"

"It's important for the Prince to know what we are doing and why. It'll justify us being here and there'll be a record of events, our work etc. We do need to be professional in everything we do. Right?"

Paula nodded.

"Excellent. I can see why you two come highly recommended!"

I tucked my hair behind my ear. "So tell us doctor, you are the Princess's private physician?"

"Yes. I hired by King Jabbar to serve him, but when his wife Liynaa became ill, I move my wife and five children from Egypt and we now live in Jeddah. Prince Jabbar also very sick, in de poorest of health, but I do what I can. He refuses to go hospital and refuses female nurses. His male servants help, but dey not nurses. I worry. De four sons, they want de best. Dey dink deir parents will live forever, but dis is not true. I try prepare for deir failure, but it is difficult. You understand. I am happy you here. Now Princess will get better care. The King refuses nurses, and dere is nothing I can do," he said, turning his palms to the sky.

Paula sat down. "Why do you call him 'King', and Prince Jabbar? Is he both King and Prince?"

The doctor laughed. "No, he King, but he *not* Crowned Prince Of Saudi Arabia. He head of dis branch of Royal family. He King of dis tribe, but a Prince in de country. You understand?"

We nodded.

"I believe there is another Princess?" Inquired Paula.

"King's second wife? Yes. Her palace here. It causes much pain for Princess Liynaa. She now in France and never comes to palace here. Only if King summons her. He hasn't summoned for years."

"I imagine it's difficult," I said.

"Yes. Yes." Dr. Keerani whispered and leaned closer. "When King married second wife, de Princess wouldn't talk to him for dree years. She speaking when he move second wife to France. She never forgive him even though it is his right." He shook his head. "Ah…dis family. Much unhappiness."

I sat beside Paula. "What do you mean?"

Dr. Keerani looked over his shoulder and bending towards us spoke in hushed tones. "Prince Turki hit by car and many broken bones. He lay around for months, and put on weight. He cannot exercise, so he got fatter." He chuckled. "He hardly walk now and sees his wife and children um…maybe one time in year. Prince Sultan. He married to very important Princess. She family much more powerful dan dis one. Shh…"

He put a finger to his lips and looked around. "She divorce Sultan. She wants to be wife of crowned Prince. Dis make Prince Sultan very unhappy. He looking for another wife, but he cannot marry unless his wife, Gooda approves. She never approve. Dey have two childrens and no woman good enough for her childrens!"

Paula straightened her shoulders. "I didn't think women had any say in who a man marries."

"Dis is so, but Princess Gooda have power." He looked behind him. "I tell you dis because you good nurse, but you must keep secret. Prince Mohammad wants to be favorable to Princess Gooda's father. She daughter of uncle to Crowned Prince. Prince Sultan feels trapped. Dey get many favors and are with powerful peoples through Gooda's father, so important to keep Princess happy." He looked over his shoulder. "But you not talk. Dis family secret. Yes?"

I nodded my head and wondered why the doctor told us so much about the family.

The curtain separating the sitting room from the Princess's inner chambers opened, revealing a Filipino woman who froze, looking surprised to see us. She pulled her shawl around her shoulders, stomped to the other side of the Princess's bed and scowled. The two American nurses huddled in a corner, whispering to each other.

"Oh. Doctor. Hi." Said Tanya.

"Everything all right?" Dr Keerani asked, sounding official.

"We have a problem this morning."

Dr. Keerani's cheeks turned red and his smile vanished.

Leslie spoke. "The Princess wet herself. She's never done that before. Her servants are upset and the Princess refuses to get out of bed."

I interrupted, "She wet herself?" Without thinking, I rushed to the Princess's bedside and put my hand on her arm. She was hot. Very hot. I took her pulse. It was racing and she was breathing fast. I put my hand on her forehead. "Princess Liynaa. Princess? Can you hear me?"

"She doesn't understand you." The Filipino woman snapped.

"You speak English! It doesn't matter if she can't understand what I say, she should still respond to my voice." Turning to the American nurses, I asked, "Did you take her temperature and blood pressure?" I turned to the Filipino woman. "Get me a cold cloth!"

She hesitated.

The doctor yelled at her and before she had time to respond, another servant came from behind a corner with a cloth. The Princess rolled her head. She was semi-conscious and pale, her fingertips, blue.

"Paula, she's going to code. Everyone back!"

The doctor yelled in Arabic. Those that had left the room returned and crowded around the bedside. The women started crying and wailing. Some put their hands to their cheeks. Others looked, gesturing, 'why, why?' Two of them read from the Qu'ran.

"Doctor, please! Can't you tell these women to stop crowding? We can't help the Princess. Paula get on the other side. I'll get at her head. Leslie, put pillows under the Princess's legs to lift them up."

The servants wailed at the top of their voices. The shrieking was unbearable. They fanned the Princess with their bodies and arms in competition to touch and be as close to her as possible. The American nurses stood back and let the servants in. One of the servants pushed me hard and I stumbled. Paula held the Princess's hand, refusing to move aside. The doctor paced, wringing his hands. I was going to say something when I heard male voices coming our way. Two Western male paramedics, Prince Mohammad, his wife Johara and Prince Sultan burst into the room. The indistinguishable clumpity clump of Prince Turki's cane and shuffling feet echoed in the hallway.

The paramedics couldn't get near and yelled, "This is impossible!"

Prince Mohammad clapped his two hands above his head and bellowed. The women shriveled at the sound of his voice and stepped back. Others slinked away and their subdued cries were heard from the hall beyond the room.

The paramedics assessed the Princess. "She has a heart beat and is breathing."

They loaded her onto a stretcher. As they were strapping her in, Prince Sultan turned to the Americans and said, "You two go with servants."

He pointed at Paula "You stay with my mother." He turned to me, "You come with me."

My heart skipped a beat. I had no choice. Prince Mohammad and Prince Sultan exchanged glances, then he and his wife followed the paramedics out of the palace. Prince Sultan hung back until everyone left the room and then signaled me to follow.

Prince Turki didn't make it to the Princess's bedroom. He struggled to breathe, his enormous stomach heaving in and out as he sat on one of the chaise lounges, calling out in Arabic watching the medical team and everyone else rush by. Prince Sultan looked at Turki and said in English, "We will let you know if it serious."

Prince Turki raised his hand and waved, gulping air and wiping the sweat from his forehead with his sleeve.

Everyone was gone by the time Sultan and I stepped outside. Sultan unlocked his car door. This time he was driving a shiny red convertible, larger than the one I rode in from the airport. I started to get into the back-seat.

"I told you. You sit in front. With me."

I didn't know if I should speak or not. I tried to look relaxed but was apprehensive about being alone with the Prince.

Sultan broke the silence. "So. You like Jeddah?'

"I haven't spent enough time here to form an opinion. One thing I know I don't like, is the humidity."

"You will get used to it. You will see." He paused. "You American?"

"No. Canadian. I come from the West coast."

"Ah. I live in California."

"My home is north of Seattle, on an island."

He looked confused.

I changed the subject. "I hope your mother'll be all right."

"She will."

"I hope so."

"No hope. You safe her. She all right. Enough of her. I want to know about you."

I took a deep breath and looked at him. Sultan smiled at me from one side of his mouth. My heart was pounding hard and hoped I wasn't blushing. I wanted out of his car and to get to the hospital, but it seemed to be taking forever. The thought crossed my mind Sultan may not be taking me there…

"Are we close to the hospital?"

"You not worry. You with me."

I swallowed hard. "Where are we going?"

He didn't answer.

I felt small and helpless. I looked out the window and watched as we left the city, passing property after property. There was no escape. I was trapped, going who knows where. My heart thumped hard, my hands sweaty, unable to think.

Sultan's cell phone rang. His face fell when he looked at it and grumbled. He answered it. He looked at me, turned the car around muttering under his breath and drove for a long time without speaking. He cleared his throat. "That Prince Mohammad. I take you back."

My heart beat high in my throat and my stomach churned, fearing Sultan's intentions. I consciously slowed my breathing and managed to find my voice. "I thought we were going to the hospital."

Sultan laughed an evil-sounding laugh. "You like a bird. You free to fly. For now."

He grinned then looking straight ahead, gripped the steering wheel and sped down the highway.

****

I walked down the corridors of the VIP unit on the fifth floor of the new hospital trying to conceal the echoes my shoes made on the hard polished tile. I came to a nurse's station centered in the middle of the unit with easy access to the suites. The counter formed a semi-circle of black marble rising four feet and its desk had a glass covering to protect the wood surface. It was equipped with the latest computers and they had the largest medication room I had ever seen. Princess Liynaa's suite was across the hall from the desk.

I walked through double doors, which opened to a short hallway with two rooms on opposing sides. The one on the right had a fully-equipped kitchen with tables and chairs scattered in the large space. The room on the left was filled with chatty female attendants, sitting on sofas lining the walls. Another pair of double doors faced me. I pushed them open and saw the Princess lying in her oversized hospital bed on one end of the room and on the other end were dark aqua-colored sofas against the wall. Paula stood by the Princess and grinned. "Where were you?"

"I think Prince Sultan got lost."

I walked past a couple of the servants who gave me dirty looks and peeked through a doorway. I saw a four-piece bathroom with a special waist-high tub that allowed a stretcher to lower a patient into the water. There were two vanity sinks, a bidet and a toilet with gold handles.

"There are no mirrors in there, Paula."

"That's because in some sects of the Arab culture to see one's image means they may lose their soul."

Dark aqua and black velvet curtains covered tall windows extending the full length of the suite. They were drawn tight, blocking out light.

The American nurses propped the Princess in bed with large fluffy pillows. I was about to offer assistance when Prince Mohammad entered the suite waiving his hands, signaling the servants to leave. They hurried out the door, keeping their heads low. They all left, except for two. Prince Mohammad looked at the American nurses and said, "Come here." He indicated we sit on the couches at the opposite end of the room, facing the Princess. "You two. Sit here."

Paula and I sat beside him as directed, then doors opened and a tall, slim woman entered the room. She shed her abaya and greeted Prince Mohammad.

"I Johara. I first and only wife of Prince Mohammad. How's my mother-in-law?"

"She's weak." Tanya answered.

The two servants moved aside as Johara pulled up a chair, sat down and stroked Liynaa's arm.

Prince Mohammad took his eyes from his wife, looked at me and yelled, "You let my mother get sick! This your fault!"

Shocked and still a little shaky after my drive with Sultan, I tucked a strand of hair behind my ear and thought hard. "Excuse me. I was not caring for the Princess when she became ill. I just happened to find her. I suspect she has a urinary infection and needs antibiotics and fluids."

Prince Mohammad stood up and leaned over me, yelling in Arabic. His words sent shock waves through me but I was determined not to be intimidated. I straightened my back and looked unswervingly at Mohammad who was not much taller than me. I waited for him to stop yelling, then said in a controlled voice, "Please don't yell at me. I'm here to look after your mother and I can't do my job if you're going to treat me like this."

Prince Mohammad blinked in disbelief. He took a step back and I wondered if he was going to strike me.

The female servants gasped. Prince Mohammad's wife Johara walked over and stood beside Paula. She looked at the women servants and spoke to them. They stopped their chatter, then left the room, bowing their heads as they passed.

I looked into Prince Mohammad's dark eyes and noticed a subtle softening. "Prince Mohammad, I understand you're worried. Let's see what the doctor says and go from there."

Turning to his wife, he asked in English "What she say?"

When Johara finished speaking, Mohammad turned, huffed and looked me up and down. He sat down on a chair at the foot of his mother's hospital bed.

"You are very brave. No one talks to my husband like that."

"I don't mean to be disrespectful, but you have to understand that we want the same thing for Princess Liynaa. We want her to be well and strong."

"That is true. Hmm...You are a guest in my mother-in-law's home and we want you to be comfortable. I will remind my husband."

Johara went to her husband and they spoke for a few minutes. I fidgeted with a button on my uniform jacket.

"You." He said pointing to the Americans. "You will stay here and look after my mother. You two. Come."

Paula and I exchanged glances and followed Prince Mohammad into the room with the kitchen. He yelled at the servants who sat at the tables. They looked stunned then scurried past, hiding their faces. Prince Mohammad pointed to an empty table and we sat down.

"You good nurses. You help her. My brothers and I pleased."

I smiled at the Prince. A chill went down my back, thinking about the impromptu drive with Sultan.

"You two go to Riyadh tonight. I will arranged."

I was bewildered.

Paula spoke. "You mean you are, uh, replacing us?"

"No!" Mohammad said. "You get things. Anything you need. You live at palace. It is reward!"

"You mean all of our things? Everything?" I asked.

"Yes. The plane leaves tonight. After supper. My driver take you."

My hair stood up on the back of my neck. "Prince Mohammad, we don't need a reward. The hospital is responsible for us. We must stay in communication with them."

"You belong here."

Paula said, "We thank you, but we belong to King Faisal Hospital. We can't leave there."

"I will make arrangements."

I hugged my waist. "No, you don't understand. We appreciate your offer, but we're here to do a job. We won't be able to do our best for your mother if you think we want rewards. Please."

"Why not? You good nurses. You deserve reward."

"No thank you. We do not work for rewards. Our reward is to see that your mother, the Princess is well taken care of. We have our salary and that's sufficient. You must understand." I felt panic rise from my center as images of a forced marriage to Sultan teased my imagination.

"Claire's right. We don't belong to this country, and we don't belong here. We're on loan short for a time then we must go. We must return to the hospital, then one day soon, return home to our own countries. It 's the way it is."

Prince Mohammad had a solemn look on his face. "Yes. What you say is true. Very well. It is as you wish. Stay with hospital, but work here."

"Just for a time, Prince, not forever."

"Yes, yes. No reward?"

"No, Prince. No reward." I said.

Prince Mohammad looked confused. I took in a deep breath and extended my hand toward the Prince. He looked at my hand for a minute, then shook it firmly. He then shook Paula's hand and chuckled.

"You go Riyadh tonight. Bring back what you need. You be back in three days. That is your reward. A holiday."

I laughed. "Thank you Prince Mohammad."

"Yes, thank you!"

Prince Mohammad left the room.

"I wonder if the Prince thinks our customs are strange?"

"He probably does. It's reassuring to know he has a sense of humor. Claire, look. Those servants in the other room are straining to hear and see what we're doing."

"I don't think they approve of our relationship and interaction with the Royal Family."

"Who cares? Let's go."

****

I entered the villa and ran to answer the phone.

"Hello nurses? King Faisal nurses? Dis Mowark. Prince Mohammad assistant."

"Yes, Mowark. This is Claire. How can I help you?"

"Mr. Anthony Herd from King Faisal Hospital on line. One minute."

I waited while Mowark switched the lines.

"Hello Claire. I'm glad I caught you. How are you two?"

"Quite well. Prince Mohammad is sending us home for the weekend and my one concern is that he wants to keep us here. Permanently."

Anthony laughed. "Yes. If you do a good job, some of the royal families want to 'adopt' you. I'll have protocol speak with the Prince."

"Is there any chance he could keep us here against our will?" I twisted the phone cord.

"It's unlikely. The family signed a contract with the hospital and if they dishonor it, it looks bad. Also, the hospital won't cooperate in loaning out its nurses in the future. However, if you decide you want to disassociate yourself from the hospital, that's your choice, but I wouldn't recommend it."

"I don't know about Paula, but that's the last thing I want to do."

"Good to hear that. I'd worry about you. Um...I won't see you when you get here. My flight for home leaves tonight."

I had no intentions of seeing him. "Have a great time at home,

Anthony. I hope everything works out for you."

"Yeah, me too. I'll be in touch soon."

I returned the receiver to its place, staring into space.

"You don't look very happy Claire. Did Anthony say something?"

"Huh? Oh. No. He's going on holiday tonight and he'll talk to protocol before he leaves. We should pack if we are going to be flying this evening."

It only took a few minutes to throw things in the suitcase. I smiled when I came out from my room and saw Paula in a similar long colorful dress.

"Modest, yet elegant," said Paula. "We can show those princesses that we're just as lovely as they are."

I jested, "Yes. We are princesses from our own countries. You are a Princess from Australia, descendent of some long lost king, and I am the Princess of British Columbia!"

"Shall we go to dinner, your highness?"

We turned to leave when Tanya came through the doors.

"Claire! Paula! I have to talk to you."

"Tanya, what's going on?"

"We came back from the hospital with the doctor to make a list of medications for the hospital nurses and we discovered the Princess is missing some pills. She's missing two ativan and the doctor wants to know what happened to them. He's irate! He's threatening to tell Prince Mohammad. The pills went missing after you sorted them."

Paula's face went white. "You count them?"

"Of course we count them! They're controlled substances. I know Leslie didn't take them, so it must be one of you."

"Just a minute. The drug cabinet is unlocked. How do you know one of the servants didn't take them?" I asked.

"Because they wouldn't. They'd be afraid they'd get their hands cut off. Come on, fess up!"

Paula put her hands on her hips. "Why do you think we took them?"

"One of you did and I'm going to find out who."

She stomped out of the villa. Paula looked at me then flopped on the couch.

"What are we going to do, Paula?"

"I don't know. Maybe return them?"

"You know what. I'm giving them back to you and you can figure it out. I want nothing to do with it."

I went into my room opened my luggage, picked up the uniform pants and rummaged through one pocket, then the other. They were gone. My heart gave one solid thump and panic raced through me. I pulled my other pants off the hangers and checked them. I stopped, thought about where I'd been and my legs nearly gave out from under me. What if they fell out of my pocket when I was in Sultan's car? I trembled. I took a deep breath and returned to the living room.

"Paula, they're missing. The pills are missing! I think they fell out of my pocket."

Paula was quiet. She looked down, twirling the cup in her hands.

"Paula, did you hear me?"

"Yeah."

"What is it?"

Her cheeks reddened. "I was having a bad time last night and when you were asleep, I snuck into your room and took them."

I gasped. "You went into my room? Why didn't you tell me?"

"Well, I…I didn't…"

"You scared me to death! I thought they fell out in Sultan's car! What's the matter with you that you not only steal from the Princess, but from me too? I tell you! I have a good mind to go and tell the doctor that you stole them and let the chips fall where they may." I paced.

"Oh no. Claire. Please, please don't. I was shaking so badly, and…"

"And you took the pills. I still don't know why you didn't tell me." I threw my hands in the air. "And why didn't you stop me before I tore everything apart?"

"Well, I didn't have much time this morning, did I? We were at the hospital, then Tanya burst in ranting and raving. I, I didn't know how to tell you. Besides, I only took one."

"That's not the point." I stopped dead in my tracks. "What? You only took one? Where's the other one?"

"You just told me you washed your hands of the whole thing. I have it in a safe place. Lookit, if we just keep our mouths shut and act dumb then they can't prove anything, can they? Tanya and Leslie are going to be leaving soon and if it's still an issue after they're gone, we can blame them."

"Paula!"

"What? We are the ones left behind in this God-forsaken country! We have to protect ourselves."

I sighed. "You are making a criminal out of me. I do not know anything, nor do I want to. Understand?"

"I understand. I'm sorry."

I went into the kitchen and waited for the water to boil. I tried to calm myself as I made the tea. I took several deep breaths and put angry thoughts out of my mind, then walked out to Paula and put a mug in front of her. I didn't know what to say.

Tanya opened the door and poked her head into the villa. "Claire! Paula! The doctor wants to talk to you. Now!"

"Tanya? On never mind!" Paula slammed her cup down on the table, spilling it. She stood up, stomped into her room and slammed the door. I took anther sip from my tea, looked at Tanya and sighed.

"Aren't you coming?"

"Yes. In a minute. I need a moment to gather my thoughts."

"Why? So you can come up with a story for the doc?" snapped Tanya, holding onto the door.

"Don't be nasty. No. I need a moment to compose myself. I've had quite a day."

She stepped inside. "Where were you today? Where did the Prince take you?"

"For a long car ride." I straightened my shoulders. "I'll get Paula and be there soon."

****

The doctor paced back and forth, his head obscured by his white headdress. He turned and looked at us when we entered the suite. "You know where pills?"

"Why would you think Claire or I took the pills? It was Claire who discovered the Princess was ill and saved her life. We didn't give the Princess her medications. We never have. Those nurses were responsible," Paula said, pointing at them.

Tanya and Leslie gasped.

"We didn't take those pills. Don't you blame us!"

Dr. Keerani put up his hands. "Ok. Ok. Ok. Please womans. Stop."

"We didn't take them!" Leslie cried.

"Doctor. Anyone could take pills. That cabinet is not locked. As I said, Claire and I didn't give the Princess any medications."

Tanya put one hand on her hip. "No, but you were looking at the bottles."

"We were recording the meds so we can organize your mess!" Paula turned her back and crossed her arms.

"Womans! Stop! Now. It is true Claire found de Princess and safe her life. She could not take pills then safe her. No, no. Not makes sense. What you say is true, Paula. You two nurses give pills. You two responsible."

"We didn't take them!"

"No shouting! Womans should not argue. You two take blame. Someone have to take blame."

"But…"

"No, no. I have plan." Dr. Keerani put up his hands. "I tell Prince Mohammad dey are missing, but not know who took them. Paula is right. We need lock. I will tell Prince you take blame, but did not take. You will get paid for contract and go home in one week. All will be ok." He paced. "I will talk to Prince and make dis arrangement. Yes? Agreed?"

The American nurses mumbled and looked unhappy. "Will this stop us from taking contracts with other Royal families?"

"I make sure not."

Tanya flopped on a chair. "Ok. We'll go along with the plan. But make sure the Prince understands we did *not* take those pills."

"Yes, yes. No problem. Now I have news. De Princess is very sick. De Prince, he provide transportation to and from hospital every day so you look after Princess. Paula and Claire you must set up routine and talk to Prince when you back from Riyadh. Must tell about emergency and plan for her to come home. I will help you. Understand?"

"Yes we do."

"You two are going to Riyadh?" gasped Leslie.

"Yup, tonight. The Prince made the arrangements. Any objections?" Paula glared at Tanya.

"Ok womans. Please, no argue."

"I'll take Paula back to the villa. We need to get our luggage." I smiled and led Paula away.

Chapter Eleven

I arched my back, feeling stiff after sitting on the uncomfortable seats of the commercial plane. I checked my watch before opening the door to the apartment. One o'clock in the morning. I didn't want to disturb Rose.

I stepped inside, dropped my suitcase and looked down the hall toward Rose's bedroom. Her door was open, and I tiptoed towards it and peeked through the crack. Her bed was made and I listened for a moment to make sure she wasn't in the bathroom. I heard nothing. I breathed a deep sigh of relief, glad to be alone then headed towards the kitchen to make a cup of tea and relax before going to bed.

I filled the kettle and put it on the stove to boil then picked up my suitcase, opened the door to my bedroom and flipped on the overhead light. I stopped dead in my tracks. The room looked naked. My bed was stripped. The pictures and nick knacks on my dressers, gone.

My heart skipped a couple of beats. Was I in the right apartment? I raced to the front door and checked the numbers. It said 525. It had to be the right one. My key unlocked the door.

I raced back and threw open my closet and saw Rose's clothes on hangers. I opened a couple of drawers, then a couple more. My things were gone. Even the computer that once sat on the desk in the corner was taken down and the keyboard, cords, speakers, and printer were missing. My heart sank. Where are my things? Where are the pictures of my family and my recent purchases? It didn't make any sense.

I sat down on the corner of the bed and looked around. I wanted to cry, but couldn't decide if I felt despair or anger.

I heard the kettle singing on the stove. I ran to it and picked it up before the piercing scream drove me to madness and made tea. I carried it to the living room, sat down then on a whim got up and opened the hall closet. There were boxes piled one on top of another, marked 'Claire's stuff'. I took one box from the top of the stack and peered inside. It was filled with my clothes. I took down the next box, checked its contents and the one after that. I left the open boxes in the center of the living room, sat down and stared at them. Why did these things always happen when I'm aching to go to bed?

I drank my tea then headed to the bathroom. I opened the door and put my hands over my mouth, suppressing a shriek. I couldn't believe my eyes. The sink and the bathtub overflowed with plants. The counters had potted plants crowding every available space. Plants hung from the ceiling and larger ones were on the floor in decorative pots.

Over wrought with fatigue, feeling invaded, I was outraged. I stomped to the living room, reached into the boxes and threw my belongings all over, not caring where they landed. I went through one box, then another in a frantic search of sheets and blankets. I found them in the bottom of one of the boxes then marched into my bedroom, whipped them open and struggled to make the bed. I thrust my pillows toward the headboard and they bounced to the floor. Frustrated, I sat on the edge of the bed, trying to catch my breath. I sighed then reached down to pick up one of the pillows and hugged it. I calmed down, vowing I'd deal with Rose the next time I saw her. I picked up the other pillow, crawled into bed and tried to go to sleep, allowing my anger to dissipate into the darkness…

****

The next morning I stepped over blouses, skirts and dresses and went into the kitchen to put the kettle on to boil. I didn't feel anger any more, just frustration, not knowing what to say to Rose. I may not even see Rose before my weekend 'holiday' was over. I picked up my belongings and carried them into the bedroom. It took me several hours to put the clothes away, hook up my computer and arrange the bedroom and bathroom the way I had them before.

The phone rang. It was probably for Rose, but I answered it anyway.

"Hello?"

"Howdy! Is this the lovely Claire?"

My heart jumped and my spirit soared. "Jake! Hi!" I glanced at the clock. It was nearly nine pm. "Where are you?"

"I'm back from a jaunt to the southwestern part of Saudi. Very nice there, actually. It's a mountainous area and much cooler than here, the heart of the desert."

"Have you finished your vaccine deliveries?"

"Oh no. Just on a reprieve. I'm on my way back to the States again to pick up more supplies. Thought I'd take a chance on you being there."

"What a pleasant surprise! And the timing. I wasn't expecting to be in Riyadh. It's a 'reward' from the Prince."

"I wish I could see you. We're fated to be separated, but I kept my promise and thought about you."

I didn't know why, but my heart ached and bitter disappointment flooded me. I could feel the tears close to the surface. "I would like to see you too. Can't we?"

"I can't leave the base. We're locked down again."

"Oh no. It's like you're in prison."

"It feels like it sometimes. But, hey. I'd like to get to know you better, but it doesn't seem like it's going to happen. Not now anyway. Maybe when we finish in Saudi we can meet up in the States."

My heart sank. Was he breaking up with me before we even had a chance? Tears rolled down my cheeks.

"Claire, you there?"

"Oh yes. Sorry." I swallowed a lump in my throat. "I suppose we can meet in the States. How do you feel about Canada?"

"I'd love to go there on a holiday, but I'm married to the military, you understand. I'm here for another 18 months or so. How about you?"

"Yes, me too. I have the option of extending this contract, but I don't know."

"I guess the smart thing is to put our friendship on a backburner. Do you have e-mail?"

"Not at the palace, but I can e-mail you when I get away from there… or how about an old fashioned letter?"

"Ha. Ha. Yeah, good old Saudi Post. Sometimes you don't get the mail and if you do, it's been opened and read. Ok Claire, I'm being summoned. We'll keep in touch."

"I hope so."

"Good-bye, Claire."

He said 'good-bye.' Good-bye…

I ran to my room and threw myself down on the unmade bed. I hugged my pillow and sobbed, burying my face in it. I screamed, using the pillow to muffle my cries, but the lump in my throat made it hard for me to breath. I felt my cheeks burn hot as my chest rose and fell in steady jerks.

Why? Why? Why? I'll never hear his musical voice again…just his voice…the sound of it lifted me so high. Thinking of him made it just that much easier living here, but now…because of this stupid assignment and because of the military we're torn apart before we had a chance to begin. Oh…it's so unfair!

I rolled on my back and stared at the ceiling. Big, hot tears fell from the corner of my eyes.

Why do I feel like this? Why does my heart feel like it's broken in a thousand pieces? I hardly know him, yet I feel like we've known each other forever.

A part of me felt like I had been ripped apart, exposing fresh wounds. I hadn't felt that kind of pain since losing my son.

Loss. So much loss in my life. Too many vacancies in my soul. Will they ever be filled? Will I ever feel happy again? I Can't stand this!

I rolled over and screamed into the pillow. I screamed again and again until I weakened from fatigue. My cries turned to whimpers. I rolled over, sat up and reached for a Kleenex on the bedside table. I breathed in little jerks, my body shuttering, sighing deeply.

Stop. Just stop.

I didn't know if this severing of my soul was profound grief or if I were in the depths of despair. How could I possibly be broken over a man I didn't know? Perhaps this gut-wrenching pain wasn't about him. Maybe it was the loss of a wish or a dream. Could it be the loss of baby Nawaar?... Was it the horrors in Chop-Chop Square?... Maybe it's the fear of not knowing what Sultan wants... or perhaps Anthony. Would he leave me alone now? Would they both leave me alone? Is that what I wanted? ...What do I want?

I leaned forward, burying my face between my knees.

I didn't know if I wanted to settle down or continue to take work assignments in exotic places, exploring, trying to satisfy some West-Coast definition of freedom.

"I don't know, I don't know!" I cried, looking up to the ceiling. "Why am I in Saudi Arabia? What have I gotten myself into? Why don't I give up and go home?"

I reclined on the bed allowing my tears to spill and the emotional exhaustion lull me into a restless sleep.

****

The apartment door slammed, jolting me awake and realized it must be Rose. I came out to the living room.

"Oh. You're back." She commented, walking to her bedroom. Rose returned a few minutes later and flopped on a well-worn chair.

"I didn't think you'd be coming back, so I packed up your things. I could use the extra space."

"If I weren't coming back, I'd tell you. Anyway, I put everything back. I don't know what to do with your plants. I found empty buckets at the back of the kitchen sink and I put them in there."

Rose was indignant. "You should've told me you were coming back. You can't be at the palace one day and then show up here."

I sat up straight. "Just a minute, Rose. I don't have to report to you my comings and goings. You have no right to assume anything about me and you have no right to go into my room."

"Fine." She snorted.

"Listen, I don't want to argue with you. Please just leave my things alone, Ok?" I relaxed. "Uh…would you like a cup of tea? I could use one right now."

"Yeah, ok."

I returned with two large mugs and placed one down in front of her.

"So, how are you?" I asked.

"Ian and I are wonderful." She put her hands over her heart. "He's the man for me! I'm going to Scotland to tell his wife about us."

"You what?"

"Yup. I've made up my mind. Ian and I should get married. He has to divorce his wife, that's all."

"Does Ian know you're going to Scotland?"

"Nope. When I can get my new passport from the embassy, I'll go to Scotland."

"My goodness Rose. Don't you think Ian should be the one to tell his wife?"

"Ian? I can't wait for him! He can be such a wimp sometimes and he'll chicken out, I know," she said, flipping her long dark hair. "He wants to marry me. The sooner the better."

I drew in my breath. "What if you were Ian's wife? How would you feel?"

"But I'm not his wife in Scotland. I'm his wife here. And I won't ever let him out of my sight."

"What about his children?" I protested.

"They can come and live with us. I like children. Sometimes." She flipped her hair again, and stood up. "I wish these stupid restrictions were gone. I want my passport and I want to be free to do what I want." She twirled around then marched down the hall and slammed her bedroom door.

I was shocked. Who was that woman I was living with? A forty-year old teenager? Could her experience in Saudi prison alter her thought processes? Or was she always impractical and self-centered? Ian's poor wife. I couldn't imagine the shock of having Rose show up on your doorstep. I worried about what Rose may say to the unsuspecting woman. Rose has a sharp tongue and when she puts her mind to something, there's no stopping her. She's the most stubborn person I ever met.

I thought about Ian. Was Rose simply a passing fancy or did he want to separate from his wife and children? And marry Rose? Rose? I doubted it.

I shook my head. Rose was strange, there was no arguing that point. My concern right now was to define my boundaries and living arrangements with this woman before heading back to Jeddah.

****

I sipped my tea looking out the window at the swimming pool, feeling rested after the trip to Riyadh. Paula sat opposite me reflecting a dreary ambience in her demeanor, staring into space. I coveted our privacy. The staff was at the hospital with the Princess, allowing this rare moment of peace. With servants behind every corner and curious eyes watching your every move, tranquil moments were scarce.

"I want to thank you for trusting me, Claire. About the pills. You know."

I frowned. "How are you feeling these days? Are you able to sleep any better at night?"

"I should be able to. Nils takes care of me. I went to see one of the Norwegian doctors with Nils. I got a prescription for the pills I need and I should be ok now." She sipped her tea.

"I hope so, Paula. Are you sure it's all right to carry them with you?"

"I have a prescription. Besides, the Arabs won't know what kind of medication it is."

We stared at the still water for a few moments then Paula interrupted the silence. "Nils wants to get me a cell phone. It's better we don't rely on the system here, but I don't think I want Nils to do that."

"Why?" I crossed my legs.

"I don't want to be attached or dependent on him."

I put my cup down. "We could always get a cell phone ourselves, then we'll have a little independence and you won't have to feel obligated to Nils."

"Good idea. Let's see if the drivers will take us downtown."

We finished our tea, put on our abayas and one of the drivers took us to a shopping area in the new part of Jeddah. He dropped us outside a newer mall, and wanted to wait, but we refused.

"That driver wasn't happy leaving us here."

"Yeah, but Claire, I don't want to rush. We can find a taxi driver to take us back when we're ready."

The mall was a maze of jewelry stores, high fashion boutiques and specialty shops.

"We need to find a communications store."

"Yeah…Oh—Claire! Look at those shoes! Let's just take a look." She pulled on my arm.

I stopped. "Paula, there's a phone store over there." I pointed. "Let's go."

"There's also one beside it and another one again."

"Let's go into that one. It looks the cleanest."

When we entered, the shoppers and merchant stopped their transactions and stared.

"What's going on?"

"I don't know. Maybe they haven't seen Western women before. We're properly covered, mind you this scarf is itchy in the heat. Common Claire. Let's look at the phones."

The customers filed out giving us strange looks as they passed.

"Something isn't right, Paula."

The merchant approached us and cocking his head to one side asked, "Welcome. I can help you?"

"Yes. We want to buy a cell phone."

The man took a half step back and let out a little laugh. He took a corner of his black checked headdress and covered his mouth to hide his smile.

"You cannot have cell phone."

We looked at each other.

"Why not?"

"You are women. Women cannot have phones."

Paula put her hands on her hips. "But I see women with phones in Saudi!"

"Yes. Yes. But you need husband or father to get phone for you. A women not responsible."

"I beg your pardon?" I asked, folding my arms across my chest.

"A woman not pay bill. She careless. A man has to be responsible for phone." He laughed and shooed us from the store.

"I don't believe this!"

"We shouldn't be surprised, Paula. Remember, women have no status in this country."

"What'll we do?"

"I don't know." I scratched my head then said, "Perhaps we can ask if the Faisal Hospital will supply us a cell phone for Royal assignments."

"It's a thought."

We wandered around the mall and I followed Paula into store after store, looking at clothes, shoes and fine perfumes. I sighed. "I'm tired of shopping. I think we should find a taxi and go back."

"Where do we go?"

I pulled at my scarf. "Hmm…Let's go to one of the five-star hotels and asked the concierge. I'm sure we can get a safe taxi at a hotel."

"What hotel?"

"I saw one across the street from this mall."

Paula put one hand on her hip. "Oh great, Claire. Cross the street? You want us to get hit by a car?"

"It'll be all right. How will we get back if we don't?"

We negotiated our way across the lanes of traffic, ignoring the horns and heckling from the Arab men. "I hate it when they do that. They think we're prostitutes," complained Paula.

" I know. Pure ignorance."

"You mean arrogance."

When we entered the lobby of the hotel, an East Indian man saw us and smiled. "Good afternoon ladies. How can I help?"

"We need a taxi, please."

"No problem."

He went behind his desk and made a phone call. Within moments a taxi pulled up and a slight Arab man with pointed features and yellowed Thobe jumped out of his car and opened the rear door, waiting for us to get in.

"Thank you. How unusual for you to hold our door." Paula said, flirting with the driver.

"No problem womans. I know what Western womens like and I, Faisal, directed descendant of De Great Mohammad Himself, like to serve."

Paula leaned over and whispered, "He means he likes the tips!"

"Where you go?"

"To Princess Liynaa's Palace."

"Prince Jabbar's wife, dat Princess Linyaa?"

Paula flipped her hair. "That's right. You seem surprised."

"Oh no! It very dangerous dere. Womens like you, whew! You very brave. No scared?"

I exchanged glances with Paula. "Why should we be scared?"

"Oh! De womans in dat palace, dey all black hearts. Very, very black hearts. You be careful. Tch, tch, tch." He shook his head. "I worry."

"But you just met us!"

"Yes, dis is true, but I can see. I see many, many peoples. Poof! I know *now* what dey like. I see people's hearts. You two. Whoo, whoo. Careful."

He shook his head, drove for a few blocks then asked, "Womans. What your names?"

"Paula. I'm Paula. This is Claire."

"Poolla. Claire. Ahh…Claire I like." He looked in his rearview mirror and winked.

"Humph! You only like her because of her blonde hair!"

"Ah, Poolla, dat may be true. I like you too… but Claire!"

Amused, I smiled and winked back at him.

"Poolla. Claire. I give number. My taxi number. You call me, ok? I, Faisal, directed descendent of De Great Mohammad give you number! Any time, I will come. I worry. It not safe at palace. You call. I take shopping or any place. Ok?"

****

I tried to shake off the sleepiness of my restless night. I wrapped my robe around my waist, stretched then opened the bedroom door. Leslie greeted me as I walked into the living room.

"Where were you two yesterday?"

Her unfriendly tone surprised me. "Why do you want to know, Leslie?"

"While you were away, the servants ran around like crazy, cleaning, scrubbing and dusting, preparing for the Princess to return from the hospital."

"When's she coming back?"

"She's already here."

Paula came from around the corner, tying the belt on her robe. "Well, since it looks like you two have everything under control we'll let you continue. You're leaving tomorrow, aren't you? Claire and I have some things to sort out, so if you'll excuse me."

She marched into the kitchenette.

"Why doesn't she like us? She's snobby and always angry."

"I don't know. Don't worry, Leslie. You're leaving."

"Not fast enough. This is our last day, thank God," she said, exiting the villa.

Paula and I ate breakfast, dressed and walked down the long hallway to the Princess's suite. Princess Linyaa was propped up in her bed, surrounded by fluffy pillows. She looked pale and not her usual self with her hair tangled and nightgown wrinkled from the night before. On one side of the bed, I noticed a drainage bag for collection of urine.

The American nurses were not there. The servants communicated they had gone shopping.

"Well, that leaves things up to us!" Paula snapped.

"I'm going to examine her while we have a chance. Paula, help me ask the servants to stand back, please."

Paula spoke to them using dramatic gestures.

"Do you think they understand? They won't stop crowding me and I can't listen to her heart and lungs with all the shoving and chatter."

"They're afraid you're going to hurt the Princess. That stethoscope is scary for them and if you remember, the other nurses didn't have one."

I looked at an older woman who had a large, square figure and shoulder breadth that would have made two of me. She wasn't fat, just had one of the largest bone structures I had ever seen in a woman. Her hands were enormous and her commanding character and harsh tone enhanced her dominance. She portrayed misery in every movement, avoiding eye contact and never smiling. I made a mental note not to get on the wrong side of her. There was something about her I didn't trust.

Another large-framed woman refused to leave the Princess's side. She possessed an authoritative persona, but not like the first woman. She focused on her tasks and acted like she was shrouded in secrecy.

"What are these women's names?"

Paula spoke in Arabic and they looked surprised, then responded.

Paula introduced the larger woman. "This lady is Affaf."

"I Samira. I care Princess night."

"You speak English."

"Little. Affaf, no speak."

"I'm Claire and this is Paula."

She nodded, then turned to Affaf and said something in Arabic. Affaf growled and turned her attention to the Princess.

"We need to examine the Princess. Could you stand over there and ask the other women to back away?"

Paula repeated the request in broken Arabic. Affaf glared, then pausing for a moment, yelled at the other servants in the room. They looked scared and then scurried away. I put the stethoscope to my ears and communicated to the Princess I was going to examine her. The Princess nodded her head. I stepped closer and Affaf and Samira stood on either side of me.

"Could you please stand back? I can't move."

The women came closer and leaned on me.

"Paula, how am I supposed to do this? They won't stop crowding me."

"Move back! Back."

Affaf looked at Paula.

"They won't budge. This is impossible."

Paula said something in Arabic. Affaf responded.

"She won't, Claire. They're afraid you're going to hurt the Princess."

"That's ridiculous. I'm getting impatient with them."

Princess Linyaa squirmed. She raised her hand and spoke. Affaff answered. Paula said something. The Princess spoke and Affaf and Samira stood back, but just enough to give me elbowroom. I lifted the Princess's nightgown but Affaf stepped in and pushed me aside, ripping it off.

"Hey! Be careful! You could hurt her."

"She doesn't understand what you said."

"No, but she can see I'm displeased. Can you tell them we have to do things slowly? It's too easy to tear her fragile skin and as you know, with her diabetes it could lead to more serious problems."

Affaff glared at me.

I went through the routine of listening to her chest, checking her abdomen, assessing the swelling in her feet and the patency of the urinary drainage bag. I rubbed the Princess on the back, trying to reassure her. The Princess smiled. I looked up and saw Affaf scowling at me, her dark eyes dancing with rage.

From around the corner a servant woman entered the room carrying a warm bowl of water to begin the Princess's bath. Affaf pushed me out of the way.

"Hey!"

Affaf picked up the cloth, soaped it up and started to scrub. Her movements were rapid and the Princess looked like she was in pain. She moaned and fresh blood trickled down her side, staining the white sheet. Paula shrieked. I pushed my way past Affaf to have a closer look. The Princess's skin was torn.

"You can't wash her like that! Look what you did," yelled Paula.

Both women looked terrified for a moment, then Affaf tried to wash her again. I took the cloth from her hands.

"No you don't. Let me show you how this is done."

Affaf was visibly angry.

"Shawaya. Shawaya." Paula said in Arabic as she bandaged the bleeding area. "It means slowly, slowly."

The Princess smiled, nodded her head and repeated, "Shawaya."

Affaf and Samira snorted and refused to look at us.

"I didn't mean to upset them, Paula."

"I know. Maybe we can get someone to explain to them."

"I feel like we're fighting a war with these women and this morning we won a small battle."

"I hope every morning isn't going to be like this. Let's step back and let those servants waiting behind the door come in and do her hair and make up."

We walked into the sitting room adjacent to the bedroom and sat down.

"Paula, do hear someone whimpering? I'm going out to have a look."

I stepped into the hall, looked around and saw Joyce hidden in a corner, crying. I walked to the young woman and crouched down to face her. "Joyce, what's wrong?"

Joyce startled and looked embarrassed. She sighed, then said, "I don't know if I can trust you, but I have to talk to someone."

"Hush Joyce." I put my arm around the frail lady and led her to a settee against the wall. "You can trust me. I won't tell anyone anything if you don't want me to."

She hung her head. "Affaf won't let me eat today."

"What?"

She looked up. "Affaf and Samira said I didn't do my work well enough. He wouldn't let me have lunch. I wish I could go home."

"They tell you if you can eat or not?" I held her hand.

"Oh yes. They bosses of us ladies. They work with Princess for many years. Everyone under them and everyone have their place."

"You mean like seniority?"

"Seniority. Yes, that is it. I one of the last ones here. It is Affaf and Samira, then Noona and the others after that. Noona is another Philippine and she mean. Real mean."

Joyce whimpered.

I put my arm around her shoulders. "Oh Joyce, I'm sorry."

"Yes. Those chi girls? The ones who give out tea? They special. They not under Affaf. They get new costumes every month. They have to look nice to serve the Princess her guests. They have bedroom over there. See," she pointed. "We are in basement."

"Yes, I know. You showed me."

"Ah, yes. That is true."

I heard footsteps and looked up to find Paula glaring at Joyce. "What's going on?"

I turned to Joyce, "Is it ok if I tell Paula? She won't tell anyone."

Joyce eyed Paula, hung her head and nodded.

"Joyce was telling me that Affaf and Samira denied her food today because she didn't work hard enough."

"What? That's terrible." She knelt down and put her hand on Joyce's knee.

"Not just me. The others. There two slaves who haven't eaten in two days."

"Listen, I have an idea." I leaned closer to Paula and whispered, "Why don't we give these women the food we don't eat from the silver cart the cook leaves for breakfast and lunch? We don't eat it all and I'm sure that food is wasted."

"Yeah. Great idea."

Joyce stopped crying. A sparkle in her eyes appeared then vanished. "If I get caught…"

Paula stood up and put her hands on her hips. "Don't worry. Claire and I'll see what we can do. We'll talk to Prince Mohammad for you."

"Oh no!" Objected Joyce. "That makes things worse." Joyce trembled.

"What's wrong?"

"If we get caught with food, we will be punished." She put her hands on her cheeks and shook her head 'no'.

"Punished how?"

"They will beat us." She rocked back and forth.

I looked at Paula then back to Joyce again. "Joyce, we don't want to make things worse for you. Not to worry, we'll figure something out."

"No. No peace here. They just do it, beat us no reason sometime. We have no choice." Joyce cried. "I want to go home. I just wanted a simple life with my husband and my children."

"Then why did you come here?" asked Paula, turning her head to one side.

"We need money."

I scratched my head. "What about your children? Who's taking care of them?"

"My mother. He is looking after them. You see, we need money for the children. My husband, she isn't working. I go to agency in the Bilipines and get this contract. I have to finish before I get paid money."

I couldn't help smiling at the way Joyce expressed herself. I found it amusing how some Filipinos got their 'he's and she's' mixed up. My smile waned thinking of Joyce in her suffering. How I could help this poor soul? I stood up. "When will your contract end?"

"In one year. And I hope my husband, she doesn't send me back. I can't stand it. I just wanted a simple life." She buried her face in her hands.

I put my hand on her shoulder. "Hmm…how about we leave the food for you somewhere."

"Where Claire?"

"Do Affaf and Samira go to the basement?"

"Very little."

"Ok. Let's leave it by the dryer in the basement. We'll make it look like we're doing laundry and leave it there for you and the others. You'll make sure everyone gets some, won't you Joyce?"

"Oh yes! You very clever, Miss Claire. Thank you." Joyce jumped to her feet.

"Paula, I believe I have some laundry to do right now. Are you all right watching the Princess by yourself?"

"Of course."

I walked through the halls to the villa, ran to my room grabbed some of my clothes then went back to the cart by the window. A roll of paper towels was left on the table from breakfast. I opened the hinged doors and wrapped the food in the towels, hiding it in my clothes and headed towards the laundry room. Joyce waited beside the dryer. She accepted the small package, bowed to me and disappeared into the darkness.

I knew several women left their families and little children to come to Saudi in the hope of making a better life for themselves. They earned a good salary, up to five times what they could earn in their own country. Grandmothers raised their daughter's children, while the daughter works. When a Filipino woman was too old to work, then it was her turn to raise the children. They come there in good faith, with so many promises, but were lied to, denied their salaries, mistreated, raped and tortured when left in the hands of the Saudis. It's a miracle any survived to tell their stories. Their useless governments. They were more interested in political ties and money they got from trading with Saudi Arabia than the treatment of their own people. Disgusting. All for the sake of that almighty dollar. Poor Joyce. I hoped she'd find happiness one day. I chastised myself for complaining. I should be ashamed of myself.

Chapter Twelve

I sat outside, sipping a cup of tea, enjoying the coolness of the evening when Paula strolled through the French doors, swinging a shopping bag stuffed with her abaya. When she saw me, she skipped and quickened her pace, flopping in a chaise lounge beside me.

"Well, did you get it?"

"Look Claire! Isn't it the most wonderful cell phone you've ever seen? And Nils got it just for me." she pulled out a shiny silver object from the bag.

I didn't want to tell my friend that all cell phones looked the same to me, but took it from her hands and examined it, then handed it back. "What made you change your mind about Nils getting one for you? When you asked me to care for the Princess today, you ran out of here so fast we didn't have time to talk."

"Sorry for springing that on you, but Nils said he was in Jeddah for just a few hours. I didn't want to miss him. You understand, don't you?"

"I guess so, but you still haven't answered my question."

She sighed, looking at her phone and smiling. "Oh, I don't know. Seemed the prudent thing to do since we can't buy one for ourselves… and the hospital will take forever to get us one, that is if they agree to getting us one at all.

Paula stretched out on the chair, keeping her eyes on the phone, allowing her purse and bag to fall on the cement. She turned it over and over in her hands, opened the flap, pressed a few buttons, then closed it again.

"You better look after that. You wouldn't want to lose it," I said, amused at the way she treasured her new gift. "Cup of tea?"

"Sure. Thanks."

I stood up, shook my head and headed into the villa. When I returned, Paula was still admiring her phone. I gave her the cup, sat down and stared at the water in the swimming pool.

"Claire, can you believe the American nurses have been gone for over two weeks?"

"Time's flying and we've changed a lot of things around here, haven't we?"

"Yeah. It is always a struggle. Affaf and Samira are impossible. Thanks for getting up and helping me move the furniture around in the Princess's suite."

"Imagine blocking out the light and obscuring the view of her pool and garden."

"Even though she's blind, I think the Princess senses the change in atmosphere."

I turned my head towards the door and saw a servant approaching. "Hello, nuses? Princess Johara he want you."

I exchanged glances with Paula.

"Just wait a minute. I need to put these things away." Paula took a quick sip from her cup, picked up her purse and shopping bag then disappeared into the villa. When she returned we followed the servant into the Princess's room.

"Good evening. The servants of my mother-in-law complain. They say you take her outside, Paula?"

"Yes, Johara. She needs fresh air and she needs to get out of her room."

I added, "If Princess Linyaa doesn't have change, she may get sicker."

Johara's eyes widened. "You mean she will get worse?"

"It's a possibility."

Johara had a confused expression on her face and looked like she was searching for understanding. I didn't know how to explain. "Um…The Princess is blind. She's an intelligent person and listens to everything. She needs to feel warmth on her skin, or a breeze on her face. It'll help her know it's day instead of night and will stimulate her senses so she can stay sharp and prevent her from being depressed. If she's depressed, she'll continue her screaming at night. You don't want that, do you?"

Paula added, "Yes and Doctor Keerani said it's good for the Princess."

Princess Johara's expression changed. She snapped at the servants and they cowered.

I noticed Affaf glaring at Paula as if giving her a warning, as she half bowed. I shifted my weight from one foot to another feeling uncomfortable and wondered if we were crossing boundaries we shouldn't.

"If this is so, we shall take the Princess for a walk now!" Johara demanded.

The servants jumped to her commands. They gathered her scarf and shoes and prepared her for outdoors.

Linyaa was put in her wheelchair with a blanket over her knees and a veil over her hair. Paula stepped forward to push the wheelchair, but Affaf protested. Johara chastised her. She bowed, backed away, giving Paula a dirty look.

We headed out the front door manipulating the wheelchair down the ramp to the driveway accompanied by Affaf, Samira, Noona, Joyce and some others. Johara walked on the right side of Princess Linyaa and I was on the left. Affaf and Samira made several attempts to relieve Paula, but Johara reprimanded them. They crowded us, pushed and smothered us with their bodies.

"Stop!" Johara yelled, looking annoyed. "If they were my servants, I would replace them all!"

"They're hard to work with," Paula commented.

As we strolled down the driveway, I saw servants peeking from around corners and speaking in hushed voices.

Johara stuck her nose in the air. "They have never seen anything like this. The Princess has never come out."

"Never?"

"No. Saudi women are hidden in their palaces. These servants can't believe their eyes." Princess Johara shook her head and adjusted her scarf.

Women and children appeared from the small housing units bordering the driveway opposite the Princess's palace, lining up along the road like they were observing a parade. They bowed in reverence as we passed.

"They are not used to this." Johara said, looking uncomfortable.

Most of the women were elderly and I recognized some from the feeding frenzy after the evening dinners.

Paula tapped her fingers on the handles of the wheelchair. "My goodness. It's like a geriatric center!"

"Geri—attic?"

"Geriatric. A place for old people."

"Ah, yes. These are the servants that are too old to work. They have permission to live here until they die." Johara huffed. "They are useless. One looks after another. Those that are too old or weak and can't come into the palace to eat are given food by those who can. Princess Liynaa has a soft heart. If they were mine, they would not be here."

"Where would they be?" I asked.

Johara looked at me and her dark eyes hardened. I knew. The desert. The answer for many of the 'problems'. I thought about baby Nawaar...

The servants focused their attention on the Princess. They constantly checked to ensure the blanket was covering her knees and her scarf was on her head. They pressed against Paula, making it difficult to push the wheelchair. The crowding didn't last long. Unaccustomed to exercise, they lagged behind, breathless in their efforts to keep up.

The Princess lifted her head and put her face into the cool evening breeze. She took deep cleansing breaths and had a radiant look of distinct pleasure. Princess Liynaa said something in Arabic to Johara.

"She says she likes this very much. You two nurses are smart." Johara sighed. "I wish you here when I had my son and daughter."

"Your son and daughter?" asked Paula.

"Prince Mohammad and I had two children together. They were only fifteen and sixteen when they had a terrible car accident. My husband and I got to the scene as quickly as we could. Our son was killed instantly. Our daughter was still alive and I held her in my arms. No mother should have to hold their child and watch them die. She was beautiful and only fifteen. She was to marry that year." She hung her head. "I have suffered so much."

I put my hand on her arm. "I am so sorry." I knew her grief. That horrible, dark void entrenched in your soul. It hovers, consumes and when you least expect, thrashes you with the fresh sting of irreconcilable pain.

"Yes. Well it is over." Johara said, straightening her shoulders. "I have many beautiful things now. I deserve all that I have. We have a house on the beach. We have a house in the United States. I have a house in France. I deserve these things. I have suffered and I deserve the best."

"But Johara, your beautiful things can't take away your grief," I objected.

Johara stopped walking and glared at me. Her expression softened.

"You do not understand. In my culture, we do not dwell on the dead. It is forbidden.

We live as if they have never existed. It is true there is a time of mourning and some even hire professional mourners who weep and wail. This period is to last for a short time and then when the mourning is complete there is not to be any more crying or sadness. They are with Allah, and it is over."

I felt sorry for Johara and studied her. I could almost taste the anguish behind her sad brown eyes and feel the struggle she was having in living up to her principals. A human heart cannot shut itself off like that. I knew the pain of death and separation lasts for many years, if not forever.

"You must come and stay at our summerhouse. It is beautiful."

Paula's eyes lit up "Oh thank you. We would like that very much."

****

"I'm not getting much sleep these days with all the social activities. People forget when you're up nights, you have to sleep all day."

"I know Claire, but this is something you have to see. The Princess is dolled up and she's in much better spirits than she was last night."

"Have you been there when the King visited before?" I asked.

"Yes, last month, after the Americans left." She huffed.

"You didn't like the American nurses, did you?"

"They're Americans!"

"Yeah? So?"

"All Americans are arrogant and think they know everything. I haven't met an Australian who likes one yet. Always poking their noses into other country's business…"

"Paula! I like Americans. I love their positive attitude and the way they aren't afraid to take a risk. Their loyalty to their country and neighbor is outstanding and they're the first to lend a helping hand if there's a disaster."

"I think they cause disasters."

"Do you know any Americans?"

"Not personally, but…"

"Well how can you say that? I know several Americans. They're great fun and great friends. As a matter of fact, my grandmother was American."

"Oh, I'm sorry."

"It's ok. We just have to be careful about stereotyping. Just like I don't think all Australians are criminals and all Arab men are pigs."

"Australia is not my heritage, you know."

"I know and being a Canadian isn't mine. My parents immigrated to Canada, just like yours immigrated to Australia."

"I didn't know."

"You didn't ask."

A servant burst into the villa looking nervous. "Nuses! Where you? He here! She here! Come quickly!"

We laughed. I put my shoes on and followed Paula to the living room. The Princess looked regal and elegant.

"Wow, Paula! She's gorgeous. I haven't seen her look so radiant before."

"I know. She's different when she knows her husband is coming."

Linyaa appeared more alert with color in her cheeks, making an effort to sit tall and straight in her chair. Her hair was freshly died with henna and in two long braids, one hanging over each shoulder. She wore the finest jewelry and dressed in one of her best gowns.

We sat down in empty chairs beside her. Paula turned to one of the servant's and said, "She's ready. You can ask them to bring in the King."

Five male servants pushed King Jabbar into the room. Like the female attendants, they fussed and fretted over him and subsided when he raised his hand and waved them away.

My heart sank when I saw the man's depraved condition. He was ghostly white and a constant stream of drool flowed from his mouth. His eyes drooped like a bloodhound's and it appeared as if he had cataracts, giving them a glassy appearance. He slumped to one side, looking exhausted from sitting in his wheelchair and weary from his main attendant lifting him to prevent slouching. Occasionally the servant wiped his mouth with a towel. My first instinct was to talk to the doctor about getting proper nursing care, but then remembered the King refused it. I now understood Dr. Keerani's dilemma.

The male servant was expressionless. He placed the Prince's wheelchair as close to Princess Liynaa as possible, being careful not to allow their knees to touch.

I smiled, in awe of the longevity of their sixty-year marriage. They never uttered a sound and I supposed neither one of them could see. They appeared happy knowing they were in each other's presence and it was enough.

The male servant looked at his watch. He pulled King Jabbar away from Princess Liynaa and centered him in the room. Children appeared from the outer hall and formed a single line. The King barked an order silencing the scruffy youngsters and another male servant rushed into room carrying a black leather bag. He pulled out a large wad of bills.

One child was forced to go towards the King, who held out his hand. The little boy hesitated, then kissed the back of it. The male servant handed King Jabbar some money and he then gave to the child. The little boy ran back to his mother and gave her the bills, hiding himself in her skirt.

I leaned over and whispered, "Isn't the King generous?"

"Generous? The King is giving the servant's wages to their children." Paula scoffed.

"What? To the children?"

"Yeah. Watch the young boys. Even though their mother earned the wage, if the boy is the eldest male in the family, he can decide if he should keep the money for himself or give it to his mother."

"What a strange way to pay your servants."

"The women who have husbands in Saudi have to give the money to them. It just doesn't seem fair. Some of them work so hard."

The children kissed the King's hand one by one and after receiving the money, scurried back to their mothers. The older boys counted it. Most gave a portion of it to their anxious mothers; others kept it. As soon as the bills disappeared, the servants and their children exited as quickly as they came in.

Prince Mohammad and another man entered the room.

I turned to Paula. "Who's he?"

"He's another one of the sons. Abdulrockman."

They greeted their father with enthusiasm, then their mother. They sat in chairs underneath their portraits and then the male servant wheeled King Jabbar to his place between them. His servant made another attempt at straightening him in his chair and wiped his mouth.

"Now what are they doing?"

"Today is the day when the subjects of King Jabbar come to plead their case. They travel from all over the country to have an annual audience with the King or his sons."

"How do you know all this?"

"Dr. Keerani told me. He had to assess King Jabbar to see if he was strong enough today to sit an audience because if he isn't, the Princes have to continue without him." She shifted in her chair. "Dr Keerani also said some families hire a representative who is a specialist, skilled in begging before the King."

"What's the audience for?"

"This is how some royal families distribute the wealth to their subjects. It's a yearly allotment for clothes, food, shelter, medical expenses and that sort of thing. If someone is sick in the family, they may get a signed certificate allowing them to go to Faisal Hospital for treatment. In some special cases, the royal family will pay for medical care in the US, France or Germany."

"Do they come all this way just for money or medical favors?"

"No. If there are disputes between families, the Royals intervene. If a father wants his daughter to marry a man who is under the authority of another royal family, they have to get permission and then the two royal families debate which royals the young couple belong to."

"It sounds complicated and an odd way of doing business."

"Yeah, but they have been doing it for centuries. Dr. Keerani also said this royal family is kind. There are some who are not so generous."

Abdulrockman looked at his father. He spoke to Mohammad and then yelled out an order. The doors to the living room closed and a man entered, bowing as he approached, greeting the royals with the customary salutations. He burst into a dramatic performance and when finished, he lay face down, motionless on the floor. The Princes whispered, then handed him a wad of bills. He backed away, bowing and exited the same way he entered.

Man after man came before the Royals, each demonstrating desperation, pleading their case.

Fascinated, I put a hand over my mouth, holding back laughter as the men spoke with exaggerated motions and hysterics, imploring, cowering and begging. It took several minutes for them to conduct their dramatic performance, looking up to the heavens, shaking their heads 'no', pleading in woeful voices then making themselves small and throwing themselves at the feet of the Royals.

"Doesn't it remind you of the Biblical Stories of the Kings of the Old Testament?" I whispered.

"Shh," replied Paula, suppressing a smile.

Face down at the feet of the Princes, they waited as the brothers discussed how much money they would give him. Most of the men appeared pleased as they exited. When the door opened for the next man to come in, I caught a glimpse of some of them in the hallway counting their cash.

Prince Abdulrockman raised his hand. "Hallas!" He turned and spoke to his servant who put the money away and wheeled King Jabbar out of the room.

"My father, he is tired." Abdulrockman said, addressing us.

I looked at Liynaa. Her face fell when she realized Prince Jabbar was gone.

"We should take the Princess back to her room."

"Let her servants. I want talk to you." Abdulrockman said, then turned and spoke to his brother Mohammad. Paula and I waited.

"So. What you think of this…this financial business?"

"It's interesting. I understand you do it every month?" I answered.

"I am Abdulrockman. The second oldest son. Next to Mohammad, you understand? I come all the way from Riyadh today just for this!"

I wasn't sure if he was angry or expressive.

"This is important. I am, how you say? Accountant. Yes, Accountant. It my job to look after wealth in family."

"My brother is responsible for a great many things. We have many people to think about."

Prince Turki added, "Yes, yes. Over ten thousand. We listen to many people. They have so much problems."

Paula flipped her hair over her shoulder. "It looks like you see several people in one day. How many families did you help today?"

"We hear over one hundred cases in an hour! We will hear more now and into the night. Then we do the same next month."

"That is enough." Prince Mohammad said. "You have report on my mother tomorrow morning. Go now!"

We looked at each other, got up and left the room.

****

"I'll keep good watch over her tonight. See you in the morning," I said to Paula as we changed shifts. I picked up the chart and flipped through Paula's notes. Nothing unusual.

Affaf came up to me holding a blanket. "Here. You sleep."

"No, Affaf." I shook my head.

"You sleep."

She knew I never slept when I was on duty and wondered why Affaf was here instead of Samira. Samira usually worked with me at night.

Affaf grabbed my arm and led me to a reclining chair in the room beside the bedchamber. "Princess Sleep. You sleep." She threw the blanket at me.

I was afraid to argue with her, especially since we were alone. I didn't trust her and Affaf seemed impatient.

I heard a door close . Samira walked into the suite clutching a large handbag under her arm. She looked at me, half smiled and sat down beside Affaf at a table in the far corner of the room. I felt uncomfortable watching Samira and Affaf engage in a hushed, but animated conversation. They kept looking at me. I wondered what they were discussing and felt my stomach knot.

An old women entered the suite. She didn't stop to read the Qu'ran or sit at the Princess's side as usual, but ignored Linyaa and huddled with Samira and Affaf in the corner, joining them in hushed dialogue. Every few minutes one of the women looked at me. A cold chill went down my back. What were they doing? I noticed the guilty looks on their faces and hoped they weren't conspiring against me.

I got up from the chair, walked to the Princess and checked on her, trying to look casual. The Princess was in a deep sleep, her breathing steady. I placed my hand on her arm. She was warm and looked peaceful.

The women stopped talking. Affaf and Samira approached me, one standing either side of me. "You sleep!"

It was more of a command than a request. Affaf reached out and taking firm hold of my arm, pulled me to the chair. "You sleep!"

Samira scowled at Affaf, then turned and looked at me. "It ok. Princess sleep. We wake if she need you. Please. Sleep."

My curiosity was peeked, but settled into the chair. I was afraid to cross Affaf; the woman could kill me with her bare hands. I sensed they were planning something and got the feeling the less I knew, the better.

They went back to the table and taking turns peering at me, continued with their secretive discussion. Samira stood beside Affaf attempting to block my view, shifting from one foot to the other. Her swollen ankles poured over her shoes and I assumed they were painful. Samira transferred her weight one more time and looked over her shoulder. I pretended I was absorbed in the chart. Samira moaned, then reached for a chair and pulled it close to the table struggling to sit down.

Another woman wandered in. She took a quick look at me and pointed. Affaf made a gesture as if to ignore me then she walked over and sat with them. Their hushed voices rose and fell in an excited exchange. It sounded like they were negotiating something, but I didn't know what. I pretended to fall asleep.

The room was dark, but the dimmed overhead lights had enough illumination for me to see what they were doing. I knew I had to be careful. I was in a darker portion of the suite, so they wouldn't be able to see me as clearly as I could see them. When I felt they weren't looking, I peeked at them through my eyelashes. Sometimes I covered my eyes with my hand and peered through my fingers. I watched and waited, forcing my breath to go in and out rhythmically. I wanted them to believe I was asleep. My interest heightened when I saw Affaf reach under the table, pull out a sum of money and give it to the woman. The woman's eyes widened. She looked around then stuffed the money under her abaya.

Woman after woman came in. They spoke in hushed tones for a few moments, like they were negotiating and then left with carefully counted bills. What were they doing?

I counted twenty-seven women parading through the Princess's chambers that evening. When they had all gone, I saw Affaf clinging onto a large stack of cash in the palm of her enormous hand. Affaff counted out several more bills and handed them to Samira, who then took them and put them in her purse. Affaf stuffed the rest of the money in the large bag Samira brought in earlier and left.

I was astonished. Where did they get the money? Why so secretive?

Daylight was seeping under the curtains. I stretched, got out of the chair and stood by the Princess. She was still sleeping. Samira pulled a chair beside her bed, opened a drawer and reached for the Qu'ran.

"Samira, I'm going to the villa. Are you all right with the Princess?"

"Yes. I call if something wrong."

I raced to the villa, threw open the door and called out, "Paula? Paula! You up?"

"Yes. In the kitchen." She came out with a hot beverage. "You want some coffee? It's fresh. Goodness! You look pale. Is everything all right?"

"I don't know. I've been scared to death all night."

"Why?"

"Last night woman after woman came into the bedroom while Affaf and Samira handed them money. I don't know what it was all about, but they didn't want me to know about it. I had to pretend I was asleep."

"What?" Paula said, scratching her head. " Oh…a check for the Princess came yesterday. I wonder if they cashed the Princess's check?"

"But how can they do that?"

"I remember Samira talking to the Princess and she got her to sign it. I didn't think anything of it at the time."

"Maybe Affaf and Samara are responsible for the Princess's finances."

"I don't think so. There was a man who came to the palace yesterday looking for the check, but Samara and Affaf had taken a taxi downtown."

I rubbed my chin. "Do you think they stole the Princess's money?"

"I don't know."

"Hmm…we should tell Prince Mohammad." I paced. "I think we have to be careful. When we have our weekly meeting with him, I will just tell him what I saw. We don't know anything more than what we saw."

"You're right. I think we better keep our ears and eyes open."

"We know nothing. We see nothing."

"Right!"

****

I nestled in bed, about to go to sleep when there was a knock on my bedroom door.

"Claire? Sorry to bother you, but get dressed and come to the Princess's room."

"Oh…I'm doomed to be sleep deprived!"

I threw on my uniform and met Paula in the hall outside the Princess's bedchamber.

"I told the doctor what you told me about last night. He wants to speak to you immediately."

Dr. Keerani came from around the corner.

"Good Morning." He said. "Come."

He rushed us into one of the rooms beside the bedchamber. He ensured no one was near enough to hear and started to close the door. He opened it again, poked his head out one more time, then shut the door tight. In a hushed voice he said, "Paula told what you see last night."

"You seem worried, Doctor."

"Yes, yes." Dr. Keerani's cheeks went red. "You must be careful. Do not let anyone know you saw dese dings."

I yawned. "What's going on?"

"Let me tell you first. De Princess, she get check every month from King. Very big money, um… One hundred dousand American dollars."

I felt my jaw drop. I exchanged looks with Paula.

"Yes. Yes. He give her dis for many years. She is free to spend her money as she wants. When Princess got ill, she trusted Affaf and Samira wid money to buy dings for house. You know, dates, tea, cleaning supplies. Dey also buy material and give to tailor to make chi girls deir dress."

"Did the Princess entrust the whole check to Affaf?"

"She not to have check! She to give it to accountant," he huffed.

I scratched my head. "I don't understand. Who brings the Princess her check?"

"The assistant to Prince Abdulrockman. He fly from Riyadh and give check to Princess. She give check to accountant."

Paula put her hands on her hips. "Well, if the check is to go to the accountant, why is it given to the Princess?"

"You don't understand. It is very important Princess hold de check, or she dink King not give her money."

I cocked my head. "But how did Affaf and Samira get the check, and how did they cash it?"

"It is not so difficult. Everyone knows dey are number one servant to Princess Liynaa. When she got sick, dey allowed to go to bank and cash check. I dink Affaf gave banker money, you know, make him cooperative."

I put my arm around my waist. "Wouldn't the accountant be looking for the check when he came to see the Princess?"

"Ah. You very smart. Some month Princess get no money, so if check not dere, he does not worry."

The doctor got up and opened the door. He stuck his head out into the hall and looked around. He shut the door and sat down. "Dis is not first time she do dis ding. She very clever. Only take um…, two, maybe dree check a year."

"That's stealing!" I protested.

"Shhh…this is very serious. You look at Affaf and Samira. Dey big powerful women, yes?"

We nodded our heads and the doctor continued, "Dey mean to others in dis house. How do you dink dey get cooperation? Samira and Affaf pay servants wid Princess's money. Dey bribe and do bad dings. You must not tell anyone of dese dings."

I put my hand on my cheek. "But Dr. Keerani, what I saw was wrong.

Shouldn't we tell someone?"

"You do not know dese womens. Dey have stone hearts. Black hearts."

Paula asked, "How do you know all this?"

"A old woman. She used to be Princess's servants. She got sick and she told me dese dings before she die. She frightened and made me promise not to tell. For many, many months now I have silently watched. Dey do not know I know them, and I watch. It has been a terrible ding."

"So you've kept her secret?"

"Yes, until now. You must be careful" The doctor leaned closer and whispered, "Others have disappeared. Dey take dem to desert."

"I still think Prince Mohammad should know."

He stepped back. "You are right, of course." Dr. Keerani paced. "Yes, yes. He should know. You must be careful. I will help, but we must wait for time to be right, so you will be safe."

Paula went white. "Dr. Keerani, if we do tell the Prince, what about the others? Are they a threat as well, or are Samara and Affaf the only ones we have to watch?"

"Dey all dangerous. No. You will not tell the Prince. Dat is too dangerous. I will tell. Affaf and Samira will be punished, de others too. You will be in danger. But if it is done right, you will be safe. You must not say anything until right time. You must not speak."

"I don't understand, Doctor."

Dr. Keerani seemed agitated. "No! You not tell. I tell Prince. You must trust me. I do right thing. I tell him and then you be safe. De servants will not know what you see. I will wait for time to be right. When next check comes, perhaps."

I stiffened. "What about you? Won't you be in danger?"

"Not if we do it right so dey caught in deceit." He paused. "I have plan." Dr. Keerani's mood lightened. "Yes, yes. I have plan! You will see."

"But Dr. Keerani …"

"Ahh." He smiled and clapped his hands together, looking up to the ceiling, "I have prayed for very long time to stop dis lies. You two are my answers! Praise be to Allah!"

Dr. Keerani leaned towards us, his cheeks burning hot, "You not tell anyone. No one. Please. It very, very dangerous."

"You have our word, doctor."

Paula nodded. The doctor seemed satisfied and opened the door. I went back to the villa.

It took me a long time to fall asleep. I understood the doctor's concern for our welfare. Money is a powerful tool and if the members of the household were cut off from their little scheme, who knows what would happen to us. We were two strangers among powerful and dangerous women. My first instincts about Affaf and Samira were correct; they were not to be trusted.

Chapter Thirteen

I snuggled into the king-sized bed, shut my eyes and drifted into a light slumber when I thought I heard something.

"Claire? Wake up."

I did hear something. I looked at the clock. It was one o'clock in the afternoon. Only five hours sleep.

"What is it?"

Paula opened my bedroom door. "I had to send the Princess to hospital."

"What?" I threw back the covers.

"No! No, it's ok. She had a reaction to a medication and the nurses on the VIP unit are looking her after. Why don't you get up? I thought we'd get Faisal, the taxi driver and go for a ride or something before going to see her."

"Oh…I need to wake up a bit."

"Don't rush. I'll put the kettle on for tea and you can make us a cup. Ok?"

"I guess I'm destined not to sleep."

"You poor thing. Now that she's in hospital, you don't have to work at night."

We had tea and then I washed and dressed. We walked out the front gate and waited in the heat for Faisal. He pulled up in his taxi, jumped out and held the door for us while we crawled in the back. I was relieved to sit in the cool of an air-conditioned vehicle.

"Where you want go?"

"Anywhere. We just want to go for a drive," Paula said.

"Ok. I take you round city. Many dings to see."

Paula wiggled in her seat, then asked, "Are you married. Faisal?"

"Ah ha! You looking for husband? I have two wives."

"Two?"

"Yes. I come from Jordan. It is beautiful place. I have one wife in Jordan. She my first cousin. I no like her." He made a sour face.

"Why did you marry her if you didn't like her?" asked Paula.

"She is my father's brother child. She not all there."

I smiled. "What do you mean?"

"There something wrong. She born with difficulties. Her mind is whoo whoo." Faisal said making circular motions with his hand, pointing to his head.

Paula gasped. She asked, "She has mental problems?"

"Yes. Yes. She also has, how you say, drool from mouth. But she knows what she wants. We fight. Every time I see her we fight."

I tilted my head and frowned. "Why did you marry her?"

"It is my duty. You see, I am firstborn son. She is firstborn daughter of my uncle. If I do not marry, she be without husband. She need husband to look after her. But I hate her."

"Oh Faisal, that's terrible." I put my hand over my mouth.

"No Claire. Not terrible. My duty. I give her house. I give her money to live. I will never give her a children!" He opened his window and spat. "She get a beat and she be good."

"You beat her?" Paula leaned forward.

"Yes, of course. Every good husband give a beat to his wife. They need know who is boss. I am de boss and my first wife needs to be told often." He said with authority. "I let her argue so much," he said putting his index finger an inch away from his thumb, representing a small measurement. He swerved, missing a curb.

"Ha! Ha. I cannot drive and dink about her. She make me angry. Very angry. We have accident." He frowned.

Paula pressed, "You said she's your cousin."

"Yes. I am directing descendent from Holy Mohammad Himself! I have special duty, in marriage to this cousin." He pointed one finger in the air. "Ah…, but I have another wife. She I like. She no get beat very much. She good wife." He said, smiling.

"What do your wives think about each other?"

"Dey not know about one another. One is in Jordan, the one I hate. One lives here. In Jeddah. We have first baby soon."

I looked out the window was thankful I was from a different society where women had choices for mates and where kinship marriages and polygamy outlawed. I thought about Princess Liynaa and how her heart was broken when her husband took another wife. She didn't speak to him for years, especially when he built her an identical palace on the same property. It was wise of him to keep his two wives in separate countries, just as Faisal is doing. Even women in this society do not want to share their man with another woman.

****

I entered the hospital suite with Paula following at a close distance. The Princess seemed comfortable but looked gaunt. Prince Mohammad was at her bedside and looked up as I approached.

"You safe my mother's life. Two times. You be rewarded."

I looked down at my feet. "No, no Prince Mohammad."

"Oh yes, yes. Ah! You don't want? Ok .ok. Just look at my mother."

Affaf and Samara huddled over her fluffing her pillows. Paula asked them in Arabic to move aside. They didn't budge. Prince Mohammad shouted at them. They hesitated, sneered, then obeyed.

Princess Linyaa mumbled. Prince Mohammad turned to me and said, "She want in chair."

"Her wheelchair?" I scratched my head. "She doesn't look well and I don't think it's a good idea."

"You put in chair!"

"We better do it Claire."

We prepared her and Mohammad left. A few moments after the door closed, some of the servants came rushing in.

Paula looked at me. "I thought Mohammad told them to get out."

"I know. Let's just transfer her, but we won't leave her sitting for too long."

The servants came close, pushing and rubbing against me. A large servant pulled a smaller woman out of the way.

Paula stopped what she was doing and said, "That's Sada. I have to fight with her in the mornings."

"I can see why. Does she understand any English?"

"I'm sure she understands 'get back'. I shout it enough."

Sada tried to push me out of the way.

"Hey, wait a minute! Get back!"

She pushed again. Paula glared at her. "Get back! Leave Claire alone!"

Sada came closer to me and stood at my right side. I noticed Affaf and Samira with smirks on their faces.

"Get back, Sada!"

She took one step back and I strapped the sling around the Princess. "Ok Paula, you can pump the lift now. I have her on this side."

We lifted the Princess from the bed using the hydraulic lift and carried her to the wheelchair. The Princess was suspended in the air and only inches away from being lowered into the chair. I was about to undo one of the Princess's safety straps when Sada reached across my face. I tried to throw the Princess into place as Sada pulled on my shoulder, spinning me around.

"She tried to make me drop the Princess!"

Paula put her hands on her hips. "I saw that! Sada, get back!"

I was angry. "How dare you do that to me. Get out!" I pointed towards the door. "Get out of this room!"

Sada pretended she didn't understand.

Paula stepped forward and shouted, "Get out! Get out of here!"

Samira said something to Sada in Arabic. She backed off a little, but didn't leave. The Princess moaned. I turned towards her to see what was wrong. Paula ignored the women and went to Linyaa's other side and as I approached the Princess, Sada stepped up and hit me.

My world went black and I was surprised to find myself sprawled on the floor. My side ached and I screamed out in pain. I heard Paula shriek. It hurt to breath in. I curled up in a ball, rocking back and forth.

"Claire!" Paula rushed over and knelt at my side.

"Oh...it hurts."

The other servants shouted, running in and out of the room.

I rolled on my back and little by little extended my legs. I was able to breath again. I waited, then sat up and stared into the icy cold eyes of Sada glaring down at me. Sada backed up. I was breathing hard and could feel pounding in my neck. I got to my feet.

Paula gasped, "Are you all right?"

I looked long and hard at Sada. I clutched my side, restraining myself from attacking the woman.

A nurse ran into the room. "What's all the shouting?" She covered her mouth and cried, "Oh my god! What's going on?"

I didn't realize I was shaking and my nose bleeding. "That woman. Sada. She struck me. I want her out of here. Where's security?"

Out of the corner of my eye I saw Affaf hanging back in a corner, laughing. Was she responsible for this attack? I turned and looked into Affaf's eyes. Her eyes glittered with contempt and she wrinkled her nose, looking smug.

Two men in dark blue uniforms charged into the room. "What happened? You Bleed!"

"Where's Sada? She's not going to get away with this," Paula said, wagging her finger.

The nurse put her arm around my shoulder, "You better sit down. Come over here."

I stopped, looked over my shoulder and scanned the people in the room. "Where's Sada?"

"She must have left," Paula said.

Paula took security to one side and explained what happened. She then turned and said, "Prince Mohammad will hear of this. There will be no more. You understand?"

Affaf's grin disappeared. She folded her arms across her chest and huffed.

"You look shaken," said one of the nurses. "Come with me. I'll get you something to drink."

The security guards approached me. "You have to fill out incident report."

As the security guards turned to leave, I overheard one Arab guard say to the other, "Just like woman to cause trouble."

I washed up in the staff bathroom and returned to the Princess's suite. Linyaa was back in bed and Affaf and Samira sat on either side of her, reading the Qu'ran. Paula was on the other side of the room flipping through a magazine. She looked up. "Are you all right, Claire?"

"Yeah, I'm fine. Just a little shaken, that's all."

"We should go back to the villa. There's nothing more we can do today and I know some of the servants are getting a ride back to the palace." She put the book down and turned to Affaf. "Affaf, you coming?"

"Um…I stay night."

"I stay too." Samira added.

"Ok. We'll see you in the morning."

They nodded and continued reading to the Princess.

Paula and I stepped off the elevator, walked to the exit and looked around. "Where's the van?"

Paula shrugged. "I was told they were waiting for us."

"Should we wait or call Faisal?"

"Let's call Faisal."

****

"Hello womans!"

"Faisal, you're always in a good mood."

"Ah, but I like to be here for you. You make my day, how you say? Happy."

I giggled.

He opened the rear door of the car and Paula climbed in first.

"Miss Claire, please come to other side."

I stepped down from the curb and felt a sharp pain go from my side into my back. I clutched my ribs. "Oh! Ow!"

Faisal grabbed my arm. "You ok?" He furrowed his brow and looked concerned.

"Thank you Faisal. I'm ok." I leaned against the car.

"She is not! One of the servants hit her and pushed her down."

"What?" Faisal jumped back. " Princess Liynaa servant? She hit you? Which, which womans did hit?"

"Faisal, don't worry about it. It's over, and I'm ok. Are you going to open my door?"

"No, it not ok. Which womans?" He made fists and boxed the air. "Which one? I protect you."

"She's not here, now get Claire into the car and let's go."

He stopped prancing. "Oh yes, yes. Miss Claire, get in. You ok? I don't like it der are problems. I worry. I worry for you Poola, but most especially for Claire."

He closed the door.

"I think he likes you, Claire."

"Oh Paula, you think everyone likes me."

"I wasn't wrong about the last one, was I?"

I gave her a dirty look.

Faisal got into the front seat and turned the key.

Paula continued, "I didn't tell you before, Claire, but I was hit hard in the ribs by a different servant the day before."

Faisal looked at Paula through the rear view mirror. "Dis is not good. You two must be careful."

"What do we have to be careful of?"

"It is a fact dat de womans of Princess Liynaa Palace have black hearts. Dey dangerous."

I rubbed my side. "How do you know about them?"

"Ah, everyone knows royal family and deir business. You forget. She have many peoples working for her. Dere are many spies."

"Spies?" I gasped.

Paula smiled. "You make it sound like we're in a mystery novel."

We giggled.

"No! No. I tell you it is true. You forget. Saudi has many tribes and people who know people. You understand? Dere is talk. We know what happens behind palace walls. It is not so secret."

"We haven't done anything. We're here to help," Paula said.

"Dat may be so, but I tell you dis. You are not Muslim. You are threat because you are pretty and smart. You have favor of Prince Mohammad and you must tell him."

I frowned. "A threat? We want to work *with* them, not *against* them."

"You know dis. I know dis, but dey do not trust. You be very, very careful."

Faisal drove in silence for a long time. He looked out the side window and chewed on his fingernails. He spit out a nail and said, "I thinking. You must tell Prince Mohammad. You need protection. Let me give you advice. Dese people like wolves. Prince Mohammad is big wolf. You understand? You little chirpy birds that sit on back of de great wolf and whisper in his ear. No! You must demand. Prince Mohammad is wolf. You must be bigger wolf. Dat is how it done."

"But that's not our way, Faisal." I cleared my throat. "We'll tell Prince Mohammad. He's kept the servants in order for us when they get out of control."

"Ha! I tell you. You like birds dat land on de back of big wolf and whisper in ear. Whisper is no good. You must be like big wolf! Bigger wolf than de Prince! You must demand and then you will see. Dese servants, Dey be good. Dey wont' hurt you. But now, you must be careful. Prince Mohammad not dinking you serious. He must beleef you serious, or dese servants won't do as he say. Dey trouble."

I was perplexed. Was Faisal making this up to scare us, or was what he said true?

"Here." Faisal said after a few moments. "Dis is my private mobile number. Here is one for you, and one for you." He gave us each a piece of yellow paper.

"You put it close to heart."

Paula reached for her purse.

"No. I say close to heart. You woman, you understand?"

I smiled and looked at Paula who was also smiling. We tucked the piece of paper in our underclothes.

****

Paula and I turned the corner to the hall that led to our villa when we saw Affaf come out of the kitchen. She seemed surprised, then brushed by. I shrugged. "I don't think I've seen Affaf in the kitchen before."

"Maybe it has something to do with her money transactions."

"Shh!"

"I thought she said she was going to stay at the hospital tonight."

"I don't know, Paula."

When I got into my bedroom, I had the strangest feeling someone had been in there. I knew the servants came in daily to make up the bed and clean the bathroom, but my clothes were disturbed. I opened the drawers in the closet and eyed my belongings. I had hidden a nurse's watch in one of my pant pockets. It was gone. I went into the bathroom and checked my makeup and other toiletries. My new facial cream was missing. I knew I left it there this morning. I felt my skin crawl. It disturbed me someone had taken my things, not that they had much value.

Exhausted, I settled into bed and closed my eyes. I just got comfortable when I heard a scream. Bolting out of bed and grabbing my housecoat, I ran towards Paula's room, coming face-to-face with one of the male servants.

"This man came into my room!" Paula shrieked, struggling with her robe.

I looked at him and pointed, "Get out!"

He didn't move. He folded his arms across his chest and grinned.

"Get out!"

"He won't move!"

"Paula, look out, he's coming at you!"

The man reached for Paula's robe and pulled on it. Paula struggled and screamed. I kicked him. He thrust me back with a sweep of his arm and I landed on the floor. Paula backed away and he chased her, making her fall on the bed. I got to my feet, looking for something to hit him with.

I ran into the kitchen and grabbed a frying pan. When I came back, the man was trying to pull off Paula's pajama bottoms. Paula screamed, struggling against him. I came up behind him and whacked him in the head. He pulled back, rubbed his head then stood up.

"Don't you even think about coming after me!"

Paula lay motionless on the bed, breathing hard.

"Paula! Get up! Kick him!"

The man tried to grab me. I hit him in the face. He stumbled back and I hit him again on the arm, then again and again, striking him anywhere I could reach.

"Ok! Ok!"

"Get out!"

"You prostitutes!"

"No! No we're not!"

He backed out of the bedroom shielding his face with his hands. "Ok. No! I leave!"

I hit him again and he turned and ran out the door.

I stood in one spot staring after the stranger, trying to catch my breath. Turning around, I saw I was alone. Where was Paula? I walked to her room. She was still lying on the bed. "Paula? Are you all right?"

No answer.

"Paula?"

Paula turned away from me and cried.

"Paula? Look at me."

She sighed then rolled over and sat up. "He…he tried to rape me."

"I know. He thought we were prostitutes. We have to fight, Paula. Fight with everything we have. These men aren't used to women standing up for themselves. That's how my roommate Rose survived the jail ordeal. She fought tooth and nail and we should do the same." I picked up the robe on the floor and handed it to her. "Come and help me. I want to move that overstuffed chair to block the door."

Paula didn't move.

"Paula, it is over. We're safe."

"I know." She put the robe on.

"Is anything missing from your room?"

"I don't know. Why?"

"Someone went through my things today. I'm not worried about what they took. They can have them, but I'm concerned our privacy has been invaded."

Paula looked shocked. "I didn't look."

"Well, after you help me push that chair, why don't you go and check your room and I'll make us a cup of tea. I don't think either one of us can sleep right now."

We shoved the heavy chair against the door then I went into the kitchen, made the tea and carried two mugs into the living room. Paula was on the couch looking forlorn.

"Paula, I think it's wise to heed Faisal's words. We have to be careful and I'm still wondering what Affaf was doing in the kitchen. We should keep our eyes open and our mouths shut."

"I think Prince Mohammad should know. I'm missing some clothes and jewelry."

"When we have our meeting in three days from now, we need to tell him about the difficulties we're having with the servants, especially the hitting and pushing."

Paula pouted. "Yeah. I also don't want any men in our villa, ever.".

"I agree."

****

Paula and I walked through the palace towards one of the sitting areas where we waited with the servants for the morning ride to the hospital. When Paula and I entered the room, the servants stopped talking and stared. Their silence was unusual.

The van arrived and the side doors slid open. The servants filed out of the palace and into the bus. I followed and started to climb in when one of the servants grabbed the sleeve of my abaya.

"You no come."

"What?"

"You no come."

Affaf came from inside the palace and said, "No room!"

She climbed aboard and closed the door. The van drove off, leaving us behind.

"Hmm. This isn't good. There was plenty of room in that van."

Paula crossed her arms. "They want the Prince to think we're late, or not coming."

"There's something we can do about that, isn't there?" I marched into the palace and picked up the phone. An Arabic male operator answered and recognizing my voice, hung up.

I tried calling him again. He hung up.

"What is going on? Why won't he answer me?"

I saw one of the tea girls. "Paula, ask her if she'll dial the number for us and connect us to Mowark."

The tea girl was happy to help. I took the phone from her when she got a connection. "Hello, Mowark?"

"Dis nurse? But how you phone? You called me?"

"Mowark you seem surprised. Is there a problem?"

"Uh…no problem."

"There's some confusion at the palace this morning. We need someone to take us to the hospital."

"I no can take. De driver having tea. When tea finished, it is prayer. No one take you."

I hung the phone up and stood motionless, staring at the receiver. "This is strange and I don't like it. Paula, they're trying to keep us away but they won't. I'm calling Faisal." I picked up the phone. "Great."

"What?"

"The phone lines are dead."

"What? What are they trying to do? Cut us off?"

"Are we getting paranoid?" I wrapped my arm around my waist.

"It's just weird. First the attempted rape, the missing articles in our rooms, refusal to allow us in the van and now the lines are dead. I'm scared."

"Don't give in, Paula. We will fight them. Stand our ground and be independent." I scratched my chin. "You have a cell phone. Use it."

" It's expensive and I'm saving the minutes for Nils."

I sighed. "I'll pay you for the minutes, but if we don't call Faisal, we're stuck."

"Oh…ok."

I studied Paula. In a crises Paula was unable to think…unable to plan…unable to react. I felt burdened, realizing I couldn't depend on her in an emergency.

****

I sensed the servant's change in mood when I stepped into the Princess's room. They appeared happier and weren't crowding me as usual. Paula stood beside me looking confused.

Dr. Keerani knocked on the door and then entered the hospital suite. He greeted the Princess and told servants to leave. They didn't budge. He shouted at them and they filed out the door.

"You too, Affaf and Samira."

Affaf crossed her arms. Dr. Keerani yelled again and they slinked away, flashing dirty looks at me, then Paula.

I shook my head. "I'll never understand them."

"Dey womans wid black heart."

He examined the Princess then went to the door, poked his head out and shut it. He beckoned to us, drawing us away from the Princess's bed.

"Dis is day."

"What day?" asked Paula.

"De day de Prince accountant leave money for Princess. Today I make plan."

Paula and I exchanged glances.

"I see no patients today. I make arrangements for Prince Mohammad to come to hospital for meeting. He will come. You must trust me. You two watch out. When you see King's assistant, call me. You keep assistant here until I come. Dat all you do. Yes? You understand?"

We nodded.

I watched him leave. No wonder they appear happier—they were expecting money. Stolen money.

"Paula, I wonder what the doctor is going to do. How can we keep the king's assistant occupied until Dr. Keerani returns?"

"I don't know. Shh…they might hear you."

The servants filed back into the room trying to pick up clues from our body language. I concentrated on the Princess's medications, concealing my mounting anxiety. I poured the last pill when the King's assistant walked into the suite.

Paula rested her hand on my arm. "Claire, go call the doctor. I'll talk to him."

I went out to the nurse's desk and used the phone then came back and observed Paula. She was a very good flirt and the assistant was amused at her attempts to speak in Arabic. The assistant laughed, turned from Paula and sat on one of the couches. He opened his black leather briefcase, under the scrutiny of Affaf's steady stare. He pulled out an envelope. I assumed the check was inside.

Affaf stood close to the assistant never taking her eyes off the envelope. She spoke to him and tried to relieve him of the check. He didn't let her touch it, pulling his hand out of her reach and walked towards the Princess. I didn't know what to do. I looked at Paula who slithered up to him blocking his path. He smiled and cocked his head. Affaf huffed. I stepped forward and pushed the Princess's wheelchair away from them.

"Princess Linyaa needs to take her medications." I said over my shoulder.

"Ok. I wait."

He sat on the sofa at the other end of the room with check in hand. Affaf and Samira followed, engaging him in conversation.

Paula whispered, "He has to hand that directly to the Princess. We have to keep him away for as long as we can."

"Where's Dr. Keerani?" I asked, concentrating hard to hide my trembling hands and feeding the Princess her pills one by one.

Paula wrung her hands and looked over her shoulder, smiling at the assistant.

The Princess swallowed the last pill. I bit my lip. Where was the doctor and Prince Mohammad?

"Ah. She finish." The assistant stood up and walked towards the Princess when the door burst open.

"Good afternoon! How is Princess?" Dr. Keerani was breathless. "Ah, you must be Abdullah, assistant to King Jabbar?"

I watched the two men go through the traditional greetings and wondered how long the doctor could keep Abdullah away from Linyaa.

Dr. Keerani busied Abdullah with conversation. I perspired. My heart pounded harder and I tried to control my breathing. Where's Prince Mohammad? I looked at Affaf who had her eyes fixated on the envelope in Abdullah's hand.

Prince Mohammad entered the room and Dr. Keerani looked relieved. The three of them greeted each other and when finished their dramatics, Prince Mohammad spoke to the assistant. The doctor also spoke, directing his comments to Prince Mohammad.

Prince Mohammad took the check from the assistant's hand. I glanced at Affaf. Her cheeks burned red and she appeared edgy. Prince Mohammad walked to his mother, allowed her to feel the check and then put it in his briefcase. The assistant bid his farewell then left. Prince Mohammad spoke to Affaf and Samira. They left the room, looking over their shoulder at the briefcase Mohammad held in his hand.

"How is my mother today?"

"She's improving, Prince Mohammad," Paula said

Dr. Keerani gave Prince Mohammad a long report, which summarized his mother's hospital stay and what the next steps in her care would be. Prince Mohammad seemed pleased. He said a few brief words to his mother and then left with the check tucked away in his briefcase.

Samira and Affaf returned to the Princess's side, looking angry and miserable. They stared after us as we followed the doctor into the room with the kitchenette. He closed the door.

Dr. Keerani smiled and clapped his hands. "It is fixed!"

"How? What did you say?"

"It was simple. Assistant ask me how is Princess. I told him Princess good, but she cannot see. He did not know dis. When Prince Mohammad came, we discuss her business and from medical viewpoint, of course, she not able to take check. From now on, assistant of King Jabbar will give check to Prince Mohammad. He take care of it. Princess Liynaa accountant will get check from Prince Mohammad himself. He will tell his mother, so she know she get money."

"You are brilliant!" exclaimed Paula.

"Yes, yes, but dis important. Listen. It is Prince Mohammad's choice to take check. Affaf and Samira can blame no one. Dey witness to dis. Deir plans ruined!"

"Dr. Keerani, you are the best!" I said. I wanted to give him a hug, but thought better of it. Instead, I shook his hand wholeheartedly.

"I wait long time for dis and now Allah answer prayer!"

Chapter Fourteen

We rushed down the corridor into the Princess's room. The surprised and curious servants stared with astonished expressions of disbelief. Paula flashed them dirty looks and I ignored them. I was angry. It was bad enough I felt stressed from yesterday, but to wake up to a maintenance man peeking in the windows of the villa was outrageous. At least he scared easily and disappeared when Paula screamed. That wasn't the worst of it. The servants left the palace without us and the phone lines were dead. Why is it so difficult? Again, Paula used her cell phone to call Faisal. I made a mental note to reimburse her for the calls.

"How you here?" Samira asked.

"When there's a will, there's a way!" I retorted. By the look on Samira's face I knew she didn't understand the cliché.

"Do they think we're stupid?"

I crossed my arms. "I don't know. I'm not going to let them manipulate me."

"You're right. We have a job to do."

I dialed the number from the nurse's station. Mowark answered. I could tell by the sound of his voice he was annoyed.

"No, you cannot speak to Prince. He busy."

"Can I leave a message for him?"

"Ok. I take message."

"Please ask Prince Mohammad to contact us as soon as possible."

"Ok. I give message."

I doubted he would. I walked towards the hospital suite. "Paula, come in here where they can't hear us." I looked around and closed the door to the room. "They're trying to make us look bad and blocking our communication. I was wondering what we'd do in an emergency and the answer came to me. I think we should talk to protocol. They're supposed to settle misunderstandings."

"Good idea. I'll ask the nurses where the protocol offices are."

I checked the Princess while Paula spoke to the nurses.

"Come out here, Claire."

I joined her in the hall.

"We take the elevators down to the second floor and when the doors open, we turn right."

As we headed toward the elevator, we walked into Sada. She carried her prayer beads in one hand and made a fist with the other. Her eyes narrowed then darkened and I heard her muttering under breath. A chill went up my spine.

Paula gasped. "She's not praying. She's cursing us. It wouldn't surprise me if she were an evil witch and the others were as well."

We found the protocol office on the second floor and an official-looking individual greeted us. "I Abdul, head of Protocol in Jeddah. You?"

"We're caring for Princess Liynaa." Paula said with pride.

His eyes lit up. "Nuses! I hear good things. Very good things. How I help?"

Paula crossed her arms. "The phone line is dead at the palace. We called Prince Mohammad's assistant and left a message for Prince Mohammad to call. We haven't heard back."

"Dis is too bad, but no thing I can do."

I leaned forward. "It's important, Abdul. What if something happened to Princess Liynaa? We can't have this delay if there's an emergency."

"Ah! Yes, dis is true. Ok, for de Princess, I help."

Abdul pulled a book from his desk with phone numbers in Arabic script. He picked up the phone, dialed a number and spoke in Arabic to someone on the other end, then waited for several moments. He straightened and recited Arabic greetings and I assumed he was speaking to Prince Mohammad. Abdul handed the phone to me.

"You speak."

Surprised, I took the phone.

"Why you not call Mowark?"

"We did, Prince Mohammad. Several times. Didn't he give you our messages?"

"No. When you call?"

"The last call was about an hour ago. Didn't you get *any* messages?" I asked again. I knew Prince Mohammad was annoyed by the change in his breathing.

"What you want?"

"We have problems we need to discuss with you. Can we set up a meeting?"

"Problems? What problems?"

"Men are coming into the villa and we are having trouble with Affaf and Samira. Sada struck us. We cannot do our job to help the Princess and the van driver isn't available for us. We can tell you more when we see you."

"Men in your room?" Prince Mohammad sounded irate. "You have meeting. Tomorrow. After dinner we have meeting."

"Thank you Prince Mohammad."

Abdul stared at us. "You did not tell dese dings to me."

"We think we need to deal with them through Prince Mohammad."

"Hmm. Yes, you are right. I know de servants hit you. I read your report. Dis is serious."

"We just want to put things right," I said.

"Prince Mohammad very generous to see you. He say you good nuses."

"Thank you Abdul. We must get back to the Princess."

Paula turned to me, "I wonder how he'd treat us if we weren't good?"

"Don't think about it. We have enough problems."

When we returned, Affaf was furious. "Where go?"

"None of your business." snapped Paula.

Affaf huffed and turned her attention to the Princess, not disguising her anger.

****

"We haven't had a meal at the palace for a long time."

"Look Claire. The whole family is here. Sultan, Prince Mohammad, his wife Johara, Turki and his wife Marion and Prince Abdulrockman."

"Makes me a little nervous," I winced.

"Why? We asked for the meeting."

"Howwddyyy!" Prince Turki said welcoming us.

Prince Mohammad stood up. "Welcome. You two safe our mother again. Tonight we celebrate. Sultan come back from hunt and we eat his kill."

Sultan looked at me askance and grinned. I felt apprehensive and avoided his eyes, taking a seat at the table.

The servants burst into the room with large silver platters of cooked carcasses of slain antelope, skinned from the neck down. Their mouths, propped open with apples and their glassy eyes staring into space made me squeamish.

"Mmm. Dis good! You try!" Turki stated. He helped himself to a large portion of the meat and scooped up generous helpings of brown rice.

Abdulrockman asked, "How's my mother?"

"She's getting a little stronger every day, but her condition is unstable. We have to watch her." I said.

A waiter pushed a platter in front of us. We exchanged glances and put small portions on our plates.

"Ha! That is not enough to feed a bird!"

"Ah, but Turki my brother, they are little birds," said Sultan. "Little birds still free to fly."

I remembered he made that same comment before. I shivered. He wasn't gong to put me in a cage. I was free. I would always be free.

The wives finished their meal and went on a tour of the palace to discuss redecorating it. We followed the Princes into the living room, feeling the eyes of the servants on us as we passed them in the hall. Abdulrockman stood by the double doors to the entranceway waiting for everyone to enter. Once we were inside, he closed the doors.

They sat in their appointed chairs underneath their portraits. I scrutinized the severe and cruel expressions on the faces of the brothers in the paintings. They looked much softer and more approachable in real life.

Abdulrockman spoke. "What is problem? Affaf, Samira and the others, they not do as you say?"

Paula answered. "They're rough with your mother. They crowd us and we can't do our jobs."

"Yes. Yes. I know dese tings from before," He said. "Why you call meeting?"

I struggled. "You must understand. Things are worse. We've been hit and pushed by some of the women."

Prince Abdulrockman was enraged. "Hit? They hit you?"

"Yes. We had to fill out a report at the hospital."

"Where is dis report? I not see this report!" Mohammad demanded.

"I want dis report! They will not hit you!" Abdulrockman shouted.

"There are other things that cause us concern." Paula continued. "The phone line in our villa doesn't work. The van driver won't take us to or from the hospital. We sometimes have to get a taxi just to do our job."

Prince Turki spoke this time. "Oh. This is not good. You need to be with my mother. You must be there, not the others."

Prince Mohammad's cheeks glowed red. "You not call my assistant Mowark?"

I mumbled, "We've called Mowark on many occasions. He promises he'll give you our messages. He says he'll speak to the drivers, but nothing is done."

"Mowark not give me messages. What else?"

The tension in the room increased.

Paula stated. "Someone has gone through our belongings. Some items are missing, but that's not important."

I drew in my breath, fearing Paula's accusations of stealing.

Paula continued, "The most serious, is that men are wandering into our villa. They peek into the windows and come in when we're sleeping and they've scared us. We had to chase one man out who tried to rape me."

Sultan's face dropped and reddened, then he mumbled to his brothers. My stomach turned. I looked from one prince to the next and realized the portraits weren't as severe as the expressions on their faces in this moment. An icy terror trickled through me, rendering me numb.

Prince Abdulrockman jumped to his feet. His neck veins throbbed and lifting his arm with one finger pointing to the ceiling, bellowed in a tone of supreme authority, "No man be in your villa. No man will touch you!"

Prince Abdulrockman marched across the room. He flung open the double doors shouting at the top of his lungs, his voice echoing throughout the palace. The servants came running. They looked terrorized, and fell at the prince's feet. Prince Abdulrockman yelled at them for several minutes then dismissed them, closed the doors and marched into the center of the room.

The brothers spoke in Arabic. Prince Mohammad addressed us. "Tomorrow, you no go to hospital. You be here. Nine o'clock!"

Prince Abdulrockman paced the floor. The Princes stood up then filed out, Sultan lagging behind Turki who struggled with his canes. Sultan paused, raised his eyebrows looking me up and down as he exited.

****

I woke up feeling refreshed and amazed I slept better last night than I had in a long time. Somehow the angry outbursts and scolding the staff gave me a sense of security. I nestled into the couch thinking that maybe now Affaf and the others would be more cooperative, making our job easier.

Paula came out from her room, yawning. I stood up and arched my back. "How did you sleep Paula?"

"Quite well. I took two of my little pills after speaking to Nils on the cell."

"Two?"

"Yeah. One isn't enough."

I didn't say anything. I worried about Paula's increasing need for drugs then looked at the clock. "We better get ready and go."

It was close to nine when we walked to the main part of the palace. We weren't sure where we were supposed to meet, so we waited on a settee in the foyer. I crossed my legs and jiggled my foot, sensing something wasn't right. Not one servant was in sight.

Prince Mohammad and his brothers entered through the main door. I was used to seeing them without anything on their heads, but today they wore traditional red-checked headdresses. A sheer brown cape with a gold braid on its edges hung from their shoulders. They carried long skinny canes, except for Prince Turki who struggled with the cape that kept getting underfoot of his walking canes. Not one of them smiled. Prince Mohammad called to us, "Come!"

We followed him into the living room. The four brothers took their place underneath their portrait and looked straight ahead, like they were in a military procession. Prince Mohammad turned and shouted, "Sit!"

We sat on chairs to the left of the four princes.

Prince Abdulrockman called out in Arabic. The men who served the dinners, the tea girls, the van drivers, the elderly women whose legs were so swollen they could hardly walk, Joyce, the slaves, the maintenance men rushed into the room. Even Affaf, Samira and Sada came. Mowark, Prince Mohammad's personal assistant was the last to enter. He closed the door behind him.

Prince Abdulrockman shouted at them and they assembled, standing in four long lines, filling the room. Some were whimpering, bowing their heads avoiding eye contact.

I was puzzled. Maybe the Princes decided to bring them together to lecture them as a group. I watched and waited absorbed by the scene yet feeling apprehensive and small. Paula reached over and took my hand.

Prince Abdulrockman turned and said, "I got report from the hospital. I spoke to the protocol. What you said is true. No man will go near your villa. We will have none of that! No one will bother you again!"

Relief flooded me.

Abdulrockman yelled and I jumped The servants were silent. Prince Mohammad took a step forward and shouted in Arabic. He bellowed for a long time, occasionally pointing to us. Although I couldn't understand his words, I knew he was relaying what we discussed last night.

Abdulrockman lectured alongside his brother. The more they scolded, the angrier they became. The servants sniveled. Sultan didn't utter a sound. He scanned the room, scrutinizing them.

Suddenly, everyone fell to their knees. The older ones who couldn't move well struggled down to the floor. Some of the women cried out, raising one hand and begging. The Princes shouted at them, subduing them to quiet whimpers.

My heart went out to them. Paula clutched my arm and squeezed.

There was a long period of silence and then a few of the men threw themselves on the floor, pleading with the Princes. They sounded desperate. I was mystified and didn't understand what was happening. Prince Mohammad, Sultan and Abdulrockman stepped forward, threw off their capes and began beating the servants with the long canes.

Paula and I jumped to our feet and gasped. Prince Turki shouted, "Silence! Sit down!"

I put my hand over my mouth and hugged my waist with the other one. I thought I was going to be sick. Paula buried her face in my shoulder then sunk into her chair, pulling me down with her. Paula was breathing hard. I couldn't look at her.

Images of the women in Chop-Chop Square floated in front of me. Their cries echoed in my memory, making the shrieking of the people in this room deliriously insufferable. I put my hands over my ears, withdrawing into the chair, rocking back and forth. My head spun round and the room went black, but only for a moment. Paula nudged me.

"Sit! Sit still!" Turki's voiced boomed in my ears.

I opened my eyes and hugging my waist watched each one of them receive lashes. The old women who could hardly walk, the tea girls, our friend Joyce, even the slaves. Some received more lashes than others The wails, screams and cries filled the room, hurting my ears. A trickle of sweat ran down my back. A pungent odor of stale perfume and sweat swirled and teased my nostrils, inducing gagging.

Whooish, then a scream. Whooish, then another scream. It was unbearable. I rocked back and forth not wanting to see any more, but couldn't take my eyes away from the scene. Horrified, I froze watching the merciless, cruel chastisement.

The sound from the whip rose above distraught cries of the people writhing and sprawled on the floor. My head swirled, my stomach turned and I felt nothing. I was an empty shell not seeing, not hearing. Mowark came into focus. He was the last one. Prince Mohammad was ruthless. He struck him over and over and over again. I saw the blood on his back oozing through his white thobe, trickling in a steady stream to the carpeted floor. Prince Mohammad stood back, grumbled something then he and his brothers returned to their positions. They sat down on their chairs, breathless. Streams of sweat ran down Mohammad's forehead. Sultan's thobe was soaked with perspiration. Abdulrockman wiped his wet forehead with the sleeve of his thobe then shouted at them. The servants and slaves who could walk, stumbled to their feet while others crawled out of the room. I looked through the doors, into the hall and saw some of the elderly women being helped to their feet. Their cries and sobs slowly died down as they disappeared into the palace.

I couldn't speak. I couldn't look at the Princes.

Sultan said, "You do not approve. I tell you dis. Dat is how we treat our servants. Important to let dem know who is boss." He said with authority.

Prince Turki added, "Like a wife, you have to keep them in their place. Ha! Ha! A beating is good. Ha! Ha! They are not important. They are servants!"

My mind and body separated. I felt nothing, but my thoughts were clear. Waves of compassion flowed from my soul to those punished, and I thought about their plight...

They have no choice. Be loyal to you, serve you or be punished by you. Not only are they dependent on the royals for their livelihood, but for their very survival. In this harsh land, power and control is in the hands of a few and life is not precious as viewed in Western societies. In the Prince's minds they were justified in their actions. It was their duty to punish and keep their staff controlled. They could even kill them if they thought it was necessary. They own these people, and their lives are of little significance.

****

I didn't remember walking to the villa. I locked myself in my room, stripped off my clothes and stepped into the shower. I let the warm water wash over me. I took the shampoo and scrubbed myself hard. I scrubbed and scrubbed and scrubbed, trying to wash away the memories of the horrendous treatment of the household staff.

I knew I wasn't going to erase memories, but I couldn't stop scrubbing. My skin was rubbed raw, but I didn't care. Why so much torture and abuse? Why? This time it was different. I felt responsible.

I leaned against the shower door. Tears rolled down my face but the running water washed them away. I cried so hard my chest hurt and a lump in my throat choked me so no sound could escape. My chest rose and fell in violent heaves. I drooped to my knees, banged on the glass, unable to console myself. What have I done? Were things that bad we had to complain?

I sobbed.

"I didn't' know. Oh God forgive me, I didn't know!" I cried.

I stepped out of the shower and dried myself. I threw on a cotton nightgown and lay down on the bed. I felt worse now than when I witnessed the beatings in Chop-Chop Square.

Did I need to complain? If I had known, I'd never allow this to happen. Those poor, poor people. No wonder they hate us!

I rolled onto my side and hugged my pillow. I thought about the struggles Paula and I had since coming to the palace a couple of months ago. Some issues needed to be dealt with… The servants pushed and hit us; the men untrustworthy. The telephones were cut off and I thought about the conspiracy against us to make us look bad in the Prince's eyes. Games. That's what they were. Dangerous games. The problem is I didn't know the rules. Neither did Paula. No. The complaints were legitimate…but I never dreamed Prince Mohammad would be ruthless…I could do nothing.

I rolled on my back and looked at the ceiling. How do I make amends? How do I make it right? Can I?

I rolled to my other side, drawing my knees to my chest.

I used to think people are people and everyone believed life was precious. How wrong I was. Not everyone values human lives. People are not all equal and not everyone has the same morals and values. What a naïve person I am. God forgive me! I didn't know, I honestly didn't't know.

Chapter Fifteen

The next few days were quiet. Even Affaf and Samira were polite, but avoided eye contact.

"Paula, don't you find the servant's cooperation unnerving?"

"Yeah. Their control over the others has dwindled since their embezzlement scheme was shut down."

"They're still powerful and dangerous women. I think perhaps the beatings have subdued them but I don't know how far their influence reaches, nor what other resources they have. One hundred thousand US dollars is a lot of money and who knows how long they've been taking those funds?"

"I don't know, Claire. Forget them." She waved her hand. "The doctors are talking about discharging the Princess soon. Her appetite is back to normal and she's able to tolerate some activity. Her medications have been reduced, or discontinued and all seems positive."

"The servants must know the Princess is going home soon too. Look at all the stuff they have to pack." I put my hands on my hips. "I think I'll go and examine her before she gets into her wheelchair." I walked to the bedside. "Paula! Her lips are blue!"

We took the Princess's blood pressure, heart rate and temperature. I ran out to the desk. "Quick! Call the doctor!" I ran back.

"Claire, help me! She's going into cardiac arrest!" Paula jumped on the bed and started CPR.

"Everyone out! Out!"

The servants looked at us with wide eyes.

"Get out!" I shouted.

They filed out. Within minutes the hospital cardiac team arrived. They attached a cardiac monitor to the Princess and prepared to give her a shock from the defibrillator. The Princess's cardiologist ran into the room and shouted out orders.

I let the team take over. Paula helped me keep the curious, wailing servants outside.

"Prepare to take her to ICU!" The doctor shouted.

One of the hospital nurses ran out to the desk and made phone calls. The nurses and doctors worked frantically. Monitors were placed on her bed and IV bags hung from poles. They covered her with a sheet for privacy and wheeled the bed out of her room down the hall toward the elevators.

"I need the phone."

I dialed the number for Prince Mohammad. Mowark answered. This time he didn't hesitate in getting Prince Mohammad to the phone.

"What is it?" I heard him say.

"Prince Mohammad, your mother is very sick and has gone to ICU."

He hung up without replying.

Affaf and Samira tried to get on the elevator with the team. The cardiologist yelled at them and they stood back, looking forlorn. Another elevator door opened and the servants pushed their way inside.

"They're going to be turned away when they get to the ICU," said Paula.

"Yeah, I know. They'll never learn they can't be included in medical matters. They'll also be angry we'll be able to go and see the Princess when things settle."

Paula laughed.

We waited for half an hour then went up to ICU. A nurse was at Princess Linyaa's side giving her medications through her IV and Prince Mohammad stood at the desk talking to the cardiologist. Another nurse behind the desk looked up and smiled. "You two must be the Princess's private nurses. Princess Liynaa is seriously ill, but the doctor is confident she'll pull through."

Dr. Umar interrupted. "Again we thank you. If it weren't for your quick action, the Princess would not survive. I told Prince Mohammad you both are responsible for her life."

I whispered, "I am glad she didn't die. I wonder how many setbacks a person can suffer?"

"I don't know. I just hope she doesn't die when she's in our care." Paula huffed.

"There's nothing more we can do here, so let's go back to the palace and relax."

As we were leaving the unit, Dr. Keerani stepped off the elevator. "Hello." He said.

"How are you, Doctor?"

"Good. Good. I must talk to you both. Meet me in her chambers downstairs."

We entered the quiet hospital bedchamber and I gazed at Liynaa's belongings scattered around the room. Her black wheelchair was in one corner and the sling lift used to transfer her from bed to chair in another. There was an empty space where the bed used to be and her creams and oils scattered on a tray. The servants had their scarves and abayas and other personal articles in one of the adjacent rooms. It amazed me how they could keep the Princess's area clean and tidy and their areas were always messy.

Dr. Keerani stepped into the suite. His cheeks burned red and he wrung his hands, checking over his shoulder.

"What's wrong, Doctor? Is it the Princess?" I asked.

"No. No. It not de Princess."

Paula went white. "Affaf? She thinks we know about the money scheme?"

"No, no. I don't think so."

He suggested we sit down.

"I tell you dis because you have good hearts." He paused and looked over his shoulder. "You must be careful. I overheard plan. Dey want to harm you."

I jumped back. "Harm us? Who? Why?"

"Dey dink you poison Princess. Dey dink it your fault she sick."

"What? That's ridiculous!" Paula shook her head.

He got very nervous. He looked at the door then leaned towards us and whispered, "Affaf and Samira have plan. I know not what. Dey have many connections outside palace. Be careful. Dere! I warn you." Dr. Keerani got up and left the room.

I felt a terrorizing chill rise from my center then dissipate.

"Claire, what's that all about?"

"I don't know."

****

We didn't speak to each other on the way back to the palace. I was in deep thought about what was going on behind closed doors. When we entered the villa I didn't bother to ask Paula if she wanted a cup of tea; I marched into the kitchen and made it. When I came out, Paula was holding her face in her hands

"I can't take it any more," she sobbed. "I want to go home. I want to go back to Australia and live my life again."

I didn't know what to say. "Here. Have some tea."

Paula took the cup from my hands.

"I want to see Nils. I don't want to be here any more. I need a drink. A good stiff one. I *need* one. *Now!*"

I cleared my throat. "I don't think that's what you need. Come on now. Things aren't as bad as they seem. The Princess is taken care of so we can relax, go shopping and take advantage of this time. Who knows? Maybe Prince Mohammad will let us go back to Riyadh."

Paula sighed, taking a sip from her cup.

I shrugged. "Lookit. It's not yet noon. Why don't we go and buy ourselves a special treat and have a nice meal in town? Would you like to, Paula?"

Paula stared into her cup. After a few moments she said, "I suppose." She took her eyes off the cup and looked at me. "I need to check out something in the Princess's suite. Um,...I heard there is a new mall here and they have the latest fashions from Milan and Paris. I could use a beautiful outfit to show off to Nils." She smiled. "Meet you in the front of the palace in about half an hour? I'll call Faisal."

I watched Paula go to her room then exit the villa with purse and abaya over her arm. I finished my tea then gathered my belongings, walked through the halls of the palace and out the double doors into intense heat. I looked in my purse, ensuring I had my scarf.

Paula opened the doors and came out after me. She shifted her purse from one arm to the other, looking flushed. She looked down the drive. "Isn't it unusual the palace gates are open?"

"Perhaps. Let's go." I said focusing my attention on the Matawa sitting outside his hut.

He smiled and waved as we approached. I was glad he was spared from Mohammad's beating and assumed because he was a holy man, was exempt from discipline.

Just as we were about to leave the property, a white van came speeding up, swerving into the driveway. Our purses flew from our grasp as the van veered towards us, forcing us to stumble and fall on the grassy slope.

"He should watch where he's going!" Paula complained, getting to her feet.

I brushed the grass from my abaya and looked into the van. Affaf was in the passenger seat looking straight ahead. Something didn't feel right.

The driver leaped out and slid the side door open. The rear seats were removed and on the rusty floor were shovels, rope and duct tape. My heart somersaulted and a surge of adrenaline shot through me.

"Paula, look out!"

The man lurched toward us grabbing hold of Paula's arm.

"Let me go!"

I pulled on her other arm. "Fight Paula! Fight!"

She screamed, her knees giving way, allowing herself to be pushed and pulled like a rag doll as the driver edged Paula closer towards the door of the van. The Matawa ran forward and grabbed Paula around the waist, shouting in Arabic. Affaf screamed at the man, opened her door and jumped out. Out of the corner of my eye I saw Faisal drive up in his taxi. Affaf turned and shouted at the man pulling on Paula.

"Faisal's here. Common Paula, Fight!"

Matawa and I yanked hard and the driver fell back against the van, letting go of his grip.

Faisal was out of his car and running toward the gate. "Come! Hurry! Run, run!"

I bent down, scooped the purses and ran. Paula was frozen. I stopped, ran back to her and hit her hard.

"Come on! Paula, Run!"

Paula came alive but the man grabbed hold of her again and turned her away from me. I couldn't reach her and horrified, watched as he shoved her in the back of the van, slamming the door closed. He yelled at Affaf as he hopped in the driver's seat and started the engine.

Faisal ran to me and reached for my hand just as the Matawa tugged on my arm. The van backed up at top speed and as it came to a screeching stop, I was pulled out of the way of being run over. I fell on the grass and clumsily got to my feet.

Faisal rushed to open the rear door of the taxi. "Hurry, hurry!" He shouted.

Affaf shook her fist above her head, cursing us in Arabic.

Faisal and I ran towards his taxi. The man was on my heels and he clutched the skirt of my abaya, choking me. I turned and pelted him with both purses until he backed off and then bolted into the car. Affaf threw the weight of her body against the taxi and grabbed hold of the open door. I clutched the handle and heaved, fighting with Affaf for control as Faisal sped away. Affaf let out a bloodcurdling shriek as she was dragged along the street, then relinquished her grasp falling on the hard pavement.

I shut the door. I turned and looked through the rear window to see Affaf sprawled out on the road and Paula in the back of the van, screaming and flailing her arms. The Matawa was in the background, clasping his hands together over his head, looking up into the sky, praying to Allah.

I was breathless and panted in the backseat. "What about Paula? Faisal!"

"Yes, yes. I follow van. I no lose."

Faisal was on the tail of the white van. It sped through traffic circles and ran a red light. Faisal followed. I held onto the front seat and braced myself as the taxi swerved with every turn. "Where are they taking her?"

"I not know. Desert perhaps."

The van weaved its way through back streets and onto a long road. There was no other traffic and Faisal drove fast, keeping pace with the van. We came to a large gateway with towering iron rod gates. The driver stopped and inserted a card into a receptacle that opened the gates, revealing a long drive bordered by green palms. It led to a pink mansion in the distance that looked like something out of a movie.

Faisal and I jumped out of the taxi and ran towards the van. Faisal tried to open the driver's door and I banged on the side, attempting to unlatch the side door.

"Paula! Paula!"

No answer.

Faisal stopped, put his arms in the air and backed up when a man from inside the gate pulled out a rifle and pointed it at him. The driver sped through the gates. The guard stepped backwards onto the drive, keeping his weapon aimed at Faisal's torso. The gates closed and the guard jumped in the van.

My heart sank as I clung onto the iron rails, breathless, watching them speed away. I felt Faisal's hand on my arm.

"Come. We can do no thing. We wait."

We were disheveled and shaken. I had no energy to cry; I was numb. We drove for a long time before Faisal said, "You ok?"

I cleared my sore throat and answered. "I'm ok."

"You lucky. Dey take you to desert. You die dere."

"Faisal? What about Paula?"

He didn't answer.

He drove to the shore, stopped the car and opened my door. I stepped out and saw several young men leaning on their vehicles watching cars go by.

"What are they doing?"

"Dey being bad. Dey waiting for women. De young women, when dey finish prayer, dey hire taxi. Two or three sit in backseat of taxi. When dose men see dey come, dey drive beside taxi and look in."

I smiled.

"No, no. It is wrong. De young women, dey bad too. Men drive up beside taxi. Taxi slows down and de young woman, if she like what she see, she remove veil from face. If boy like what he see, he give young woman card. She call him on mobile and sometime dey meet."

I couldn't help but laugh. Was it nervousness? Worry? This new information about Saudi customs was a reprieve from the anxiety I was feeling.

"Oh! So the youth of this country are curious about one another."

"Yes, yes. Curious. But for Muslim, dis forbidden. It very dangerous. If dey caught, dey in trouble."

"Have they ever been caught?"

"Yes. One young woman I know, her father kill her. He accuse her of dishonor and prostitute. Dis behavior forbidden in Islam."

"What about the young men? Are they punished?"

"No reason for men to be punish. De woman tempt him. It her fault."

I tilted my head. "Oh Faisal, you don't believe the woman is completely responsible, do you?"

"She take off veil. She bad."

"Do you drive any of these young women in your taxi?"

"Sometimes. I say 'it is wrong', but dey ignore. I do not like, but what I do? I need money for my family."

"Do the taxi drivers ever report these things to the police?"

"No. If dey do, dey not drive taxi any more. No more business. You understand?"

I sighed and thought about how brave the young women were and if I were in their place, would I flirt with the young men knowing there may be a penalty of death if caught?

"Come wid me."

I followed him, climbing over boulders, logs and other debris the sea washed in. He took me to a single bolder obscured from the view of onlookers, behind a large palm tree that bent so far over it almost touched the ground.

"Sit here."

I sat down and he sat beside me, his knees touching mine.

"I sorry about Poola. Tch, tch, tch. I toll you dese people have black hearts."

I looked out over the water and allowed the rhythmic waves to lull me into a hypnotic state. The panic I felt earlier had gone, leaving a void. I couldn't think or feel, and allowed my mind to drift.

"You shake. You cold?"

I swallowed hard and looked at Faisal. I was trembling, but wasn't cold. I felt hot tears nearing the surface and turned from Faisal, burying my face in my hands.

"Claire! Please, no cry."

I felt his arm around my shoulders. I shook my head and forced myself to stop.

"I didn't think Arab men are allowed to touch women."

"Ha! Ha! No, we not, but dis special."

"Oh?"

"I from Jordan and I know Western womens from movies. You like man to touch like dis when you sad."

I smiled then shivered. Faisal put his arm around me and squeezed. I felt safe and comforted by him. I rested my head against his chest and he brushed a stray lock of my blonde hair. We sat in silence, staring at the water.

Three men dressed in uniform leaped in front of us, pointing guns.

"Ahh!" We both screamed.

Faisal jumped to his feet. They shouted orders.

"Dey want us to follow."

I froze. I felt my heart beat in my chest and I was in a thousand pieces.

"Yella! Yella!" One of them shouted, pointing a gun at me.

I got to my feet and followed one of the armed men with a second one poking a gun in my back whenever I slowed down. We walked onto the pavement of the parking lot. The young men we had seen earlier turned their attention away from the traffic, pointed at us, laughing and jesting. One of the guards shouted. They looked back with sly grins on their faces, muttering to one another.

Faisal stopped, causing one of the guards to stumble into him. Faisal turned, grabbed the rifle and struggled for control. A shot fired into the air. I screamed. A guard grabbed one of my arms and forced me into the back of the van. Faisal managed to get free. The young men laughed and the guards let Faisal go.

I sat on the metal flooring of the van. I saw shovels and duct tape and realized I was in the same van that carried Paula away. They got me. What did they want with me? Where were they taking me? I thought of Rose. Should I fight men with rifles?

As the van pulled away, I managed to look out the window and saw Faisal standing beside his cab with a distraught expression on his face. I felt a blow to my head. Everything swirled then went black.

****

My head hurts. Oh, it's so painful... Is someone calling me? Open my eyes? But why? It's excruciating...Who's calling me? Where am I?

"Claire, are you all right?"

"Paula?"

"Yes, it's me. Are you all right?"

"Paula!" I tried to sit upright, but a sharp twinge traveled down my neck and back. I fell back on the bed and opened my eyes. The light hurt, but squinting helped.

"Where am I?"

"You're at Prince Sultan's Palace."

I sat straight up. "What am I doing here?" I remembered the beach and realized Faisal was followed. I rubbed my eyes then looked at Paula. "What are you wearing?"

Paula twirled. The almost skin-colored garment barely covered her. Little diamonds in the sheer fabric caught the light and glistened.

"Isn't it beautiful?"

"It's, it's a negligee!"

"Yes, and you should see it without the robe."

"No thanks. What do you have that on for?" I rubbed my temple. "Oh my goodness, you're not? ...You're not!"

Paula sat down on the bed beside me.

"I had no choice." She hung her head and I could see tears building in the rims of her eyes. "Remember when I said I had to go back to the Princess's suite and check on something?"

"Yeah?"

"Well...I needed them!"

"Needed what?" I rubbed my head. "Oh no! Not the pills?"

"Mine ran out and my nerves were so bad...and there is no alcohol and..."

"And you took them. How dare you!"

"Claire, please don't be angry."

"Angry? I'm past angry. I'm past livid. I could strangle you right here and now!"

"I don't blame you, really, I don't! I know sorry isn't enough, but don't worry, we aren't going to be in trouble."

"We? What's this we? I had nothing to do with your burglary."

"No, I know. I meant me."

"How do you know we aren't going to get our hands cut off? Or worse? And Sultan was in the Princess's suite? And you still haven't explained the negligee."

"No, he wasn't in her suite. When I was kidnapped yesterday they found the Princess's pill bottle in my pocket. Affaf and the driver said they were going to take me to the desert, but when they discovered the pills, they brought me here instead. They told Prince Sultan. I think they were hoping he would have me beheaded."

"Paula! That' frightening!" I put my hand over my heart. "How did you…"

"Prince Sultan of course was angry, and threatened to have me arrested but then I made him an offer."

I was flabbergasted. "You offered yourself to him? Yesterday?"

"What choice did I have? Besides, he's not so bad looking, but he's pretty lousy in bed."

"Paula!"

"They were going to send me to the desert, but the pills saved me. Affaf wanted me beheaded. That would give the servants much more pleasure than dumping a person off in the middle of nowhere."

"Good grief! Behead you! I…I can't think." I put my hands on my cheeks. "You said yesterday?"

"Yeah. You've been unconscious for a while. I was worried about you."

I rubbed my aching head. The door burst open to the room. Prince Sultan marched in followed by one of his male servants. He looked at Paula and half smiled.

"Come here!"

Paula went to his side and snuggled against him.

"Ah, you see Claire. I am not such a monster."

I looked at him, full of contempt. "Why did you bring me here?"

"I told you. I capture little bird, now you in cage. I not capture one, but two!"

"There is no way, Sultan. Let me out of here." I threw back the blankets.

"Ah, but your friend here, she like it, do you not?"

Paula batted her eyes. "Oh, you must let me go too, Sultan."

"Why? I make it nice for you, yes? Why you womans want go? I not taste dis one yet!"

"Taste me! I'm not a food!"

"Ha, ha! She funny one!" Sultan left the room followed by his servant.

"Now what are we going to do? There must be some way out, that is if you want to leave." I frowned.

"Of course I want to leave. I did what I had to do so I wouldn't be charged or left to die. You know that don't you Claire?"

"I don't know anything any more. I have to get my head in order. If only it would stop pounding so I could think."

"Claire, Prince Sultan left these clean clothes for you. Perhaps you'll feel better after you wash up? Why don't you go into the bathroom over there." She pointed.

"I'm not wearing those. What am I wearing anyway? A hospital gown? Where are my own clothes?"

"They've been laundered and they're here. I had to put you in something."

I went to stand but my legs were like rubber and I slinked to the floor.

"Are you all right?"

"Just weak, that's all."

I pulled myself up and consciously placed one heavy foot in front of the other, heading towards the door. There were two doors, one on the left and the other on the right. I chose the one on the right and looked in the mirror.

Think, Claire, think… I looked at the lump on the side of my head. It was huge… How do I get out of here?

Tears were close to the surface. I knew I had to be the planner. But how? I'd never been in a situation like this before…I had to be strong…I had to fight my fear. I thought of Rose. Fight like Rose fought.

Paula was so weak. How could she give in like that? One thing was for sure…I was not going to be mistress to some misguided, selfish, spoiled rotten Prince.

"Claire! Get out of there!"

"What do you mean get out?" I said from behind the door.

"That's the Prince's bathroom. You went through the wrong door."

I poked my head out.

"You're supposed to be in our bathroom. There." She pointed. "Hmm…Prince Sultan usually keeps that door locked. Get out before he finds you."

"Just a minute."

I closed the door and looked around.

His bedroom is next to this one? He doesn't let Paula in here? I wonder what he's hiding…

I checked the door on the other side of the bathroom. Locked. I couldn't get into his room. I made sure the locks on the doors were securely fastened on the inside of the bathroom then opened the door to the medicine cabinet. Nothing. I rummaged through the cupboards, then the drawers. I didn't find anything until I pulled a little too hard on one of the drawers. It fell out hitting the marble the floor, making a thud. I noticed it had three sides; the back was missing. I bent down peering into the hole where the drawer rested and saw a panel in the rear. Reaching in, I pushed, opening a false door and pulled out a shoe-sized box. I opened it. It was full of pill bottles. Some were labeled, some weren't. They were narcotics. The Prince is an addict!

I put things back the way they were, took the box and came out of the bathroom.

Paula looked upset and wrung her hands. "I'm glad you're out. It's unusual that door is unlocked. When I first got here Sultan gave me strict warnings never to go in there."

"Well I know why."

She looked at the box in my hands. "What did you take?"

"Our ticket out of here. Now help me find a place to hide it."

"How about between the mattress?"

"The servants will find it, Paula."

"Not this afternoon they won't. They come in the morning, and we're expected to go for tea in a few minutes."

"Tea? You're going like that?"

"No, I'll change. What's in that box?"

"The less you know the better. You're going to have to trust me, Paula. You owe me that much."

There was a loud bang on the door, startling me. Paula jumped to her feet and helped me put the box between the mattresses then opened the door.

"De Prince ready. Chi."

"We have to go."

"That doesn't look good. There's a big lump in the middle of the bed."

I threw the covers off the bed piled them up with the pillows, obscuring the lump in the middle of the bed. "No one will see anything but an untidy bed. Ok Paula, hurry up and change."

I sat on the edge of the bed feeling nervous, crossed my legs and shook my foot as Paula slipped on a pair of tight-fitting black slacks and a sheer blouse. I fought the mounting feeling of desperation, wanting to formulate a plan of escape, but how? Now I had Sultan's drugs. Would he attack me? Would he take revenge against both of us?

"I'm ready," Paula announced, jarring me from my thoughts.

I looked at Paula and couldn't help thinking she'd make a good call girl.

Someone pounded on the door. Paula unlatched the bolt and before she could turn the handle, three servants rushed in, pushed their way past Paula and focused on me. My heart leapt and I stopped shaking my foot. They marched towards me and took hold of both arms, forcing me out the door.

"Claire!" I heard Paula scream behind me.

I struggled, kicking and fighting as they dragged me down the hall and through another door.

"Ah. There you are!" A voice said in the darkness. "Come here." He turned on a light. Prince Sultan grinned.

I couldn't look at him. Cold shivers ran through me making the hair stand up on the back of my neck. My breath was rapid and shallow. I wanted to run, but where?

"You no wear clothes I give. Shame. Come."

My stomach turned over and felt faint as I followed him into a darkened foyer. He took me through a hallway and then stopped and looked me up and down. "Come!"

I saw the lust in his eyes but was determined not to succumb to his desires. Sultan opened a brown door that led to a room lighted by candles. He leaned in the doorway and rested one hand above his head, forming a human arch. He signaled I pass under his arm. My heart beat hard and my legs already weak, felt weaker. I could hardly step forward, afraid of what he had planned. I took one step towards him, stopped and looked up. He grinned, revealing a devious sparkle in his eye. My skin crawled, raising goose bumps all over my body.

"Go. It ok."

I ducked under his arm and entered the room. It was a small square space with red and gold cushions placed on the floor. A low glassed-top table with lit candles, cheese, green grapes and figs was in the center. The walls were painted a muted brown and decorated with tan colored sofas and overstuffed chairs. It was void of the heavy Arabic flare and looked like a room in a decorator's magazine.

I felt Sultan's hand on my shoulder. He stepped in front of me and pointed with his other hand, indicating I sit. Sultan walked ahead and stretched out on one of the cushions.

"Lie there!"

I didn't lie down, but sat with the table separating us.

"Eat. It is good." He said pulling grapes apart and popping two of them into his mouth. "Do not be afraid. No harm will come to you. Eat!"

I looked down at my folded knees. I closed my eyes and took a deep breath. I had to think. I could do it. Think, think.

I remembered a lecture from a self-defense class from years before… observe your surroundings…don't let your enemy see your fear… Sultan already knew I was afraid. I had to fight my fears, like Rose fought. That's it! Fight.

I shook my head and cleared my throat. I gathered my strength and looked into Sultan's eyes. "Why did you bring me here?"

"Why do you think?"

"Don't play games with me Sultan. I don't like this. I should be at the hospital with your mother."

He sat up straight. "I told you! Enough of my mother!"

"No! Not enough! I'm here to help your mother, not be with you."

"You with me! I tell you want to do!"

I jumped to my feet. "You do *not* tell *me* what to do! You do not own me!"

Anger flashed in his brown eyes, then they softened. He laughed. "You are right. You my guest. Now sit down. Eat. Enjoy food. I prepared especially for you."

I looked hard into his eyes and sank into the cushion. "Why did you do this?"

"I thought you would like."

"I don't like it"

"But you not work. It like holiday!"

"Sultan, I want you to take Paula and I to the hospital. To work. To look after your mother."

"Yes, yes. But first you eat. I want talk."

I didn't move. I glared at him.

"I check on you."

"What do you mean?"

"You have mother and father, brother and sister. You have one son. Other son dead."

I gasped.

"You single. Time you marry."

"You did a background check on me? How…"

"Of course! I Prince. I can do anything." He smiled from one side of his mouth.

A dark wave of fear washed over me.

"I live in California. I know Westerners. You *date*. You like date?"

"What? What are you asking me?" I shook my head. "This is supposed to be a date?"

"Of course!"

"This is not a date! You didn't ask me if I wanted to be with you. You kidnapped me."

"This is Saudi. We not date. You be my, my…how you say?"

"Girlfriend? No way!"

"You will! I command it!"

"You cannot command something like that and I told you, you can't tell me what to do."

His eyes darkened and he spoke in a low voice. "You do as I tell you. You be my girlfriend. I know about these things. In America it means a man can have woman without marry. You be my girlfriend."

"Just a minute. Not every woman does that! No, Sultan, no!"

He jumped up and grabbed my arm, forcing me to my feet.

"You not argue! You do!"

He shook me. I pushed him away. He threw me down. I picked myself up from the floor and looked into his face.

"Perhaps you like lowly taxi man!"

"What?" I said taking a step back.

"Ha! Ha! I know dese things! You want taxi man over Prince!" he spat on the floor.

I was breathing hard and could feel my cheeks burning. "I don't want any man!"

Keeping my panic under control, I scanned the room and my eyes rested on a long cane hanging on the wall. It was the same cane the matawas used to hit women to make them behave.

"You lie! You want taxi man!" He laughed.

I dashed past Sultan and pulled it off the wall. To my surprise, a long sword-like knife slid from an encasement. Sultan came up behind me and grabbed me by the shoulders. I elbowed him in the stomach making him release his grip. I turned, holding onto the sword with both hands. Sultan's eyes widened and rested them on the weapon.

"Get back! Don't touch me!"

"Put down!"

A servant ran into the room shouting in Arabic. Sultan stood in front of me with his hands on his hips, refusing to move. I waved the sword in front of him and he sneered. The servant looked like he was going to pounce on me like a cat after its prey. How could I fight off two men?

Sultan raised both his hands as his servant leapt towards me. I whipped the sword, slicing a long tear in his tunic. The servant jumped back and Sultan yelled.

"Ok, ok. Put down."

I raised the sword waist level, pointing it at him. "You let me go."

"No. I capture you!"

I waved the sword and it made a whoosh. Sultan took a step back. I pressed forward. "What do you want with me?"

"I told you. Girlfriend. I buy jewels, clothes. Whatever you want!"

"No. I don't' want anything! I want to go and look after your mother. That's all! You understand?" I waved the sword again.

Sultan looked confused. He put down his hands then waved the servant out. The servant hesitated before closing the door behind him. Sultan sat down and had a look of calculating sadness in his eyes. I lowered the sword.

"You very brave. You fight with Prince." He shook his head and laughed. "Sit. Please. Sit and eat."

Clinging to the sword, I approached the table and sat on the cushion. I wasn't sure what I was going to do now. We were still trapped behind palace walls and I didn't trust Sultan. I laid the sword across my lap and glared at him.

"How I make you girlfriend?"

"You can't."

"I want girlfriend!"

"No!"

He shouted in Arabic. The servant returned carrying a small, black box in his hands. He tried to hide his knee, which poked through the tear I made in his thobe. He handed Sultan the velvet box and then stood back a few feet. Sultan had a smirk on his face, opened the box then turned it towards me. An emerald and diamond necklace sparkled in the candlelight, taking my breath away. I refused to be tempted. I took the box from his hands, snapped it shut and threw it at him. "I am not a prostitute. You cannot buy me!"

Sultan looked stunned. He picked up the box and tossed it to his servant. I stood up, armed with the sword.

"Ok. Ok. You be my wife."

"No! I'm not a Muslim and I won't be your wife, or girlfriend or anything!"

He laughed and said something to his servant.

The servant turned to me and said, "He say you like bird. Free to fly this day, but one day, perhaps tomorrow, caught and put in cage."

Sultan ate the cheese and figs.

"Your friend. She not like you. She know what is good for her."

I said nothing.

"Why you not like her? Why you not want to please me? Hmm?"

"You expect me to sleep with you? You are a pig!"

Sultan brushed his arm across the table, sending the figs, cheese and grapes flying. I jumped. He called out in Arabic and three servants burst into the room. Before I had time to react, they came behind me, pinned my arms against my side and reclaimed the sword. They picked me up and I kicked and screamed as they dragged me down the halls. One of them punched me then heaved and I landed on the floor in the bedroom.

"Claire!"

I was breathless. I wiped my tear-stained cheeks with my sleeve.

"Claire. Let me help you up. What happened?" Paula reached for me, but I pulled away.

"This is all your fault! I want out of here, and I want out now!" I shouted, then stood up.

Paula backed away. She had a helpless look on her face.

I was dizzy and my head pounded. I put my hand to my forehead and stumbled onto the bed, feeling the lump from the shoebox underneath me.

"Can I get you anything?"

"I wish I could have a cup of tea!"

There was a loud knock on the door.

"What do you want?" Paula asked.

"De Prince. He want Miss Poola ready. Hurry."

"What does he mean by that?"

"You know, Claire."

I bolted upright. "Paula, you're not!"

Paula changed into the negligee.

"Paula?"

"I don't have a choice. I'll bring you back something to eat."

****

I didn't remember falling asleep. I rested in bed not wanting to open my eyes, aware of my hunger, but my head hurt more than my hunger pangs. Am I really trapped inside a Prince's palace? Can this be happening? I felt like an imprisoned maiden in a fairy tale, waiting for my knight in shining armor to rescue me. Who was my knight? Faisal? Jake? No…it wasn't that simple. I had to find a way out myself. I had to fight for both myself and Paula. Poor Paula. Poor weak, vulnerable Paula…

"Claire? Are you awake?"

I forced myself from my dream-like state and opened my eyes.

"Claire you slept for over four hours!"

"What?"

"Yeah. It's nearly dinner time."

I sat up and looked around.

"Where's that box we hid?"

"In the same place. You're lying on top of it"

"Sultan wasn't looking for it?"

"Not as far as I know. Anyway, the Prince wants us both at dinner. Go and get ready."

I felt shaky and weak leaning against the white marble sink, filling it with warm water and forcing thoughts through the pain in my head. I needed to comprehend what happened. How would I escape? The palace was a fortress. I thought of the tall iron gates and the high wall built around the property, locking people in and keeping intruders out. I dried myself and walked towards a dressing table on the other side of the bathroom. I fingered the fine silk and cotton garments Sultan purchased for me. No way was I going to succumb to his demands. I was not going to be anyone's mistress. I came out of the bathroom.

Paula looked up from reading a book. "Why aren't you wearing your new clothes?"

Before I could answer, someone knocked on the door. Paula opened it. A servant brushed by her and said, "Yella, yella," and signaled we follow him.

He led us into a formal dining room. Sultan watched us, licking his fingers. A half eaten leg of greasy chicken lay across his plate.

"Come. Sit. You there. You there."

I chose a different seat than the one Sultan pointed to. His dark eyes showed disapproval but he didn't say anything.

I looked at the place settings and when no one was looking took a steak knife off the table. Paula saw me and smirked. I leaned over and whispered, "I don't have a pocket. Will it fit in yours?"

Paula took the knife and hid it.

I greedily devoured the steamy food, satiating my hunger and when finished, I felt better and stronger. My head still ached, but my mind was clearer.

A servant whispered in Sultan's ear. I watched the color drain from his face. He jumped to his feet, yelling. He pointed at us and I thought I heard the name 'Mohammad' from his lips.

"Claire, he wants us out of here."

"My body isn't responding quickly."

Sultan seemed panicky and shouted, "Yella! Yella!"

The servants had looks of desperation on their faces as they tried to herd us to the other side of the room. Double doors burst open, stopping us in our tracks. Turning around, I saw Prince Mohammad greet his brother with enthusiasm, not noticing Paula and I standing dumb-stuck by the rear exit. Mohammad went through the ritualistic greetings and after kissing his brother on the cheek, spotted us. He looked puzzled. "What's dis?"

A tall woman dressed in a flowing green silk gown, bustled into the dining room, inspecting the surroundings with her eyes, then rested them on us. "Who are they?"

Sultan shrugged one shoulder.

"We are the nurses for Princess Linyaa." Paula stated.

"Yes, but what are you doing here?" She asked in very good English.

Paula stepped forward, but I spoke. "He brought us here!" I pointed at him. "He kidnapped us!"

"Kid... What is kidnap?" Mohammad asked.

"He brought us here, but we didn't want to come."

Mohammad looked at Sultan. "Dis is true?"

Sultan shrugged, sat down and spoke in a nonchalant tone, waving one hand.

"This is unacceptable! Sultan, what is this?" The woman demanded.

Mohammad's face turned red and he slammed his fist down on the table making me jump. The servants looked fearful and hid. Sultan rose to his feet and yelled. Mohammad yelled back. Their harsh voices bounced off the walls as they flailed their arms over their heads, arguing venomously.

"She must be Gooda, Sultan's wife," Paula whispered. "Her family is more powerful than this one."

"I think you're right." I scratched my head. "Hmm...I have an idea. Paula, how do we get back to the room?"

Paula led me to the bedroom and I took the box from between the mattresses. "Come on, let's go back there."

"What are you doing?"

"You'll see."

When we returned, the two men were still arguing and the tall woman argued with them. The knife Paula hid in her pocket fell on the hardwood floors making a clatter. Mohammad turned his attention to her. Sultan saw the box I carried and stepped towards me.

"That is mine!"

"I know."

"You stole! You stole from me!"

"I did not steal. Prince Mohammad, look what your brother has." I opened the box and put it on the table in front of Mohammad, exposing his stash of pills.

Sultan stepped back.

"Dese yours?"

"She lie!" The color drained from his face.

"You just said they're yours. I found them in the bathroom. " I reached in and opened one pill bottle, pouring the contents into a glass of water.

"No!" Sultan moved forward but the woman blocked his path.

She picked up a bottle and examined it. "It is true. They are yours, Sultan. They have your name in Arabic on the label."

Sultan fumbled, "Yes, yes. The doctor give them to me."

"Why so many?" She shook her head and her chestnut curls bounced off her face. "No, no this is not right. I will not have my children exposed to this!"

Sultan yelled at her in Arabic. She yelled back. Mohammad raised his voice. I tucked a loose strand of hair behind my ear, feeling awkward. I wanted to bolt, my mind racing, wondering how to get out of this situation.

"You not get any favors from my family! Nothing!" the woman shrieked.

Mohammad's face went from red to white and then red again. He trembled with rage then turning, struck Sultan across the face with the back of his hand. Sultan stumbled back, falling on the floor. He looked up at his bother, holding his hand to his face and yelled as Mohammad knocked the box of pills off the table with one sweep of his arm, sending pills flying in every direction.

"You!" The woman pointed at Paula. "You! You take drugs from my mother-in-law?"

Paula's face was white and I could see she couldn't speak. "Why would Paula take medications from Princess Linyaa?" I fumbled for words. "She saved her life."

The woman spoke to Mohammad in Arabic. Mohammad squinted his eyes and sighed. "Dis is true. Day safe life. Two time."

"Well then. It is decided. These are very good nurses, but they need... let me see..."

She turned to Mohammad. The exchanged a few words, then she continued, "They need a holiday. That is why they are here. Correct?" She looked at me then Paula. She turned, glared at Sultan and spoke harshly to him in Arabic. She then said, "It is agreed. You need holiday. You go back to palace and we make arrangement for four nurses."

"Four?" asked Paula.

"It is reasonable that if you are the best, then it takes two to replace one. Yes?"

Paula and I exchanged glances.

"You and you!" She pointed at us. "Get your things. I will make arrangements for ride back to the palace, yes? You cannot be here with my husband. It is forbidden and it is bad for my children. Now hurry!"

Relieved, I slipped my arm through Paula's and allowed her to lead me back to the bedroom. I gathered my purse and slipped on my abaya. I felt stronger knowing Sultan's wife was helping us escape. I wanted to get away as fast as I could but Paula was taking her time. I felt impatient watching Paula pull a shopping bag from one of the dresser drawers and filling it with clothes and a black velvet box.

"Hurry, Paula."

"I am."

I paced. "Where do we go? How do we get out of the palace?"

"I don't know but I'm not leaving all these beautiful things Sultan bought for me!"

"What's in that box?"

"Oh, look!"

She opened it and showed off a glimmering emerald and diamond necklace. The same one Sultan tried to give me.

"You're taking that?"

"Of course! It must be worth a fortune and he owes me."

"I guess he paid you in full for your services."

Paula gave me a dirty look.

A servant knocked on the door, entered the bedroom then directed us to the entrance of the palace. He led us through the front doors and we stepped outside just in time to watch two silver cars pull up and stop in front of us. The drivers of both vehicles got out and one of them opened a rear door. We climbed in the back seat and fastened our seat belts. Mohammad charged through the door of the palace and got in the other car. We pulled away, but not fast enough for me. I wanted to get away. Far, far away. I stared out the window at the palms bending gracefully in the wind as we drove down the long drive leading to the tall iron gates, hoping I would never see Sultan again. Ever.

"Where are you taking us?" Paula demanded.

"Where you want?"

"Claire and I want…"

"The hospital. We want to go to the hospital to see Princess Linyaa, then talk to protocol."

"Protocol? Dere is problem?"

"Um…we need to let the hospital in Riyadh know where we are."

The driver picked up a cell phone and spoke to someone.

"Yes. It is done."

When we arrived at the hospital, Mohammad got out of his car first and waited for us. We entered the hospital vestibule and ran into a small group of Linyaa's servants. Affaf was among them and her jaw fell open at the sight of us. Prince Mohammad shouted and they moved away.

Prince Mohammad walked into the protocol offices. He spoke to the secretary, and then a protocol officer came out from his office. He ushered the Prince in, leaving Paula and I in the reception area.

"I wonder what that's all about?"

"I don't know. I still can't get over Gooda's involvement and Mohammad striking his brother."

"Paula, do you remember what Dr. Keerani told us when he first met us? Sultan's wife has a lot of power and I get the feeling she is milking her position for all its worth. She seems to have it in for Sultan for some reason. Besides, her children would be around Western woman. We'd be bad influences."

"Yeah. Also, we're not rich enough or powerful enough to be Sultan's wives." She scratched her head. "Um…Claire, how did you know Mohammad would go against his brother when you exposed his drug habit?"

"I didn't, really. I think Prince Mohammad is trying to make us feel comfortable, but he keeps running into obstacles. He's an intelligent man and I think he has, as they say, a good heart. Just like his mother. He doesn't want to lose favors with Princess Gooda, either."

"Yeah, I think you're right."

"Ladies? Come here please."

I walked into the protocol office where Prince Mohammad waited, tapping his fingers on the arm of a leather chair. There were no other chairs in the room. I felt weak and leaned against the wall, rubbing my temples and wishing the pounding in my head would go away.

"The Prince, he tells me you two saved his mother two times and he wants to apologize for his brother's psychological problem."

"Psychological problem? You mean drug problem, don't you?" Paula blurted.

"No! No Prince have drug problem. There no drugs in Saudi Arabia! It is forbidden. No Prince of his standing would go against the laws of Allah! Enough now. Prince Mohammad have me call supervisor, Anthony. He know you are safe."

Prince Mohammad stood up. He looked at me and smiled. "You let me go to work now?"

I laughed and Prince Mohammad left the room. I sat in the chair.

"Can we talk to Anthony?"

"Not now. You go back to palace and everything will be all right. You will see."

He ushered us out and closed the door.

"I'm not going back to the palace. Did you see Affaf's face?"

"She's scary. Let's call Faisal."

Chapter Sixteen

"Womans! Ah ha! I so happy to see my friends! I so scared. Oh Praise Allah! He keep you safe. Praise Allah!"

He danced around the taxi, opening one door for Paula and another for me. We climbed in the backseat and I watched Faisal in the rearview mirror. He smiled from ear to ear, hummed a tune and tapped his fingers on the steering wheel.

"You left something in my car last time, yes? You forgot womans bags. I dink dey very important."

"Our purses! I thought we lost those." Paula reached into the front seat and opened her bag. "I was going to sell the necklace to get us some money, now I don't have to."

"Necklace? What is dis necklace?"

"Prince Sultan gave me a necklace. Let me show you."

She pulled it out of her bag, opened the black velvet box and leaned over the seat so Faisal could see. He gasped. "It too expensive. Why he give?"

Paula looked embarrassed and hung her head. Faisal's expression changed.

"It's not what you think, Faisal."

"You sleep with Prince. I know dese things. You did too, Claire?"

"No! I would never!"

He studied me in his rearview mirror, his expression softening. "I beleef you. You like little flower, in bloom and beautiful."

Paula leaned over and whispered, "He sounds like a lovesick puppy."

"You Poola? You be prostitute?"

"Faisal! I'm not a prostitute."

He drove without speaking. Frowning, he rolled down his window and spit.

Paula was despondent and shrunk into her seat. I studied her. She was shaking. Was she going through withdrawal, or was she going to have a nervous breakdown?

"You no go back to palace. It not safe."

"You're right.," I said "I think we'll have to go to a hotel, Faisal."

"You need walk."

We stopped by the beach and I got out. I had to encourage Paula to get out of the car then linked my arm through hers and led her down to the shore. We stepped over logs and debris to the water's edge. Paula sat on a big rock and stared at the water. I sat beside her and took off my sandals, digging my toes in the sand then stood up, lifted my skirts to my knees and waded into the water. It was refreshing.

Paula copied me. I splashed her and a few drops of salty water landed on her abaya. She smiled.

" That's enough or I'll soak you," she said.

Amused, Faisal walked towards us laughing. "You crazy womans."

He reached out and took me by the hand and led me to the bent tree.

"Isn't this spot dangerous? This is where they took me away."

"No. We ok now. I pay those mans to look out. We safe." He looked deep into my eyes. "Um... Prince Sultan, he no touch?"

"No way! I'd kill him first."

He laughed. "You not little chirpy bird. You grow into big hawk!"

I smiled, tucking a strand of hair behind my ear and looked down at my feet. He reached up and brushed my hair back. I looked up at him and he ran his hand along my face, sighed and suddenly turned away.

"We go now."

We gathered our sandals, walked back to the parking lot and climbed into the car.

"I think we should go to a hotel now." Paula stated.

"Dat good idea, but please, listen. You single women. You have no, how you say, bags? Dat cause suspicion."

"We need to go and buy a suitcase. We also need to buy a change of clothes, a toothbrush and other things," I said.

Shopping seemed to lighten Paula's spirits and while we shopped, I thought about how we were going to get back to Riyadh. We couldn't go to Prince Mohammad and risk being around the servants. They were angry with us. Very angry, and in one respect, I couldn't blame them. Still, we needed someone's help.

My heart skipped a beat. Travel documents! We had no travel documents. Single women can't go to a hotel without permission. Women in this country belong to someone and we 'belonged' to the King Faisal Hospital in Riyadh. How do we prove ourselves?

I looked at Paula. She looked like she was about to fall apart. I couldn't mention this to her, it could push her too far.

When we finished making our purchases, Faisal met us outside the mall. Faisal helped Paula into the car. I held back. He went to open the door on the other side of the taxi but I didn't follow.

"You ok?" He asked.

"Faisal, come here for a minute." I pretended there was something wrong with my sandal. I said to him quietly, "We have no travel documents. Will a hotel let us register for the night?"

"Oh! Let me think."

"I don't want to upset Paula."

He looked inside the car. "I understand. You no worry."

He drove us to one of the nicer hotels in Jeddah. I didn't care how much I spent. I wanted a place to stay for the night and to be safe.

"I know manager. He good. You stay here."

Faisal disappeared into the hotel while we waited in the taxi. After a few minutes, Faisal returned with a big smile on his face.

"It ok. You go in."

Paula headed towards the lobby. I whispered to Faisal, "We owe you for this."

"You nice ladies and you my friends." He winked.

I thanked God for Faisal and our safety.

****

The room was small and plain, but clean.

Paula flopped on one of the beds. "I'm glad we're not in the Palace. I'm tired of looking over my shoulder, closing curtains to peeking toms and always being watched."

I didn't answer. I sat on my bed then said, "Paula, I think we better call protocol."

"Protocol? Whatever for?"

"Someone needs to know we're safe."

I made the call to the Faisal hospital in Jeddah. Abdul answered the phone.

"You not at Palace? Prince Mohammad, he not be happy."

"I think he'll understand. It isn't safe for us."

"I do not understand."

"Um…How is the Princess? We need rest to care for her and we won't get it at the palace."

"Oh. Ok. I talk to Prince Mohammad. Hold phone, please."

I paced the floor while I waited.

"Hello? You stay there tonight. You come and see me in office at hospital tomorrow morning. Where you stay?"

"We're safe and we'll keep in touch." I hung up the phone before answering his questions, determined not tell anyone where we were.

I was restless. The day's excitement played in my head over and over again. I felt I was going to explode at any moment and trying to stop my racing mind and thinking about the last few days, made me nauseous. I wondered if we were in danger. Would Sultan be looking for us? Would life ever be normal again?

I watched Paula sleep, her breathing, deep and rhythmical as if she were in a drug-induced sleep. She probably was. Did she take pills every night?

I crept to the window and parted the curtains. Our room overlooked a quiet street. I stared at the road and sighed, thinking of Faisal. Such a sweet man. If it weren't for him, heaven only knows what would happen to us. "He's special," I whispered and looked into the sky.

How do I feel about him? His ways are so different to mine. We could never…could we? Faisal already has two wives…me be a third? No, no it would never work…

****

The phone rang, waking me out of a deep sleep.

Paula answered. "Anthony? Hello! How did you find us?"

"It's Anthony?" I jumped out of bed and across Paula's taking the receiver from her hand. "Anthony? It's Claire. How…"

"I'm worried. Sounds like you two have been through an ordeal. Someone's looking for you and Paula. They want to finish their business. Please be careful."

"I don't understand."

"Protocol told me the household blames you for the Princess's illness. They believe your little jaunts into Jeddah were acts of treason and when she took a turn for the worse, they believe you cursed her and in essence, poisoned her."

"Prince Mohammad doesn't believe that, does he?"

"No. He's an educated man but some of these people are highly superstitious. Protocol is working hard to make them leave you alone."

"It isn't just the household you know. Prince Sultan kidnapped us. By the Grace of God, Prince Mohammad and Princess Gooda rescued us from him and now we're on the run."

"You're lucky the Prince and his brothers liked you and respected the work you did for his mother. From what I understand he wanted to reward you both on several occasions, but you declined."

"Yeah, well, we were there as professionals, not to see what we could get out of him."

"The Prince felt he had to repay you somehow. When he learned of the pushing, shoving and hitting he knew there was much more to it than that. There's a network of people who are either loyal to the royal family or against it. There have been many assassinations in this country. Brother against brother, cousin against cousin. You never know who your enemy is. King Faisal himself, the man responsible for the hospital you're working for was assassinated at its opening. He never got a chance to see what he created but his family was powerful and his dreams were carried out. You're witness to that or you wouldn't be working here."

"I still don't understand what all of that has to do with us."

"I don't know all the intricacies, but there are organizations that have connections throughout the Arab world. The Royals themselves and business people both inside and outside the Kingdom fund these groups. The groups have military ties and have caused disruptions in places like the Gaza Strip and started wars in this region. You must understand the men in Protocol aren't going to give me more information than they want me to have. What I do know is there is an 'Arab Brotherhood' and its members have deep alliances. Not being an intelligent agent, I can't tell you much more."

I frowned. "I can't believe simple servants from the palace could have networks as large and dangerous as what you just described. It's craziness."

"I know. These are tribal people and their roots and influences spread far and wide. Just be aware your 'freedom' has been bought by the Prince."

"What if Sultan tries anything? He must be really angry."

"Yes, I know. Sultan has a drug problem, but the royals have a way of covering that up. They call it 'psychiatric problems' to avoid prosecution." He cleared his throat. "I've arranged with Abdul the protocol officer in Jeddah to give you air tickets home and travel documents. There are still a few things to work out, so you won't be coming back to the hospital yet. The hospital owns some villas near the French Quarters in Jeddah. After you meet with Abdul this morning, you go there until it's time for your flight."

"Sounds good. I can't wait to get out of here. By the way, you never told us how you knew we were here."

"I just told you. There are networks. Everyone knows everyone else's business. Um…Claire, I have to thank you."

"What for?"

"For being a person who sticks to her values. My wife and I have worked everything out and I'm grateful nothing happened between us. I'll be leaving the Kingdom in six months to go home."

"I'm happy to hear that Anthony." I hung up the phone.

But I wasn't happy he was leaving. Why this sense of loss? How could I hate him when he was pursuing me, and now feel sad? Loss of a friendship, maybe? Then there's Faisal. Dear sweet Faisal…

"Claire, what are you thinking?"

"Uh, oh nothing." I shook my head. "I'm looking forward to going back to Riyadh."

"I just want it over. I want to see Nils and be happy again."

"We'll be back soon"

"I want to go now!"

She threw herself on the bed and cried. I stood over her wanting to chastise her like a mother would a child. I sighed and sat down. "We've both been through a lot and are under a great deal of stress."

"Yeah but you didn't have to sleep with him."

"It seemed to me you were enjoying yourself."

"I was pretending! I didn't want to die." She pouted then flipped her hair over her shoulder. Tilting her head to one side, she said, "I like it when a guy comes on to me like that. It makes me feel…"

"Paula! Do you hear yourself? You mean to tell me you'd sleep with anyone?"

"You make it sound dirty! I was trying to save my life."

"I know that, but what a terrible choice you made."

Paula pouted. "You are so high and mighty. I bet you were a goody, goody in school, weren't you?"

"Why are you mad at me?"

Paula turned her back and cried. "I can't go on. I just can't do it. I want to go home."

My shoulders slumped forward. "You'll be there soon."

She sat up. "Claire, you won't tell Nils, will you? I mean, what happened here in Jeddah is our secret, right?"

"No Paula, I won't tell anyone anything."

Paula paced the floor. "I need…I need a drink, or one of those pills. My nerves are so bad. I think I have a couple in that bag."

I watched her. Her hands trembled as she reached for her purse. She looked like a walking glass house about to shatter any moment.

****

Faisal paced in front of his taxi after I told him about my conversation with Anthony.

"Dey know you here last night? You talk to supervisor? Dis is bad. Someone I cannot trust, now I have to find who. But, dat is my problems. For now, I take you to hospital to get papers and den, I, Faisal directed descendent of de Great Mohammad will take my womans friends for lunch!"

"But Faisal, isn't that dangerous?"

"Ah, but we be careful. Dis is lunch and I take to modern part of city. You will see."

He drove us through the busy streets of Jeddah, weaving in and out of traffic, while we held our breath. Paula protested and asked Faisal to slow down. He did, but only for a moment. When we arrived at the hospital, Faisal and Paula waited in the taxi while I went into the building. I took the elevator to the second floor and rushed into Abdul's office. I was glad to find him pre-occupied with other business; I didn't want to answer questions. I accepted the envelope containing the travel papers and airline tickets and then rushed outside.

Faisal continued his hellish drive through the city, coming to a less congested, quite area in Jeddah. He parked the taxi and we walked into a bright restaurant. There were several empty tables and the only other patrons were two Arabic women sitting in a corner smoking a fruit tobacco, hubbly bubbly and eating dainty sandwiches. Faisal led us to a table away from them. We sat down and before I could relax, I checked my bag ensuring the travel documents and plane tickets were safe.

"Claire, they don't have hot dogs. I'd like a hot dog."

"That's a strange craving."

"You want *dog*?" Faisal wrinkled his nose.

I laughed. "It's a piece of meat like a sausage and you eat it in a bun."

"Ah! I thought you want eat dog. Whew! Dogs dirty, filty animal."

"But I love dogs."

"So do I. I have a little brown one waiting for me in Australia."

"Dog filty beast. No dogs in Saudi Arabia." He shuddered. "Dey dirty. Only dogs allowed are hunting dogs. Dogs dirty like pigs. Dey unclean."

"Oh no, no, no!" I shook my head. "I had a little dog, a Jack Russell. You should have seen her! She loved to run and chase a ball like she was playing soccer. She'd run and bark and have so much fun."

"Dis dog. She play soccer?" He scratched his head.

"Oh yes! One time a group of boys were playing basketball, bouncing the ball around the court and she took the ball away from them. They had a terrible time getting it back. They chased her for over an hour in a big field, but she outsmarted the lot of them."

Paula added, "Mine loves to dig stones out of the sand and he carries them home and sleeps on them. He must think they are eggs or something. He only brings the round ones home."

Paula and I laughed. I saw Faisal smile.

"Ah ha! Faisal you laugh!"

"No! I no laugh at dog."

"Yes you do!"

"Dis dog, it is beast dat goes whoof, whoof?"

"Yes. Faisal, don't you know dogs are special in other parts of the world?" I asked.

"Yeah. You can buy sweaters for them, beds, toys…"

"Don't forget the gourmet doggy stores where you can get special treats."

"And the pet cemeteries."

"What is dis ceme…"

"Where you bury your dead dog."

Faisal shook his head and smiled. "You whoo, whoo!" He said making a circular motion with his finger close to his ear. "Ah, you see. The Saudi man, he is too pure to have such filty beast."

"What do you mean too pure?"

"De Saudi man, he dink he most superior being on earth. He is because he guards two most Holy cities."

"So everyone else is less than him?" I asked.

"Er…yes."

"Even you?" Paula teased.

"I Jordanian! I directed descendent of The Great Mohammad! I not lower dan any Saudi."

"Well, I believe no one is above another. We all have different talents and everyone is special."

"No Claire. Not every man equal. Not Filipino. And dose, dose Jews! Dey not equal to man!"

My stomach turned as he choked on the word 'Jew.' He shuddered as if to shake the thought of the Jewish people from his mind.

"Even dog and pig better. But Jew?" He spit on the floor.

I never witnessed pure hatred before. I was exposed to prejudice and bias, but not abject hatred. The depth of this man's loathing was so well-founded it changed his appearance, leaving me with mixed emotions of amazement and disgust.

We finished eating and Faisal drove for a long way outside the city until coming to the French Quarters.

"Claire, you come back and go wid me? Ok? I want talk."

"Ew! Lovebirds," Paula teased.

Faisal waited outside the gate while we walked a short distance to the villa.

"You go ahead Claire. I'll see you later…. And don't be late or I'll leave for the airport without you."

I walked back to the taxi, sighing, perplexed by Faisal's attitude toward Jewish people. I climbed into the back seat, deep in thought as we drove in silence. He brought us to the beach. "This seems to be your favorite spot, Faisal."

"It is good. Most times no persons come. Just dat one time, but we followed. Come."

He led me along the shore then up the rocky embankment leading to the bent palm tree. I stepped over the loose stones, struggling to keep pace with Faisal. We slowed when we came to a log underneath the tree. I sat down, resting my hands in my lap acutely aware of how close he sat beside me. I tried to focus on the beach, staring out over the glistening water and into the starry night sky. My heightened senses absorbed the beauty of the evening and the tranquility I longed for was replaced by my sensitivity to the excitement radiating from Faisal. My heart pounded and I felt nervous about what he wanted to tell me. Faisal reached over and took one of my hands. I felt a gentle breeze surround us, playing with the loose skirt of my abaya.

"Claire, you no like other womans. I see heart. I see everyone's heart and I know what dey do, what dey dink. You understand? Remember, I know dese things. I tell you, my heart, it feels like it heavy rock all de time and I so sad. But it is like feather when I see you. Whoo, whoo! I so confused. I think, think, think at night and cannot make it stop. I see you. I see you when I wid my wife, when I sleep. You everywhere. I no feelt like dis before. You nurse. Tell me. I sick?"

I looked at him, embarrassed by the earnest expression on his face and saw his eyes filling with tears.

He wasn't sick. He was in love. I studied his face and I knew I liked him very much, but love? No, never. Especially after I saw him shudder with hatred…what could I say to him? How could I be gentle?

He took my other hand and held both my hands in his.

"I not know how to make you happy. You be good wife. Dat I know."

"Faisal, I can't be your wife. We're too different and you would end up hating me."

"I, Faisal would never hate! You my flower…" He sniffed my hands then kissed them passionately.

I looked out over the water then cleared my throat. "You know we're leaving for Riyadh tonight."

"Dis I know. I come to Riyadh. It no problem. I drive taxi dere."

"What about your wife? You said she's about to have a baby."

"Ah, she taken care of. She ok."

"Faisal, we can't."

He sighed and hung his head. "Dis I know too. I want... I want you to know my heart. You Christian, yes? I, Muslim. In our religion we no believe in, how you say, re..rein..recarton..."

"Reincarnation?"

"Yes! Dat is it! Perhaps if dis reincar...how you say?... it true, we married in past? Maybe have marriage in future?"

I smiled and squeezed his hand. "You never know, Faisal."

He looked at his hands and a tear rolled down his cheek. I reached over and brushed it away. He looked at me, smiled, went to reach for me then pulled away.

"No. Dis cannot be. You good womans and I not spoil you. You always be my flower, yes?"

As we walked back to the car in silence, I thought about Faisal's words, wishing things were different. I questioned myself, mulling over a familiar feeling brewing in the pit of my stomach. I didn't want to run away from Faisal, did I? I knew I cared deeply for him, but not in the way he would like. I was glad I was leaving for Riyadh in a few hours, hoping to avoid those dreaded feelings of awkwardness and the instinct to flee.

I heard male Arab voices discussing something in the near distance, close to where we parked the taxi. My heart somersaulted when I focused on armed guards standing around Faisal's cab and beyond them, a van with its side door open. They shouted something and Faisal turned white. He trembled.

I couldn't move. An icy chill went down my spine and my legs became cement. Unable to think I stood motionless, staring at the men in front of me. A guard came from behind and poked me in the back with his weapon. I jumped but didn't advance towards the van. He then reached out and grabbing hold of my shoulder, lurched me forward. I took a couple of steps then froze, unable to think or process what was going on. The guard shoved me and another one grabbed my arm, forcing me into the back of the van. They groaned and heaved, throwing Faisal face down beside me. Faisal sat up and crawled towards me. We huddled together on the floor in a corner of the van with a barrel of a gun pointing in our faces. The guards sneered, waiting for three others to climb in the back.

Faisal was shaking. He swallowed then whispered, "Dis is my time. I see death in dese men's hearts. Remember, you are now hawk, you free to fly. Fly Claire and perhaps I see you in future and you be my wife. My one wife."

"What do you mean it's your time? Faisal?"

One of the guards hit Faisal hard in the head, knocking him out. I screamed and reached for him but was pulled back. The guard dragged me from the rear of the van and forced me to sit with my back against the driver's seat. Where were we going? I couldn't see outside. My only view was Faisal's limp body on the bare van floor, guarded by three armed bullies. I trembled. I wanted to run to Faisal to help him, comfort him, but the guard blocked me. I felt small and weak, combating encroaching panic. An image of Rose at Chop-Chop square floated into my consciousness. I had to be strong. I had to fight, but who am I fighting?

We drove for a long while before I felt the van go over a bump then come to a stop. The door opened. Someone reached in and pulled on my arm, causing me to lose my balance. I tumbled out and fell face down on the ground. Picking myself up I realized I was standing in front of Princess Liynaa's palace.

A man pushed me and dug a long-barreled gun into my back, forcing me through the double doors and into the living room. Prince Sultan sat underneath his portrait, looking suave and calculating.

I felt a sudden surge of electricity pulsate through my veins. I wondered what he was doing. Was he going to beat me like he did the servants? One of the guards tossed my purse at me.

Two muscular guards had Faisal by the arms and threw him into the room. He landed on his face at the foot of Prince Sultan. He shook his head and when he saw the Prince, he bowed. Sultan stood up.

"See what happens to little birds who leave their cage! Get down! On your knees little bird!"

"I will not bow before you! You have no right…"

"Enough!"

Sultan walked over to Faisal and kicked him. I ran to his side and Sultan yanked me back.

"You prefer taxi man to Sultan? You could be my wife! But no! You Prostitute!" He spit on the floor.

"She no prostitute! She pure, like flower!"

Sultan kicked him again. Faisal curled into a ball, clutching his stomach.

"No, please! Stop! What do you want?"

"I want nothing. You garbage!" He turned his back and yelled.

Two guards came in and picking Faisal up by the arms, dragged him out of the room.

"Fly Claire! Do not be sad for me! I tell you, it is my time! In future…"

"Faisal!"

A guard prevented me from running after him.

"Faisal!"

I hit and kicked the guard over and over again, desperate to follow Faisal. He tried to grab my arms, but I moved too quickly.

"Faisal!"

He disappeared into the darkened corridors.

The guard overpowered me and threw me on the floor in front of Sultan. I reached out and grabbed his thobe. "Where are you taking him?" I said pulling myself to my feet. "Where?" I screamed, thrusting myself against Sultan, pounding his chest. "What are you doing to him! He's an innocent man!"

Sultan grabbed my arms and threw me down. "Innocent! Ha! Ha! The desert is big place! He is gone! Forever!" He laughed.

I couldn't move. I lay breathless, facing this monster.

"Why? Why?" I cried, getting to my feet.

"No taxi man better than Prince!" He spit.

I looked at him and an overpowering red rage ascended from the pit of my soul, flashing, blinding, filling my mind and staining it with its red torrent. I flung myself at the Prince and wrapped my hands around his throat, squeezing, wanting to feel the life drain from him.

"Die, Sultan! Die!" my mind screamed.

Sultan, reaching up, grabbed my wrists digging his fingernails into me. I screamed in pain. Desperately, I clawed at his throat and we wrestled until he stretched my arms apart and flung me to the ground. I landed face down, sprawled out, seething with hatred. I rested on my hands, eyes focused on the floor. My heart pounded hard, my cheeks burned hot and breathless, my mind and thoughts returning, leaving me petrified. Petrified I could kill Sultan; astonished I wanted nothing more in that moment other than to see his lifeless body collapsed on the floor. The depths of my emotional eruption scared me and I shook my head… Faisal… Where is he? Where did they take him? I trembled, unable to move.

"Get up!"

I couldn't respond. I concentrated on clearing my mind. I needed to think.

"Get up!"

I looked up at the Prince towering over me. I got to my feet, staggered then straightened.

"You have ticket? You have ticket!"

"Huh? Ticket?"

"For airplane? Find ticket!"

I was shuddering in rapid jerky tremors. I wanted to cry, but couldn't. My mind was still separated from my body... Where's Faisal? What are they doing with him? Where are they taking him?

"Ticket! Where Ticket?"

I picked up my dusty purse, rummaged through it and showed him the ticket.

"Good. My driver take you to airport."

"What?"

"You free from cage! Go!"

****

Paula was waiting for me at the airport.

"Where've you been? I was worried you wouldn't make it. Claire? Claire are you all right?"

I couldn't speak and was struggling, holding back tears and fighting the lump in my throat. I rubbed my bruised wrists.

"Claire what's wrong?"

I swallowed hard and looked at Paula.

"You're so pale. Are you ill?"

I shook my head. "Its...Its Faisal. He..."

"He what? Is he ok?"

I shook my head no. The tears flowed.

"What happened?"

I heard the announcement for boarding for first-class passengers.

"That's us, Claire. Come on."

We climbed aboard and I sat in a window seat. I couldn't talk. Didn't want to talk. I stared out onto the black tarmac watching the attendants load the plane with suitcases.

"Claire what happened to Faisal?"

"They took him."

"Who took him?"

"Prince Sultan. They took him away."

"Claire, you're not making any sense."

"They found us and took us both to the palace. They beat him and took him to the desert!" I snapped in an unexpected burst of anger.

"What? To die?"

I nodded my head. I looked out the window and let the tears fall. They dripped on the fiberglass frame of the window and ran down the wall exposing the discoloration from cigarette smoke. The lump in my throat was so painful I couldn't breathe.

Is it my fault they took Faisal away? Is it because I wouldn't do what Sultan wanted me to do? Was he trying to save face, punish me or prove he has control over me? Oh Faisal, Faisal…I am so sorry.

"It's not your fault you know."

How did she know what I was thinking?

"It's not your fault."

"How can you say that? Sultan wanted me and I refused him. Even fought him. When I was at the palace I felt such rage. Paula…I didn't know myself. I could have killed Sultan! I could have strangled him to death with my bare hands! He's so…so arrogant. He thinks I chose a taxi driver over him, now Faisal has to suffer for our friendship. Oh Paula. I don't know how to live with this. This is torture! Pure torture!"

I wept.

Paula pulled away and after a few minutes, cleared her throat. "No Claire. It's my fault."

"Why do you say that?"

Paula's voice was faint.

"I can't hear you."

She cleared her throat again. "When I was with Sultan he'd go on and on about how to win you over. I told him he never could because you were in love with another man."

"What?"

"I told him you loved Faisal. I never thought…"

"No you didn't! Paula!"

"I didn't know he would go after Faisal. I didn't! You have to believe me. I liked Faisal too. He was my friend, too!"

"I don't know what to say." I turned and stared out the window. I didn't know what I was feeling. Anger? Pity? Frustration? Betrayal?

"You don't trust me, do you?"

I looked at her. "I know you don't mean to harm others, but I think your little drug habit is out of control."

"How dare you!"

"You placed us in danger from the very first time you stole the Princess's pills! If you didn't steal them a second time, Faisal would still be alive!"

"You're *blaming* me?"

I let out a sigh and bit my lip. I stared out the window into the black night. I turned to Paula. "I'm sorry. I just…oh, I don't know."

"Well, it is my fault."

Her voice sounded faraway. "Today after you left someone phoned."
"Who?"
"I don't know." Paula dropped her chin to her chest and mumbled. "They were looking for you and I told them you went for a drive in a taxi. I said you would go to the beach. It's my fault. Everything is my fault."
I went numb and couldn't look at Paula. My mind blank and my soul empty, I stared straight ahead, motionless, thinking of nothing.

****

I hardly said a word to Paula when we left the airport and no one spoke on the long ride back to the hospital. How could this happen? How could people be so cruel? I crept into the apartment and tiptoed down the hall to Rose's half open bedroom door. I poked my head in and saw her bed was made. "Alone. Good."
I threw my purse on a chair and shed my abaya as I made my way to the kitchen. I passed a note propped up by the phone. It was addressed to me.

Claire. I never know if you're coming home or not. I'm in Scotland to talk to Ian's wife. There's a guy named Jake who keeps calling. I left his number in your bathroom. See you soon!
Rose.

Jake. I hadn't thought about him in a long time...
The phone rang.
"Hello, is dis Claire?"
"Yes, who's speaking?"
"Dis Joseph from security. You have friend, Paula?"
"Yes?"
"She in emergency and wants to see you."
"Oh my! I'll be right there!"
I snatched my abaya and ran to the emergency department across the street. I burst through the doors.
A man behind a desk looked up.
"How can I help you, miss?"
"I'm looking for...
"Claire, is that you?"
I whirled around. "Anthony?"
"Claire, come here."
He led me to a private room and closed the door.

"Where's Paula?"

"Claire, sit down."

Anthony was as white as a sheet and trembling.

"What's wrong?"

"Claire, I'm so sorry…"

"What? Where's Paula?"

A lump formed in my throat and tears ran down my face. I jumped up and grabbed Anthony by the shirt, trying to shake him. "Where is she? Where is she? No! No!"

"Claire, Claire!"

I fell into his arms, sobbing. He held me then I pulled away, took a deep breath and sat down. "Tell me. Wha…What happened?"

"Paula was found wandering the street, delirious. Someone mistook her for being drunk and brought her here. She took an overdose of pills. She's barely conscious, but will pull through."

I slumped and turned away, covering my face with my hands. I knew Paula was fragile and about to come apart. I never dreamed she'd try to commit suicide. I don't blame her for any of this. How could I? What we lived through! The tremendous battles, foreign thinking and traditions, language barriers, royals, peasants, slaves…too much. How could she blame herself? How could I blame her? We were both so tired…scared and frightened…stressed beyond belief…

I cried for a moment then took in a deep breath. "Did she say anything?"

"She said to tell you everything is her fault and that she's sorry."

"Oh, no. It wasn't her fault. She was pushed too hard, suffering from extreme grief and she couldn't take it any more. Oh Poor Paula! Poor, poor Paula!"

"Claire!"

I jumped to my feet. "Oh please! Let me see her. I have to speak to her."

"Claire I don't…"

I walked behind the nurse's station and looked behind curtains separating one patient from another. I found Paula in a room by herself, hooked up to monitors. I ran to her and held her hand.

"Paula?" I whispered. "Paula. It's me. Claire. I'm here, dear. Can you hear me?"

Paula groaned and turned her head towards me. "Oh…I'm sorry. I'm responsible…"

"Shh…none of this is your fault." I stroked her forehead. "Come on now. You have a lot to live for."

"I don't want...too much pain..."

"Shh...we can deal with this. We can get through this together. We've come such a long way already, haven't we?"

Paula smiled weakly and feebly squeezed my hand.

"That's a girl. Be strong. I'm here for you."

"Excuse me miss? You have to leave now."

"Oh. Ok. Paula, I'm not faraway."

I wiped the tears from my face and met Anthony who was still waiting for me in the hall.

He straightened his shoulders and said, "I'm walking you home."

****

I stood in the middle of the apartment. I felt detached. Detached from my surroundings, detached from myself, detached from the world. I sighed heavily.

This is where it all began. Rose's arrest. The disappearance of Nawaar... The beatings at Chop-Chop Square... The struggles at the Palace... Twice Sultan kidnapped me. Twice!

I sighed and threw my abaya on the chair and poured myself a hot bath, allowing hot tears to drip, drip on the floor. I was empty. Void of energy, void of emotion.

Faisal. Dear Faisal. How did he know he was going to die? He said he knew things...He told me not to be sad for him... Ok Faisal. For you, I won't be sad, but I miss you. I miss you very much.

I lay down allowing the warm water to sooth me.

Paula? Poor, poor Paula. I'll always mourn for her and for lost souls like her. I don't know how to help her...

I stepped out of the bath and slipped into my nightgown.

So much suffering. Too many deaths. It's a harsh, cruel society, one I'm just beginning to understand. Do I want to understand it? Do I want to live through the drama and struggle to survive in this strange and exotic land? No one outside the borders of Saudi Arabia could understand this life or its people. Life is surreal in Saudi. Ah... Maybe I should pack my bags and go home. Maybe this is enough, there's nothing more for me here. Nothing...

I sighed, hugged my waist and paced the floor. A single tear crept down my cheek, forging a path to my chin where it rested before falling and making a cool splat on my arm. I loosened the grip from my torso and wiped the wetness away then walked into the living room. I stretched out on the couch, fluffed a pillow for my aching back then rested my face in my hand.

The phone rang. I got up and wandered by the desk. I stared at it, allowing it to ring a second time, then a third.

"Hello?"

"Howdy!"

My heart stood still and recognizing the musical voice, drew in my breath. "Jake!"

Maybe there's something in Saudi Arabia for me after all...

THE END.

Printed in the United States
70724LV00003B/181-210